What I Never Said

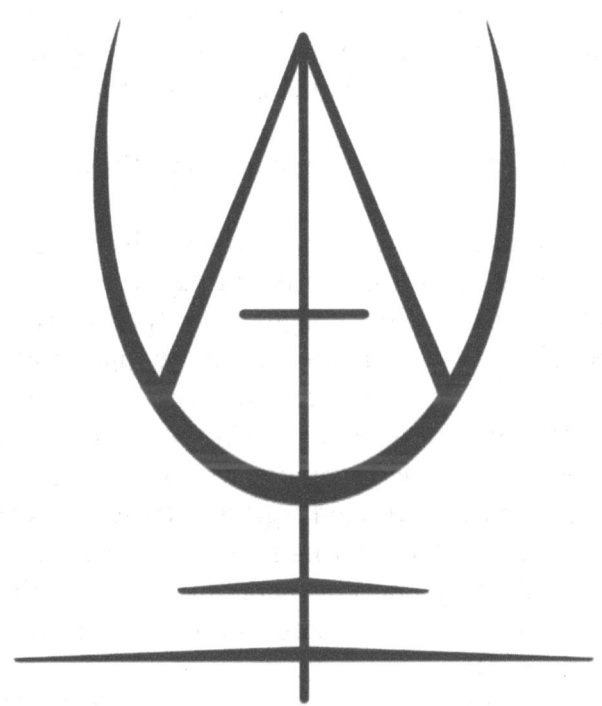

C.J. Phillips

Trigger Warnings

- Death of a spouse and sibling
- Grief
- Murder (parent/child)
- Mentions of Bi-Polar Disorder
- Mentions of Schizophrenia
- Drug use
- Alcohol use
- Attempted Suicide
- Many Explicit Sexual Encounters
  - Possession Kink
  - Brat Kink
  - Altocalciphilia
  - Anal Sex
  - Breath Play
  - Begging
  - Sensory Deprivation
  - Spanking
  - Praise Kink

For those of us brave enough to look beyond the scars.
To see into a person's soul and not be scared of what
is sitting in the shadows. Loving them entirely,
obsessively, impulsively.

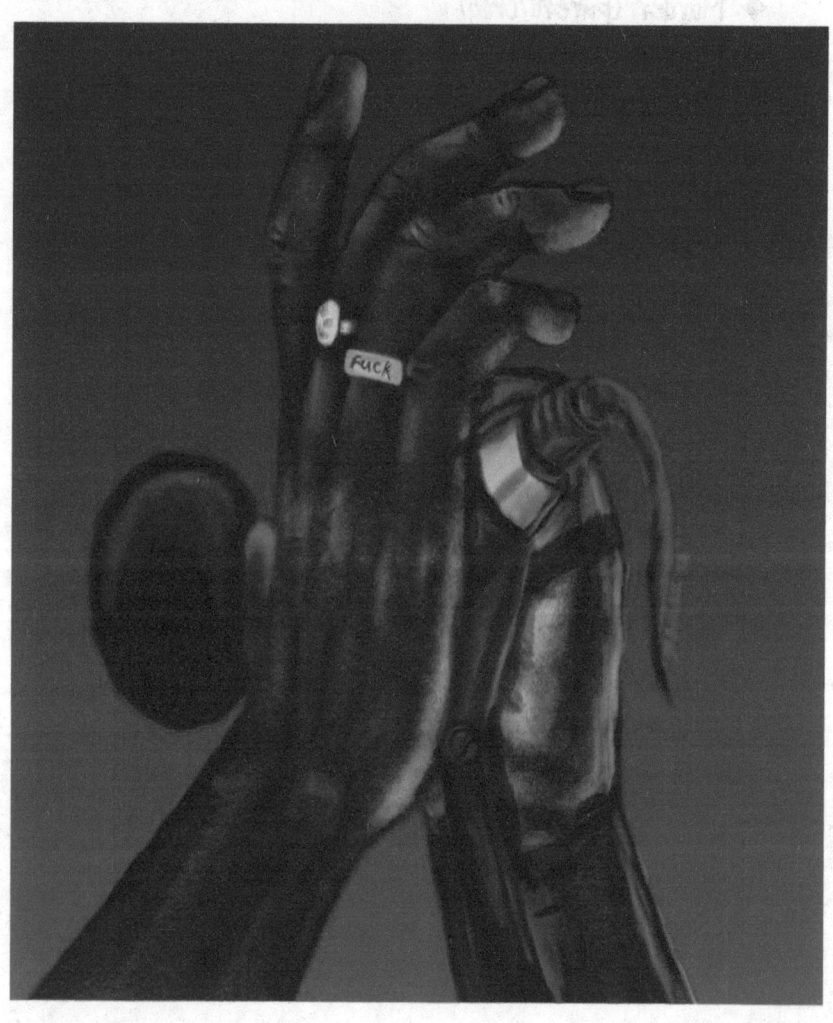

Playlist

Gone Away - Five Finger Death Punch

Past Self - Sleep Token

run for the hills - Tate McRae

Dangerous - Sleep Token

The Lion's Roar - First Aid Kit

I WANNA BE YOUR SLAVE - Maneskin

Indigo - Sam Barber, Avery Anna

WILDFLOWER - Billie Eilish

Dynasty - MIIA

Alkaline - Sleep Token

Intrusive Thoughts - Natalie Jane

The Sound of Being Alone - Tenille Townes

THE DEATH OF PEACE OF MIND - Bad Omens

Ascensionism - Sleep Token

Shame On Me - Catch Your Breath

All Around Me - Flyleaf

Fuck Me Like You Hate Me - Jutes

Leave a Light On - Tom Walker

The Way That You Were - Sleep Token

Read All About It, Pt. III - Emeli Sandé

Emergence - Sleep Token

DIE 4 U - Kami Kehoe

Sleeptalk - Dayseeker

Pretend My Pain Away - Citizen Soldier

Someone To You - Banners

Hold Me Down - Halsey

Blood Sport, from the room below - Sleep Token

Infinite Baths - Sleep Token

Lily
Gone Away - Five Finger Death Punch

I never imagined that at the age of 34 I would be a widow. Mark and I were supposed to be together forever, not just 8 years. Now, here I sit in the front pew of this ridiculously elaborate church, staring at a pearl white coffin in front of me.

I have just sat here staring at the seriously overdecorated pulpit for more than an hour now. The priest did his sermon which was more like a congressional speech to get more attendees into church then actually talking about Mark. That unfortunately only killed about a half hour. Very little pun intended. The man didn't even really know Mark. Not the real Mark. Just church Mark.

Church Mark had always been prim and proper. Speak only when spoken too. The real Mark was so much more than that. He was funny. He was always so full of spirit. He loved my dark humor. He loved me for me.

Mark had always been so healthy, like granola for breakfast kind of healthy. He ran 2 miles every single morning since the day I met him. Even on our honeymoon, he was up at the ass crack of dawn running around the hotel and down the beach. Even though I begged him to stay tangled up with me in the sheets, he was still out burning off the excess nerves. I guess that is who I get it from.

He ate right.

He lived right.

He barely drank and when he did it was never to the point of being drunk. He was a corporate attorney for Christ's sake.

And a good one.

One of the good guys, which are in very low supply these days if we are being honest. He was devoted to a fault. He was generous, kind and reliable. But none of these qualities are even mentioned by the preacher. But I am sure everyone in the building knows what time mass starts on Sunday, since it was mentioned a half dozen times.

No one could have known that the cancer would take him so quickly. It honestly feels like we found out one day that there was a tumor, then the next day he was gone. I know there had been 6 ½ months in between but those 6 ½ months were the longest of my life.

194 days is all I was given with him after that day at the ER. When we thought he had just fallen because he got dizzy, not from the ever growing tumor in his brain.

I look around the obscenely elaborate church at his family and friends. My now ex family and ex friends. You can visibly see the sadness around the room. Most of the people are just sitting with their heads down, shoulders slumped. I look around the room and the sadness is just hanging over the entire congregation, like a thick fog that is blanketing everything and everyone in its path. Everyone keeps walking by me, leaving me with their condolences.

Their prayers and sorrows.

I want to tell them all to shove their pity up their asses but I don't. I am still playing the dutiful mourning wife. I honestly feel like the majority of them are here because they feel obligated to be. Either by family or work connections. Sure, I believe they are sad, but is it sadness that has their heads hung low or is it their own struggles with immortality? I am going with the latter for the majority of them. I could count on one hand the people I believe are actually sincere in their grief right now.

I am one of the few on that list.

Of course I am sad. I'm shattered if we are being honest. But more than that, more than anything,

I'm pissed.

I'm pissed at Mark for leaving me here all alone.

I'm pissed at God for taking him away from me.

I'm pissed at *myself* for allowing him to go.

Logically, I know there is nothing I could have done. Hell, even the dozens of doctors and surgeons that were called in were unable to do anything.

But still I am angry.

Susie makes her way over to me, smiling and nodding her head to each person as she passes them like she is Miss America accepting her title on national television.

I swear to fuck if she starts waving like the queen I am booting her ass from the building. Best friend or not, I *will* do it. She sits down solemnly beside me, though no longer acting like royalty. The floral scent that follows her wherever she goes envelopes me and I instantly feel comforted again.

I feel her put her hand on my thigh and I lean into her, placing my head on her shoulder so I can whisper in her ear,

"I should have hired some big burly Italian guys to come to the funeral."

She lets out a small snicker, whispering back, "Why?"

I turn and look at Mark's mother, my no longer mother in law. She is sitting there all proper and straight-laced in her cashmere Mcqueen wrap dress. With her perfect manicure, perfect posture and perfect resting bitch face.

"Cause Maureen would have freaked the fuck out when they leaned over the coffin and said, 'We are gonna miss ya boss', then just walked back out of the church."

Susie clenches my thigh, nails digging in deeply, trying to pretend that her laughter is just a cough caught in her throat.

"Maureen would have lost her shit. We should have thought of that days ago!"

Susie is turning a shade of red that I have never seen on her before. Which is saying a lot considering she is a natural redhead and somehow still more porcelain than me.

Susie knows that I only deal with emotions with either inappropriate humor or dark jokes of some sort. Or on the really bad days when I completely shut down and think about all the different ways to just run away or disappear, she is the only one who has ever been able to pull me out of the fog. She has known me since 9th grade.

She has been here for every break up, every death, every nightmare. She is the only person that I actually trusted at the age of 13 and allowed myself to be open with.

She is the first person that I verbally spoke to in more than 7 years. That first day of school we sat next to each other in study hall and she asked me if she could borrow an ink pen. She wouldn't let me *not* answer. She stared directly into my eyes, unblinking until I finally blurted out "Sure!" out of sheer anxiety

She is the only one that was able to help me walk out of that darkness I was left in at 6 years old. She is the one that showed me that sometimes it is okay to be broken.

4

She saw me in my shell, then she watched me claw my way out of it. She knows every single side of me and still accepts me for my faults as well as my strengths.

She is my rock.

She is the only person under the sun that knows all of my secrets. Everything I still keep hidden deep within.

Even though Mark couldn't stand us when we were together, I never cut her out of my life. He always said we acted like annoying little sisters when we were together.

I smile at the thought of him avoiding us like the plague when we were together. If he could see us right now he would sit up out of the coffin and shush us.

I let out a heavy exhale,

"I have to say goodbye. This is too real now. If he thinks for one second that he is going to haunt my ass, I will hire that priest to come to the house. I swear. Exorcise the fuck out of it, remind me to buy sage tomorrow."

I feel her hand tighten on my thigh again, "Do you want me to come with you?"

I give her a weak smile, "No, this is something I have to do alone. But thank you."

Susie gives me another sympathetic frown of the eyebrows, "Of course babe. I will be right here waiting for you when you are done."

I tilt my head at her then take a deep breath before standing up. I can feel everybody's eyes on me. It feels like a million little needles are being slowly shoved into my back all at the same time. They are all judging me. They are all watching my every single move just waiting to see the cracks in the plaster start to open up. The entirety of the church seems to have fallen silent now. Because staring down their noses at me isn't enough, they need to have creepy church silence too.

It even feels like Jesus himself is watching me slowly move towards the open casket. There is some natural light shining in through the stained glass windows that line the congregation hall. The light reflects off of the satin casket turning each ray into a rainbow effect. The colors swirl and dance, creating a delicate ensemble of light that is painting the walls in this gentle spectrum.

That explains Mark to a T.

He could take something so ordinary and make it sparkle—make it shimmer.

I move toward the casket, seeing Mark come into view. His face pulled taut with layers upon layers of makeup on him. I guess he looks as natural as possible. But he had lost so much weight before he passed that he just looks like a shell of the man that is supposed to be there. I am glad I have chosen the dark blue Armani suit for him though. It always looks the best on him. It had always made his crystal blue eyes pop as well.

But now I will never get the chance to see those eyes again. I place a hand on his chest, wiping away a piece of invisible lint from the fabric. I let my fingers roll across the silky softness of the jacket as I feel the tears start to stream down my face.

I look at his gold wedding band, embossed in diamonds, gleaming in the light. I slide my own matching wedding band off then slip it down into the breast pocket of his suit jacket.

It's his now.

I feel my shoulders start to shudder. I have been strong all day. Why the hell am I breaking down now?

In front of everyone?

I lift my face to the ceiling, praying to whatever god is listening to help me make it through the next 5 minutes without a complete emotional breakdown or falling on my face.

6

I have to find the strength to walk away from this casket. To say goodbye. I look back down at the sweet, compassionate face that I promised my forever too.

He finally looks at peace.

He has been in so much pain, torment for months. I give him a soft smile before I lean forward, kissing him one last time on the forehead.

I stand back up then look at the preacher, nodding at him ever so slightly. Signaling that it is time. Time for this to finally be done.

I turn to see Susie standing right behind me, reaching her alabaster arm out for me to steady myself on. I take her offering, not letting my gaze completely meet hers. Silently, we walk down the aisle then out the front doors of the church.

I can't handle the procession that is about to take place. I move towards the limo that will be following the hearse to the cemetery. Susie stands back, giving me some space but keeping her eyes on me at all times. Just in case.

Reaching into my handbag, I pull out a pack of Marlboro's. The irony that my husband has just died of cancer and I am lighting a cigarette does not fall flat on me. Susie gives me a side eye but isn't about to lecture me right now. But I have full confidence that once she makes it back to the house after the burial, she is going to rip me a new one. Just like every other time when she sees me light one up.

I just need to get through today. Then I will quit. Or maybe plan to quit. I quickly light the cigarette while attempting to hide behind a shrub so I am not seen by the judging eyes of everyone making their way out of the church.

I take a few quick drags off the cigarette before stomping it out beneath one of my leather Jimmy Choos'. I spray some body spray on me quickly then turn to watch Mark's cousins and brothers carry his gleaming pearl casket out of the church and place it into the back of the hearse.

I let out another deep breath before popping a breath mint in.

Mark's parents, Maureen and Paul are walking towards me, both somber, both beside themselves with grief. They never imagined they would be burying their youngest son at the age of 35.

Paul immediately steps up to me and gives me a warm hug. Paul has always been the best to me. Maureen can barely stand me on a good day but Paul, he has always just accepted me for me. Accepted our marriage for what it was. A form of love with a healthy dose of respect.

I did love Mark, in my own way. I just never planned to fall in love with him, or with anyone for that matter. I saw at a very young age what love can do to somebody.

Why would I willingly walk into that kind of agony?

I planned to spend the rest of my life with Mark and him with me. But I don't think anyone would have been writing love songs about our earth shattering relationship.

Because that wasn't what it was. We loved each other, we respected each other, and we were both comfortable with what we had. None of that changed because I had never uttered the phrase "I am *in* love with you."

Susie had always worried that I was just settling but she never understood that the mutual respect and the easiness that filled the gaps in our relationship rounded us out. It was all I had ever looked for in a partner honestly.

I slowly pull away from Paul, looking up into his saddened face, "I can't believe this is actually happening. I mean, we knew it was going to but I never actually believed it was going to happen."

8

Paul places a warm hand on my cheek, giving me a weak and weathered half smile, "Mark loved you so much Lily. You were his world. He would be so proud of you for being as strong as you have been."

You can see the stress and remorse etched in Paul's face. He seems to have found a dozen new wrinkles overnight. I hope he is pacing himself, getting some rest at least. His heart has not been good for awhile now. I am worried that the stress of today is going to push him past his boundaries.

I feel another tear start to slide down my cheek as I turn towards Maureen. Whether we like each other or not doesn't matter right now. We are burying my husband, her son. The time for uncomfortable silence has passed.

Maureen looks at me, hesitating for just a moment before I lean into her, gently wrapping her up in my arms. I can feel her silently sobbing into my shoulder. We may not have always gotten along but one thing we always had in common was how much we both loved Mark.

I let my hand stroke the back of her head, smoothing her long grey hair, "He loved you so much Maureen. He never not once had a bad thing to say about you. He would tell me stories all the time of when he was younger and all the things you two would do together.

"The picnics, the vacations, he cherished every single memory of you two together. He loved you so, so much. You were a wonderful mother to him, thank you for that. For helping to mold him into the man that he became."

Maureen lets out another short shudder, then slowly pulls away from me. She gives me a soft smile, the lines in her face barely evident from the copious amounts of botox she receives, probably weekly,

"Lily, we may not have always seen eye to eye but I know how much my son loved you. Hell, even a stranger could have

9

seen it. I am so grateful he was able to know that kind of love. I am so glad that you were the one to show him that."

Maureen has never been this nice to me before. I am completely certain it is just because her emotions are getting the best of her at this moment but I don't care. She may have even had an extra Lithium in her morning cocktail, but either way I am going to take full advantage of it. A win is a win.

Paul pulls open the door to the limo for Maureen and myself to slide in. I take one more look back at the hearse as they are shutting the big back door on it. I give another small smile to Paul then push myself into the limo beside Maureen. It is time to finally put Mark to rest.

4 long hours later, I'm finally home. This big house seems so cold now, hollow even. I sit my purse down on the table inside the front door, slowly sliding off my shoes. I roll my ankles one at a time out in front of me, stretching the arches of my feet and my neck at the same time.

I reach down and pick my shoes up then slowly start to make my way upstairs to our bedroom.

What in the hell am I going to do with this house now?

We had plans to fill it with laughter and love. Children and grandchildren. Now here I am, 34 fucking years old with a 3 story brownstone with 5 bedrooms and absolutely nothing to fill them with. Nothing besides sadness and fear.

I drudge myself up the stairs, rounding the corner slowly. I leisurely take my time walking down the long hallway to the bedroom. The walls are lined with our wedding photos. Smiling images trapped behind glass and wood. Just a reminder of how alone I really am now.

I finally make it into the master bedroom and round the corner into my closet. I slowly slide out of my mourning dress, throwing it into a heap in the bottom of my closet.

I never want to see it again.

I don't even care that it is a beautiful Dior now wadded up in the corner. I throw my Jimmy Choo's right on top of it. Susie will find a use for them I am sure.

I walk to the dresser, pulling out a pair of sweatpants and Mark's favorite Yale Law t-shirt. I dress slowly, almost robotically then make my way back downstairs.

I pad my bare feet over to the wine refrigerator but quickly decide that wine isn't going to cut it today. I definitely need something a bit stronger to get these clouds out of my head tonight.

I close the refrigerator door and move to the bar in the living room. I pour myself a rather large glass of 40 year old Dalmore. I let the rich, oaky aroma of the whisky take over my senses. One sip from it leaves me with the taste of citrus and black tea lingering on my tongue. The warmth rolls down my throat coating my stomach with a desperately needed hug.

I walk towards the living room then to the wall of windows that overlooks the backyard. I had thought about going up to the rooftop deck and just staring out over Central Park but I don't want Susie to show up thinking I am about to jump or something.

You can see a random star here and there but even on a clear night there isn't much to see over Central Park. I instead look at the skyline, the tall metal coffins that seem to hold us all hostage. Maybe I should move to the country, where there is no one for miles. No reminders of this house and its empty rooms.

I hear the door knob jiggle signaling that Susie has made it home. I had given her Mark's key when he first went into hospice. She has stayed with me almost every day since. I smile as I hear the door shut and her throwing her keys into the small dish on the table inside the front door.

I continue to sip my single malt until I feel her step up behind me and wrap her hands around my waist to meet at my stomach. The embrace of the rose petal scent that follows her. It always brings a small smile to my face. Immediately, the anxiety starts to drift away again.

I can then feel her resting her chin on my shoulder,

"How are you holding up Lily?"

I let out a small chuckle,

"Wonderful. I am thinking of running a 10k in the morning."

I can feel her smile at me while taking my whisky from my hand then taking a long draw from it,

"Not a chance. We are having brunch at Upland tomorrow. You will have to start your training some other day."

I snort at her then walk over to the bar and pour another glass. We both sit in comfortable silence on the couch, just staring at the wall in front of us. She is probably counting the bricks in the wall but I am sitting here thinking about how much I hate the bricks in the wall. How they are keeping me contained in a life that I don't fit into anymore.

"I think I am going to sell the brownstone."

I can feel Susie's green eyes on me. I know she is thinking it is an emotionally fueled decision but really it isn't. Not completely at least.

This is the home that Mark had wanted. He dragged me all over Manhattan looking for the perfect house. The one that he envisioned us growing old in. When he saw it, he knew it was the "one". Yes I love it, but it holds too many broken promises. Now, we will never fill this house with the love we promised to give each other for the rest of our lives.

I can feel Susie's eyes on me so I glance towards her,
"Don't look at me like that."
She gives another small laugh, "Like what?"
I turn fully to face her on the other end of the couch,
"Like I am making a stupid decision."
She shakes her head as she takes another drink of Dalmore, "I never said it was a stupid decision."
I sit my glass down on the coffee table then cross my legs underneath me, "Your eyes are saying what your mouth won't."
Susie lets out another deep laugh,
"I just don't want you to make any rash decisions. I mean, damn the man hasn't even been in the ground for 24 hours yet. And before you say that is harsh, you know I am right."

Dammit, she's right.

I roll my eyes at her sarcastically,
"I just see him everywhere here. I can feel him in every single room of this house. I am not saying I am wanting to forget him. I never will. But I don't want to wake up to the reminder every single day that he is actually gone."
Susie gently reaches out and places her hand on my knee, rubbing small circles on it,
"Sweetie. I know you are never going to forget him. No one is asking you to just move on immediately. I think you should just wait. What you feel like is too much right now may not feel as heavy in a few months. Ya know?"
I shoot her a brief grin, picking my glass back up,

"Yeah. You're right. I know you're right. It's just the silence here, it is just screaming at me. Maybe I will just travel a bit. I always wanted to do that. We just rarely could because of Mark's work. He was always in court, then he was in the hospital."

I can still feel Susie's eyes on me as I down the last of my whisky then stand up to pour another. I wave the empty glass around the room as I walk towards the bar,

"I have no fucking clue where I will go though. Every single vacation destination I have ever looked up was for some type of couples retreat. I don't even know where to start."

Susie stands up and walks over to me, setting her empty glass down beside mine,

"Let's just drink our whisky. Listen to some music and just be. At brunch tomorrow, we can pull out that little black book of yours and start writing plans in the date boxes. Okay?"

I smile and nod at her as I fill her glass as well,

"Sounds like a solid plan."

Susie grabs her drink then turns to the stereo. She always knows exactly what I need to hear. I need the music that Mark never liked. I need something resounding, something heavy, something tormented.

Something louder than the voices already screaming in my head. I just need to not feel anything, just a little bit. At this point, I will take a 5 minute reprieve and be eternally grateful. I would possibly even be open to a back alley lobotomy. She hits the shuffle option before we both sit down, quietly sipping our whisky.

I'm exhausted. She looks just as exhausted.

We sit in comfortable silence as the music soars loudly around the room. Each song is a bit more devastatingly beautiful than the last. I glance over at Susie and notice her eyes are heavy and her arm is barely holding up glass.

14

I smile at the sight of her. Long red hair twirling around her face in beach waves. Her perfect ivory skin is speckled with small brown and orange freckles. She is a stunner, the bad part is she knows it.

It isn't 20 minutes later and I am taking her glass from her sleeping hand then covering her up with a blanket from the back of the couch. I quickly finish my glass then stand to take the empty vessels to the kitchen sink.

My ears quickly perk up to the sound of a haunting piano coming from the speakers. I glance into the other room at the stereo as if I am going to see a live concert in front of me. Interestingly enough, I have never heard this song before.

I continue my journey to the kitchen sink, listening to the dark rumble of the singer's voice. He has to be British. I can hear the accent in between the growls.

"Hold me, we're eclipsed in reverie,
Surrendering our souls to the night.

Drowning in the abyss of ecstasy,
In your arms, I find my light."

I quickly throw back the last of her whisky as well. I roll my head across my shoulders as I really set in to listen to the voice coming from the speakers.

The man's tone is picking at my soul. You can hear the emotion, the resistance in the soft falsetto of his range. Then the next moment you will hear him screaming into the microphone with this torment and torture that just feels like home.

It is somehow comforting.

Like his soul is somehow connected to my own. I feel like I can take all that rage he is emitting and hold it close to my

15

own heart. It has a calming effect on me that is surprising but welcomed.

> *"Let the moon bear witness to our descent,*
> *As shadows dance along these sacred walls.*
>
> *In the heart of the night, I flourish with you,*
> *In this beautiful waltz, we come alive."*

The way his voice mixes with the synthesizer then moments later the guitar is taking over. The drumline is loud from the back then disappears to just his voice again. It is constant and it heavily reverberates in my head.

I sit the glasses in the sink then slowly make my way back to the living room. I curl up on the other end of the couch from Susie listening to the lyrics.

> *"As the dawn unravels soft and slow,*
> *Remember this love, where only we go.*
>
> *Eclipsed in time, where shadows caress,*
> *In silence, my heart finds its rest."*

A small smile falls over my face as I close my eyes. His words flow over me like smooth velvet, wrapping around my soul. There is this captivating tone and rasp to his voice. Like the sound of distant lightning crackling against the night sky. But it is still just so smooth. The way he can fluctuate the lyrics through his chest. It's enchanting.

He is singing about heartache. Mistakes that were made, feelings that were misunderstood.

I unfortunately know those emotions all too well.

16

2
Lily
Past Self - Sleep Token

"Lily, you have to go. It's Mark's will reading. You have to at least make an appearance."

I glance back at Susie, rolling my eyes at her.

Why she feels the need to constantly tell me I need to do something that I have already agreed to do, I have no idea. She has been here for over a week now. I mean, I love her but she needs to go get laid or something. Just spend one night away from me for fuck's sake. That is not too much to ask for.

For both of our sanities.

I reach into my closet pulling out a beautiful Carolina Herrera sleeveless dress. It has a drop waist and a gorgeous flower pattern. I hold it up at eye level then glance towards the shelf behind me until I find a pair of Louboutins' that will match perfectly.

I grab the heels and make my way out of the walk-in closet, clad in nothing but my underwear,

"*I know* I have to go. I never said I wasn't going to go. I just know everything that is in it though. It just seems like a technicality that I could honestly be fine skipping out on."

I slide the dress up over my hips and position it on my shoulders while staring in the full length mirror. I waggle my shoulders at Susie and she steps up behind me to zip the dress up,

17

"Yes, but you have to make sure that the money gets divided out to the right places. He had specific shelters in mind for that money."

I nod into the mirror in front of me. Susie's smiling face beaming over my shoulder. She worries too fucking much. She pulls my hair back around and flattens it down my back as I give her another quick leer then slide my heels on,

"I will make sure the money goes to the correct places. It is just 2 hours of my life I may never get back is all."

Susie reaches behind me, grabbing my clutch to hand to me, "Here. Don't forget this."

She glances at her watch yet again, "The driver is going to be here any minute. Are you ready? Do you have everything?"

I turn to face her, placing a hand on each shoulder,

"Yes, Mother, I have everything."

She laughs and slaps my ass as I turn to walk out the room, "I would have been the coolest mom ever and you fucking know it."

I raise one hand with a perfectly manicured middle finger in the air over my head as a goodbye,

"Get the fuck out of my house tonight. Go find Brian, get laid or something. I love you but you need some ♪dick♪." I make sure that last word is in song form so the sarcasm can really set in.

Her laughter surrounds me down the hallway as I walk down the stairs towards the front door. I step out onto the front stoop just as the driver pulls up. I carefully make my way towards the car then slide into the open seat waiting for me.

"Murphy, Bryant, and Wades, please."

I know that Garrett, the driver, knows where to go. He has been working for Mark for a while now. I still just feel awkward getting in and not speaking though. The silence is still deafening.

He nods quickly as he shuts my door and makes his way to the driver's seat. I put my airpods in my ears and turn Spotify on.

I have been listening to Carnal Decay for over a week now. Ever since I heard them the night of the funeral.

The song begins and I hear that familiar cadence fall over my ears. I smile, closing my eyes to let myself get lost in the words flowing from the lead singer.

"Skin like silk, the truth feels like sin,
Drawn to your flame, the burning begins.

In every heartbeat, I feel the chains,
The echo of longing — the sweetest of pains."

I have never heard music so soothing before. I don't think I will ever get tired of it. I wish I was at home right now so I could be painting. I have found this offering of inspiration in the chords they play. I have painted almost a dozen pieces in the last 8 days alone.

"So hold me with poison, and bind me in grace,
In the fabric of life, I find my true place.

Embraced by the shadows that bask in my delight,
In a universe of stars, only you feel right."

We arrive at the law firm 20 minutes later, though it feels like only seconds have passed. I huff as I turn the music off reluctantly then put my phone and air pods away.

Garrett graciously opens my door for me. I step out onto the busy street, looking up at the large glass building in front of me, "Time to finish this."

3 hours and 30 million dollars later, I am back in the car heading home. The meeting went exactly as expected. I am now the sole owner of the brown stone and the vacation home in the Outer Banks. I also take over sole ownership of a very well padded checking and savings account. Plus multiple stocks and other bonds.

The reserved 30 million has been divided up between 8 different shelters across New York and Boston. They are all shelters for abused women and children.

Mark had always held a soft spot for the topic. He had heard what I was raised in. He said from the very beginning of our relationship that he would donate every last dime he had if it meant that some little girl would not have to live through what I had.

Thankfully, Susie actually listened to me and decided to spend some quality time with Brian. The note she left though expressed that she would come back in a moment's notice if I needed her. Also, that she would be here promptly in the morning to check on me.

I roll my eyes as I toss the note in the trash then walk to the refrigerator to find something to eat.

There is a caesar salad in there calling my name. I have honestly been thinking about it for the last 2 hours. I am just happy that no one seemed to notice the rumblings from my stomach as I sat at the long boardroom table earlier.

I sit at the counter, grabbing the stereo remote. I turn on Carnal Decay again. I sit in silence just eating and listening.

Every single song feels like it is being sung directly to me. Like the lead singer is sitting across this very counter from me.

"In shadows the whispers echo,
Where the light dares not tread,

I'm tethered to the silence,
Of the words that were never said."

Most of the songs have a deeper meaning probably than how I interpret them. But that is what I think makes them so popular. They have obviously intended for the lyrics to mean one thing but there are so many paths you can take with the words they are stringing together.

Loss can mean so many different things.
Death.
Heartbreak.
Inability to allow yourself to live in a situation any longer.

"Tell me where the lost souls go,
When the night takes its final bow.

In the stillness, I feel the undertow,
Veiled whispers, come find me now."

Every single song talks about some type of inner conflict, some turmoil that is just begging to be crushed. It feels like thick waves of tension running through my veins. But the pressure, the crushing weight of it, somehow soothes my own demons. Like the weight of his words is what is actually holding me together.

I finish up my dinner and wash the few dishes sitting in the sink while still listening to the haunting lyrics. I tilt my head, I wish I knew exactly what he is singing about.

"Submerged in pain, the silence screams,
In this garden where dreams slowly vanish,

Are flowers born from ashes of fate,
The love we lost, too pure to wait."

I want to understand the lyrics from his point of view as well. He sings them with so much passion, it's overwhelming. Some of their songs hit a bit harder than the others. I love them all though.

I know if Maureen was to walk in right now though she would try to call a priest or something. She would probably expect me to be committed for some type of trauma induced psychotic episode.

This was one side of me that she luckily never saw. Mark saw it but he never really understood it. When I would lock myself away and play haunting tormenting music, he would normally just leave me to sit staring out the window. He never really figured out how to save me from drowning in my own demons, my memories.

I smirk to myself as I head upstairs to put pajamas on. I change into my silk set then grab my robe to head back downstairs.

I stop at the end of the bed, looking over at Mark's side. His phone is still sitting there. His Breitling Top Time lies right next to it. There is also a half read novel with his glasses resting on top of it as well. I let out a sigh looking at our bed that I still haven't brought myself to sleep in yet.

22

It is still impeccably made. Untouched for months now. I need to fucking do something with his stuff. I can't just leave it all sitting here like he is going to just show back up. He is gone. I know he is gone. I need to just accept that and move on.

I let my eyes still there for just a moment longer before letting out another heavy breath and head back downstairs.

I throw my robe over the back of the couch, then grin at yet another ballad from Carnal Decay coming from the speakers. I should probably stop fixating on them. But there is just something about their music that I just can't shake. I actually feel a sense of belonging when I hear their music. I have only ever felt that with Susie before. It comforts me. I smile at the lyrics then suddenly realize, I don't even know his name. The singer that is.

I move across the hall into the study and grab my laptop off the desk before going back to the living room and settling into the couch. I promptly flip it open and do a broad search for the band. I click on an image and quickly fall into a rabbit hole so deep even Alice wouldn't be able to find her way out.

There are 5 members in the band. It seems that none of them go by their real names. They don't even show their faces. They all wear masks, even during their live shows.

The lore behind the band is fucking intense. There are so many different avenues that people have taken to try to figure them out. It is honestly impressive the lengths some fans have gone to just to convince themselves that their ideals are correct. The most convincing theory that I have read though is that they all channel the powers of whatever god they are representing.

They take on these personas and they become that god or goddess for whatever amount of time they need on stage. It is a bit insane to imagine. I can only envision what one of their concerts is actually like if they are truly channeling the persona of the god they are imaging. Just seeing stills of them is overpowering, emotionally charging, breathtaking. I can't imagine what they are like live.

From the images on the screen, it seems like at least 2 of them are females. I look them all over intensely. Their masks are fucking majestic. Everyone has their own style of mask but they blend together so well as a group. There are 5 gods that they have deemed worthy enough of channeling it seems.

Hestia, Apollo, Dionysus, Hera and Ares.

Ares being the lead singer. He stands tall with a slender frame, yet there is a certain strength to his physique. He is lean and toned, like an athletic swimmer or something.

His mask is fucking terrifying though. It makes him look fearless and resolute. It has a crack going down the middle like some type of sharp blade has tried to break the damn thing right off his face. There is blood splattered across it like he has taken his own blade and forced an artery to spray out across his face.

The photo hints at the long, sinewy muscles beneath the hooded cloak and body paint he wears. He seems confident and honestly, terrifying.

I sit there following the lines of his body with my eyes. You can't see his face under the mask but the body paint that covers his torso leaves me with nothing but deviant thoughts.

He is towering over the others in the photo with a formidable presence. I couldn't look away even if this damn house was on fire.

24

I take a deep breath imagining running my hand down that long, toned torso. My eyes close, their lyrics flow from the speakers and has my mind going down a descent I do not expect.

"Can you feel the weight of the silence?
The echoes of promises we lost in violence.

I reach for your ghost, but the void draws near,
In the depths of my sorrow, I drown in my own fear."

What would his hands feel like touching my skin? Wrapping around my neck?

I quickly shake my head to try to make the images disappear but they won't budge. I can still hear his voice in my head.

I swear if I ever heard him say my name I would die on the spot. I laugh at the hilarity of the situation. One, he is way too young for me and Two, I don't think I will be running into him at the corner grocery store so even letting myself get lost in these fantasies is ridiculous. But I guess that's why they call them fantasies. It's not like I can dream them into existence.

I let my eyes run over the others in the band. It is hard to see a lot of any of them but from what I can tell they all seem young and intense. A lethal combination. At least that is what it looks like from what little can be seen.

Hestia and Hera stand together on one side of the image. They hold hands like sisters. I look over their clothes, their stance.

They seem so self-assured. I wish for just a moment I could have a fraction of their confidence. Hera's mask is the most colorful of them all. It is a kaleidoscope of colors with a lighting bolt stretching from the left side of her chin up to the right side of her forehead. The colors all mold together in perfect unison.

Hestia's mask is a bit haunting if I am being honest. It looks like the face of an old porcelain doll that has been kept on a shelf for the last millenia. It is weathered and cracked with age but still looks like a young cherub faced girl staring back at me.

Behind them, Apollo is standing tall with a drum stick in each hand. I lean in to look closer at his mask. There is a sun emanating from the center of his forehead. The rays from it stretch in every direction and seem to wrap around the edges of the mask itself. It is one of the most beautiful things I have ever seen.

Dionysus stands to the right of Ares, turned slightly away from the camera. Dionysus looks fucking terrifying if I am being completely brutal. He looks to be just a smidge shorter than Ares but more built. His mask is green and looks to have the faces of many different souls trying to claw their way out of it.

I let my eyes go back to Ares. Standing tall and proud in the center of it all. It is intense. But also enticing.

I cannot pull my eyes away from him. It feels as if everything in the room is orbiting him. Those vacant slats staring back at me, covered in blood, unwavering in his claim on any soul he sees fit.

I can understand the reasoning behind wearing the masks. This way they could still live their lives. Have some small glimpse of normalcy.

The band itself is not really huge yet but I can see that easily happening. They truly are phenomenal. From what I can tell from Google and Youtube, their following is growing by the thousands, if not more every day.

I click on another photo of Ares. This one has him towering over the camera, looking down onto it. I enlarge it then sit the laptop on the coffee table so I can just stare at him as I hear his words float around me.

I softly lean back into the couch falling asleep to the sound of his bewitching voice.

"The moonlight weeps as I trace every scar,
An elegy sung beneath a lone star.

Your name is a song whispered by quivering lips,
A delicate reminder of our fleeting eclipse."

I finally wake up around 9 am. Somehow, I have lucked out and Susie has not arrived yet. The music from the stereo is still playing on a loop but the laptop had gone into sleep mode hours before. I let out a yawn, stretching and cracking my neck as I sit up. I reach over, grabbing the stereo remote to turn the music down a few notches.

I lean over to the laptop fully intending to turn it off and return it to its home in the study but as the screen wakes up from the movement, I see a pop up that has sprung up over the picture of Ares.

There is a banner across the screen reading Carnal Decay has a concert coming up in Philadelphia. In less than a week's time, they are going to be live at the Fillmore.

I smile to myself as I feel a warmth roll over my chest. Before I lose my nerve, I instantly go to the website that is advertising the concert.

A tight frown instantly covers my face when a huge banner pops up on the screen stating "Sold Out".

That sounds like my fucking luck.

I am finally able to find some solace and peace in something only to not be able to experience it first hand. Literally, the story of my life. I sit the laptop back down and head upstairs to shower then dress for the day.

A half hour later, I am trotting back down the stairs to the living room when I hear Susie singing from the kitchen. She is still listening to Carnal Decay.

I step around the corner silent like a ninja, "Whatcha doin?"

Susie belts out a scream that sounds like a damsel in a horror movie, throwing a half peeled orange onto the ground so she can clutch her neck as if someone is trying to strangle her.

I smile wider as I step through the door and pick up the orange as it rolls across the floor. I laugh maniacally at her as I rinse the orange off in the sink then sit it back down on the counter in front of her.

Susie is still struggling to breath between the fear and the now laughter tearing from her throat. Her face and neck have turned a deep shade of pink.

She shakes her head at me, "You really are a bitch you know that?" I fucking love catching her offguard. Any chance I get to make those freckles on her face stand out, I take.

I give her a smile and a nod, "Yup, sure do."

I stroll past her and pour myself a cup of coffee before settling in at the kitchen island opposite of her. Susie is still breathing heavily, shaking her head, trying to calm her nerves.

She gestures her chin towards the stereo in the other room, "I didn't know you listened to Carnal Decay. I mean don't get me wrong, they definitely sound like a band *you* would love. When did you hear about them?"

28

I lean back on the barstool a bit,

"I first heard them the night of the funeral when you passed out on the couch. I have kinda been obsessing over them ever since."

Susie gives me a quick nod, tossing a slice of orange in her mouth, "Yeah, I have listened to them a few times too. If I was 10 years younger, I would definitely try to scoop up that lead singer. He is fucking hot."

I smile into my coffee mug, "You and me both, babe."

Susie smiles back as she puts another slice of orange in her mouth. She gives me a slight side eye as she walks past me and into the living room. I watch her walk back into the kitchen holding my laptop, "What are you doing with that?"

She smiles back at me, "Don't worry about it."

I give her another questioning glance as she types away on the keyboard. I continue to sip my coffee watching her type like a woman possessed.

Then I watch her take out her phone. She types something on it then smiles as she sits the phone down on the counter in front of her.

"No seriously, what are you doing?"

She lets out an evil laugh, "You are going to Philadelphia this weekend."

I shake my head, "Uh, no I'm not."

She gives me the classic Susie evil grin as she turns the laptop towards me, showing me that I am now the proud owner of a front row VIP floor seat at the Carnal Decay concert.

I feel my jaw almost hit the counter,

"What the fuck? I thought they were sold out!"

Susie flashes me another grin waving her hand at the laptop, "Venues always hold back tickets just in case. If they don't sell them grossly overpriced before the concert they sell them dirt cheap the day or so before."

I shake my head at her, "I can't go to Philadelphia by myself! I don't even know anybody there."

Susie reaches out and squeezes my hand, "Sweetie. You have to venture out a bit. You have to do these kinds of things on your own now. You are strong. You are smart. You are capable. Go, have fun, spend a few days there. I mean why not? You don't have to work. You don't have any pets or children. This could be the start of that traveling you said you wanted to do."

I glance questionably from the laptop screen to Susie's face, "I mean, yeah but, come on Susie. I am thirty fucking four years old. I am going to be the oldest god damn person there."

She laughs out loud at me, "I highly doubt that. And yeah, you are *only* thirty fucking four. You are far from old. Just go and have fun. Don't worry about everyone else. Just go and enjoy yourself."

I shake my head at her then look back at the screen. I mean. I guess it wouldn't hurt to go to one concert.

3
Lily
Run For The Hills - Tate McRae

Four days later, I am checking into the Cambria hotel in Philadelphia. I am still shocked at myself that I am actually going through with this. Susie didn't really leave me much choice though. It was either this or fucking online dating apps. I choose the lesser of the two evils. I picked the nicest hotel I could find as close to the Fillmore as possible.

  I only really have two requirements, a bar and a gym. I can live without everything else. I have to feed my cardio addiction then ruin it with a nice whisky. So, the hotel itself is perfect for my short stay. I have also luckily arrived right at check in time so they have my suite ready and waiting.

  The concert isn't until tomorrow so I decide I will grab a bite to eat tonight, maybe get a drink at the lounge then tomorrow work out and go shopping for something more appropriate to wear to the concert. I brought a few outfits with me but all of them just seem too ostentatious for an alternative metal concert. I don't think there is going to be a lot of Ralph Lauren or Tom Ford being rocked there.

  I am not a prude by any stretch of the imagination but in the last 8 years my clothing styles have most definitely changed. I used to be tight, black, with holes and no designer labels. Now it seems my closet could probably feed a third world country.

I had to change with the situations though. Mark was an extremely successful lawyer. He also came from a very prolific and wealthy family. I had to fit into the crowd I had begun to run with.

I still miss the days of being a struggling artist though. I miss the smell of the paints as my brush runs across the canvas. The feel of the rough fabric under my fingers when I would smear pastels and charcoals. Somedays, I can still feel the grit of a piece of charcoal in my hand.

I laugh to myself as I open my suite door. Now all I want to do is rush back home and paint. It seems my new happy place is painting while listening to Ares sing to me. He has this ability to make me tune everything out. I just channel him, the music and I am instantly teleported to a place where there is peace, calm, and acceptance.

It doesn't take me long to get settled into my suite. It is nicely designed, decorated in modern simplicities. All clean lines and white slabs of marble. It even has a pretty decent view of the city. Well, I assume it is nice, I have never been here before so I really have nothing to compare it to.

I stare out at the city for a bit before deciding I am hungry. I haven't eaten anything since I shared an English muffin with Susie this morning at breakfast. I grab my phone and send her a quick text letting her know my plans for the evening. I step over to the vanity as I pull my long black hair up off my back and put it into a messy bun on the top of my head.

I try to contain the wild fly aways since I haven't actually straightened it today. I put on minimal makeup but for some reason feel a bit sassy and decide to paint my lips red.

I smile into the mirror, taking in the face of the woman before me. I feel a lot older than I look. I run my fingertips over my sharp cheekbones, I could probably pass for my late 20's. I look into my steel grey eyes again, maybe I should look into botox when I get back home.

Take care of the fine lines starting to appear on my forehead. Even though I am completely aware that the fine lines that look like deep crevices are not even noticed by anyone other than myself. I let out a heavy sigh staring at the stranger before me in the mirror. I am a far cry from the girl I was back in college. Even more different from the mute child struggling to survive at St. Francis.

I quickly dress in a one shoulder wide leg black jumpsuit. It's luxurious but not completely dripping with pretension. I grab my clutch then quickly make my way down to the street level to have an uber take me to a nearby steakhouse.

The restaurant is nice, just different. It has the atmosphere of an old established tavern. All rich dark woods and linens on the tables. The lighting is set low and there is some hint of a pop instrumental coming from the hidden speakers. I have become very accustomed to the finer dining experience. This place is still fancier than most but I instantly feel overdressed.

It doesn't help that I am currently being stared at by nearly every single person as I walk in alone. The women are giving me evil sneers while the men are ogling my every step.

It is terrifying. Being alone now. No one here to put his hand on my lower back and lead me into a room. Navigating this world alone is quickly becoming a deafening experience. I know that I will find a groove eventually but I had latched onto the security that my marriage had provided. It is just terrifying to try to maneuver life alone now.

I was just going to find a seat at the bar. But my nerves are getting the best of me so I decide to request a small table in the corner for some privacy. I am still not completely ready to come out of my bubble yet.

I sit and enjoy my dinner and drink. I mostly stare out the window onto the street. People watching has always been a passion of mine. I can honestly sit on a park bench for hours happily just watching the hustle and bustle as it passes. I see a group of twenty-somethings make their way in the front door. I wish I still felt as young as they appear to be.

I finish my salad but decide to order another glass of whisky. I lean back in my chair just watching the crowd around me. Everyone is so alive. So excited to just be. I remain here watching their expressions wondering when I will ever feel that again. *If* I will ever feel that again.

It doesn't take long and my drink is gone. I have already paid the bill. All that is left to do is to head back to the hotel. I let out a soft exhale as I stand up and smooth down the legs of my jumpsuit. I slowly make my way through the maze of tables to pass the bar and head to the front door. I quickly realize about half way that I have forgotten my clutch at the table.

Maybe I shouldn't have had that second glass of whisky. I laugh to myself and slap my hand on my hip, "Shit!"

I turn to run back to the table and catch the gaze of one of the men sitting at the bar. His dark eyes hold mine for just a moment before I turn and veer back to my corner table. He is strikingly handsome, though way too young for me. His face is holding no expression but something seems to lock in within that half a second we spend enveloped in each other's gaze.

I quickly pick up my clutch then swivel to head back towards the front door. I look back towards the bar but the guy has already turned his back to me. I don't even give him a second glance as I walk out the front door and back onto the city street.

I decide to have just one more drink at the hotel bar before I go upstairs for the night. Why not? It's not like I have to drive anywhere and I still have plenty of time to kill. I sit at the far end of the bar, by myself, staring into the amber liquid in the bottom of my glass. I wonder how many of these I am going to have to ingest tomorrow to have the nerve to go to this concert alone?

I let out a small laugh at myself and the absurdity that is this entire trip.

"Something funny?"

I hear a deep voice resonating from my left.

I look up to see the most beautiful yet haunted eyes I have ever seen in my life. They are as black as a moonless night sky.

It's the man from the restaurant. The man from the bar.

He was one of the twenty-somethings that had walked in while I was eating. I sit up a bit straighter, "Uh, no. Not really. I was just thinking to myself is all."

He nods his head towards me then looks up to the bartender, "I will have a whisky sour and another of whatever the lady is drinking."

His voice is melancholy to my ears.

It has a hint of gravel to it but it is smooth as velvet at the same time. I smile at him, "Thank you but you don't have to. I was about to call it a night anyway."

He looks down at his watch then smiles back up at me, "It's 10 pm." I let out a small chuckle as my eyes scour the room.

He is right, it is still early. At least to everyone but me apparently. I give him another smile and a small nod, "Okay, maybe one more then."

He motions to the seat between us, "Do you mind if I sit here?" I feel my breath catch in my throat, why the hell am I nervous? He is just being nice is all.

I put another small smile on my face and nod back to him, waving my hand towards the empty seat, "Sure, that would be fine."

He slips into the seat next to me and his scent falls over me in waves. He smells like the ocean after a fresh storm has passed. I close my eyes trying not to make it look so obvious that I am obscenely attracted to this man.

I look down at my drink and nervously down the last of it before the bartender even has a chance to sit down the next one. I glance up at the stranger again and see he is staring right at me, "Uh, hi."

I am so fucking awkward.

I know that I am awkward.

I am half drunk and fucking awkward as shit. This dude needs to run away and fast.

The man smiles back, "Hello."

I fold my hands together on top of the bar. Nervously, I look around the room then back at the dark eyes staring at me, I point to my own throat, "The accent. Where are you from?"

He nods and smiles at the bartender as he sits our drinks down, "Thanks mate." He slides my drink over to me then gives me another dazzling smile, "London."

I nod my head as I wrap my hands around my glass, "London is beautiful. I love the architecture there. Something about the history in the bones of that city. It just does something to me."

36

I realize quickly that I am rambling. He is staring at me like he is trying to figure me out. Good luck with that buddy, even I can't figure myself out most days. He gives me another sly smile, "Where are you from?"

I smile back then take a small sip of my drink, "New York City now. But originally from Boston."

He takes a drink from his glass, smiling at me, "You don't have a Boston accent though."

I smile towards the bar top, "Yeah, I haven't been there in years. Probably since before you were even born."

My eyes close hard as I instantly regret my words.

I sound like I should be wearing Depends and living in a fucking retirement community. I give him a quick side glance before raising my glass to my lips and taking another long nervous drink.

He smiles, letting out a small but deep laugh, "I highly doubt that. You are not nearly old enough for that."

I feel my palms getting sweaty. I quickly put them in my lap, trying to wipe the sweat onto my pant legs without him realizing.

I let out another nervous laugh, "I am older than I look."

What in the actual hell am I doing? I could have babysat this kid while I was in high school. I may not be exactly old enough to be his mother but I know I am too fucking old to be sitting here accepting free drinks from him. This is just an uncomfortable situation but there is just something about him. I don't want to get up. Even though I feel awkward as shit, I feel some type of pull towards him.

He shakes his head, tilting it to the side a bit. He is looking me over, making my palms sweat even more. I can feel his eyes landing on different parts of my body while he apparently is judging what my actual age is. The heat from his stare is stirring up certain emotions and none of them are

37

appropriate. He gives me another coy smile, "I would say you are what, maybe 31? 32? At most."

I look back up at him, "And you are like what, 21 maybe 22?"

He smiles at me again as I raise my glass to take another large swallow of whisky, "I am 26 actually."

I nod my head sitting my glass back down on the bar without making any kind of eye contact with him, "34."

He turns towards me smiling again, "See, my guess was way closer than yours."

I grin and look a bit deeper into his face. He is an attractive man, I will give him that. He has sandy blonde hair and these dark bottomless eyes. I could swear they are onyx. They look like two black orbs just floating towards me. I can also see a small dimple in his left cheek when he grins at me.

He is tall with a slender build but he doesn't seem like he is a runner. I let the thoughts run rampant in my head. I smile again but quickly shake all those images away.

I have been a widow for less than a month. It doesn't matter that it has been almost 8 months since I have gotten laid. I cannot be thinking about another man like this. Especially not one that is 8 fucking years younger than me.

I let out one last nervous giggle before drinking down the last of my whisky. I smile and grab my clutch, "Well, thank you very much for the drink but it is definitely time for me to head to my suite. I have a long day tomorrow."

He nods while giving me a small smile and stands up at the same time as me, "I hope you have a good evening then."

I smile and step around him still smelling the ocean waves again. My eyes instantly close as I take the scent deep into my senses. If this was Bridgerton my name would be Anthony right now. My heart is hammering in my chest and I have no real idea why.

"What is your name by the way?"

I stop in my tracks, feeling a giddy smile come over my face. What in the actual hell is wrong with me? It's just a damn name woman, it's not like you are giving him a key to your house.

I turn back to him slowly, staring up into those sad eyes, "Lily. My name is Lily."

He smiles and sticks his hand out to me, "It was definitely a pleasure meeting you Lily. My name is Gideon."

I reach out and take his hand. He has strange calluses on his hands. Not in the usual places you would think to find a callus. I feel little bolts of lightning shooting into my palm. I stare at our joined hands expecting to see little bands of electric running between our skin.

I smile back at him, "The pleasure has been all mine Gideon. Good night." I pull my hand back, clenching it into a fist trying to keep ahold of the lightning running through it as I make my way to the elevator.

I steal one more glance at the bar as I head to the foyer and notice that Gideon is now at a table with all the other twenty-somethings. I hurry to make my way back to my suite, locking myself in and cringing at the memory of almost every single word that has come out of my mouth in the last half hour.

The next morning I decide to pretend like meeting Gideon has never even happened. I am here for just one more day. My flight is leaving tomorrow morning, taking me back to New York. I am going to stick to the plan. Go to the gym, do some shopping then enjoy the concert. No unplanned activities with hot guys I meet in a bar. No matter what my vagina says.

Tomorrow, I will be back home trying to not tell Susie all about my run in with the mysterious soul at the bar. And the embarrassing aftertaste it left in my mouth.

I eat a light breakfast in my room then put on a pair of leggings and a sports crop before heading down to the small gym.

I am surprised but grateful that I am the only one here. I step up onto a treadmill, sliding my airpods into place. I turn on Carnal Decay and start my jog.

I keep an eye on the clock. I have 8 hours until I have to leave for the concert. Plenty of time to shop still. I decide to run an extra mile. I crank up the speed on the treadmill and just moments later I am running like I am being chased by a masked serial killer.

After last night, I have some pent up nerves that really need to be released. I can feel the burn of the run in my calves then up into my hips. I fucking love the pain of it. The more it burns, the easier it seems to be able to get through the day. 48 minutes later the cool down of my run finally begins.

I gulp down half a bottle of water as I bring down the speed of the treadmill. I gently step off the machine and turn around to see Gideon and 3 other guys working out on the weight machines behind me.

I instantly freeze in my spot.

I didn't even notice him come in.

I turn quickly and pace over to the shelf on the far side of the room that holds the clean towels. I know I look like a deer in the headlights. I had honestly planned to run the memory of him out of my body completely but apparently the fates had a different idea. I begin wiping down my neck when from close

40

behind me I hear, "I do not believe that you are 34. I honest to god believe that it was all a lie now."

I smile down at myself as I turn around, still wiping the sweat away from my chest, "Why is that?"

Gideon lifts his hands, putting them on his very toned hips, his eyes following the towel across my chest,

"I swear I just saw you run full speed for a mile or more. You never faltered. And I am pretty sure you were singing while you did it. That doesn't sound like something a 34 year old, one foot in the grave woman would do."

I let out a loud cackle and pull my airpods out, "I never said one foot in the grave. And also I don't sing."

Gideon leans in just a bit until I can feel his breath on my cheek, his voice low, almost a growl, "Yes, you do little one."

My heart starts fluttering just like it had the night before. I feel something awaken deep in my core. I turn my face just a bit towards his and his eyes meet mine. I could stare into the void of them for hours, days even.

I turn in the opposite direction and throw my towel into the dirty hamper, "Well, even if I was. That doesn't make me any younger."

Gideon is standing back up to his full height now, which is easily a foot taller than me. He looks back over his shoulder at his friends then back to me,

"You believe what you must, Lily. I am glad we ran into each other again though. How long are you going to be in town?"

I feel like my legs are going to give out on me at any moment.

What the fuck is wrong with me?

I glance down at my feet then back to Gideon, "I fly out tomorrow. I would say we could meet up at the bar later but I have a full day and long night ahead of me."

Gideon nods his head at me again, "Plus, you don't stay out after 10 pm so...."

I laugh and out of just a natural reaction flip him off.

He lets out a deep laugh, a comical look of shock on his face, "Oh, so that's how it's gonna be?"

I smile back. Are we flirting right now?

I have not flirted with anyone in over a decade. This has to all be in my imagination. Gideon steps a bit closer to me, "So how am I to get in touch with you when you are back in New York?" I look up into his gaze.

Yep, this is flirting.

I take a deep breath, trying to steady my nerves, "You aren't."

Gideon's face falls into a shocked and confused frown, "Are you in a relationship or something?"

I smile over his shoulder at the young guys waiting for him, "No. No, I am not in a relationship anymore. But I am 8 years older than you. You should be out hitting on someone closer to your own age, don't you think?"

He tilts his head slightly to the right, giving me a panty dropping smile that has that dimple popping out at me again, "What if I don't care about any of that?"

Stunned, I look into his eyes again, "Look, Gideon. You seem really great and please do not take this the wrong way because honestly I am very attracted to you. It's just I have a lot going on in my life right now. I am only in town for a short time and then I have to get back to the chaos that is my everyday life. I have really enjoyed meeting you. It has been a very flattering experience but I think it is best if we just leave this as it is. Nothing more than a little flirting."

I smile at him, then gently touch his bicep as I step around him. I can almost swear I hear his breath catch in his throat when my fingertips meet his skin.

42

For me, it feels like little zaps of electricity are running up through my fingers. Just like last night when I shook his hand.

I look at my hand then up to his face. He is still facing the wall of mirrors but his eyes are closed. Like he is in pain under my touch. Or maybe he feels the lightning too. He slowly turns his head and opens his hooded eyes towards mine. His smoldering gaze is rousing something from deep within again. He doesn't even blink as his eyes scour my face like a long lost lover.

I want to run my hand down his arm but instead I give a short smile to his friends, quickly retreating my hand then leave to go back to my suite. I run from the gym so fast I don't dare stop and turn to look back. I am just not strong enough for that. If I was to turn around and he was watching me, I don't know that I would be powerful enough to not fall at his feet.

I am panting in full panic by the time I shut the hotel door of my suite behind me. I run to my suitcase and grab my little friend out of the side pocket. I am in a complete frenzy over this man. I can't get his eyes, his scent, his body out of my head. I can still feel his breath on my cheek. The electricity when I barely even touched him.

I close my eyes, seeing the sweat trickle down his neck and onto his chest. I quickly kick my shoes off and yank my leggings down. I don't even bother to take them off completely before I am parting my legs at the knees and pressing the vibrator hard to my clit.

My eyes roll up in my head as my shoulders cave in around my breasts. I am still panting at the thought of him touching me back.

I close my eyes again imagining him running his nose up my neck. His fingers tracing the curve of my ass. His hand gripping my neck tight as I clench hard around his dick. It

43

doesn't take much at all and I am cumming all over myself. Screaming at my release. That is the first time I have had a real orgasm in almost a year.

I laugh to myself as I get cleaned up then take a shower.

A few short hours later, I am walking around Saks just trying to find something to wear to the concert. I have looked over my shoulder at least a dozen times, expecting Gideon to be standing there.

Or even somewhere off in the distance just watching me. I peruse the clothes, finding absolutely nothing that feels like I need to wear it.

Normally, when I go clothes shopping I can imagine myself in the item, in the moment. But for this experience, I am coming up empty. Defeated, I leave the store and start walking down the street. There has to be another store or boutique here somewhere that will have something appropriate.

I glance up and down the street trying to catch a glimpse of a sign that would draw me in when I see it. There is a small boutique across the street that I have never heard of.

Rae's Secrets.

I quickly make sure there are no cars coming as I cross the street to look in the window. The entire vibe of the window display is "window shopping appropriate BDSM". There is leather and buckles and chains. Velvet and sin smile towards me at every turn. I give the window a slight grin as I turn and step through the door to go inside.

The amount of leather and lace in this store is fucking mind boggling. They literally have everything. I take my time, checking every single rack before coming to the conclusion that I am probably going to buy out the entire store. A young girl, with piercings and many, many tattoos steps up to me. She has soft violet hair with silver streaks in it and is wearing a plaid schoolgirl skirt with chains and leather straps wrapping around it. Her makeup is actually quite beautiful. I can see the artistry it took to paint it on. It is a work of art in itself.

She looks me up and down before letting a smug grin fall over her lips, "Are you lost?"

I turn to her fully grinning at the attitude. I can't blame her. I know I don't look the part of her normal customer base I am sure. She is just reading the room, no harm in that.

I smile widely at her, "I am not lost but I do need help."

She crosses her arms and juts one hip out to the side, "With what?"

I let out a long sigh, allowing my eyes to scan the items around me, "I am going to the Carnal Decay concert tonight and I have absolutely nothing to wear."

The girl stands up a bit straighter, "You? You are going to the Carnal Decay concert tonight? At the Fillmore?"

I let out a soft laugh, "I know. I don't look like their normal type of fan, but yes. I brought some clothes with me but I don't want to stand out like a fucking idiot. I want something that is comfortable but at the same time appropriate for the moment. And even something to make me feel a little bit, I don't know, sexy? Maybe."

The girl smiles, nodding her head as she looks through the rack beside her, "I get it. You are going on a cougar hunt tonight."

I cover my face with my hands, I knew this is what people were going to think. I am too fucking old to be behaving this way.

I have missed the chance to be young and carefree. I debate the entire fucking trip in this one moment.

I feel the girl touch my arm and I part my fingers to look at her. She smiles at me through the cracks in my hands, "There is absolutely nothing to be embarrassed about. You are not even old. I just like giving people shit. Keeps the day interesting.

45

Honestly, I can't blame you. I could be 90 and still have a thing for Ares. He is a fucking god after all."

I let out a small laugh as I drop my hands, "Right? There is just something about his voice. I don't even care what he looks like, if he could just sing to me all day, every day I could die happy."

The girl is laughing and nodding along with me,

"Personally though, I am a fan of Dionysus. Yeah, Ares can sing but have you seen the way Dionysus plays that guitar? Tonight, just watch his fingers work. If that doesn't give you ideas, nothing will."

I laugh nervously at her then see a peculiar look come over her face. Like she is thinking intensely when a lightbulb finally illuminates in her brain. She grins then grabs my hand tightly, "Follow me."

She quickly drags me towards the back of the store. She is obviously on a mission so I just hold on for the ride. She turns to me, "What size skirt are you?"

I look down at myself then back up at her, "Normally an 8. I kinda got an ass."

She looks around me briefly, nodding along, "And bra size? I am gonna guess, like maybe a 32C?"

I nod back at her, "Yes, but I don't need a bra. I need something to cover my bra."

She smiles as she walks over to a wall of clothes, "Trust me."

She is gone for maybe 42 seconds when she turns back towards me. She is holding a mid-shin cream colored pencil skirt and a cream colored bustier, with a corset back held together with a black satin ribbon.

There is no way in hell I can wear that.

46

That is just not me. She smiles as she walks up to me, pointing at the mirror behind me. I turn around and she holds the items up close to my body. I feel a shiver run down my spine.

I can do this.

I can be someone else for just one night.

I smile at her reflection in the mirror in front of me, "I'll take it."

I pay for my items then make sure she has my contact information. I let her know if she was ever in New York to call me.

We could get lunch, maybe do some shopping. She smiles though I have the feeling she will never actually reach out. I don't mind though.

2 hours later, I am staring at myself in the mirror of my hotel room. I look fucking hot. I turn so I can see myself from every angle. I can not believe I am going to wear this out in public. I instantly imagine what the look on Gideon's face would be if he happened to catch a glimpse of me walking through the lobby or something.

I smile to myself, making sure my hair is perfect then I add another layer of red to my lips. One of my favorite features of the skirt is the hidden pocket on the inside front of it.

I slide my id and some cash into it before straightening my tits. Making sure they are in there securely. The last fucking thing I need is a nip slip mid concert.

I look back at the mirror one last time and smile to myself, "Let's do this shit."

I grab my phone and turn to leave the room.

4

Ares
Dangerous - Sleep Token

Why can't I get this woman out of my head?

I feel this pull to her—something I have never really felt before. There is just something about her, I just can't get enough of it. There was just something so familiar about her, like our souls had met before on a different plane of existence or something.

Every fucking time I close my eyes, I see her. I hear her laugh. I smell her skin. When I leaned into her neck at the gym, she smelled like cherries. She touched my fucking arm and I wanted to pin her to the god damn mirrored wall so I could watch myself fucking owning her.

I close my eyes as I feel Simone start to roll the small paint sponge over my skin. The rough texture painting the dark armor onto my exposed flesh. I have to find a way to get her out of my head, at least for a few minutes. I am finding it impossible to focus on what I need to do right now.

I look over at the table behind me in the mirror, seeing our masks lying there. Another night, another show. I still can't believe we are on an American tour. We are fucking headlining an American tour. I turn my eyes back towards the mirror, arms straight out from my sides.

Simone has been the one to paint me before every show since we started touring. Each of us paint each other, for fear of anyone outside of our little circle knowing our true identities. The only thing we really have is our anonymity. It is something we will not give up, no matter what. There are less than a dozen people in the entire world that know who we really are. Family included.

I close my eyes again and Lily immediately pops into my head like a siren. Fuck that woman and the god damn power she has over my subconscious. The way she was singing while she was running. She was singing my songs.

She is a fucking fan of ours.

That was the most unexpected thing from her. Of all people. She looks like the kind of person that would do yoga to like Adele or maybe she could be a hard core Swiftie.

Not that there's anything wrong with Adele or Taylor Swift, they are both mega talented. But Lily just looks like she is more into soft love songs.

Not so much the music we create. Maybe not so much into the thoughts rolling through my head. But then there she was, running full fucking speed on an incline singing my lyrics, perfectly I might add. Then another quick thought runs through my mind, making me smile.

What if she is in town just for our concert?

She was singing our songs. So maybe, just maybe?

I quickly shake these thoughts out of my head.

Stupid.

I can still hear her words in my head from earlier in the day, "I am very attracted to you." When she had been speaking to me in the gym, I could see the vein in her neck pulsating faster.

I had nearly died when I walked into that gym and saw her running on the treadmill.

She had been gorgeous the night before but at that moment I had never seen anything sexier. The way her tits rose and fell as her chest heaved from the workout and the singing. Her long black hair pulled into a tight ponytail, swinging back and forth with every step she took. I could have stood and watched the sweat trickle down her neck for the entire day.

I wanted to step up behind her and wrap that ponytail around my hand. I imagined myself tugging on it roughly, making her back arch as her eyes were forced to reach mine.

The way she ran the towel over her chest, with her head tilted slightly away from me. She has no idea what she is doing to me.

Or does she?

I don't know how I was able to keep my hands to myself. I just felt this uncontrollable urge to grasp her soul tight.

Making sure the world knows that she is mine—But she isn't.

Not yet.

I shake my head, I have to stop this. The last thing I need is to walk out on stage rock fucking hard. I glance down at myself in the mirror, down boy.

"You alright Gideon?" I turn to look at Simone's painted frame standing to the left of me.

I give her a soft smile as she starts to paint my neck and face, "Yeah, I am alright."

She pulls back looking into my eyes, "You are full of shit. What's wrong?"

I give her a small chuckle as I look back at my reflection in the mirror, "Nothing is wrong. I just have something on my mind is all."

50

From the other side of the room I hear Apollo chime in, "Something or someone?"

I look past my shoulder in the reflection and see Apollo in full gear, paint and all staring at me, "Someone."

He nods at me as he picks up his drumsticks then starts walking towards the door, "Get her out of your head. At least for the next 4 hours. Got me?"

I watch him as he walks out of the room. Nodding at him because I know he is right. I look back at myself in the mirror. It is time to get my fucking head on straight.

It doesn't matter right now how much I want her. It doesn't matter that I can't think of anything but her lips, her eyes. That one single strand of hair that always seems to fall over her cheek. The intensity of the feeling that she is what I have been looking for, waiting for my entire life. That she could be the one to shine some light on the darkness that I have been living in for the last 26 years.

A half hour later we are all standing stage left, nervously trying to get ourselves pumped for the show. We are here for one night only then we will be in South Carolina, then New York City.

My mind wanders back to a set of crushing grey eyes.

I wonder what she would do if I found her when we were in New York in a few weeks?

If I just randomly show up at her doorstep.

I could see her in my mind's eye, smiling at me as she opened her door for me. Those cherry red lips biting down on my neck. Those short black nails running down my back. She has to be mine. I am hopelessly obsessed. How can I even find her though? Maybe tip the bartender from last night, get her full name off the card she used.

Would she even actually want me though? Me, not Ares. I battle my own thoughts. What if she thought I was crazy? What if she would get one look at me then call the cops or push me out of the door, never wanting to see me again? But what if she opened the door further, smiling and invited me in? The pull of the unknown is the only thing making me smile right now.

Maybe I can just scour Insta for her. I am sure she has an account. I let the small smile creep further over my face as I slide my menacing white mask down. The lights go out in the arena and I hear the crashing screams of the fans.

Their echoing wails fueling us forward.

We all slowly make our way out onto the stage. The crowd can't even see us yet but you can feel the energy as it charges through the arena. The excitement and overwhelming sense of panic crackles through the air like lightning over the sea.

The entire building is dark except for the glow of the blue signals on the floor showing us our marks. Hera and Hestia make their way to their spots at my left.

Simone has already pulled her Hera mask down, glancing out to the crowd with a small tilt to her head.

Mona's Hestia mask looks back at me from the keyboards, like a menacing little cherub faced sister. Matthew has been in full Apollo mode since before the green room. He is already seated comfortably behind his drums.

Dionysus is back to wearing his green mask that looks like a million crazed men trying to climb out of the depths from within. He swings the guitar at me.

His sign that he is ready to begin.

I stand there, rolling my shoulders under the long black hooded cape covering my body. I reach up and grab the mic as

52

Apollo starts to count me in. I start lightly singing the words to Peripheral,

> *"Her fingers wrapped around my soul,*
> *like lightning strikes.*
>
> *I want to own you from the inside,*
> *I want you to run and hide."*

The stage lights instantly fire up sending beams of lasers stretching across the building. Licking every single corner with light then quickly dissipating.

I immediately lose myself in the words. I always feel so free up here on stage. I run back and forth, screaming, lunging, jumping. I have almost no control over my own body when the beat starts to hit.

An hour later, I am standing behind my piano. I take a few hurried breaths before starting the first few keys of The Descent. It is the closest thing to a love ballad that we have. It always makes the girls in the crowd fucking feral, which Edge loves.

For me though, it is a story about my first and only heartbreak. How she was able to so easily just walk away from me, from the life we had built together.

> *"In the chambers of heartache, I breathe your regret,*
> *An altar of longing, where love's a threat.*
>
> *I'm a ghost in your garden, where roses decay,*
> *In the feast of your indifference, I starve every day."*

I sing the first few lines while playing the piano. No other noise besides me and the keys. After I feel the anger and emotions start to take over, I grip the microphone and slowly step up to the front of the stage.

I lift my leg up on the small ledge that runs the front of the stage and lean forward into the microphone, screaming my emotions to the masses.

"So let the stars witness, the tale of the lost,
In the expanse of your absence, I count every cost.

When love's just a whisper, and shadows align,
I'll cradle my sorrow, because your heart was never mine."

My eyes scan the front row. Just a sea of people crammed together chanting our name, singing the song along with me.

My eyes roll from person to person.

Then as I turn to stand, I catch the glimpse of a woman standing by herself in the VIP section. Far enough away from the pit that she has room to breathe and enjoy the show.

I know her instantly. I continue to sing but I feel as though my body has turned to stone at the sight of her. It feels like a boulder has landed squarely on my chest. My spine compresses from the force of the realization that it is Lily standing out in the crowd watching me. I feel it roll across my skin in waves.

I blink repeatedly but Lily is still standing there. Not the mirage my brain is trying to convince me of. My dream is standing stone still watching me, watching her. In the front fucking row in the VIP section. She stands right behind the low barrier that separates the VIP from the mass hysteria that is currently happening in the pit, making her easy to spot and follow with my eyes.

Her long silky black hair pulled over her left shoulder, showing me that she is wearing a cream colored bustier and skirt.

Every single fucking curve she has is being hugged by that fabric. My eyes travel up her body catching a hint of her abdomen then the ample top sides of her breasts. Her skin is perfect like an alabaster statue.

My brain shuts down immediately.

All I can focus on is her chest heaving into the night.

When my eyes reach hers, I can see that she is crying. She is smiling and swaying to the music now but she is utterly weeping. I hear the twinge of a guitar and immediately know that I have missed my mark.

I recover as best I can, the crowd not seeming to notice.

Thankfully.

The rest of the night goes off without a hitch. During every single song though, I can feel myself gravitating to the left side of the stage. And every single time I look down and see her standing there.

Alone.

Content.

Happy, yet still sad.

While the other fans are screaming, jumping, singing all around her she seems to be in her own little bubble. No one dares to touch her.

She just stands there, swaying.

Sometimes singing, sometimes just crying but every single moment a smile is covering her face.

She is fucking perfect. She is so reserved on the outside but I just fucking know there is something below that skin.

Something barely beneath the surface, just begging to be set free. She has a darkness in her. I feel this sense of possession come over when I realize that I have to claim that darkness - make it my own. She is too pure to hold that much within herself. She needs someone to help carry the weight of it.

When the show ends and we are all standing on stage, bowing, showing our gratitude to our fans I feel an urge come over me. I look across the crowd then quickly to Apollo.

I have to do something.

Now that I know she is here I can't just let her leave. So I do something I have never done before.

I jump down off the front of the stage. Fans losing their fucking shit the entire time. I can feel hands reaching for me, swiping at my arms and body. They don't even phase me as I keep my eyes locked on her.

I walk swiftly in the small gap between the short metal guard rail and the stage. The guards don't dare to stop me as I briskly pass by them. I can feel a sea of eyes staring at me as I walk up to the short barrier that is holding back my queen.

I stop directly in front of her and bring my hand up. I turn my palm to the ceiling as the air around us stills. She looks from me to my hand then back to my covered face.

She is stunned.

Her eyes are blown wide and her mouth hanging open just slightly as if she herself can't believe what I am doing either.

I smile to myself at the naivety on her face.

She reaches up, swiping those beautiful tears from her cheeks before placing her hand gently in mine. I don't say a word as a little burst of energy passes between our skin. I take her hand in mine and slowly guide her to the end of the guard rail, holding onto her as she walks through the now open gate.

She nervously steps up to me, looking up into my mask while blinking rapidly, "Hello."

She can't really see me but I am smiling. The mask covers everything except my chin and even that is painted black so she can't really see the expression on my face.

56

She has no idea who I am.

I smile wider as I feel the blood starting to course through her palm as her heart rate ticks up. I hold onto her hand but let our arms fall as I turn and lead her towards the green room behind the stage, still clutching her hand tightly in mine.

Silence falls over everyone as we walk through the door, still hand in hand. Dozens of eyes are on us as I let the door slowly close behind us. This never happens.

I do not bring women back here.

This is normally just a space to decompress after the show. Sometimes there are fans with VIP access, this is where they get to mingle with us.

Even though they do all the talking, no one seems to mind.

I hear a small chuckle come from Apollo when he realizes who I have brought back into the room with us. I give him a one sided smile then turn to her and gesture my hand towards the room.

Inviting her in.

She watches my hand, my arm as it sweeps out before her, then those fog covered storm clouds in her eyes follow my arm all the way up. Focusing on the mask on my face. I have to physically keep myself from shivering after being exposed to the power of her stare.

Lily gives me a soft smile then slowly starts to walk towards the corner of the room. Reluctantly, I let her hand fall from mine then walk to the other side of the room, sitting in a chair perfectly arranged for me to keep an eye on her through the mass of people.

She is so out of her element.

She has no clue how to act, what to say. She smiles sheepishly at everyone, excusing herself for even the slightest touch. I just sit here memorizing her every gesture.

Just as I had last night in the bar. She is exactly the same as she was then. Always giving a shy smile. Always looking at her hands like she is trying to decide in her head what is actually appropriate to speak out into the world.

Her eyes travel across everyone in the room. I see her look at Hera. A small side grin comes over her face as she looks her up and down from head to toe. Then her eyes are scanning the crowd again, never really settling on one person.

I could have sworn I had asked her why she was in town.

Why didn't she just tell me she was here for a concert?

I pull up my right ankle, resting it on my left knee as I slowly lean back in the chair. My long torso, covered in smeared black body paint and sweat.

I put one hand on top of each arm of the chair and take in a deep breath. I feel the cloak fall around me as I settle in to watch my little one as she nervously tries to find her place in the situation I have handed her.

I continue watching her awkward movements, realizing quickly that I can happily watch her in any and every situation.

My eyes follow her walking silently over to the bar counter that is covered in bottles and cups. She grabs a large bottle of whiskey from the back of the table and pours herself a cup. She looks at the bottle only seeing maybe a shots' worth left in it.

As if in slow motion, she lifts the neck of the bottle to her lips and tilts her head back, letting the amber liquid roll down her throat. Her back is arched, tits pressing into the void in front of her. Some guy beside her, watches her with an intent in his eye that makes me want to snap his fucking neck. I glance back at Lily and see a small stream of whiskey run down the right side of her lips and down her neck. My knuckles turn white even through the black paint covering them, as I grip the arms of the chair tighter.

I am now battling within myself. I want to walk over there and lick that whiskey all the way from her collarbone to her mouth. My heart is beating like a ticking time bomb. I hear nothing around me, just the steady beat of it increasing in speed as I watch that liquid run down her chin onto her neck.

She brings her head back down then just as slowly pulls the neck of the bottle away from her lips. My eyes continue to roam the curves of her face, imagining those lips wrapped tightly around my dick. Those pouty rubies wrapped around my cock as she smiles up into my eyes.

There is a desire within me wanting nothing more than to storm across the room. The pull of it almost overpowers me. She sits the bottle back down and uses her pointer finger to wipe the small stream of whiskey from her chin.

Lily turns and looks directly at me as she slides that perfect little finger into her mouth to suck it clean. I feel a moan sitting in the back of my throat. I can feel myself thickening just watching her.

She jolts alive again.

Back into normal speed like she is alarmed when she realizes I have been watching her the entire time. The need to march over there and crush her lips with mine is becoming overwhelming again.

But I can't.

It was one thing when I thought she was just a random woman at a hotel bar. But now, I know she is a fan. And fans already have the tendency of being a bit crazy sometimes. Sure, I have hooked up with a random girl here and there but this is Lily.

There would be no "hooking" up. If I ever get my hands on her, I may not ever be able to let go. I have been drowning in the need to possess her every breath since I first met her. I can't shake her. I don't want to shake her.

She turns her back to me then starts to make her way to the corner opposite of me. Seemingly not being able to decide which path she wants to take, she takes a few steps in one direction then turns and takes a few more in the other.

I smile at her awkwardness.

It's almost as if I can read her mind, the nerves that are rolling around inside. Each misfiring synapses, confusing her on which direction to go.

I watch as her expression changes. Her eyes as they travel across every single person in the room. She looks like she is analyzing each and every one of them as she gives them a small smile then slips past them. My little one finally settles into a corner, her back shoved into it so no one can possibly step up behind her.

I wonder what it would feel like to kiss those lips. Just her fingertips alone are able to jumpstart a car with the amount of electricity they pass through me. I stare at her mouth a bit longer, imagining the offering of heaven that those lips may hold. Like my own demented version of the pearly gates.

She quickly drinks down the whiskey in her plastic cup like it's fucking water. I see her look into the cup in her hand and then a small frown comes over her face.

What's wrong little Lily? Has your liquid courage all run out? I can feel the grin spreading over my face as I wonder what exactly will she do next? I pray it will be to get another drink so I can continue to watch her every move. Continue to study her.

She sits the empty cup down on the table beside her before nervously checking her surroundings. She looks down at her phone as the frown deepens on her face.

Her eyes come back up and meet mine.

I watch her as she slowly, methodically sways her hips over to me. She walks with her head pointed at the ground, not for lack of confidence, but because she is trying not to bump into anyone around her. I continue to smile at her inability to just own the fucking room like I know she can. She has that power within her. I just don't think she has ever had anyone point that out before. She has never been shown what she could be. What she is.

She stops just a few feet in front of me. Her eyes slowly rising from the floor to look into my mask again. I run my own eyes up the entire length of her body once more, shuddering a breath.

She truly has no idea just how mesmerizing she is.

I stand up, towering over her even with her heels on. I try desperately to not imagine her in nothing but those damn heels. Still, her somber eyes look up at me. To where she seems to imagine my eyes are under this mask.

I watch the grey orbs start to sparkle with more tears as she softly whispers, "Thank you. For everything."

Why is she so emotional right now?

Does she not want to leave me either?

My stomach knots up at the thought of her walking away from me and never being able to look into those eyes again.

I nod my head as she starts to take a step backwards.

Unable to control myself any longer, I reach my painted hand up and drag my thumb down her milky white cheek then across her plump bottom lip. Her wide eyes instantly try to reconnect with mine.

I watch my thumb as it glides back across her bottom lip. The pull of the energy between us becoming too strong to resist, I lean forward giving her a kiss.

It's not a crushing kiss like what my dick is begging for. But instead it is soft, sensual. Something I assume is more to her liking. I don't want to completely scare her senseless with what I really want to do. I try to keep some level of decorum about myself.

It honestly feels like a million nukes are going off in my head. I feel her fingers as they touch my bare chest. Sending goose bumps across my flesh. It's like a culmination of every dream, every wish, every yearning combining into a powerful chokehold on my soul.

My eyes close again as I feel the electricity surge through me like it had earlier today in the gym but this time a thousand times stronger. Unable to control my demons any longer, I turn my head just a bit to get a better angle.

It is nearly impossible to kiss somebody with this fucking mask on so I roughly take my other hand, placing it on her lower back, just trying to get her closer. I can feel the spikes of energy that pour into my lips from her own. I notice she has goosebumps on the exposed flesh of her back as well.

She lets out another small gasp as I pull her in closer to me. Feeling her molding her body into mine. Her heart is beating like a drumroll, vibrating through my own chest as well.

I part her lips with my tongue, running it along her teeth until she opens her mouth wider for me to enter. She tastes like whiskey and cherries, just as I had imagined she would. I feel my eyes close as a deep growl starts to rise from the back of my throat.

She glides her hand up my chest, onto my neck.

And for just a moment, I think she is going to try to take my mask off. Reluctantly, I pull back, looking down at her expressionless face. I don't know that she was going to actually try to remove the only thing protecting me from this reality. I just know that I can't reveal myself to the world. I am not ready to suffer the negative consequences that go along with social expectations. We have created a world that gives us comfort in anonymity.

62

Lily opens her eyes and gives me an unapologetic expression, "Goodbye." Her hands slide back down my chest and fall to her sides. She wasn't trying to unmask me. She just wanted her skin on mine. She wanted to feel the rush as much as I do.

With that she turns away from me.

I watch her as she slowly makes her way towards the door. I want to run and stop her. I want to show her who I am. That I am just Gideon. Just the guy from the bar.

But there are currently about 35 people in here that have no idea what our real identities are. I can't just reveal myself here in front of everybody, ruining everything that we have built. Destroying this world we have created, not just for us but for our fans. They don't really want to know who we are. They enjoy their own perceptions of us too much. They would only find versions of disappointment in the reality of who we really are.

I take a step towards her, to follow her as I watch her open the door and step out into the hallway. She doesn't look back once. Would she find a disappointing version of what she wants if I was to remove this mask? Something rips through me.

How can she so easily walk away from this? Why can't she see that I am dying here? Can she not feel how much I need her? Does she not realize that she belongs to me now?

I know she feels something too.

I glance at Apollo. Even through the mask, I can see he is smiling at me. He nudges his head towards the door, telling me all I need to know.

63

I cross the room in only 3 steps, set in my mission. Stepping out into the hallway, my eyes are everywhere at once looking both left and right. I see her about 20 feet down the hall about to turn out the exit door.

It suddenly feels as if the energy around us is thick and heavy. Hearing my boots as the crash from them ricochets down the walls, she turns her face towards me.

Seemingly surprised to see me stalking down the hall after her. I forge my way in her direction, with the passion of a thousand deaths pushing me towards her.

Oh, she is not leaving.

Not yet.

I decide to stop in front of her, so she doesn't think I am trying to murder her. I am sure I probably look like a psycho stalker at this point. Smiling widely she reaches her hand up, wrapping it around my neck bringing my lips crushing down into hers.

Her lips slam into mine with a strength that I never knew someone so small could ever possess. I brace my hands on the wall behind her, pinning her between my open arms and chest. Lily pulls me in closer as I feel her tongue exploring mine.

I push myself into her, knowing damn good and well she can feel me hard and wanting against her stomach. I feel a groan leaving my throat as her tongue entwines with my own. She takes her other hand and wraps it around my back, still trying to pull me in even closer.

Like she is trying to make my skin her own.

I release my hands from the wall around her head, grabbing her wrists from my body. I slowly raise them up above her head, smiling down at her.

Those big eyes twinkling up at me from below doing things to me that even I didn't even know could happen. I firmly pin her arms to the cinder block wall behind her. I smile again

64

as I hear a small gasp escape her mouth when her arms slam into the wall. Her mouth is slightly parted as she raises one eyebrow at me.

I pull back to try to read her expression. Try to make sure I haven't scared my little one already. I scavenge her face like a man starved looking for any sign of salvation. She grins devilishly at me, "Do it."

I take a deep breath. Hearing her want me was not something I was prepared for tonight. The hunger from not kissing her envelopes me as I crush my lips back into hers. When I hear a small whimper escape her lips, I realize immediately that she has claimed my soul.

Without even trying it seems.

I am hers.

She continues to hold her arms pinned above her head as I let my fingertips slide down the underside of her arms. I pull back a bit to watch her face as I let my large hand slide across the tops of her breasts.

She parts her mouth ever so slightly then closes her eyes leaning the back of her head against the wall. Her eyes are clinched together so tight that I can see little lines stretching back to her temples.

She smiles briefly then looks up into where she seems to believe my eyes should be. Lily leans forward, pressing her lips to mine again with a force that could stop an army. She is finding it just as hard to let go as I am, it seems.

I grab her by her hips pulling her roughly into mine.

I can feel myself trying to thrust into her. But I would be damned if I stood out in this dingy ass hallway and dry humped her into the wall.

She deserves so much more than that.

65

I feel her teeth as she lightly bites my bottom lip sending shivers down my spine. I let another growl leave my throat. God, I want this woman so badly. She opens her eyes leaning back into the wall again, smiling at me wickedly.

My hands are still on her hips as she runs one finger from the base of my neck, down my exposed chest, stopping at the buckle of my belt.

I can feel and hear myself panting at her touch. I couldn't pull my eyes from her right now even if I tried. Her eyes smile along with her lips this time, "Good night Ares."

She swiftly ducks underneath my arm then slams herself out the exit door.

Again, never looking back.

She knows my fucking names. Both of them. I stand there, leaning up against the wall in front of me. There are so many thoughts, emotions running through me that I can't do anything besides stare at the wall before me.

I let my head fall forward as I try to bring my breathing back to normal. I hear the exit door close beside me and I let out a deep breath. I look up at the wall, speaking to nothing, "Jesus fucking christ."

I can't go back into that room with a raging hard on. Honestly, I don't want to go anywhere at all without Lily. I let out a small laugh as I turn, deciding to walk back towards the stage area. I walk around the small barricade and take a seat in the vip area. Right where she had been standing earlier. I can't wrap my head around everything that has just happened, still in a trance from her.

I watch the crew breaking down the stage, glancing over at me every few moments. I don't even acknowledge them. I am too far into my own head trying to figure out a way to find Lily again.

This is not over.

Not by a long shot.

5
Lily
The Lion's Roar - First Aid Kit

Two weeks have passed and I still am not entirely sure why I haven't told Susie about my night with Ares.

When she had asked, I told her that the trip was fine. That the concert had been great. And that was it.

I haven't told her about Gideon hitting on me. I haven't told her about Ares pinning me to the wall. I haven't told her about his very impressive length as he pressed into my stomach. I haven't breathed a word about the 3 hours I spent afterwards with my little friend either.

And I definitely haven't told her about how I have been stalking their fan pages for the last 14 days and rubbing one out every other day. Nor about my thoughts that Gideon and Ares could very well be one in the same.

I have spent hours every single day going back over the entire trip in my head. My thoughts, my fantasies, ping pong back and forth between Gideon and Ares. I know that it isn't possible. I know that it's just my brain playing tricks on me, but I felt the same electricity when I touched both of them. I can't imagine Ares just out and about, going to dinner, working out at the gym, talking to widows in bars. But something keeps nudging at my subconscious telling me that there is more there. It is getting harder to shut down those thoughts.

Susie slams the front door behind her, entering like her name is on the deed, "Hey Lucy, I'm HOOMMEEE!"

I smile to myself as I hear her throw her bag on the hall table, "Where ya been?"

She grins at me as she rounds the corner holding a manilla envelope, "Nope, it's my turn for questions."

I give her a puzzling look as I sit down the knife I have been chopping up baked chicken with. I grab a towel and start wiping my hands off, "Uh. Okay."

She lays the manilla envelope down on the counter then takes one finger and pushes it towards me, "What the fuck is this?"

I look down at the counter, immediately recognizing the emblem on the envelope.

It's the Carnal Decay logo.

I stare at the picture of the god Pan, horns and all as he sneers up at me from the envelope. I feel my eyes go wide. My breath instantly catches in my throat. I immediately feel like my heart is going to explode out of my chest.

I reach down, barely touching the envelope afraid it is going to burst into flames, "I don't know what the fuck that is."

Susie puts her elbows on the counter and leans over onto her forearms, "LIAR!"

I "pfftt" at her, smiling at her dumbass remark while I pick up the envelope. I turn it over to unseal it.

As I run my finger under the glue, I look up at her, "Where was this?"

She nods past me towards the front door, "Looks like someone had just slipped it through the slot."

I nod again, confused but looking back down at the envelope in my hands. I reach in slowly, grabbing another envelope out. I am staring at just a plain white envelope now.

Nothing written on it.

69

No emblem. No logo.

Just blank white starkness staring back at me.

I unseal it and pull out a folded paper that is inside. Two tickets flutter to the counter.

Susie quickly reaches out snatching one off the counter from in front of me, "Bitch, this is a front row fucking VIP ticket to Carnal Decay tonight!"

Dropping the folded paper onto the counter, I rip the ticket from her hand, "No fucking way!"

I glance over it quickly. It is indeed a front row ticket to tonight's very sold out concert. I reach down, sliding the other ticket off the counter as well.

A quick scan of it shows that it is also another front row seat ticket but instead of for tonight it is for tomorrow night's show. I hold them up looking back and forth between them.

What in the actual fuck is happening right now?

Susie clears her throat as she looks from the paper now unfolded in her hands then up to my face, "Lily, I have not stopped thinking about you since that night in the hallway. I have to see you again. Please accept this invitation. Ares."

My jaw officially drops open as I look from Susie to the paper then to the tickets.

I think I am going to fucking pass out.

Ares.

Mother fucking Ares has not been able to stop thinking about me! Me! Of all fucking people!

I let out a nervous giggle and quickly sit down on the stool behind me. This can't be real. This can't be my reality right now. I instantly start sweating and get the chills at the same time. What the hell?

Susie quickly rounds the island, clipping it with her hip then wincing through the pain as she waves the letter in front of me, "What the fuck happened in the hallway? With fucking Ares? Wait....did you fuck Ares in a hallway?"

I laugh at her then snatch the handwritten letter from her grasp. His handwriting is beautiful.

Almost like calligraphy.

Susie waves her hand in front of my face, "Um Hello? What the fuck happened in the hallway?"

I let out another heavy sigh, sitting the letter down on the island in front of me, "After the show that night, Ares jumped off the stage and brought me around the guardrail. He took me back to the green room with him."

Susie is now hopping back and forth from foot to foot as she starts clapping and giggling. She looks like an over enthusiastic soccer mom at a regional competition.

I let out another nervous laugh, "Nothing really happened in the green room. Just some casual looks and stuff. I went to tell him goodbye and he kissed me."

Susie squeals, smacking my thigh repeatedly, "Why the fuck didn't you tell me any of this?!"

I shrug my shoulders, still in shock myself, "I thought it was like a fluke. Like something he did a lot. How the fuck would I know if he did?"

Susie leans back frowning at me then points to the letter lying open in front of me, "Obviously not or he wouldn't have invited you back for seconds. Also, that doesn't tell me what happened in the hallway!"

I exhale, defeated as I lay my forehead on the island then turning my head to plant my cheek on the cold marble as I look up out of the corner of my eye at Susie, "He followed me after I said goodbye. When he caught up to me in the hallway, he leaned into me and I don't know what happened. I just reached up and slammed his lips into mine."

I sit back up rolling my eyes up into my head. I lean my head back to rest on my shoulders, slowly dying of embarrassment from my admissions,

"The next thing I knew he had my hands pinned above my head and his dick was hard on my stomach. I turned into a fucking feral teenager in less than 2 seconds."

Susie slowly sits down on the stool across from me with her eyes wide, "Did you actually fuck a rock star in a hallway Lily?"

I hear myself belt out a loud laugh, "No! Susie! I didn't fuck him. We just made out for a few minutes then I left. That was literally it. I didn't look back, I literally ran to find a cab and went back to the hotel. Nothing more."

Susie leans back on her hands, laughing and shaking her head, "You little whore."

I laugh back at her.

I forcefully slap the island countertop, "I am not a whore! I am a cougar, get it right."

I continue to stare at the tickets in confusion, "I never told him my name. How the fuck did he know my name, let alone where I live?"

Susie raises her eyebrows at me, "I mean, it's not hard to figure out. He probably found out from the venue who had VIP tickets in that spot. Then the process of elimination from there. It's not like you don't have any social media accounts."

I nod back at her, I mean I guess it makes sense, "That seems like a lot though, right? For someone to just look up?"

Susie jumps up laughing, then turns to me quickly, "What are you going to wear tonight? What did you wear last time?"

I shake my head at her, "I don't even know if I am going tonight. And what I wore last time doesn't matter. It's not something I can ever wear again."

Susie puts her hands on her hips, pouting at me in a confused stare, "Why the fuck not? To all statements."

I sigh again rolling my eyes at her, "Because I am newly widowed. Also, because he rubbed black body paint all over me last time and the clothes were cream colored."

Susie's jaw nearly hits the ground in shock or maybe horniness, "Don't give me this shit about newly widowed. No one is expecting you to marry him. Just fuck his brains out. And as for the outfit, where is it? I need to see it."

I look towards the ceiling as Susie takes off running out of the kitchen and up the stairs. Giggling like a fucking girl scout the entire way.

I follow behind her slowly. My thoughts are scattered everywhere. I can not believe he wants to see me again. This whole experience feels like a dream. Like one of those dreams you vaguely remember when you wake up, half confused and in a frenzy.

I feel this flutter start in my chest. Then a heavy weight in my stomach. This is not familiar to me at all. I have to get a fucking grip on myself. I already know he isn't going to want me when he learns the truth. He probably only wants one thing from me anyway.

I finally make it to the bedroom and see Susie digging through any pile of clothes she can find. I quickly grab the 'never gonna come clean' clothes from beside the hamper. I whistle loudly at her to get her attention.

She turns her gaze to meet mine, her eyes blowing wide and her jaw dropping a bit. She stands up and slowly walks over to me, taking the garments out of my hands, "God Damn Lily! Who knew you had it in you?"

I slump down on the floor against the wall, "Not me apparently."

Susie smiles as she throws the top and skirt into a pile next to my vanity then barrells arms stretched out wide into my closet. I can hear her yelling to the clothing hanging on all sides, "Come to me my lovelies! No. No. No. What the fuck is this? No. No. Here! Yes! You! This is perfect!"

She comes marching out of the closet holding up a dress that I had bought on a whim a week ago. It is Dolce and it is fucking stunning. Just a short little tease of a cocktail dress.

The thing is, it's also sheer. You can basically see right through it because it is mainly made of tulle. I shake my head back and forth, "Nope. Not happening. Not now, not ever."

She drops the dress a few inches, frowning at me, "Then why the fuck did you even buy it?"

I shake my head at her, hearing the whine in my own voice, "I don't know why I bought it. It just screamed at me at the store so I brought it home with me."

Susie walks over and crouches down in front of me, placing one hand on my bent knee. Her voice low, she commands my full attention with her gaze, "You are going to break his heart if you don't go. He sent you tickets. He wants to know you, see you. This will be good for you sweetie. Mark would want you to be happy."

I give her a dirty look then turn my head towards the vanity.

She is right.

Mark told me to continue to live after he was gone. He wanted me to find somebody, but I don't really think this is what he meant. I let out another sigh and reach for the dress, "Go find me some matching heels."

74

Susie releases the dress and jumps up, shouting into the ceiling, "Fuck Yeah!" I laugh at her as I stand up and look at myself in the mirror.

What the hell am I doing?

Susie comes charging out of the closet just a few minutes later holding a pair of open toe Louboutins' in her hand. She sits them down beside me then stalks over to my dresser, "What bra set are you going to wear?"

I look over my shoulder at her as I pull my shirt over my head, "I don't care, just grab something."

Susie slowly turns back to me, glaring, then points at the dress, "Bitch, that is see through. You need to be making a fucking statement right now."

I feel my shoulders tense up as fear falls over my chest again. This is torture.

Plan and simple torture.

I close my eyes, "The red lace set, with the thong."

I don't even bother to open my eyes when Susie yet again screams, "Fuck Yeah!"

An hour later, I am fully dressed and ready to leave. I have a small clutch this time since there are no secret compartments in my dress. Fuck, can it even be considered a dress when there is barely any fabric, nothing else? Maybe one single solitary string holding it all together.

I make my way downstairs as slowly as Susie will allow. I can feel her hopping on the stairs behind me. Can't she just go get laid on her own and quit living vicariously through me? I grab the ticket off the counter then a long coat off the coat rack by the door.

Susie, standing on the bottom step tilts her head to the side quizzingly, "Why are you taking a coat?"

75

I smile as I slide it up over my shoulders then pull it tight in front of me, "Because if I step outside like this right now, Garrett and all the neighbors might have a coronary. Don't worry. I am going to leave it in the car before I head into the arena."

Susie smiles and steps down in front of me, "Good. Now remember, have some fucking fun. You deserve it. I will be here tomorrow expecting a full fucking report on everything that happens. I am going to need you to literally grab that bull by the horn. Mkay?"

I smile and nod at her. I slowly turn to face the door, quickly losing my nerve by the second. As if she can sense it, Susie opens the front door and "lovingly" pushes me out of it.

I look from the closing door then down the front stoop. Garrett is standing there smiling as he waits for me. As I step closer, he smiles wider and opens the door to the car. I quickly thank him then climb into the SUV.

The drive to the arena feels like it takes a fucking lifetime. The concert will be starting soon. And I am literally fidgeting with anything I can get my fingers on. I feel like I have little tiny gremlins running through my veins, randomly attacking me with pickaxes.

I slide my phone into my clutch after turning the ringer off, trying to breath through the impending panic attack. Garrett parks right in front of the building then quickly jumps out and opens my door. I slide out and stand there staring at the large stadium in front of me.

There are people stretched for what seems like miles. I take another deep breath trying to steady my pulse, "Miss Lily. Are you okay?"

I glance at Garrett with a smile and then a nod, "Yes, Garrett. I am fine. Thank you. Please wait nearby to take me home. The concert should only be a few hours. I will text you when I am ready to leave."

Garrett gives me a curt nod and smile. He holds his hand out to allow me to balance with it as I step onto the sidewalk from the roadway. I quickly throw one finger in the air after stepping onto the curb then place my clutch in his still outstretched hand. I pull the jacket away from shoulders revealing the tulle dress and what lies beneath it.

I throw the jacket into the back of the car then turn to retrieve my clutch. Garretts' eyes are as round as saucers. I smile bashfully as I grab the clutch out of his hand, "Thank you Garrett."

I slowly look towards the entrance doors, squaring my shoulders, trying to at least fake some confidence. I take a few steps towards the door before automatic kicks in and I am hurling full steam towards the arena.

I hear the car door shut behind me but I don't dare look back. Only because I know I would see Garrett staring at my very visible ass.

I fake confidently stroll up to the VIP line and hand my ticket to the person working the door. She does a quick one over on me and smiles, "I guess security won't need to search you, huh?"

I give her a tight smile then step through the metal detector before turning towards the open hallway leading into the arena. I turn to my left and head straight down to the main floor. I can hear people whispering as I walk by.

At one point, a man that has just walked out the bathroom stops and I hear, "God Damn!"

I blush but keep my head held high as I continue down to the stage area. I walk around the rail to the VIP area and stand right up against the low guard rail. Just like last time there are seats and other luxuries for the VIP crowd. I bypass them all and stand where I know I will have a perfect view of the stage.

Some man that looks to be around my age, wearing an Armani suit steps up beside me smiling. I can read this schmuck like a book as his eyes roam my body, "Would you like a drink or a seat?" I glance over at him then give a small smile, "No. I am fine, thank you."

5 minutes later the lights start to go out across the entire arena. The crowd around me loses their fucking minds.

I look to my right and see a girl jumping up and down so hard she is most likely going to knock herself out with her own tits. Right beside her, a guy is doing a quick hit of coke from a little tube he pulls from his pocket.

I feel myself staring at the man and his brazenness before I turn my attention back to the stage. It's about to start. I can hear noises and shuffling on the stage in front of me.

I know he is up there. I can feel him.

I can feel his energy radiating towards me.

Can he see me?

I take a deep breath and close my eyes as I hear his raspy voice as he leans into the microphone.

6

Ares

I Wanna Be Your Slave - Maneskin

I talk Simone into painting me 15 minutes early tonight so I can spend my last moments before going on stage pacing back and forth behind the doors. Because it's only normal for a 26 year old man to have fucking anxiety over a woman like he is a teenager again, right?

I still can not believe that the lady at the Fillmore gave us Lily's full name. I guess it didn't help matters that Simone and I were still in full makeup when we approached the woman. The poor chick would have handed us her own fucking passport if we asked. She looked to be shitting bricks at the sight of us. She didn't have an address for her because apparently someone else had bought the ticket.

But that was okay, I had her name and I easily found her on insta, then the fun really began. It is still a bit terrifying how easy it was for Simone to find out every last little detail about where she lives and her daily routine. But luckily for me she had helped me, because I would have never been able to find her in a city the size of New York without that information.

I shake out my shoulders. I am starting to get nervous again, pacing incessantly.

What if she doesn't come?

What if she does come but only because she feels obligated to?

I am so fucking twisted up in knots over this woman. I have been for weeks if I am being honest. My every waking thought has been wrapped around her smile. Fuck, I have found myself waking up in the middle of the night panting with thoughts of her. The amount of times I have jerked off to the thought of her smile and her lips is fucking laughable. I rub my palms together then turn and walk through the door towards the side stage. My eyes instantly start to scan the crowd.

Then I quickly remember that the VIP area is to the left of the stage. I stealthily run up behind a speaker and glance around it.

There she is.

Lily is standing there in a fucking see through dress. It is tight, short and very tempting. She is also wearing another pair of heels that are begging me to walk over there and fuck her in front of everybody.

I feel the familiar chill of nerves run down my spine. The same feeling I get every fucking time I catch a glimpse of her. If she only knew the power she has over me.

I smile until I see a man, easily 10 or more years older than myself step up next to her and start talking. I feel the heat roll up my spine as the anger in me surges. Who the fuck is this guy? Did she bring a fucking date? Is he the one that bought her ticket the first time? I am not entirely sure what he is saying but she turns and gives him a small smile before turning back towards the stage.

What he didn't see was the roll in her eyes when she did it.

She is here entirely for me.

I smile again as the lights go out across the stadium. The crowd going fucking wild. I worry a bit that the knowledge that she is standing there watching me is going to hold my attention more than it should. That I may be so concerned with her presence that I won't perform the way I should. I have never been this obsessed before. I have never allowed myself to imagine that I could some day actually be happy.

Surprisingly though, I seem to breeze through the show as normally as any other performance. It's keeping me more on track if anything. I smile to myself as I sing through the song list.

> *"Veiled in silence are the secrets we share,*
> *Revealed realities in this bittersweet space.*
>
> *In moments of longing, in every stare,*
> *We dance on the edge of eternal grace."*

Then I feel the peace that falls over me when I am in my own mind. Just me and the music. I easily lose myself in the atmosphere around me. It is so easy to lose myself in the lyrics that cradle my memories, my most painful horrors.

I have the piano positioned differently tonight so I am facing her when I sing a few of the songs. Every time I look at her, she is smiling but crying. Swaying peacefully unaware of the chaos just a mere 20 feet to her right. She is completely wrapped up in her own imagination. I just pray I am there with her. The real me, not just this mask.

> *"In shadows deep where whispers dwell,*
> *I've carved your name in the breath of night.*
>
> *A ghostly kiss sent from the swell,*
> *Of ancient stars that caught our light."*

The last song finally ends and the lights come up. We do our final bows then just like before, I jump down with the guards and walk over to Lily. The man from earlier is standing beside her again. Whispering in her ear. But she doesn't even seem to notice him there as she grins at me while I walk straight to her. I step in front of her and hold my hand out, palm up.

The man turns then quickly realizes who it is standing before him. His face is one for the books. A mix between fear, shock and sadness. He backs off with his hands up in surrender then sits down behind her.

Lily looks into my mask, a hint of a smile on her lips, "Hello again."

I stick my hand out a little closer to her chest and she smiles as she takes it. We turn in unison as she lets me lead her out of the VIP area. I keep my eyes on her the entire way. I watch her walk with so much poise and confidence it is honestly a bit surprising. This is a far cry from the timid woman 2 weeks ago. We pass through the door and she turns right to lead me to the green room.

How the fuck does she know where the green room is?

I let my eyes roam down her body, realizing that not only is the dress see through but that she is wearing a red fucking thong underneath of it.

I can see the swell of her ass right in front of me and I almost cum right on the spot. I look up to see another small hallway leading to the right. I step in and quickly pull her in behind me. I just need her all to myself for a minute. Before all the eyes set on us in the green room.

She squeals as I pull her into my arms. She is smiling but panting up into my face. I turn her, pinning her back to the wall like I did weeks before. This time she lifts her arms on her own with a sly smile on her lips as I lean in and crush my mouth into hers. I feel her tongue run across my bottom lip and my eyes roll up in my head.

I smile into her lips. Into the salvation that is reaching out to me and offering me a slice of paradise. I have been starving for her for days now. The feeling of my love back in my grasp is an emotion that I have no idea how to describe.

Her hands come down behind my neck as I run mine up and down her body. Her dress is black so I don't even bother to hold back because of the body paint. I grab her tit and feel her moan into my mouth. I growl back into hers in return.

I turn my head and start kissing down her neck then across her collarbone. I knead both her breasts the entire time as she lets her head fall back against the wall behind her. The small little moans coming from her throat are pushing me to the point of no return. My entire body feels like a bottle rocket that has been lit but hasn't taken off into the night sky yet.

I look into her eyes, seeing no hesitation looking back at me. I stand back up to my full height then pick her up behind her thighs. Her eyes bore into me as she places her hands softly on my biceps before the wall meets her back again. She lets out another small gasp when her back hits the wall. A wicked delicious smile forming on her face.

As I pin her to the wall with my body, she quickly wraps her legs around my waist. She takes her hands and runs them up my arms then around my neck. She is practically humming with need. I can feel the heat radiating from her pussy.

I bet she is dripping wet for me right now.

I stop kissing her for just a moment. I stare into her face as her eyes roam the mask in front of her. I want to show her who I am. I want her to see it was me the whole time but I am afraid.

What if she doesn't want me then?

What if all she really wants is this alter ego?

I run my left hand around the outside of her thigh then back towards her center. Goosebumps follow the path of my fingers as they trail around her outer thigh. Her mouth falls open just slightly but she holds contact with my eyes the entire time.

I stare at her lips as I start to stroke her lacy thong. I was right. She is soaked right through her panties. She bites her bottom lip but does not look away from me. Her eyes scan the mask in front of her like she is trying to decipher some hidden code.

I want so badly to fuck her up against this wall but I am not going to do that.

Not like this.

She seems to have the same thought as me. Her eyes are feral but I can see a hint of withdrawal in them. I slowly lower her back down to the floor. She is still panting as she reaches into her purse. She smiles as she pulls out a phone then texts someone before putting the device away.

I am instantly confused. Is this really the time to be just sending random texts to god knows who? She smiles as she grabs my hand then leads me back out into the main hall.

Instead of turning towards the green room though she turns to the left. I have no fucking clue where we are going but I am certain I will let this little minx lead me straight into the gates of hell if she wanted to.

A few moments later, she is pushing on an exit door that leads us into the cold alley beside the arena. She stops long enough to look at me and smile then a door is being opened to an SUV.

She climbs in and slides over into the far side of the seat. The next thing I know I see her hand outstretched, palm up.

Inviting me in. I look down the alley, unsure if I should go with her or not. The rest of the band will be looking for me.

I look back down at her hand. I smile as I think 'fuck em' to myself. I lift my hand to hers and slide into the seat beside her.

The driver shuts the door then moves around to the front seat of the SUV. He has to be shitting himself right now. Especially if he has never seen one of our shows before.

And by the looks of him, he definitely has not.

I point to her purse then hold my hand up to the side of my face like a phone. Lily smiles as she reaches into her bag. She gives me another soul melting grin as she hands the device over to me.

Still no fucking clue where I am going, I type in Matthew's number and send a quick text to let him know that I am okay and I will reach out later.

I hand her the phone back and she reads the message smiling. She slides the phone back into her purse then grins at me as she leans back in her seat as the car accelerates around a corner.

I turn my face towards her. I know all she can see is the mask but I don't care anymore. I tilt my head slightly to the right and I slide my right hand across her bare thigh.

I watch her eyes close and her mouth fall open slightly as she feels my fingers slide in between her legs. God damn those red lips.

I turn to face her fully and slam my mouth into hers. I don't care what the fuck the driver sees. I feel us moving down the street but all I can think about is her tongue in my mouth right now.

I need her more than I need air.

I take my hand from between her thighs and wrap it around the back of her neck holding her mouth to mine. Then I slide my left hand between her thighs, pushing them apart roughly. She lets out a small moan from the back of her throat.

I pull back and watch her face as I push her underwear to the side and slide my finger lengthwise down her engorged clit. Lily lets out a noise like her breath has caught in her throat and lets her legs fall open a bit farther.

I kiss her hard as I slide a finger inside of her. She wraps her hands around my neck, kissing me harder and faster.

Almost to the point of my mask falling off.

I did not envision this for the evening. I thought maybe we would have a drink. Maybe just maybe at the end of the night we would agree to meet up tomorrow.

But here I am in the back seat of her suv with two fingers pumping inside of her as she rides the palm of my hand.

The car itself comes to a stop and I hear the driver clear his throat. I pull back and see that her face is flush and she is breathing heavily. I let a small smile roll over my lips knowing I am the one making her this uncontrolled.

Lily clears her throat, smiling at me, "Thank you Garrett. You are done for the evening. I will reach out tomorrow."

I look over my shoulder at the driver.

He doesn't even bat an eye, not even glance in the rearview mirror, "Yes, Miss Lily. Have a good evening."

She smiles at me as I slide my fingers out of her. She bites her bottom lip again then opens the door and climbs out.

I follow her, standing up fully as I look up and down the street. I glance in between the houses as we step towards what I am assuming is her front stoop. Did I just fucking see Central Park behind her house?

I glance at her again then up towards the enormous brown stone in front of us.

Who the fuck is she?

86

This house has to be worth millions.

She stops at the top of the steps and looks back down at me, "Are you coming? Or do you want me to have Garrett take you back?"

I let a low growl leave my throat as I make my way up the steps. She smiles as she turns around towards the door.

She unlocks the door then holds it open for me. I step inside swiftly, letting the door close behind me. She reaches around me and locks the door then looks down the hallway towards the back of the house, "This is home. For me at least."

She is nervous. I can feel it pulsating off of her in waves.

I watch her as she turns her back to me then steps through a doorway into what looks like the kitchen. She settles up to a marble island and drops her purse onto it letting out a huge sigh.

This house if fucking immaculate. There is fancy white wainscoting on the walls. Real hardwood floors. There are a few pieces of art hanging down the hallway. It looks cozy if you aren't afraid of looking at price tags. I am sure her decor alone cost more than we made on our last album.

I reach up and unchain the hooded cloak from around my neck, letting it fall into a heap on the floor. We are finally alone. I can finally be for her everything I have wanted to be since the night our eyes met in that fucking restaurant.

I step into the kitchen behind her, placing my hands on her hips and slide my foot in between hers, lightly kicking her legs apart. She lets out a gasp as she grips the sides of the island.

I smile knowing I have caught her off guard again. I reach my hand up and gather her long black hair pulling it all around her shoulders and down the left side of her neck. I decide right then that it is time for me to claim her.

She is going to be mine. Whether she realizes it or not. I roll my eyes into my head as I lean into her neck breathing her in deep. I groan at the scent coming off of her skin, like cherries and need.

Fuck, I want to bite her fucking neck and make her scream. But this fucking mask won't let me. I stand there staring at the back of her head, at that silky black hair as I slide the mask off and lay it on the counter in front of her.

I see her face turn to it but she doesn't even attempt to turn around to look at me. I reach down to the hem of her dress and pull it up around her waist roughly.

She lets out as gasp as the fabric bunches above her hips. I hook a thumb in each side of her red lacy thong and pull it down swiftly. As soon as it hits the floor, she steps out of it widely, leaving her legs spread for me.

I reach down and unbuckle my belt, quickly letting my trousers bunch around my thighs. I lean into her neck again and run my nose from her shoulder all the up to her ear.

I see the goosebumps raise on her skin. She lets out a soft moan as I put my left hand in the center of her back and push her forward over the counter. I run my other hand across her bare ass, grasping her cheek tight before I wrap my hand around my dick and slide into her roughly.

Her scream pierces the room.

I freeze. Fuck, I hurt her.

I am still inside her, trying not to push too far then I see her arms reach out and grip the counter on either side tighter. I watch her paste herself to the countertop in front of us and push her ass higher into me.

Inviting me in deeper.

I can feel my brain about to explode as I start to push myself in and out of her tight little pussy. I wrap my hands around her waist trying to steady myself so I don't pass out on the spot. I continue to slam into her from behind as my gaze goes towards the ceiling. I listen to myself moan into the room around us. It feels like nothing I have ever experienced before. Every single squeeze of her pussy sends pulses through my dick and straight to my spine.

I hear her cry out and I start to lose all hope of walking out of here unscathed. My heart is hammering in my chest. I knew she was going to feel this fucking good. I just fucking knew it. I grab a handful of her hair, pulling hard enough to make her back bow. Her tits rubbing across the top of the island.

God damn, she is so fucking perfect. I can hear the want, the need in every single breath she lets out.

I continue to slam into her, trying not to let myself go too soon. I want her to see me. I want to look into her eyes, so she can feel the claim I am laying on her soul right now.

In a last minute decision, I withdraw myself from her quickly. She lets out a small whimper as her head starts to lift off the counter to try to see what I am doing.

I grip her hips then spin her around, quickly lifting her up under her arms. I sit her down roughly on the edge of the counter.

I grab her ass and pull her to the edge before looking up into her eyes. I see the realization in her face when she recognizes me.

Fear grips my chest. The look on her face is somewhere between relief and shock.

Is this what she wants?

Will she accept me for who I really am?

I am standing in front of her, rock hard wanting so badly to slam back into her. My dick is hesitating at her entrance, pulsating with want. She lets out a small shudder, "Gideon?"

I blink as I lean in to kiss her again.

She pulls back slightly and runs her finger down the side of my face then looks deep into my eyes, smiling slightly, "I wanted it to be you."

I growl into her mouth, "Fuck, yeah you did little one."

I slide her closer to me and slam back up into her. She screams again but this time wraps her arms around my neck and pulls her face into my shoulder.

I continue to pummel her as I feel her cunt start to flutter around my dick faster and harder.

Fuck me.

I have never been with someone so responsive before.

I push her lower back into me a bit further as I slam into her again and again. I am grunting into her with every stroke as she moans into the skin at the base of my neck.

Lily leans back with her hands bracing her body on the countertop behind her. I look down at where we are joined then meet her gaze. She smiles at me and I growl at her as I start to thrust into her faster than before. She lets out a soft moan, pulling my attention back to her face. She is watching me destroy her pussy then she gives me a half grin, "Fuck me harder Gideon."

I smile into her eyes as I pull her hips closer to me then surge into her harder than before. Her mouth slightly parts and her breathing is becoming deeper, raspier. I smile at her, "Use your words baby." She lets out a small whimper.

Within just a few minutes, I feel her pulsate again then clamp down on my dick as she screams, "Fuck Gideon. I am cumming. Fuck me."

I hold her hips close to mine as I continue to slam into her vice like pussy. It honestly feels like my entire body is on fire. I feel my blood pumping through me. I almost swear my vessels themselves are going to erupt at any moment. I can feel myself bordering the line into ecstasy, "Baby, you're doing so good. Taking all of me so deep. You're so tight."

Lily lets out another deep moan as she sits up wrapping her arms around my neck. I feel her breath on my shoulder. I can feel myself hitting the walls inside her as she clenches down on me harder than before. Lily screams into my shoulder then bites down on my neck, hard.

I hold onto her tighter, "Lily, I'm about to cum." She whispers in my ear, "Do it baby. I want to feel you everywhere." then she bites down on my neck again. I growl my own release just a moment later, "Fuck Lily. God dammit."

I continue to spear into her until every single drop has left my body. I pull back and look into her hooded eyes. I reach up and move the hair away from her face then lean down to kiss her sweetly again.

I pull back a moment later, out of breath but still inside of her. She smiles up at me, "I wasn't lying. I wished it was you from the first moment you spoke to me."

I smile back at her, "I haven't been able to get you out of my head since I met you. I have never wanted to possess someone before. I had to find you."

She smiles as she leans into my chest, "I am glad you did."

I grin into her long black hair then slowly remove myself from her and pull my trousers back up.

I have no idea what to do now. I look around her kitchen. There is a huge restaurant style refrigerator next to the fanciest gas stove I have ever seen in my life. The countertops and island are all a beautiful cream colored marble with flecks of black in it. The sink alone looks big enough to bathe a German Shepard in.

I am literally blown away by the extravagance of it.

I continue to look around the room then towards the open living room a few steps away. This is definitely not the kind of place I grew up in. I give her a bit of a side eye, "Are you in the mafia or something? Should I be worried right now?"

Lily smiles as she slides off the counter. She pulls her dress down around her thighs then retrieves her underwear from the floor, "No, I am not a part of the mafia. Calm down, there are no Guido's waiting outside the door with a baseball bat."

I give her another small nod, looking around the kitchen and into the living room, "Good...Good..."

I turn back towards her, "Do you want me to leave now? I mean now that, well that has been done?"

Lily grins wickedly at me, "You mean since we fucked? Do I want you to run out the door before I even have my underwear back on?"

I stare into her eyes, unaware that my little one has this side to her. I smile as she walks over to me then wads her red thong up in a ball and slides it into my pants pocket. I look from her hand back to her face, smiling just as wickedly back at her.

Oh, I am definitely using those to jerk off to later.

She leans her back against the marble kitchen island. Her eyes flash with an expression that I am not familiar with, "I thought young spry guys could go all night? Or was that just another myth?"

I step up to her so she has to crane her neck to look up at me. I grin down at her and narrow my eyes, "Oh you're in for it now. I may never leave."

She smiles as she turns and walks towards the staircase in the foyer, "We'll see about that."

7

Lily
Indigo - Sam Barber feat. Avery Anna

I can feel Gideon watching me from the other side of the kitchen. He is so fucking nervous. I bet he thinks I want him to leave now that we have fucked. But no, I don't.

No matter how many times my brain has told my heart not to get involved it still did. I am starting to think this heaviness in my chest might be addictive. Like I won't be able to handle my day to day life without it after tonight.

I wanted Gideon to be Ares.

I had already thought through all the similarities but I was always quick to run a red line through them in my head. When he spun me around and pulled his face to mine, I felt nothing but relief. I had known there was something about him from the beginning but never let myself imagine this.

Never this much.

I feel this pressure in my chest, something I have never really felt before. It doesn't hurt. I am not scared of it either.

It just feels like something is changing within me. Unsure of what it might really be, I round the corner to go upstairs. I can feel him running down my leg and it is making me want to do just fucking feral things to him. Gideon steps into the foyer and looks up the stairs at me. I smile back down at him, "Do you want a shower?"

A devilish grin comes over his face as he starts to slowly follow me up the stairs. I feel like a schoolgirl. Like a little fucking teenager with a crush.

It is heavy.

It is real.

It is honestly crushing, but still welcomed.

And that is the scary part, because it's new. I have never felt like this before and the fear gripping my chest has me believing it may be nothing but a dream.

I am about to turn the corner into the bedroom when I hear Gideon behind me, "Uh, Lily?" I turn around, feeling the smile drop from my face.

Fuck!

I didn't even think about him seeing the pictures of Mark and I when I decided to bring him home with me earlier. I breathe out a sigh and step back up to his side. He is still pointing at my wedding photo with his long black finger.

His eyes not daring to meet mine, "Are you fucking married?" I look at the wedding photo hanging in the hallway, "No. Not anymore."

He turns and looks at me, questioning everything I can tell, "So if you are divorced, why do you still have this photo up?"

I look at the photo of Mark and I, then back to Gideon. I close my eyes, breathing deeply then turn to continue to the bedroom, "We aren't divorced. He died."

I round the corner into the bedroom then right again towards my closet. I didn't expect to be having this conversation 5 minutes after having Gideon's dick inside me but here we are. I am standing in front of my full-length mirror when I see Gideon step up behind me.

His eyes are hard on mine, "When?"

94

I look to the ceiling then back at his reflection staring at me in the mirror, "A little over a 6 weeks ago."

I throw my hands up in front of me defensively because I know how that sounds, watching his eyes go wide in the reflection in front of me,

"But, in my defense he was sick for a very, very long time. We said our real goodbyes months ago. I had already begun to move on long before he was even gone. He let me go months ago."

I know it sounds horrible. But it is the truth.

Mark refused to let me take care of him. He refused to let me sit by his side while he wasted away in hospice. He wanted me prepared for his departure.

He made sure I knew he loved me but he also made sure that I would let him go and continue moving forward with my life.

Gideon tilts his head to the right, "How did he die?"

I blink long and hard before turning around and facing him, "He was beaten to death by the lead singer of an alternative metal band. It was tragic." Gideon's eyes fly open and I just smile widely at him, "It was brain cancer."

I watch his eyes roam my face like he is trying to read some indecipherable language. He is looking at me differently. Not bad, just softer. I can already feel it, what we had, is changing. He pities me. I instantly start to build my walls back up. I knew this was too good to be true.

Gideon turns and looks around the room. I can tell he is noticing all of Mark's things still here. He looks at the bed, the nightstand, then I see his eyes move to the closet on the other side of the room, filled to the brim with Mark's clothes.

Gideon turns his head back to me and I give him a small shoulder shrug, "I haven't brought myself to get rid of his stuff yet. I don't even sleep in here anymore. But this is where all my clothes and things are so I come in here for the basics then just keep to the rest of the house.

"Sometimes, I sleep in the guest room, sometimes downstairs. Honestly, I want to just sell the god damn house and start fresh somewhere new."

Gideon turns to me, placing his finger under my chin and bringing my gaze back to his. He leans in and kisses me gently on the lips, "You do whatever you need to do for you. If that means stay, then stay. If that means go, give me a forwarding address. Either way, I am here for it."

I smile back up at him, my heart fluttering. Not really sure if I can believe his words or not. But either way the hammering of my heart becomes louder.

I am so screwed.

I grab his hand, "Come on, the bathrooms in here."

We round the corner and he stops abruptly again, "Okay, was Mark in the mafia then?"

I turn to see his eyes wide scanning the extra large bathroom with rain shower capabilities, large oval soaking tub, and gold fixtures. I laugh again, "No, Mark wasn't in the mafia either. You're still safe."

Gideon nods his head as I turn my back to him, "Could you please unzip me?"

I feel his fingertips brush the skin between my shoulder blades as the other hand slowly lowers the zipper of my dress. My breathing picks up again as the goosebumps spread from my shoulders and down my arms.

I hear his breath catch in his throat as I let the dress fall to the floor. I look up into the mirror to see him staring back at me.

I reach up behind me, never breaking eye contact with him as I remove my red lace bra next. I turn around now

96

completely naked and smile up at him. I can feel his eyes watching me as I reach down and unbuckle his belt then pull it through the loops.

He slides out of the boots he is wearing tucked up underneath his pant legs. I run my hands down his waist, moaning as I feel the muscles on his hips then thighs. I follow my hands all the way down his legs until his pants are at his ankles and he is stepping out of them.

I look back up his lean body, seeing him growing hard again. I smile as I slowly raise back up, letting his dick graze my cheek, then my tits.

Gideon lets out another growl as he bends in the middle and pulls his socks off. I laugh to myself as I walk around him and turn on the shower. I smile into the water falling as I reach my hand in to test the temperature. It feels powerful and scary at the same time. Seeing his expressions to the subtlest of actions. I step inside letting the water fall all around me.

The water feels fucking amazing.

It is hot but still somehow still lowering my body temperature. I reach my hands up and slick my wet hair around the back of my head. I lower my eyes as Gideon turns towards me then steps inside the shower in front of me.

I grab a wash rag and lift it to his skin. The black paint is starting to melt off of his skin under the heat of the water. It looks like a dirty window being hit by rain. I take in a breath, holding the rag as I start to wipe the black paint off his face then neck.

His dark eyes never leave my face. I am actually surprised this stuff is wiping off as easily as it is. I bring the rag down to his chest then see his hand come over top of mine.

I stop, staring at his hand as I feel the tremors start to take over my heart again. I look back up at him. I feel all of my resolve flowing off my body with the water streaming down my

97

skin. He smiles as he takes a step towards me, making me back up.

He puts his hand on my face as he takes two more steps towards me, forcing me to back into the wall behind me. I feel the cold tiles at my back and I smile into his chest. I look up into his eyes then drop the rag onto the floor of the shower.

Gideon smiles like the devil himself as he reaches down and picks me up by the back of my thighs. I wrap my arms and legs around him as he pushes into me, settling me into the tiles behind us.

He leans into me, kissing me roughly. I grin at him as I feel his hands around each wrist then bring them up over my head. I smile into his lips then open my mouth to let his tongue explore mine.

I am panting with need again.

I want him to fucking throttle me as hard as he can into the wall. Instead, I feel him pull back gently and I know he is staring at me. I can't bring myself to look into his eyes though. I know he is looking at me differently now that he knows about Mark. I knew this was going to happen.

I told myself not to let him in. He is already gone even though his body is still right in front of me. I am beginning to feel like a pity fuck. Not really something a girl ever wants to feel like.

I open my eyes and pull my face back a bit staring down at his chest, "We really should get you cleaned up. This body paint can't be good for your pores."

He snorts out a laugh but allows my arms to fall back down to my sides. I unwrap my legs and settle my feet back into the floor of the shower. I put two fingers in the center of his chest then start to push back slightly.

Gideon looks at my fingers with a smile on his face but continues to take small steps until he is back under the water.

I turn around and bend back down to get the wash rag. I don't even realize what I have done until I feel his very large hands on my bare ass.

I let a smile fall over my lips as I feel him caressing me. Why does this feel so fucking right even when I know something has changed in him? Why do I still fucking want him when I know he is only here out of infatuation? There can never be anything more than this night. I look over my shoulder back up at him, "Sir, do you have untamed thoughts running through your head?"

I see him smile back at me, "Maybe."

I smile a bit bigger, nudging my ass back into his dick, "What are you going to do about it then?"

Gideon's eyes go feral then he starts to rub his dick up and down my center. I can feel his eyes on the back of my head as he slips the tip of his dick into my ass. He pauses as if he is waiting for my permission to continue.

I let out a small breath, "I'm okay. Keep going."

I feel him run his hand down my spine starting at the base of my neck then wrapping each large hand around my waist as he pulls me closer to him, sending him deeper into me. He is gentle, taking it slowly, inch by inch.

I look back over my shoulder and see his face leaned back into the water as he starts to slowly pump inside of me. I let out a low moan and I see his eyes open and land on mine, "You like this don't you?"

I bite my bottom lip and nod my head at him. He smiles wildly again and slams harder into me. I let out a scream into the shower as I brace my hands on the glass wall in front of me.

I feel him picking up his pace so I look back at him again, "Jesus Gideon your dick is so big. Fucking destroy me."

99

I see him look into my eyes then I feel his hand slap my wet ass hard. I let out another moan as he starts pumping into me faster. I just want to feel free again. Like earlier in the kitchen. I want him to not look at me like I am some breakable little porcelain doll. I feel him lean over me a bit then his fingers slide around my hip and towards my heat. I roll my neck to the side as he quickly starts rubbing his fingers over my clit.

I push my ass back into him as he continues to grip my hip with one hand. I smile again as I feel my release starting to grow deep within me.

Gideon pushes himself all the way inside me and holds himself there as he furiously continues to circle my clit with his fingers. I feel myself start to quiver inside and I know I am about to hit my peak. He lets out a deep moan as I start to cum all over his hand.

I cry out again as my hips start bucking back into him. He puts both hands back on my hips and rocks into me repeatedly until I hear him let out another growl. I can feel him swell inside me before he leans his head back, "Lily. Jesus fuck." He continues to slowly pump in and out of me until his waves have passed.

I smile back over my shoulder as he slides out of my ass then takes the rag from my hand and runs it over my center. I stand up straight and turn to him. His smile reigns down on me, "Well this might just be the best damn shower I have ever had." I smile back at him as I open the shower door briefly and grab another rag off the shelf.

I turn to him, lathering up the rag with my body wash, "Sorry you might smell like rose petals after this."

He smiles widely at me but nods his head giving me the green light to finish cleaning him. He watches me as I clean all the paint off his body. I hand him the rag then grab another to quickly clean myself. I can't even bring myself to utter a word to him.

He brings me so much physical pleasure but he is not going to stick around. I can see it in his face every time he looks at me. There is something there. He looks at me like he can't figure me out. And maybe that he doesn't want to. It is obvious that he is attracted to me, it has been from the beginning. But that is all this is for him. Just a physical release. There is something darker than the shadows hiding behind the ink in his eyes.

Something lying just below the surface. He has secrets.

I step out of the shower then reach for a towel to hand him. I grab a few for myself, wrapping one around my body then another around my hair.

I step up to the sink and look in the mirror to watch him wrap his towel around his waist. His eyes meet mine as he steps out of the shower. I settle into my after shower care routine. I brush my teeth then grab my few little bottles of serums, toners, and moisturizers.

Gideon slides up onto the counter and watches me. I smile into the mirror at his reflection, "You always watch old women do their skin care routine?"

I look over at him but he isn't smiling back, "You know the age thing doesn't bother me right?"

I smile back at the reflection in the mirror, "Maybe not right now but what about when you are 35 and I am 43 or you are 41 and I am turning 50?"

He shakes his head, "It's not going to matter to me then either."

I slap the last of my moisturizer on my neck and face then turn to him, "You don't know that. Plus, it doesn't even matter. We probably won't even know each other by then anyways."

Gideon slides off the counter and walks briskly from the room. I hear myself utter the words that I wish were not true. I can feel myself pushing him away. If I push first then maybe it won't hurt so bad when he inevitably leaves.

Right?

8

Ares
Wildflower - Billie Eilish

This self deprecating bullshit is starting to get really fucking old. I slide off the counter then step into her bedroom. It physically hurt me when she said that we wouldn't know each other in 10 years time. But why? Why did it feel like my soul split in half when she said that? I barely know her.

I crack my neck and let out a low grunt. I try to get my thoughts arranged in my head. I am falling for her, fast. Faster than I should. Faster than I thought possible. I have felt this coming on for days now. I knew as soon as I laid claim to her that shit would change.

I just didn't expect it would be her trying to push me away.

Everything about this whole situation has screamed disaster since I saw that photo in the hallway. But my fucking soul just won't let me walk away from her. She is the air I breathe.

How am I supposed to just willingly give that up?

I look around the room, my eyes landing on the nightstand to the left of the bed again. I walk over and pick up the book that is laying there.

A Civil Action.

I sit the book down next to a watch that looks like it cost more than my car. I glance into the closet beside me. Nothing but Armani suits and more than likely overpriced ties and cufflinks. I step back out into the room then spin on my heels and walk across the hall. I quickly decide this must be the room she sleeps in.

There are some of her clothes lying on the back of a chair. I run my fingers over the soft fabric, bringing it to my face and smelling cherries. I sit it back down then step up to the night stand, seeing a book entitled, Broken Whispers.

I stand there with my arms crossed in front of me.

I can't give her this type of life.

She obviously has come from a background grossly different from my own. I can't give her the million dollar mansion.

The "diamonds dripping from everything" lifestyle she seems accustomed to. I hear Lily clear her throat behind me as I turn around. She is smiling, wearing a white tank top and black underwear. I can see her nipples pebbled underneath and I forget about everything I can't give her.

She places a hand on my chest when I step up into her bubble, "Are you mad at me?"

I smile down at her, shaking my head, "No, Lily I am not mad at you."

She nods her head then turns to make her way down the hallway and back downstairs. Something is different about her. She is pulling back, the fire seems to be dying from her eyes. I follow behind her but take my time, looking at all the pictures in the hallway. The door on the last room to the left is cracked open so I slowly open it to take a peek inside.

I step in, dumbfounded by what is in front of me.

There are so many fucking paintings in this room. Some finished but most only half started. Yet no matter the progress of them, they are all beautiful. I take a step closer to the one on

104

the easel. I run my fingers over the wavy paint brush marks left on the canvas.

It is a woman dressed in all black, free falling into what looks like the fires of hell. Her hair is fanned out around her body as she smiles at me. Her arms spread wide as she is willingly letting herself be consumed alive.

In the top left hand corner there is one word.

Ares.

My eyes memorize every last centimeter of the masterpiece in front of me. The details in the design. The way she is able to blend and transition the colors into the next. It is fucking breath taking. I look around at some of the other paintings. Her work is fucking marvelous. She has so much vision. So much depth.

Her paintings are like lyrics to my eyes. I can literally feel every single emotion with each brush stroke. I can just imagine her painting. As she smiles into her work. She is a fucking genius. I look around the room and immediately start to feel unworthy.

She has real talent. I put words to music. But what I do, it fades. In 20 years, no one will remember us. They won't remember Ares. Lily puts real beauty into the world. Her work will hang the halls of peoples homes, line the walls of museums, hell maybe even pass down in families as heirlooms. She deserves so much more than I can ever give her. More than me.

I should fucking feel blessed to even be standing here in her private space. I am literally standing in a room filled to the brim with multiple levels of beauty. So why do I feel so defeated?

I step back out into the hallway. I look towards the stairs but then quickly turn back to her bedroom. I gather my clothes, throwing them back on as I move towards the stairs.

This is quickly becoming something that I am not going to be able to control much longer. She has to still be in mourning. She must be looking at this as just a lonely rebound type of situation. She literally just lost her husband.

But Lily is everything. She is beautiful. She is so alive. She is talented and smart. She is soft and kind. She is so easy to trust but that just makes her easier to break.

I need to end this. I need to end this now before it becomes something I can't walk away from. Something I won't allow her to walk away from. There is no way she is feeling for me what I am feeling for her. I am fucking toxic and she is pure white life in it's simplest form. She is just too fragile right now. But the thought of walking out that door and out of her life terrifies me. She has quickly become part of my DNA. It literally hurts my soul to think that I am going to have to walk away from this, from us.

I stop in the hallway looking at the picture of her and Mark on their wedding day. That was the love of her life. Not me. Never me.

That man smiling back at me from his framed prison.

This is too much, it is too soon. She isn't ready for anything with me. I reluctantly attempt to make my brain try to understand that. No matter what my demons are screaming at me over the roar of the ocean running through my head. I have to let her go. I have to walk away. I just have to do it gently. I don't want to hurt her.

I round the bottom of the stairs and see that my cloak is now laying on the table at the front door. I walk down the long hallway, peeking into an office on the way. I round the corner into the living room and see her standing at the back wall staring out the floor to ceiling windows.

She turns to me, taking in that I am fully dressed again, handing me a glass of whisky. I smile, "Thank you."

Lily gives me another distant smile then turns around and looks back out the window, "You don't have to stay. You are free to leave whenever you want."

I watch her face as her smile slides into an expressionless stone wall. I step up beside her, looking out the window into the night, "I know. But maybe I don't want to."

She makes this snickering noise in the back of her throat then downs the rest of her glass before turning to me and grabbing mine. She steps around me and sits her empty glass on the table then downs mine, sitting my glass down as well.

She clears her throat quickly, "I am sure you are tired. You have had a long day, tomorrow will be just as long. Do you want me to call Garrett to have him take you back? Or to your hotel or wherever?"

She won't meet my eyes.

I step up closer to her, placing my hand on her cheek.

She looks past my shoulder into the room behind me, not even acknowledging my touch, "What is this? What are you doing?"

She sighs and rolls her eyes at me, "We both fucking know that nothing can come from this. We live in two completely different worlds. You are some kind of rock god. I am a middle aged widow with a fucking trust fund. We could not be any more different if we tried. I don't see the point in pretending that this is anything other than what it is."

I take a step back, staring at her, wondering where in the hell all this is coming from. She turned so cold on me out of nowhere. Why is she so upset right now? She turns her back to me and looks out into the black abyss again.

She is pushing me away on purpose.

Why? Because of Mark?

Does she feel the same as me?

That it is too much too soon?

107

Why does that piss me off? Why does it hurt?

I hold my breath, "So you don't even want to try? Because you think that we are too different, you don't even want to attempt to find a common ground?"

Lily turns back to me and I see a tear rolling down her cheek. I take a step towards her but she breathes deeply and takes a step back away from me.

She wipes the tears from her cheek, "Gideon. Ares. Whatever you want to go by. You and the band are going places. You are growing and becoming larger every fucking day. I don't want anything with me to hamper that progress."

I step up to her and place a hand on her cheek, "Why do you think that it would?"

She looks up at me with pleading eyes. Like she is shocked that I don't agree with her, "Cause you are going on tour and you are going to be out in the world making music. Changing people's lives. Making fucking history and I will still be here.

"I don't want to be a distraction for you. I don't want you to feel like you have to live your life any differently than you did yesterday just because we had a little fun."

I swallow hard, instantly pissed at her words. It feels like she just ripped my heart out. I pull her face towards mine, growling, "Is that all this was to you? Just a little fun? Because it is a lot fucking more to me Lily. So much fucking more."

I take a deep breath, trying to calm myself. I step up to her again, "What if you come with me?"

Her eyes whip to mine.

She starts to shake her head so I cup her cheeks and make her look at me. Everything I had just thought about not being with her has already flown out the window.

The minute she thought she wasn't enough for me.

I stare down into her concrete eyes, "Just come with me. Just for a few weeks. You can see what it's like. You can meet everyone in the band. You can decide for yourself then what is best for you. Don't just write us off without giving us a chance."

Lily looks up into my eyes as another tear rolls down her cheek. I swipe it away with my thumb. I lean in and kiss her hard. I feel her smile back and I know I have gotten through to her.

I pick her up and sit her down in my lap straddling me as I sit back getting comfortable on the couch. She leans back softly smiling at me, balancing on my thighs, "So what now?"

I let my hands creep under the sides of her tank top, "It's still early."

My eyes rise to meet hers as she smiles back at me with a sparkle in her eye. She stands up in front of me and slowly peels the tank top off of her body. I shudder as she pulls her underwear down around her feet then uses her toes to toss them over with her shirt.

I quickly undo my trousers again, wishing immediately that I had never put them back on to begin with.

Lily straddles me then lifts slightly using her free hand to steady my dick as she slides down on it. Her head falls back between her shoulders as I lean forward and take her nipple into my mouth.

I roll my tongue across her tender skin making her slip out a low moan. She slowly slides up and down on my cock.

Most women would move front to back, but not Lily.

She wants that friction you could only receive by sliding up and down a man's dick. I grip her hips as she starts to slide a bit faster. She leans down and kisses me forcefully. I pick her up and turn her body so her back is now on the couch.

I hold her hips down with my hands as I start thrusting harder into her. Her mouth slightly parts as she closes her eyes.

I lean forward a bit, "Do you like that Lily? Do you like the feeling of my cock railing you into this couch?"

Her eyes open slightly, smiling she says, "I have never been so satisfied in my life. I can feel you everywhere."

I smile as I thrust up into her harder. She lets out another moan as I feel her start to clench down on me. I smile again, "Are you trying to cum on my cock already, Lily?"

Lily opens her eyes then looks down to where our bodies are meeting into one. She holds her gaze there for a minute before she lays her head back again, "Fuck Gideon. I am going to cum soon."

I lean down and kiss her harder as my thrusts become more frenzied. I feel her clamp down on my dick and look at her face.

Her mouth falls open as her eyes close, "Fuck Gideon. Fuck me hard. Oh my god. Gideon!"

I slam into her harder watching her fall apart beneath me. I continue to thrust into her as I feel my release growing deep in my spine. I have no idea how I haven't exploded inside of her yet. She starts to come down and I reach down between us and start rubbing my finger in tight circles over her clit.

Her eyes come back to mine as I smile at her, "One more baby. Cum on my cock one more time."

She smiles and leans forward to kiss me. She moves her head back a few minutes later as I watch myself slamming into her, "God dammit Lily you are so tight. You feel so good wrapped around my dick, baby. I am so close."

She smiles at me as she starts rubbing her own finger over her bud. I feel her start to flutter again, "That's it baby. Cum on my cock. Please. Please fucking cum on me. I need it. I need to feel you."

I open my eyes to see her looking into mine, a dark expression over her eyes, "Say it again."

I look at her still trying to claim my orgasm, "Say what?"

She smiles back at me again, "Beg for it."

I smile as I slam my dick into her again, "Please cum on my cock baby. I can't cum until you do. Please baby. Let me cum."

Her chest convulses forward as I feel her clamp down on me, harder than before. I lift her hips slightly off the couch and start thrusting into her harder than ever. It hits me a moment later and I scream my own release. I lay there inside of her for a long time after, just trying to catch my breath.

I can feel myself pulsating inside of her and every time I do she whines just a bit more. I listen to her soft moans for a few minutes longer before I finally pull out of her and cradle her close to my chest.

Before I know what is happening, I have her completely enveloped in my arms and we both doze off to sleep.

I wake up on my own before Lily. She is still sleeping soundly curled up into my chest. I smile as I wipe the stray hair away from her eyes. I look at the wall past her and feel a familiar sensation roll through me.

The nausea is hitting. I sigh heavily knowing it won't be long before the anxiety and sweats follow.

I look back down at the beautiful face in front of me. Those dark eyebrows framing that perfectly unpainted face.

Will she stay with me when she finds out the truth?

Will I let her stay with me?

▍▍

She deserves so much more than some coked out fucking musician running rampant through her life. I feel the cold chills run down my back, forcing me to let her go. I am going to go to the hotel. I am going to get a fix.

Then I am going to spend the day figuring out when would be a suitable time to detox. It will suck yes, but I have done it before. I know the process. This time, using was just to get through the tour anyways.

She is more important. I just need to keep fueling the flame until there is enough of a break in the tour to do this shit successfully. I can't let it get in the way of the band.

I kiss her on the forehead and gently get up off the couch. I dress quietly so as to not wake her. She looks like a porcelain doll laying there curled up into the warmth where my body had just been. I grab the blanket off the back of the couch and cover her gently before walking away.

I turn into the kitchen, finding some paper and a pen in a drawer. I quickly leave her a note telling her my hotel, the room number, and also how to get to my dressing room at the arena.

I also tell her if she doesn't show up tonight, I am hunting her down. I will do it too. I don't care how far I have to search. I will find her. She is mine now.

I smile as I lay the pen down then look back at her sleeping peacefully on the couch. I turn to walk out of the kitchen into the foyer and I see a red headed woman standing there smiling at me.

I stop abruptly.

She is beautiful as well with long red wavy curls and neon green eyes but something about her scares the absolute hell out of me. I know it has only been a day since I used, but I have never had hallucinations this fast before.

I look back towards the living room then back to the red head. She steps up to me gingerly then notices the mask laying on the island.

She picks it up, smiling at me, "Your Ares aren't you?"

I give her a soft smile in return, "And you are?"

She lets out a moan as her eyes roll up in her head, "God dammit I knew you were British. I'm Susie. I am your little sex toys' best friend."

Oh, Edge is going to love this woman.

I let out a laugh then nod my head, "Hello Susie. It's a pleasure to meet you. Though I was just about to head out. I have another show tonight that I still need to prepare for."

Susie just smiles at me and slowly hands my mask over, "Don't worry. She will be there."

I smile back at her, taking the mask, "Thank you."

She grins again as she moves out of the way. She sweeps her arm out to the side to allow me passage beside her. I grab my cloak and head outside.

Luckily, it doesn't take long to find a cab.

I find Matthew as soon as I get back to the hotel. He opens the door to his room, letting me slip in, "So....how was it?"

I smile back at him. I know I am radiating with energy right now. I step over to his coat and pull my stash out of the inside pocket. Hidden right where it always is. I grin over the little white baggie, "She is fucking amazing. Honestly, I have never met anyone like her before."

Matthew smiles at me, moving to sit at the end of the bed. I quickly reach down, picking up the ink pen off the table and taking the cap off. I dip the long end of the pen cap down into the baggie, bringing a hit back up to my nose. I feel the burn of it releasing into my system. I smile again as I dip in for another hit.

"Seriously. I don't even have the words to describe what she is really like. I mean I thought I knew but I had no fucking clue. She is fucking beautiful and god damn viscous at the same time." I bring the next bump to my nose, inhaling it deeply.

I quickly tie the bag back up and slide it into my pants pocket. I wipe my nose quickly with my fingers and roll my neck as the ease of the high starts to take over my body.

I grin out the window, "Dude, we took a shower together. The things that woman let me do to her. Wanted me to do to her. And she wanted it to be me. Not Ares. She wanted it to be me. She told me this."

Matthew smiles back at me, pulling a cigarette out and lighting it, "So, are you going to see her again?"

I turn back towards him, smiling as I cross my arms on my chest, "I asked her to come on tour with us for a few weeks. Just so she can see what it is like. So she doesn't have to worry about me being out on the road."

Matthew's eyes go wide as he smiles and inhales his smoke, "Well fuck me, I guess it is serious then."

I nod my head back at him then slowly turn back towards the window, "Yeah. It is. I need to figure out a good time on the tour to try to wean off the coke though. I don't want her to know about it. I want to be clean when I have that conversation with her. I don't want to lie to her but I am afraid it will really scare her off."

Matthew stands up, stretching his arms out to the side, "Yeah, we can do that. Shouldn't be too bad. Last time was pretty fucking intense but you were using alot more then. I think this time it should be a lot easier. All things considered."

14

I grin back at him before turning towards the window, "As long as she doesn't find out, I don't care how tough it is. I just want her. And I can't really have her, not fully if I am hiding shit from her."

Matthew moves up beside me, looking out over the city as well, "It's 100% your call man. I will back you with whatever you need. If Lily is what makes you happy then I am happy with that. You deserve some fucking peace and happiness. You have been through fucking enough."

I feel a sense of peace fall over me as we nail down a good break in the schedule for me to kick this. I just have to try to keep it under wraps for a few weeks. Until she comes back home, then I will get clean and stay clean. She means too much to me. I can't risk losing her.

She has somehow taken my very fucking essence and wrapped it around her own. I can't think a single thought without her being in it. I thought at first that this was just my infatuation with her but it is so much more than that. I wanted to fucking claim her as my own but in all reality she has claimed me.

We make it to the stadium and I go to my dressing room to finish getting ready for the show. Lily is going to be here soon I am sure. It's only a little over a few hours before the show starts. I am going to tell her the next few stops on the tour, maybe take her home and explore that shower some more before we pack her up for a mini vacation. I can't stop smiling.

Simone steps up to me with the small container of body paint and a brush. She does my face and arms then slowly starts on my sides, "So, what is your new girl like?"

I smile down at her, "You will meet her soon. I think you will like her, Simone. She is unlike anyone I have ever met before."

Simone smiles back up at me, "Will she be the one taking care of your coke dick from now on?"

I smile down at her as she cups my dick in her hand then stands up smiling into my face. She gives me another squeeze, feeling me harden beneath her hand.

I smile down at her when I hear the doorknob click.

I look up to see Lily standing in the doorway in a long satin red dress, completely fucking mortified. I have never seen pure shock on someone's face before, at least not outside of the movies. She looks like she is going to throw up.

I smack Simone's hand away and try to run around her. Lily lifts her hand to her chest, "I am so sorry guys. I didn't realize you were busy. I will leave."

Her voice is breathy and broken. Her eyes seem unable to pull their gaze away from Simone's hand. She turns and runs out the door before I can even make it across the room.

Fuck! Fuck! Fuck!

What have I done? What fucking shitty ass timing to walk into a fucking room!

I am screaming for her to come back by the time I reach the door. I swing it open and see her running around the corner to the left. I take off in a sprint down the hall after her, "Lily! Lily! Just wait please. Let me explain, please Lily!"

I finally catch up to her at the end of the hall. I grab her by the shoulder, spinning her around to face me.

Her eyes have rivers running out of them.

I stop breathing as I see the hurt that I have caused.

116

She wraps her arms around herself like she is trying to keep herself from falling apart. She is pacing the width of the hall, not even able to reach my eyes with hers, "How could you? You were just with me this morning and now...her? Just. Ya know what, just forget my fucking name, Gideon."

She turns and looks at me with this ferocity I have never seen in my life, "I can't believe I fell for all that bullshit you fed me last night. No, I can't believe I let a fucking child into my heart.

"Because that is all you fucking are. You are a goddamn child. How can you just fucking play with people's emotions like this? I am so fucking stupid. You don't fucking deserve me."

I feel myself trembling. I am shaking my head back and forth, just begging for a chance to explain, "It isn't what it looks like. I swear Lily."

She steps up close to me. There is a steel in her gaze that has never been there before. If her eyes were daggers, I would be dead right now. She curls her lip at me then grabs my dick, "Simone wasn't offering to take care of your, what did she call it, coke dick?"

I stare down at her face, trying to will my dick to stay down but with the cocaine in my system it is not wanting to agree with me. She can feel me starting to harden under her grasp.

Lily puts her hands on my chest and pushes me away from her, her face folding in on itself like I am disgusting to her, "I am such a fucking idiot. I believed you. I trusted you, I trusted this. I can't believe that I let myself have feelings for you. Did you even fucking want to be with me or was it just the coke talking the entire time? I knew this was a fucking mistake. I should have never gone to that first concert."

I just stand here staring at her. Unable to come up with one useful thing to say. She rolls her shoulders and angrily

17

swipes the new tears from her face. She looks me square in my eyes and with the softest, saddest whisper I hear, "I wish I had never fucking met you."

I feel the dagger laced with her words pierce my heart. I watch the new rivers starting to form under her eyes as she turns and storms away from me.

Leaving me completely hollow and broken.

9
Lily
Dynasty - MIIA

Susie meets me at the brownstone after a very abrupt phone call from me. I am so fucking angry. More than that. I am fucking destroyed.

I really actually felt something for him. I can't stop the fucking tears from flowing. I run past Susie up the stairs to my bedroom. I rip the satin dress from my body and pull on some jeans and a t-shirt.

I then start grabbing clothes and other items, throwing them into a suitcase. I can't believe I am such a fucking moron. I let his words encase me in this little bubble that was just us. I fell for it. It was all just a fucking show. I wipe the tears away from my eyes again as I try to focus on what I need to do.

I look around the room, practically fucking destroyed by me already. I look at Mark's glasses laying on the table. I turn around and scream into the center of the room. Into the nothingness that my life has become. I am so fucking stupid. Of course he was playing me. Of fucking course it was all bullshit.

Susie is standing at the door watching me the entire time. She sees me throw things, she hears me scream, she watches me as I collapse into a heap in the middle of the floor.

Only then does she step in and wrap her arms around me.

I am crying so hard I am starting to give myself a headache. I pull back and look into her eyes, "I think I love him."

Susie just nods her head at me and strokes my hair with her hand. I feel the tears streaming down my face again. Susie gets a text notification and quickly pulls out her phone. Her eyes fly wide in shock.

I sniffle, "What? What's wrong?"

She looks at me then turns her phone towards me. Gideon has cancelled the show. She had gotten an alert from a friend who knew I had a ticket. Panic attacks my chest. I feel like I am going to pass out as I start shaking my head, "No. No, I don't want to see him and he is going to come here. I have to get out of here. I can't be here when he gets here."

Susie pulls me back into her arms, "It's okay. If he shows up I will tell him you are gone. I won't let him find you, I promise."

I shake my head again, standing up and then throw the half packed open suitcase into the closet.

I turn back to her shrugging my shoulders and throwing my arms wide, "He is a fucking coke junkie Susie. I mean, what the fuck? Why? Why does every fucking thing in my life always end up like this? I wrote that shit out of my life years ago. YEARS! I can't do this again. I can't fucking be around that shit again. This is why I never wanted to do any of this from the beginning. I fucking knew I was going to get hurt. I knew it."

I stomp from the room and head straight down the hallway to my art studio. I look around the room at all the half finished pieces I have begun when the inspiration from his voice would hit me. I grab them one by one and start throwing them across the room. I reach over to the palette, grasping a paint knife in my hand tightly. I turn to painting after painting tearing holes through them while screaming at the top of my lungs.

120

I have never felt this empty before. Never this hollow. It is like he took everything from inside me and set it on fire. My soul, my essence, my heart. It's all just gone. Ashes scattering in the wind.

I turn and see the painting of me falling into the abyss that is Carnal Decay. That is Ares.

I grab the painting on both sides and slam it down on top of the easel. I watch the canvas stretch then rip apart.

"I knew he was going to hurt me. He didn't even feel anything for me. He just used me to take care of his fucking coke dick. I never even mattered to him."

I pull it back off of the easel and start slamming it into the ground. Unable to handle the pressure anymore, I crumble to my knees, crying uncontrollably again. I start ripping the canvas apart by hand, "I can't fucking believe I fell for his bullshit. His FUCKING LIES!" I am shaking with anger now, or maybe it is just the rejection that is hurting so bad.

Susie and I both turn our attention to the hallway when we hear the doorbell. Susie puts her hands up, "I will get rid of him. I promise. Just go hide somewhere he hasn't seen yet. Okay?"

I nod my head to her and run across the hallway to a linen closet. I leave the door cracked and I hear her downstairs answering the door. Then I hear Gideon's voice as he walks into the foyer, "Where is she?"

I hear Susie behind him, following him, "She isn't here. She came home and grabbed a bag of stuff then left. She is gone."

I hear his loud boots march across the hardwood floor, "I don't fucking believe that. She wouldn't just run away."

I hear him climbing the stairs then walk quickly past the closet door I am hiding behind. I hear him start cussing as he checks both bedrooms, not finding me inside.

I listen closer at the door as I hear him coming back down the hallway. He slams the art studio door open, "What, what happened?" I then hear Susie, "You Gideon. You happened."

I feel the tears fall down my cheeks again. I can't just sit back and let Susie fight all of my fucking battles for me. I have to get rid of him. I have to get him out of my home then I have to get the fuck out of here.

I am 100% selling this house now.

I open the closet door slowly. I step into the hallway, looking into the studio. Gideon is holding what was left of my Ares painting. He turns, his eyes going wide when he sees me standing there in front of him.

I watch a tear slide down his cheek as he turns and looks back down at the destroyed painting. I take a tentative step in and nod at Susie letting her know I am okay. She turns and steps out into the hallway but no further.

I let out a heavy sigh, trying to sound more assertive than my heart is actually feeling, "Gideon it's over. This, whatever it is, it's over. I don't want you here. I don't want to see you again. Please, you need to leave."

He turns screaming as he slams the already destroyed painting into the corner of the closet until it breaks into a dozen different pieces. I flinch at the sharp crack of the wooden frame falling apart. I watch him as he throws the painting down into the same heap as the others.

He turns back to me, crying harder, his face red, "She means fucking nothing to me like that. She is just a friend that would help me out on tour from time to time. There has never been nor will there ever be anything between us!"

122

He stalks up to me. But somehow I stand tall against him. I stand my ground. I look him dead in the eyes, "I don't believe you. You're a liar. Every single word that has come out of your mouth since the moment I met you has been a lie."

I have no idea how I am keeping my voice so neutral. Gideon reaches out to grab my hands but I pull them back, "No."

He looks up at me with a broken expression, "You can just turn your feelings off like that? You can just throw us away like these past few weeks haven't meant anything to you?"

I look into his eyes as I feel more tears leak from my own, "Yes. I have too. But just to make everything perfectly fucking clear, you are the one throwing us away. You did this, not me. So yeah. I am done. I am throwing away what is left of us."

He shakes his head at me, "No Lily, you don't have too. You can forgive me. We can figure this out together. I don't want to lose you."

I take another step back from him, my voice starting to rise with the anger still coursing through my veins, "You never had me. Not really. I knew to keep my guard up. I knew that this was going to end horribly. You just somehow convinced me that it was all gonna work out."

I look down at the floor feeling my skin turning crimson from the anger and stress. It is boiling in my veins and suddenly I am charged with the fire of a thousand suns. I start beating myself in the chest with my closed fist, screaming up into his face, "You ripped my fucking heart out Gideon! You gave me hope and then you fucking threw it away, threw me away like I was nothing. You used me, Gideon. You used me and you didn't even care. I saw your face when she was standing there gripping your dick. You were fucking smiling at her, enjoying it!

"If I had not walked into that room when I did, you would have fucked her. I know you would have. Like you probably have a million times before. And coke? Fucking coke? Were you even going to tell me or were you going to just continue to lie to my fucking face? That is not something you do to someone you allegedly care about Gideon!"

Gideon is shaking his head at me.

He steps closer to me, putting his hands together as if in prayer, "I swear to you Lily. I swear I wasn't going to sleep with her. You are it for me. You are the only one that I want."

I take another step back, "I don't believe you."

He moves forward and tries to pull me into a hug as I throw my hands up in defense, "Stop trying to fucking touch me. I don't want you here. I don't want you near me. I don't want to feel your fucking hands on my skin. Don't you understand that?"

Gideon looks at me as if I have slapped him, his face turning red, "So that's it. Everything that we talked about. The plans we made. Everything about trying to find common ground that is all out the window then?"

I wrap my arms around myself, feeling my resolve trying to break with every word he utters, "Yeah. That's over. I can't be with someone that I can't trust. And I can't trust you Gideon. Your a fucking addict. How am I supposed to trust anything that you say? I gave myself to you. After I have gone through some pretty fucking tragic shit in my life, I gave myself to *you*. I swore to myself that I would NEVER let myself fall in love. I swore when I was just a little girl that I wouldn't give myself, my heart to anybody. And I gave it to you. I just willingly handed it to you with no armor to protect it. And you, you destroyed it. You crushed it with your bare fucking hands Gideon. You ruined everything."

My words end in a whisper. Gideon stumbles back a bit. He is looking at me like he is just realizing something within his own mind, "What about Mark?"

124

I look up slowly at him from the floor, feeling the pain of my own words, "I said I loved Mark. I never said I was in love with Mark."

Gideon's hands are shaking now, "But me? You're in love with me?"

I look past him, out the window, "It will pass."

I look back to Gideon as the tears slide down his face, "Please Lily. Please. Please don't do this. I love you too."

I hear my breath catch in my throat. He said he loves me. He means it too. I can see it on his face. Unless it's just the coke talking. I mean, how can I know for sure? I don't even really know him at all.

"I can't believe that. I won't believe that. You don't love somebody then sleep with someone else. You don't love somebody and let someone else rub themselves all over you. I thought I was the blind one, but apparently it's you who doesn't know the meaning of the word love." I take a few steps back and then turn, storming from the room.

I round the stairs to the third floor and run past all the boxes of stuff I had never unpacked from my previous homes. My previous life. I run past the empty rooms that I will never hear filled with laughter and love. I run straight out the back door onto the rooftop patio.

I step over to the BBQ and lift the lid to grab my secret cigarette stash. I pull out a Marlboro and light it quickly.

I throw the lighter down as I shut the BBQ. I calmly step around the corner and then curl up on the ledge, with my back resting against the chimney. My eyes are swollen as I stare out over the park, completely fucking vacant of all emotions. I just want him to fucking leave.

I hear him approaching but I don't care. I can't even fucking look at him. I take another long drag off the cigarette, "I didn't know you smoked."

I flick the ashes onto the rooftop, "There are a lot of things you don't know about me." Gideon steps closer to me, "Will you please get down off the ledge? I am afraid you are going to fall."

I laugh and take another hit off the cigarette. He looks at me defeated. In a huff I reply, "I am not going to fucking fall."

Gideon takes another nervous step towards me as I turn and slide my feet in his direction, "Fine. Anything to make *you* feel better right?"

I turn towards him and stand up. I take one last drag then flick the cigarette off the rooftop onto the ground below. I instantly wrap my arms back around my middle as he tilts his head to the side,

"I was going to tell you. About the coke. I went back to the hotel this morning and figured out when there is enough time in the tour to get clean. I know I need to quit."

I blow out the smoke from lungs then look up at him, "Gideon. It's too much. It's too late. I'm done. I can't do this. It took a fucking lot to get past my own insecurities about this relationship. Then you went and destroyed it.

"I can't let you back in. I can't let you continue to hurt me. Cause that is what would happen. If I forgave you, I would just be hurt again tomorrow or in a week or a month. Who knows when, but it would happen. You chose it, her over me when you went back and took another fucking bump. I just can't do this, okay?"

Gideon steps up to me, his voice shaky, "Can I at least give you a hug goodbye?" I squeeze my arms tighter around myself. I hate myself for being so fucking weak, "Yeah."

He steps up and wraps his arms around me. I circle my arms around his waist then take in his scent one last time. He still smells like the sea.

I feel myself start trembling and crying again.

126

Gideon kisses the top of my head, "Please don't cry Lily. I am not worth it. Don't waste your tears on me, okay?"

I pull back and look up at him, "You are worthy of love. I have never given my heart to anyone. Ever. And you took it without even letting me offer it up. You had me from that first night at the bar. I didn't know it then but I felt it. It was new and raw and heavy. I just didn't know it was love until last night."

I reach up and wipe a tear from his cheek. He looks back down at me, "I am so sorry."

I nod as I go up on my tip toes and give him a brief but deep kiss. I pull back and look into his eyes, "You know your way out."

I hear his breath pick up like he is trying not to lose it as I step around him and walk back into the house alone. I go to my bedroom then lay down in my own bed.

For the first time in months.

I hold my pillow close to my body as I convulse and let my tears stain the pillowcase. I hear the door downstairs shut then Susie is laying down right in front of me.

She runs her hand up and down my arm, "Sweetie, are you okay?"

I lift my burning, red rimmed eyes to hers, "No."

10
Ares
Alkaline - Sleep Token

Matthew and the rest of the band are fucking furious with me for cancelling the show but I don't care. We agreed to do the concert for free after the tour to make it up to all the fans.

I know I am letting people down but right now the only person I am concerned with hurting is Lily. Anyway, there is no way that I am in any shape to perform right now.

I felt the pain radiate from her when Lily kissed me goodbye. Her lips quivered with emotions that she was obviously trying to keep from me. She is so fucking strong but still I was able to shatter her. I saw her crumble into pieces right in front of me.

The fire that was in her eyes when she started beating her chest, screaming at me. I never imagined that I could have that kind of effect on someone. I agree with her, I wish she had never met me. Then she wouldn't be in so much pain right now.

I walk the streets back to the hotel, not even bothering to find a cab. I need the time to think this all through. I am not worth her pain.

How am I supposed to get through this when I don't even know how to wrap my head around what just happened?

I saw the light leave her eyes.

She is right, I gave her hope and then just destroyed everything. The rain is falling all around me but I don't even feel it as it touches my skin. I only see her face when she looks at me with Simone.

I only see the betrayal that I left in my wake.

I only feel emptiness.

All the rage that I have held within me for so long feels like it is starting to rush to the surface. I have been so dark, so callous for so long it never occurred to me that someone might actually love me someday. That someone might connect with my soul on anything more than a physical level. I honestly felt the need to possess her but she is unattainable because she already possesses me. She somehow slipped through the cracks in my armor and imprinted herself onto my soul. And now I am empty. A hollow shell of the man I could have been with her by my side.

I step into my suite hours later to find Matthew and Simone sitting there waiting for me. I look up at them both then turn and walk past them into the bedroom. I know they can see the result of the night written all over my face.

Mona and Edge are standing over by the window and turn to look at me as I march past them as well. I can feel everyone's eyes on me. Judging me, questions hanging in the air around us.

Matthew follows me, Simone not far behind. I throw my coat into a heap in the corner then slide down onto the floor at the foot of the bed.

I put my elbows on my bent knees then cradle my head in my hands, letting out barely a whisper, "It's over. She can't trust me. She *won't* trust me, ever again." I hear Matthew huff as he sits in the chair across from the bed.

Simone and Mona sit down on the floor in front of me, rocking back at forth. Simone leans forward, "I can go to her. I can explain it all to her. That it was just a joke. That none of it was real."

I look into her eyes, seeing the concern behind them, "Thanks Si but she knows the truth. About everything. About me. About you. About us. She knows it all."

She lets out a sigh and leans back on her hands, "Did you at least tell her it didn't mean anything? That there were no feelings behind it, like ever?"

I look up at her briefly, "I am sure if I would have said that she would have said something about it being the same between me and her." Simone shakes her head and looks out the large window on the other side of the room. I look up at Matthew. The merciful look he is giving me is undeserved.

I can feel the anger at myself rising within me again, "She was married. She was married for 8 fucking years. Her husband just died not long ago actually. And do you know what she told me tonight?

"She told me that she had loved Mark but she was never in love with him. That I was it. I was the only person in this entire fucking world that she ever trusted with her heart. Can you believe that shit? Me. And what did I do? I went and flushed it down the fucking loo the first chance I got."

Simone reaches out and places her hand on my knee as I continue to let my tears hit the floor between my legs. Mona sighs loudly, "That's a fucking lot of put on a person. Why would she even tell you that if she had already decided it was over?"

I look at Mona, giving her a brief smile, "So I would know that I was the only person in the world she ever fucking took a chance on. The only one she will ever give a chance to. So I would remember her as the one person I fucking destroyed completely."

I look down at my feet before sighing and leaning back against the bed. I look at Simone again and see the tears falling from her face as well as my own.

I place my hand on hers, "It's not your fault Simone. I promise it's not. This is 100% on me."

She sniffles and looks at Matthew. Her eyes close as she whispers, "I didn't know she was there. I wouldn't have made the joke if I knew she was there." Matthew scoots down to the floor and wraps Simone up in a hug. Edge is still leaning into the doorway. He hasn't even attempted to even look in my direction.

I stand and walk over to the bar. My only want right now is to not feel anything. I grab a bottle of Jack Daniels, fuck the glass. I open the bottle and start drinking straight from the mouth of it.

I take a deep breath in between swigs, looking at the bottle in my hand, "Did I tell you she is an artist? Her work man, her work is fucking brilliant. There is this one.

"It was her but she was free falling backwards into these flames that were just licking up from the bottom of the canvas. She said I was those flames. Ares, that is what she named the painting. It was fucking beautiful."

Edge steps forward, placing a hand on Mona's shoulder, "Maybe we can buy it from her. Make it some cover art or something."

I laugh long and loud, raising the bottle back to my lips, "She destroyed it. It looked like she shredded it with her bare fucking hands. She destroyed everything in her studio. There wasn't one fucking canvas in that room that didn't have a hole in it."

I feel Matthew remove his hand from my shoulder as I continue to chug straight from the bottle. Matthew moves back to the chair then turns towards the window.

I chug another 8th of the bottle, "What am I going to do Matthew? This is new. I have never felt this empty before. Never this lost."

He nods at me then looks at Simone. He walks to Simone and Mona then reaches out his hands to help them back up to standing, "Here is the plan. You are going to give me that bottle then you are going to go to sleep. In the morning, bright and early, all of us are going to go over to her house. We are going to give her the full story on everything. The coke. Simone. Everything.

"If she truly loves you as much as you say she does, maybe just maybe we have a chance of her coming back to you. If she sees that truly the only threat to your relationship is the cocaine and she knows you are wanting to quit then you may have a shot to save this yet."

I snort at him as he takes the bottle from my hand. I sit down on the edge of the bed and look out the window, "It will never work."

It is 8:30 in the morning when our cab rounds the corner onto Lily's street. I step up onto the curb immediately noticing the moving truck.

I hear a low whistle as Matthew looks up at the brownstone from the sidewalk. I have zero desire to stand and ogle at her house. I look in the back of the truck and see that it is already half full with boxes and some small furniture pieces.

I turn and run up the steps then through the open front door, frantically looking in the kitchen before moving down the hall towards the living room, "Lily? Lily?"

Susie comes around the corner with her hands up in the air, "Hey, Gideon calm the fuck down. She isn't here."

I nod at her then round the stairs to head up to her bedroom, "You said that last night too."

She leans over the railing, her eyes following me up the staircase, "I was lying then. I'm not now."

I run past the studio and straight into her bedroom. I turn the corner to look in her closet. The majority of her clothes and shoes are missing. My eyes scan the empty shelves then I open a drawer from a shelf built into the wall, but it is empty as well.

I turn and look at the room again, panic fully setting in.

I start shaking my head, "No. No. No."

I turn, running into the bathroom. I open the drawer that I know she keeps all of her makeup and lotions in. It is empty.

I start opening all the other drawers. The only things left were unused men's products. Probably Mark's stuff.

I turn and walk back out of the bedroom, completely defeated. I glance into the spare bedroom, her clothes and book are gone from there as well. I look at the wedding photo hanging on the wall of the hallway. She is so happy there. She is smiling and leaned into Mark's side but there is a fire missing in her eyes.

She did love him but she didn't lie, she was not in love with him. Only I know what her eyes look like when she loves somebody.

I also know what her eyes look like when she is destroyed by the person she loves. I turn my head as the tears start to form. I take a few steps then turn to my left to see the art studio is completely fucking empty. She got rid of everything.

Every painting, every brush. There is literally nothing left in the room. She got rid of every single reminder of me. Of us. Not even a splinter of a wooden frame from the destroyed canvases remains.

I round the bottom of the stairs and walk into the kitchen. I see Susie sitting in the living room with Edge and Matthew. No one is speaking. I look to my left and see the girls standing out on the front stoop. Probably afraid of Susie just as much as I am. I turn back towards the living room and Matthew's eyes connect with mine. I want to punch the pity and sympathy out of his face.

Silently moving behind Susie I ask somberly, "Where did she go?"

I see Susies' shoulders raise then lower as she takes a deep breath, "You know I can't tell you that."

I nod my head and look out the back windows, into her back yard. I turn as I feel the tears start to fall again, "Can you tell her again that I am sorry. And that I love her. Please?"

I don't even turn around to hear her response.

I walk back out the front door and sit on the stoop to wait for the others. I have lost her.

She is gone.

Matthew comes out and sits down beside me. We sit in silence for a long moment, only hearing the sound of my breath. Finally he pats my shoulder lightly, "Come on man. Let's go."

I nod to him then stand to follow him back out to the main road. Simone and the others following close behind Matthew. I can feel their eyes on me but I don't want to talk to anyone.

I don't want to look into anyone else's eyes and see more disappointment waiting for me. I don't even smile when I hear Simone whisper to Matthew, "Do you think maybe she is the mob or something? Her house is fucking huge!"

Finally back at the hotel, I continue to ignore everyone as I walk into my room, shutting the door without even a goodbye. I toss my jacket back onto the floor as I sit in a chair facing the window. The city looks so big beyond the thin pane of glass holding me contained on the 12th floor of this hell.

She is out there somewhere. She is probably scared, sad and alone. And it is all my fault. I feel this overwhelming assault of emotions take over my chest. My eyes close as I stand and roar out into the room around me.

My fist instantly connects with the wall beside the window. I look at the wall, not affected by my fist so I punch it again.

Then again and again.

I collapse into the chair. My chest tight. I touch my sternum, rubbing where the pain is most prominent. I feel this deep well of something open up within me. Grabbing paper and pen I start writing. Everything. It is like this genesis has opened up inside my chest. The ink is being fueled by the darkness that has been collecting there, just waiting to be released.

I write about my fears, my love, my mistakes.

My hand is throbbing by the time I am done. I look at the lyrics I just put onto paper. I see the drop of water from my face as it hits the page. I shut the book staring back out the window. Finally calm enough to think straight, there is only one thought left in my mind.

I walk into the bathroom and pull a small baggie out of my pocket. I let myself stare at it one last time. I toss it into the water then reach over and push down the handle on the toilet.

I am fucking done.

No more. I cannot keep living this fucking cycle of chaos.

135

The next 8 days are the worst days of my life. The first few days were the hardest. Just like they always are. Every fucking time I do this shit to myself I say never again.

I can't eat.

I can't sleep.

I can barely keep clothes on because all I do is sweat.

I know it will pass but honestly there are a few moments when I wish it wouldn't. I wish that I was strong enough to just let the darkness take over me. I am stuck in my own head, trapped in the memories of what I have done.

Every time I close my eyes, I see her face. Her eyes in shock when she walked into my dressing room. The way her mouth contorted into disgust when she was yelling at me. The tears that drenched her cheeks. I can't get her pain out of my head. I will never be able to forgive myself for this.

We have to reschedule two shows but I don't care. Not as much as I should at least. I have to get clean. If I want any chance at Lily ever forgiving me I have to.

I also find someone else to paint me before every show. Simone is of course still with the band. She is the bassist after all.

Lily doesn't even know that Simone is actually Hera. She didn't even stick around long enough to meet the band.

The days turn into weeks, which then turn into months. I am so fucking grateful we only have a few stops left on our tour then we will have 3 months off. We have already made up the rescheduled shows thankfully. Now I just sit in my own mind.

136

My thoughts overtake my brain again as I stare at the wall. I no longer just see the pain on her face when I close my eyes.

Now, honestly, it is even worse. I see her smile, I hear her laughter. It was so much easier to imagine her angry, hurt, than it is to remember her being happy. It is just a waking reminder that I am the one that stole that happiness from her.

Maybe I can find Lily. Maybe I will get lucky and enough time will have passed. Maybe she will forgive me now. We have this show in Norfolk then another in Savannah next. That is it. That will complete this tour.

I can take a break for a minute. Find a way to be at peace.

As I always do, before each show I sneak out and take a peek into the VIP area. She is never there though. I hold out hope but just like all the other times the void is filled with unfamiliar faces.

I let out another sigh, at least today's show is outdoors. It is fucking sweltering hot right now but in a few hours when the sun finally sets it is going to feel amazing.

We open the show just like all the others before, but this time there is no need for the lights to be down. The sun has only begun to fall close to the horizon. I enfold myself into the music, the moment. About an hour into the set I address the crowd, which I rarely do.

"I have something to say. Something to get off my chest." That is it. I never give them too much, never enough for them to figure me out. The roar that ripples through the crowd is intoxicating. They can recognize the rarity of the moment. The heaviness of my words start to set in and the entirety of the crowd begins to fall silent. They can feel that something is about to happen.

I close my eyes as I lean into the mic, hearing the new chords for Firestorm begin. I look to Matthew on drums then to

137

Simone. I turn around and nod at Edge on guitar to my right.
Then Mona kicks in on the keys.

They have all allowed me artistic discretion to get these
fucking feelings out of my head and heart. I close my eyes as I
lean into the microphone.

I start the song with a heavy sigh, laced with tears
already starting to fall,

"I danced on the shards of your fragile dreams,
Chasing echoes of trust that slipped through my grasp,

In the darkness, where light bleeds at the seams,
I carved a grieving fate into this faithless mask.

These fingers once gentle now tremble with shame,
Crimson stains linger on the veil's cold embrace,

In this temple of sorrow, I whisper your name,
A prayer for redemption, but darkness leaves no trace.

In the embrace of the night, a penance unspoken,
These words are the chains that I wear on my soul,

I broke you in whispers, I fractured the token,
Now I'm searching for fragments, to make myself whole."

The crowd is completely silent as the song comes to an
end. Randomly, you hear a scream but when I open my eyes,
looking out over the crowd, they all seem to be standing still just
staring, some even crying.

I feel my own tears as they slide down my face
underneath the mask. I am breathing heavily into the mic,

trying to get a grip on myself. I scan the crowd one more time, seeing Lily standing right in the fucking middle.

I shake my head and blink. I have to be hallucinating again. She isn't in the VIP section. Every time I have seen her in my mind, she is always in the VIP section. She wouldn't just stand in the middle of the pit, would she?

I look up again and see that she is still there. The sun is setting behind her, leaving the sky in a swirl of blues, purples and pinks. She is crying. Her chest heaving as emotions take over her body.

She is wearing a long flowing white cotton dress, buttoned down the front. Her shoulders bare to the elements. The wind whips around her dress and her hair, making the image seem like a dream, a mirage. I watch the tears as they roll down her face and onto her chest. She looks destroyed again. I feel the pull to jump off the stage and run to her.

I turn to Apollo to see he is staring at her as well. Dionysus starts to count us into the next song as the lights go down. It is becoming just dark enough that it takes me a few seconds to readjust to the lighting change. 20 seconds later the lights come back up and I begin the next song.

Lily is gone.

Lily
Intrusive Thoughts - Natalie Jane

It has been almost 2 months since I left New York. I have zero fucking desire to ever go back. That city has left me with nothing but heartache. Susie said she would follow me wherever I go but I can't even tell her where I am going to land yet.

I have been staying at the summer house in the Outer Banks. No one here bothers me. There is only one person here that I know and she is just a house sitter. She checks on the place from time to time. I have had the chance to just let the silence and sadness swallow me whole. I have the beach to myself most mornings. I can just sit and wallow in my own self pity and no one will know the better. Sure, Susie calls me daily. Sometimes multiple times in a day. But even with her, it is always short choppy answers to her questions. I don't know where to start glueing the pieces of me back together.

I sold the brownstone. Happy to walk away from the memories that place held. All the broken promises. No memories of Mark holding me down. No regrets about Gideon except for the ones now living rent free in my head.

I have decided that a life with love just isn't in the cards for me. How could it be? The first time I give my heart away it is pureed. I am better off alone. It isn't even that lonely. I have all these ghosts to keep me company.

Carnal Decay is still touring.

I tell myself I don't care. Which is a lie. I tell myself that it is over and done with. But every single time I close my eyes, I see Gideon there.

I hear his laugh, I see his smile, I smell the sea.

Most nights, I wake up crying, still hearing my name falling from his lips. I didn't know that love would hurt this fucking bad. I knew that it made you do stupid things.

Crazy things.

I had seen what it did to my parents.

My mother.

But I never imagined that an actual heartbreak could make you feel so hollow. So alone, even if you are in a room full of people. I really do try to not think about him. About how easily he was able to wrap me up in his life, tucking me neatly into his pocket.

I want to hate him. I want to curse the very fucking ground that he walks on. But I just can't. Honestly, I fell in love with him the moment he sat down with me at the bar. When I heard his voice and he looked at me with those obsidian eyes, I know now, that heavy feeling. That was love. That is why it was so new. I had truly never loved until I met him.

Then he took that love and he shit all over it. He wadded my love, my dreams, my hopes, my everything up then just tossed it in the trash. I know he didn't mean to hurt me. But when someone says they want to start a relationship with someone, they don't just immediately jump into bed with someone else. That is not what love is. Love would not allow you to do that to begin with.

And if he truly loved me, he would have never kept the secret of his habit from me. He didn't even respect me enough to let me know there was shit going on in his life. Even after I told him about my reservations, my fears. He still chose to willingly lie right to my face.

I know that I have to find a way to move on. I know that this isn't healthy. Locking myself away from the world, afraid to live. But I am empty. I have nothing to offer anyone. Not love, not friendship, not even a smile. I wish he would have never sat down with me at that bar, then I wouldn't be so lost. If I had never seen a peek at his soul, I wouldn't feel like mine had been so exposed. I wish he still didn't have such a hold on my everything, because I know. I just fucking know that I don't have a hold on his.

Susie has sent me a few messages about Carnal Decay in the weeks since the breakup. Gideon had to reschedule some shows. I was worried until I saw that their new dates were being kept. I could smile at least knowing that he is moving on.

At least one of us is.

I try to keep myself occupied. I started baking, thinking that would help. It didn't. I fucking suck at it. Everything either burns or never rises to begin with.

I bought a new easel, paints and canvases but they all sit collecting dust out in the sunroom off the side of the house. I haven't touched them since I had them delivered. I have no desire, no inspiration anymore. I spend the majority of my time sitting and staring at the walls, drinking my weight in whisky.

I don't even dare turn the tv or radio on for fear I am going to see his face or hear his voice. I am back in that shell I had crawled out of all those years ago. I am back in hiding. Unable to be any version of myself anymore. I'm shattered. Completely irreparable, unrecoverable, splintered into pieces.

My cell phone rings. I sigh as I look down seeing an unknown number on the screen. I hesitate to answer it, but it might be Susie. Something may have happened. There could be an emergency of some sort.

I let out a reluctantly heavy sigh, tapping the screen and bringing the phone to my ear, "Hello?"

I hear someone clear their throat on the other end of the line, "Hey. Hello. Is this Lily?" I turn my head to the side slightly. Why is there some British dude calling me?

Sitting up a bit straighter in the chair I hold my breath, "Yes, who is this?"

It sounds like the guy on the other end of the line is walking away from a loud gathering. I hear a door shut abruptly then silence falls around him, "Hi. I am so glad you answered. I didn't know if you would. This is Matthew. Matthew Kirkland. You might remember me better as Apollo."

I feel my heart start racing. My cheeks flush as I feel the blood still in my veins. I sit up quickly in my chair, bringing myself to the edge of the cushion, clenching my shirt on my chest. Fear grips my heart tight, "Is he okay? Please tell me he is okay."

I plead to him. Beg him not to tell me what I am fearing.

My eyes close, please god, please don't let him be gone.

I am scared to fucking death that I am getting another phone call that someone is gone. That the world has lost him entirely. I try to take a breath but I am already crying so hard that my sobs choke in my throat.

"He is okay. Lily, he is fine. I promise." Matthew is trying to be as considerate and consoling as he can be.

I let out a whimper knowing he can hear me through the phone, "I thought that you were. You were calling to....to tell me he was...."

I can't breathe. I can't even fucking speak. My lungs feel like they are about to explode.

"No Lily, that is not why I am calling, I swear. He is fine. He is healthy. He....he is clean. He has been for awhile now. We had to reschedule a few shows but he kicked it."

Matthews' voice is so raw and real. I let out another whimper as relieved tears run down my cheeks. I feel my pulse starting to die down again. For just a split second, I thought that it was really all over. His demons had finally taken him from the world. From me. I have never been so afraid in my entire life. And that is saying a lot considering. The fear that clinched my soul for that one moment was the most powerful thing I have ever felt in my life. Why does he still have this strong of a hold on me?

I smile into the phone, "Thank god. Good. Thank you for calling and telling me that. I appreciate you doing that." I feel this relief lift off my shoulders. He is clean. He is getting better. He is alive.

I wait for Matthew to end the call but instead hear, "We are going to be in Norfolk tomorrow. We have an outdoor show at a festival. I wanted to see if maybe. If you wanted to maybe come see it. See him. I thought maybe if you saw him with your own eyes you could see how much better he is doing."

I let out a sigh as I turn and look out the window at the ocean crashing against the beach.

Norfolk is not far from me.

I close my eyes, letting more tears fall, "Matthew, I don't think that would be a good idea. I appreciate you telling me how he is doing. It is more than I deserve, honestly. But I just....I don't think I can see him. It just hurts, too fucking much still."

I hear him shuffle around on the other end of the phone, "He still loves you, ya know. He looks for you at the beginning of every show. After, he just sits and stares at the green room door just waiting for you to walk through. I have never seen him like this. All he does now is drink and smoke weed then stare at the wall."

I let my head fall back on the chair, "I know that feeling well."

I hear Matthew pacing on the other side of the phone. Somewhere near him a door opens and I hear Gideon, "Hey, Matthew, are you wanting food?"

I let out another strangled cry. I throw my hand over my mouth as the tears fall and my throat closes up. I can hear Matthew covering the speaker on the phone as he mumbles something I can't understand. I try to stand to pace the room but my legs won't hold me up. I land in a heap on the floor. I have spent the last 8 weeks not even listening to the radio for fear of hearing his voice.

Now here it is.

He is so fucking close I could reach out and touch him.

I let the sobs reach my throat, unable to stop crying. I am now laying in the fetal position in the middle of my living room. I am a complete mess. Matthew just seems to sit there, listening to me.

After a few minutes, I hear him speak again, "Listen. Obviously, this is just as hard for you as it is for him. I mean fuck you barely heard him speak just now and lost your fucking mind. You love him. He loves you. Just please. Come and see him. Come see for yourself that he is okay. That he is clean. Please."

145

I nod into the phone, maybe he is right. Maybe closure is what I need. I close my eyes, hanging my head in front of me, "I will think about it." I don't even wait for a reply, I hang up the phone and continue to cry for the next hour.

I wake up the next morning with more clarity than the day before. I look up the festival information online. There are no more vip tickets available but there is lawn space. I buy my ticket before I can talk myself out of it.

Now I am standing at the door to my closet, staring in but really seeing anything at all.

How am I going to be able to see him and survive this?

I want to see with my own two eyes that he is better, but what if he is? What kind of cost will that have on my soul?

What if this is still destroying me and he is moving on?

How am I supposed to endure that?

The feelings of dread and excitement are battling each other in my head and I honestly have no idea which one is going to come out the victor.

It is only a little over an hour and a half to get to the festival site. I take my time, trying to enjoy the scenery as I drive there but I have this rock sitting on my chest. I know it is because my heart has turned to stone.

I shouldn't be doing this.

It is only going to make it harder.

But yet here I am 2 hours later, standing in the middle of a crowd staring at an empty stage.

I am here early enough that there are only a couple hundred people in front of me so I am able to get a decent spot in the crowd.

I stand in center view of the stage. I am only about a hundred feet away from where he will be standing soon. The lights flash and my breath catches in my throat.

It is still daytime so though the lights are kicking on, but I still have a full view of the stage. I see Ares as he walks, head low then leans into the microphone. Anyone else looking in would think everything is fine but I know him.

I can see the small subtle differences in him now compared to 2 months ago. He is still confident but there is something else there. He is holding onto the microphone like it is his only life line. Apollo counts in the first song and Ares is off like a rocket.

It is entrancing to see him in his element. He was born for this. His voice carries across the crowd like a warm blanket tucking us in for the night.

Depending on the song, I can hear the rasp in his voice when it hurts. He has this way of conveying every single emotion imaginable with the use of just a single common word.

I am crying before the set has even really begun.

I stand out in the crowd just staring at him. He runs from one side of the stage to the other. He is up, he is down, he will dance, he will kneel. He is everywhere and everything all at the same time.

I feel the sun starting to set behind me and I know the concert will be over soon. I am going to have to find the courage to walk away. The strength to run back home and not crawl to him in the green room.

I know I could easily get back there if I wanted to.

But I can't. I can't allow him back in.

147

I am not good for him.

He is doing better.

He has kicked the coke and he is back on the right path for him and the band. I feel a calm start to fall over me as I realize Matthew was right. I did need to see him. I needed to see with my own eyes how much better he is doing now that I am gone.

It fucking hurts like hell but it still brings a smile to my face as I accept the truth that has been presented to me. He is going to be okay. Maybe, eventually I will be too.

The lights come down on the stage again and I hear someone breathing heavily into the mic. I turn my head slightly to the right, this is new. I have never seen them do this at a show before.

Curious, I take a few more steps forward and the lights come back on. Ares is standing center stage, cradling the microphone stand like a lover, "I have something to say. Something to get off my chest."

My hand flies to my throat.

I feel myself choke up.

It feels like he is speaking directly to me.

He is upset. He is crying.

I can't see it but I can hear the tears in his voice. There is a slight falter when he begins to sing. Like he is trying not to scream his words to the gods themselves.

Every single sentence that comes out I know is about me, about us. I am crying so hard that my chest is heaving into the crowd around me. It feels like my walls are starting to close in around me. I wish my heart would just explode and I could just collapse right here in the grass.

"I danced on the shards of your fragile dreams,
Chasing echoes of trust that slipped through my grasp,

148

In the darkness, where light bleeds at the seams,
I carved a grieving fate into this faithless mask.

These fingers once gentle now tremble with shame,
Crimson stains linger on the veil's cold embrace,

In this temple of sorrow, I whisper your name,
A prayer for redemption, but darkness leaves no trace.

In the embrace of the night, a penance unspoken,
These words are the chains that I wear on my soul,

I broke you in whispers, I fractured the token,
Now I'm searching for fragments, to make myself whole."

By the time the song ends and his voice has died out from the microphone, I am delirious in my own emotions. The wind has picked up, skies threatening to open up the gates of hell at any moment.

I just stand there, still as night. I am unable to move as I watch him be overcome with emotions as well.

I knew he was crying.

I can see his chest heaving just like mine.

He stands up and goes as still as a statue of the Greek god he is portraying. His hands fall away from the microphone. He shakes his head like he is seeing a mirage, but instead I know he has spotted me in the crowd.

He turns, looking at Apollo and I know he is trying to get confirmation that I am really here in the mob of fans enjoying the show.

I can't fucking do this. I am not strong enough to do this.

How am I supposed to live with myself knowing what I have done to him? How the fuck was I supposed to know that I had that kind of power over his mind, his soul?

I am crying so hard that the images on the stage are starting to blur together. I am broken.

Again.

As I see him start to turn back around, the lights go down again and I hear a new song about to start. I turn and run. I run until I feel like my legs are going to give out on me. I run until I reach my car then sit inside trembling.

He is so broken.

I knew this entire time that he was hurting as well but I never imagined that he was just as destroyed as I am. That song, it said everything I wished wasn't true. We have broken each other's hearts.

We have both loved each other with equal amounts of fire and intensity. What if he still loves me? How can I just run away knowing that he is in this much pain?

I look at the fabric lining the roof of my car.

Can I really just walk away after that? I love him. I love him so fucking much. He saw through me, my bullshit and still wanted me. He loved me without pity, without fear. Didn't he?

Could he still feel that way?

Tears are streaming down my face as I shake and pick up my phone. I let out a shuddering breath directed towards the phone as I start a text to Matthew.

Tears roll down my cheeks as I type and send,

"1928 Rye Street, Nag's Head N.C."

12
Ares
The Sound of Being Alone - Tenille Townes

I search for her for the remainder of the show. I run all over the fucking stage just praying for a glimpse of that porcelain skin, the long black hair. But she is gone. I should have just jumped off the stage and ran to her when I saw her.

If she was even really even there.

It doesn't even feel real. Why would she be standing out there in the middle of the chaos just staring at me? Was she there the whole time? Have I missed her at other shows? I feel overwhelmed with some type of emotion that I am just not familiar with.

Less than a half hour later, I am walking off the stage. Still staring out into the dispersing crowd. But she isn't there.

I stand at the bottom of the stairs waiting for Apollo.

He isn't even fully down the steps and I yell at him, "You saw her right? It wasn't just in my head? She was out there?"

Apollo steps down the last bit of the stairs and nods at me. I follow him into the green room behind the stage.

It is just the band now. No one else has made their way in yet.

I round on him again,

"Do you think she is still here? Do you think she would want to see me? Should I go back out there and look for her some more? She might be waiting for me."

I turn to run out the door and Dionysus grabs me by the arm, "Dude. Breathe. Fuck." I shake out of his grip and turn back to Apollo.

"What do I do?"

I am completely unequipped to handle the emotions flowing through me. My thoughts are anywhere but here. Hera and Hestia come walking over from the other side of the room, handing me a cup of straight vodka, "Here, drink. Calm the fuck down."

Apollo smiles at them through the mask, "They are right. If that was her. And I am pretty sure it was, then she knows you will be back here. If she wants to see you she knows where to find you. Just give her the chance, man."

I nod my head at him then sip the vodka.

I thought I was getting better.

I thought it was getting easier to push her out of my head.

But one glimpse of her and I am tripping over my own fucking heart just trying to get one more peek at her face. She doesn't even have to speak to me. If I can just look at her.

I just want to see her.

I step to the side and start fidgeting, trying to refrain from pacing around the room. I look at Apollo as he pulls his phone out of his leg pocket. His face pulls taut and his mouth drops open slightly, "Oh Shit."

I stand up a bit straighter, "What? What happened?"

He steps over to me, turning his phone around.

I read the address on the screen aloud, "1928 Rye Street, Nag's Head N.C."

I look up at the name and number to see who it is from but all it says is Aphrodite. Understanding rips through my brain. I look at him, anger starts to flow through me, "Is that her?"

Apollo nods at me. "How the fuck do you have her phone number? Why haven't you given it to me?"

I throw the vodka on the ground and push myself into his face. He has seen me suffering for months and he had a way to find her this entire goddamn time?

How could he fucking do this to me?

Apollo puts his hands up as Dionysus starts to pull me back, "Whoa. Calm down. You texted me from her phone like months ago, remember? I never deleted it. I, actually, called her. Yesterday. I told her about today's show. I thought maybe if she could see you. See that you are better. How much you miss her. Maybe it would help."

I shake my head at him, confused, "She was here because of you? Why didn't you tell me she was coming?"

He raises his arms out to the sides, "Dude, I didn't know she was. She never said yes or no. She said she would think about it."

I start to pace in front of him. I will deal with him later. Right now, I need to figure out what my next move is. I have her number. I can find her.

I turn and point at the phone, "Well, what the fuck is that then? What did she send you?"

He pulls the phone back up to his face then turns it to me, "Didn't you tell her to leave you a forwarding address?"

I feel my heart drop into my stomach.

I point to his phone, "Text that to me. Right fucking now!"

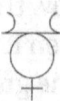

I turn and run out of the green room. I round the back of the building jumping into our SUV. The driver jumps in just seconds after me. "Take me to the hotel. Now."

I swear he drives 100 mph the entire way there. My heart is about to jump out of my fucking chest. She wants to see me. She sent me her location. She wouldn't do that if she didn't want me right? I jump out of the car and run up to his window, "Wait here. I won't be 20 minutes. Look this address up."

I throw my phone into his lap and run into the hotel up to my suite. I am back downstairs 15 minutes later. I am clean and out of costume. I am just Gideon again. I run back to the SUV and jump into the back seat again, "Go. Now!"

The further south we drive the darker the skies seem to get. There is a storm moving in. I can feel it in the air.

I had always heard Americans talk about how they could smell the rain in the air before it would hit. I always thought it was a myth but after being here for almost 7 months I fully believe them now.

It is a little over an hour and we are stopping in front of a beautiful yellow wood sided house. It has big white picture windows and even what looks like a Victorian style tower on one side.

I jump out and walk up to the driver's window. I hold up my phone, "If you don't hear from me in 15 minutes, just go back to the hotel. Tell Matthew I will text him later."

He nods at me then rolls up the window.

I turn back to the house and take a deep breath. It feels like all my nerve endings are firing off at the same time. I slowly walk up the steps and look in the window of the door. I can't see anyone inside. The lights are all off except for one towards the back of the house. I take in a deep breath, praying I have the right address.

I run back down the steps and check the numbers on the house again, confirming I am in fact in the right place. I step back up to the door and feel my palms start to sweat as I rap my knuckles on the glass.

I take a step back, but nothing happens.

No one ever comes to answer the door.

Why would she send me an address and not even be here? None of this is making any sense at all.

I knock again, a bit more urgent this time but still I am left with nothing but silence. I turn the doorknob and the door slowly opens for me. I step inside, quietly shutting the door behind me, "Lily? Are you here?"

I look into the dining room on the left but the room is empty. The house is furnished a lot like the brownstone was. Clean lines, but stylish furniture. A lot of white, open and airy settings. I look up the stairs, my voice echoing down the halls, "Hello?"

Still, I am returned with nothing but silence. I step into the sitting room on the right of the stairs and walk straight back into the kitchen. There is a comfortable sitting area around a massive fireplace. There looks to be a sunroom off to the side with an empty easel set up. The kitchen looks like a mirror image of the brownstone. From the marble counters down to the oversized sink. Where the hell is she?

I look out the window over the kitchen sink and see her standing near the waves lapping up on the beach. She has a blanket wrapped around her and she is just standing there, staring out into the stormy ocean before her. The moon is illuminating her as the light from it rolls across the waves lapping around her ankles.

She looks so small. I smile to myself as I stare at my little one.

My heart starts to hammer in my ears as I run to the back door and pull it open.   I step out onto the porch and take a deep breath before screaming into the wind, "Lily?"

She turns and her eyes lock with mine.

I smile at her and she starts crying and laughing at the same time. I take the stairs two at a time as she throws the blanket off her shoulders and runs full speed to me, sand flying behind her bare feet.

By the time I make it off the porch steps, she is on me. She throws her arms around my neck and starts sobbing into my chest.

I hold her tight, taking in her scent, "Baby, it's okay. I am here now. It's okay." She pulls back, staring into my eyes. Her chest is heaving with emotions again and she can't seem to stop weeping.

I wipe her tears away with my thumbs then tuck a strand of hair behind her ear, "Lily. I am here baby. It's all gonna be okay now. Alright?"

She nods her head then takes in a rattled breath, "I love you."

I feel my knees go weak.

I am nodding my head, trying not to cry, "You love me? Are you sure?"

She nods her head rapidly back at me, "I tried not to but I just can't stop. I love you so fucking much."

We both hit the sand on our knees. I feel her wrap her hands around my neck and then she is kissing me.

Fiercely.

Forcibly.

Ferally.

I wrap one hand into the hair at the base of her neck and the other around her waist pulling her closer into me. We kiss for what feels like hours. Just holding each other. She finally pulls away, smiling at me, her lips now red from overuse. I smile at her as she stands up.

It finally feels like my soul is complete. She has been my missing puzzle piece for months now. I feel her quivering around me as my hands wander the length of her body. This little one has etched herself into my bones. I will never be able to let go now.

She puts her hand out to me, palm up. I look up at her, smiling again as I take her invitation. I stand up in front of her then pick her up. She wraps her legs around my waist and nuzzles her face into my neck as we make our way up the stairs.

She slams the back door shut as I carry her back inside. She smiles down at me then kisses me again. I part her lips with my tongue and began exploring. She still tastes like cherries.

I let a small moan leave the back of my throat as her hands grip my hair pulling my lips forcefully into hers. I turn to take her upstairs but am not totally for sure I can make it that far without being inside of her.

I lay her down on the steps and she immediately starts to unbutton her dress down the front. I take my jacket off, tossing it on the floor behind me. I lean into her and kiss her again as she reaches behind me and pulls my shirt up over my head.

Lily pulls her dress open showing me the white satin underwear set she is wearing underneath. I reach up slowly pulling down on the center of the bra allowing her tits to fall out the top. My pulse is so fast I could honestly have a heart attack at any moment.

She is fucking stunning.

I scan her body with my eyes before leaning in and taking a nipple in my mouth. She lets a moan leave her throat as

I roll my tongue around its peak. She screams into the stairwell when I bite down on her soft skin then start working my way back up to her neck, marking her again.

I can hear her panting beneath me. I feel her reach behind her back and unhook her bra. Then I am pulling her underwear down her toned legs and throwing them behind me.

I pull back from her briefly to watch her smiling at me as she slides the bra off and throws it over the railing of the stairs. She leans up into me as she reaches down and unbuttons my jeans then pulls the zipper down.

I stare her directly in the eyes as she reaches in and grips my dick in her hand. I moan, closing my eyes as the bliss from her touch rolls over me. She leans forward and starts kissing me forcefully again. I reach down, sliding my jeans down my thighs then hook my arm under her left knee.

She spreads her right leg open for me as I wrap my hand around her neck then slam into her a moment later. She clenches around me tight at the forcefulness of my intrusion.

Stars explode behind my eyelids as I try to regulate my breathing while slamming into her. I feel her running her short black fingernails down my arms, "Fuck Gideon. Oh my god."

She thrusts her hips up into mine in the same rhythm as me. I grip her a bit tighter, not enough to cut off her air but enough to leave her gasping for more. I turn my head towards her then kiss her roughly as I continue to slam into her.

She bites my lip hard, moaning at the same time. I can taste copper in my mouth as I smile into her kiss. She is fucking mine. I am home and I am never fucking leaving again.

I pivot my hips and start to hit her at a different angle. Her back arches into my chest and her head goes back onto the steps as she screams into the openness around us.

I lick her neck from her collarbone to her ear then bite down on her earlobe. I feel her starting to quiver around my dick. I slam into her harder as she screams and moans underneath me.

I slide out of her abruptly and she looks down at me as I slither down her body. I smile into her eyes as I part her with one hand then lick her straight up her center.

She sits up a little straighter, opening herself fully to me. I feel her grip the hair on the back of my head tightly as I continue to feast on her. I flick her clit with my tongue then pull her bud in between my teeth. The taste of her sweet center is never going to leave my thoughts after tonight.

She starts to roll her hips towards my mouth, chasing her own release. I continue to flick then bite at her until I feel her hips shuddering around my face. A few seconds later she grips both sides of my head and pushes me back a bit. I look up into her unmerciful stare.

I smile at her a devil's grin as I feel her release running down my chin. She stands on the step above me, letting the dress fall from her body. She takes my hand and starts up the stairs, completely fucking naked.

I follow closely behind, still smiling, dick out with zero shame. She rounds into a bedroom then turns around to face me. She reaches down, starting to stroke my cock before falling to her knees and starts to pull my jeans the rest of the way off.

I kick off my shoes onto the other side of the room. I look down watching her every movement. She smiles up at me with those pouty red lips leaning towards my dick. Lily grips me at the base then licks me from her hand all the way to the tip. Her tongue follows a large throbbing vein from base to head. My eyes roll up in my head as she flicks her tongue across my tip. She takes me into her mouth then starts to bob up and down on my cock.

I lower my face to watch her. The warm heat of her mouth wrapped around my cock is one of the best sensations I have ever experienced in my entire fucking life. She slides her hands around to grip my hips, sending me deeper into her mouth.

She looks up at me and smiles as I feel my dick hit the back of her throat. I let out a loud growl into the room as she continues to suck on my cock, rolling her tongue around the head of it. She hollows her cheeks out, letting her tongue massage my dick as it slides in and out. I grip the hair on the back of her head tight as I slam her face into me as I thrust my hips into her face.

I look down at her seeing tears coming to her eyes but I can't stop. I continue to slam into her mouth as she lets a small moan leave her throat. I growl down at her, slamming into her again, "I am going to cum Lily."

She smiles again and takes me deep into her throat. I grip the back of her head as I slam into her mouth again and again. I feel myself let go. I scream my release as she continues to suck on me until she swallows every last drop down her throat.

I reach down, pulling her chin up to look at me. She smiles as she lets my dick slide out of her mouth.

She runs a finger across her bottom lip collecting my cum that seeped through her lips then stuffs it into her mouth as her eyes close and she moans up at me.

I reach down, pulling her to her feet as I pick her up into my arms. I step over towards the bed and lay her down on her back. I lean into her and slide two fingers inside her.

Lily smiles as she moans, letting her head sink back deeper into the bed. I lean in and kiss her hard as I hook those two fingers inside of her. I find her release waiting for me there.

She screams around my lips and grips my wrist with both hands. I look down and watch her riding my hand as I feel her starting to clamp around my fingers.

I kiss her roughly again as I slide another finger in. Feeling her stretch around my fingers, continuing to ride them as the orgasm begins to overtake her body.

I watch her right hand go to her clit and she starts rubbing it in tight little circles. She screams out my name as she clamps down harder on my fingers.

"Fuck Gideon. I'm cumming. I'm cumming."

I continue to thrust my fingers in and out of her tight little pussy until her breathing starts to come back down.

I slide my fingers out then bring them up to her mouth. She smiles as she parts her lips and I slide them inside. She sucks them clean, just like she had my dick a few minutes before. I pull my fingers from her mouth then kiss her mercilessly.

I feel her smile into my lips as I pull back and look into her eyes, "I have missed you so fucking much."

She grins back as she runs a finger across my cheekbone then up the dip at my nose between my eyes. She then traces across my brow bone and down the other cheek and I smile at her, "What are you doing?"

She smiles back as her finger crosses my chin and back up around to the spot where she began, "I am drawing your face. So I will never forget it."

I sigh and lean in to kiss her again.

I finally pull back and she raises her arms above her head then stretches, arching her back. I sit up and slide to the end of the bed. I step over to get a view of her from the other side.

She glances over at me, laughing, "What are you doing?"

I lean my back into the wall behind me, "Do that again. Stretch again."

She smiles as she stretches her arms out again.

I let out a breath, "Arch your back."

She gives me a quick side eye and arches her back. Her head is pressed back into the comforter. Her thighs are pointed to the ceiling while that tight little cunt is pressed down as well at her hips. Her knees are bent and just barely parted as if she is just waiting for me. I let out another held breath, "Jesus Fuck Lily. You are fucking magnificent."

I wish I had even a hint of artistic ability. I want to draw her. I want to look at her form every single day for the rest of my life. I walk back over to the bed and slide in beside her.

13

Lily
The Death of Peace of Mind - Bad Omens

I lay here staring into a face that I never thought I would see again. At least not this close. Gideon's eyes explore my own just as much as mine does his. I smile, realizing that he has little gold flecks in his iris.

I can't believe he is here. He is here, in my bed. In my home.

I run my finger across his collarbone, then into the little divot at the base of his neck. I look back up to him, "I am really glad that you came over."

He leans in and gives me a soft kiss, "I am really glad you gave me that forwarding address."

I smile widely back at him, "I wondered if you were going to figure it out."

He runs his nose up the side of my face before kissing my temple, "Matthew figured it out for me. I was still trying not to pass out from seeing you on the lawn."

I scoot a bit closer, "I didn't know if you would actually show up or not. I honestly assumed you wouldn't. So I didn't get my hopes up."

His eyebrows cinch together like he is confused, "Why wouldn't I show up, Lily?"

I shrug with the one shoulder I am not laying on, "Because of the way everything ended. I know that I am a lot. I know that I have storage units filled with emotional baggage. I honestly, I wanted you to just take care of you. I didn't want you to care about me anymore. I am not good for you. I truly don't think I am good for anyone. Not now. Maybe I never was."

Gideon raises up and balances on his forearm, "Lily. Why do you think so little of yourself? It is something that I have noticed before but I just don't understand it. You put too much weight on your own shoulders. I didn't show up before now because you told me to let you go.

"Plain and simple. It wasn't because I didn't love you any more. It wasn't because I didn't want you. It wasn't because I thought you were too much. It was because you asked me to let you go. And I tried. God help me, I tried. But I just couldn't."

I look into his eyes, seeing the truth lying within them, "I just, I don't know. I have never really felt like I am good enough. For anything. For anyone. I know it is my own brain doing it to me. I know it isn't logical, but sometimes the little devil on my shoulder wins out over the other voices. The ones telling me I am okay."

I close my eyes trying to hold back the tears. After letting out another hesitant breath, I look to the bed between us, "I'm sorry."

Gideon's hand comes down and he slowly lifts my chin back up, "You have nothing to be sorry for. I was the one that broke us. I was the one who was hiding shit and just hoping for the best. I took our time apart to accept accountability for the mistakes that I made. You did what you had to do to protect yourself. There is absolutely nothing wrong with that.

"And as for that little devil on your shoulder, you need to tell him to kick rocks. You are perfect just the way you are. You are literally my dreams come true. Never listen to him when it comes to us. Okay? Can you do that for me?"

I give him another soft smile then nod and roll onto my stomach. I bring my hands up and rest my chin on them, looking straight ahead at the wooden headboard before me.

I let out a soft sigh as I feel his hand trace the curve of my ass into the dip of my lower back, "Was that song about us?"

His hand stops briefly before starting up again. I can feel his eyes on me so I turn my head towards him, "The new one, you sang tonight? Was that about us?"

He gives me a slow nod, "I wrote it the night you left."

I nod my head and turn my face back to the headboard, "Honestly, I assumed you were fine with everything. I thought you would just move on. Find someone else to pass the time with. I figured you were with Simone or someone else by now. I didn't want to know if you ever thought about me or not. It was easier on myself to think you just wrote me off. I didn't know that everything weighed on you as heavy as it did."

Gideon grabs me and turns me towards him, pulling me in close, "I have burned for you every moment of every day since you left. I have never felt this before, for anyone. Every single second you were away from me was pure torture. You are my soul, Lily. You were gone and I was just fucking empty. One minute I had you and then in the blink of an eye you just disappeared. I didn't know how to find you. I didn't know if you were okay. You were a ghost. Just gone. I felt like I was never going to smile again, baby."

I feel a lone tear roll down my face towards my temple, "When I was on the phone with Matthew last night, I heard you ask him a question. I totally lost my shit. Right down in the middle of the living room floor. You sounded just like I remembered. I have heard your voice in my dreams for weeks but when I actually heard the voice come from your body I lost control of my own.

165

"I thought I was strong, I thought I was dealing with the situation but when I heard your voice I just crumbled into the floor. I couldn't even hold myself up. I was so upset. I cried so fucking hard. I am surprised the neighbors didn't call the police or something."

Gideon wipes the tears from my cheeks again, "Never again little one. I don't want you to ever miss me that much ever again. I am not going to give you the chance too. You are going to be begging for me to go back on tour."

I laugh at him, "When are you going back?"

He lifts his fingers up and puts another stray strand of hair behind my ear, "Our UK tour starts in a little over 3 months. The tour itself is only 2 months long though. After that, there will be another break. I think about 2 months before we start another American Tour. At some point, we have to get back into the studio as well. Get the new album finished."

I nod my head at him, then let my voice drop a bit, "No matter how much time you think you are going to annoy me with. I will still miss you when you leave. Especially if it is for 2 months. I know we will still talk and stuff but I have learned that it is a very, very long time to go without you."

Gideon smiles and brings his lips to mine. He looks into my eyes while he kisses me then pulls back a fraction of an inch, "Then come with me."

I pull my head back, laughing at him, "What?"

He smiles as he pulls my hips closer to his, "Come with me. I mean why not? What is keeping you from coming?"

I grin shyly back at him, "You don't think the others would mind? I mean, I didn't see a whole bunch of significant others in the green room."

He smiles as he kisses me again, "They will not care one fucking bit baby. You are with me. That is all that matters. Fuck them all if they are shitty about it."

166

I smile again, "But I don't want them to be shitty about it. I don't want to intrude on what you guys have going on. I don't want to be in the way."

He wraps his hand around the back of my neck, "You will be fine. You are coming with me. That is the last of it."

I smile as he pulls me close and kisses me. I wrap my arms around him, pulling him tight against me kissing him back.

Gideon runs his free hand down the small of my back and across the curve of my ass again. I smile into his mouth as I push him onto his back and crawl on top of him.

"I don't know if you will be able to keep up with me. I have an insatiable appetite for your dick. I hope you are aware of that."

I start to rub myself up and down his cock, feeling him start to harden beneath me. He smiles wickedly back at me then puts his hands on my waist, "Oh, I think I can manage."

I pull all my hair to the right side of my body and lean down to give him a kiss. He grabs my ass, squeezing hard as I gasp into his mouth. I smile as I start to slither back down his body.

He watches me as I let my tits graze over top of his dick. He lets out a small moan when I kiss the head of his cock while looking straight into his eyes.

I smile at him again, "Insatiable."

I lick my lips then turn my head to slide his dick into my mouth. His hands instantly come down and wrap around the back of my head. I continue to take him in deeper until I feel him hit the back of my throat and his legs start to tremble.

I look back up at him, smiling as his dick slides out of my mouth with a pop. I crawl back up his body and position myself on top of him. I slide down onto him slowly. The feeling of him stretching me is welcomed like a memory that had been lost. I

67

settle in with him all the way to the base inside of me, smiling into the nothing as pure ecstasy starts to take over my body.

My head falls back between my shoulders as I slowly raise up and down on him. I feel his hands wrap around my tits as he starts to squeeze them roughly.

I bring my hands up and wrap them around his, making him squeeze me harder. I look back down at him as he stares up at me with his mouth slightly parted open.

I lean forward and kiss him deeply.

I start to speed up the motion of my hips, riding him like a fucking carnival ride. He is panting into my mouth by the time I try to pull away. He wraps an arm around my waist, "No, stay there."

I smile at him and keep my chest pressed into his as I continue to slam my hips into his in short bursts. His breathing is becoming erratic as I stop moving.

His eyes slam to mine immediately, "What's wrong?"

I look back at him and slide down onto him slowly again. Watching his face cringe and melt. I breathe into his chest as I pull up then slide back down on him slowly again, "Say it."

He opens his eyes and looks at me sinfully, "Make me cum baby." Shivers run down my spine.

I smile as I pick up my speed, "How bad do you want it?"

He grabs my hair at the base of my neck, bending my head back as he bites the soft spot between my shoulder and neck.

I feel myself starting to build up inside, "Oh Fuck Gideon."

I start to move more erratically as I look back down at him, "How bad Gideon? Tell me."

He grips my ass hard with both hands, slamming me down onto him, "I want to cum so bad baby. I can't cum unless you do. I want to feel that tight little cunt clench down on me. I want to feel you break around my dick baby."

I hiss into the room as I speed up my thrusts on top of him. I pull my mouth away from his, panting into the night air, "Oh Fuck Gideon. Fuck. Fuck. Fuck."

I feel myself about to lose control on him. He leans forward, growling as he slaps my ass hard, "Cum on me baby. You're so good Lily. Taking all of my cock. Cum on me now. Please baby."

As soon as the word please leaves his lips I feel myself break around him. I scream into the headboard as he grips my hips and we are slamming into each other recklessly.

He belts out a scream at his own release, "Jesus Lily. Fuck yeah. Don't fucking stop baby."

I continue to slam down onto him thinking the aftermath is already hitting when another orgasm rolls through me out of nowhere.

I scream again, my legs almost locking up. He rolls me underneath of him then starts to slam into me harder than ever before. I am crying because his dick feels so good.

He is stretching me and slamming into me with enough friction to start a wildfire. I can't even open my eyes, as I feel myself continue to clasp onto his cock, "Gideon. God dammit Gideon."

I grab his ass and push him all the way inside me and hold him there as I feel my core beating all around him. He lets out another growl into my neck as I hold onto him for dear life. Finally, I start to come down from it.

I look up to him with hooded eyes, "That has never happened before baby. I have never been fucked like that. Ever." He smiles widely as he leans down and kisses me rough and hard.

He pulls away from me and rolls onto his back beside me, "God Dammit Lily. That was fucking amazing."

I smile at the ceiling, barely able to keep my eyes open. I let out a small snicker, "I think you just fucked me into a different universe. Or into submission or something."

He lets out another laugh as he pulls me into him. He wraps his arms around me, spooning me close as we both drift off to sleep.

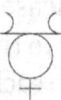

I wake up a few hours later. Gideon is still lightly snoring behind me as I slide out from under his arm and climb out of bed.

I slide my robe on just staring down at him. His naked form laid out like Adonis in the middle of my bed. I smile as I look over every inch of him. This is happening. He is really mine again.

I can't believe he is actually here. When I saw him standing on the back porch earlier, my heart clenched in my chest. Just to hear my name fall from his lips, it is the happiest I have ever been in my entire life.

I turn around and slowly pad my feet downstairs. I grab my cell phone from the coffee table in the sitting room then step into the kitchen. I dial Susie's number not giving a fuck about what time it is. I put it on speaker as I pour me a glass of water from the tap.

I stare out the window at the endless ocean stretching out under the moon. "What in the actual fuck are you doing calling me at 3 a.m.? You better be dead or thoroughly fucked right now."

I smile out the window, "Well I am not dead so...."

I can hear Susie trying to sit up in bed, "Wait, What? Is he there? Ares? Gideon? Whatever we are calling him this week?"

I laugh and take another drink of water, "Yeah. He is here. He is laid out naked in the middle of my bed right now. He got here last night."

I can hear the smile in her voice, "Lily! Oh my god. I am so fucking happy right now. How are you? Are you okay with everything?" I smile down at the phone and click the facetime option.

I sit the phone in the windowsill in front of me as I see Susies' half asleep yet still beautiful face pop up, "Damn girl. Have you looked in a mirror?"

I laugh back at her and flip her off, "Actually, no I haven't. And I am alright with that."

She laughs at me, "Seriously though, are you okay? How is he? Is he really clean?"

I nod and sit my glass down, "He is. Matthew even confirmed it for me. As for me. I am good. I am better than good. I just....I just fucking love him. And I know that it is stupid and I know that I am more than likely setting myself up for failure but I just can't stop. Ya know. I just want to be with him."

Susie makes little lovey noises as I see her curl up into a little ball against her headboard. I roll my eyes as I look down at the strings on my robe. I let out another sigh, "You don't think I am making a mistake do you?"

I am afraid to look her in the eye. She is the only person on the earth who can see straight through me. She knows me better than anyone ever has in my entire life. I hear an intake in her breath, "No. I really, really don't think you are making a mistake."

I smile down at the floor then pick up my glass to take another drink. I sit the glass back down on the counter, "You promise you aren't just saying that to make me feel better?"

I hear her let out a soft giggle, "I promise you, from where I am sitting it doesn't look like you are making a mistake at all."

Confused, I look up at the facetime call and see a totally naked Gideon standing behind me. Dick out there for the whole world to see.

My eyes blow wide as he smiles and steps up to the phone, covering himself with the counter as he waves, "Hello Susie!"

Susie lets out a laugh that is deep and gutteral and fucking terrifying, "Hi Gideon."

I slam my face into my palms as Gideon squeezes my shoulders over the counter, "Heya love. I just came down for a drink."

I watch him as he walks his bare ass to the fridge and pulls out a Pepsi before turning then heading back to the stairs.

Susie lets out a loud whistle, "Nice Ass!"

I turn back to the phone, "Jesus Fuck Susie!"

I see Gideon still retreating towards the stairs as he throws two fingers in the air making a peace sign. I glare back at Susie, trying not to laugh as well.

She starts laughing uncontrollably, "You should see how red you are right now. Oh, this is fucking amazing. I think I love this guy! I mean, I definitely see why you love this guy but I think I love him for a whole different reason."

I laugh at her and pick up my phone, "I love you bitch. I will call you tomorrow."

I hang up the phone while Susie is still cackling. I finish the last of my water and then make my way upstairs. Gideon is laid back on the bed, with just a sheet covering him. He is

172

looking through a photo album he must have seen on my dresser.

I sit my phone down on the dresser, "Well, Susie wants to fuck you now. Thanks for that."

He lets out a chuckle into the air, "Sorry to disappoint but I only have eyes for you love."

I smile as I slide my robe off and settle under the blankets next to him, "You don't really want to look at that do you?"

Gideon smiles and sits up, leaning forward into it, "Of course I do. This is you. This is your history. I want to see it all. I want to know everything."

I smile as I sit forward a bit with him, "Do you want to hear something completely fucking insane?"

He sits the book down in front of him then smiles devilishly as he looks at me, "Always."

I laugh back at him, "We don't even know each other's last names."

His eyes go wide as the realization hits him, "Holy Fuck your right! Well mostly right. I know your full name, I think. That is how I found you in New York."

I turn towards him and stick my hand out, "Hello. My name is Lilith Marie Banks, formerly Murphy."

Gideon smiles as he turns to me, shaking my hand, "Hello Lilith, My name is Gideon Jonathan Taylor. It is a pleasure to finally meet you."

I laugh as I lean in and give him a kiss. He smiles as he pulls back and picks up the photo album again, "So you took your maiden name back? I thought most widows kept the married name."

I sigh as I look over his shoulder at the photos, "I would have if we would have had children but we didn't so, I didn't. I just thought it would be easier to start fresh. Ya know? If I had

173

kept his name I would have just thought of him every time I said my own name or signed my name or whatever. He wanted me to move on and be happy. No matter what that took."

Gideon just nods and smiles as he continues to look at the album. I watch his expressions change with every turn of a page. He is going to want to know everything. I have to prepare myself for what that reaction might be. What it might change.

14

Ares

Ascensionism - Sleep Token

I flip through a few more pages. I can feel it makes her uncomfortable that I am looking through the album. Though I am not entirely sure why.

Maybe because it is mostly pictures of her and Mark. But I want her to know that I am not hung up on her past. She was married. Now she is not.

He was alive, then he wasn't.

That was all before me.

Plus, in a fucked up twisted way it all worked out for me. Had he not passed away, she would have never been at my concert that night. I would have never seen her in the restaurant or bought her a drink at the bar. I would not be sitting next to her in the bed we just fucked on a few hours ago.

I turn the page and see a picture of a young girl smiling, standing in front of a church. The church is huge behind her and you can see a few nuns standing by the door. The little girl seems happy but you can see distance in her eyes, in her smile. She is wrapped up in a cardigan that is way too big for her and she is holding a basket with some daisies in it. Her hair is cut short around her ears and she is missing a few teeth, "Um, is this you?"

175

She looks over my shoulder and groans while trying to rip the book from my hands. I laugh, "Oh no. Oh no no no. I need answers. Now."

She laughs again as she puts her cheek on my shoulder, gazing down at the photo with me, "Yes, that is me. I am like 7 or something. I am standing outside of the orphanage."

I lean back and look down at her, "You were adopted?"

She gets a bit of a haze over her eyes when I ask. She looks down at her hands, "Well, no. Not really. I lived at the orphanage until I was 18. I was never adopted."

I look back down at the smiling girl in the picture,

"Why the hell wouldn't anyone want to adopt that little cherub face? Did you smell funny? Eat your toenail clippings? Some other kind of freaky shit?"

She laughs as she smacks my bicep, "No! Nothing like that. It was just complicated is all." She looks back at me from the photo. I see the vacancy in her eyes as she looks back down at the album again, "I had some issues growing up. I didn't really speak to anyone until I was like 13, almost 14. I mean I spoke when I was younger but something happened when I was 6 and I kinda shut down. I didn't really interact with people well after that. And when I did start speaking again, it was only to Susie. As you can imagine, she would not allow me to not talk to her. Classic Susie."

I stare into the haze that has fallen over her eyes. Something happened to her. Something fucked. I run my hand over her cheek bringing her eyes back to mine, "Can you tell me what happened to make you close off like that?"

Lily gives me a small questionable smile then shakes her head no. I run my thumb over her cheekbone, "That's okay little one. Just know I am here. If you ever need to get anything off your chest. I will always listen."

176

Lily stares at me with this force so powerful that it seems like my heart is going to explode with just this one single glance. She starts to blink rapidly, like she is trying to keep herself from crying, "So, when did you start singing?"

I close the book and place it on the nightstand.

I lean back into the pillows putting my arms behind my head, "I started playing piano first. That was when I was about 7, maybe 8. Then moved onto guitar a few years after. I studied classical music during most of my secondaries. I didn't even know I enjoyed singing until secondary school.

"We started Carnal Decay about 8 years ago now. We were nothing when we started. Just a group of misfits trying to find our niche basically. All the pieces just started to fall into place a few years ago. This past year we really blew up though.

"It has been amazing but stressful. No one really explains to you the amount of pressure it puts on you, that you put on yourself. Some days it can be really overwhelming. Most days though I really enjoy it but other days, it feels like I don't even know myself anymore."

Lily looks at me with concerned eyes as she scoots over to me and lays her head on my chest. She starts to draw little shapes on my chest with her pointer finger, "So why the gods? What made you choose them?"

I smile up towards the ceiling. So many people have asked that very same question. There are so many different rumors behind the lore that is Carnal Decay. I run my fingers down her spine, "Truthfully, we wanted a way to keep our anonymity. And we decided the best way to do that is with masks. Matthew and I came up with the idea of using Greek Mythology. We all choose whichever god we felt like we resembled or wanted to emulate the most. It took us quite a bit of time to really nail it down.

"I knew from the jump that I am Ares. God of War. Because I have always been at war with myself. For years. I have been torn between so many different paths. I decided to be Ares because he carves his own path. That is what I want to do. That is who I want to be."

Lily is looking up into my face now. Her eyes are searching mine for some answer to a question she hasn't even asked me. She has no expression on her face as she continues to stare deeply into my eyes, then nods and lays her face back on my chest. "What kind of war have you always had with yourself?"

I let out a heavy sigh, where to even fucking begin, "Well, okay long story short, my da he left when I was maybe 5 or 6. I blamed myself for the longest time. That is what kinda started the broodiness within me I guess. As I got older, I did finally start to realize that it wasn't about me at all. It was about him and what he wanted for his own life. But by that point, I was already blaming everything on myself. My mum's sadness, world hunger, climate change, ya know, everything.

"It has been a struggle to truly allow myself to just be me. Mainly, because I never really knew who I was. Everything else was always more prominent than just being me. Taking care of my mum. Being the man of the house. I took more on than I should have. I let the responsibility of being an adult weigh me down before I even know what being an adult was about. When we started the band, these words that I had held in deep just started to flow out. I had found my voice, my actual voice, not the one that my brain had been disguising. It was liberating.

"From there I just kinda said fuck it. If shit happened, it happened. Yeah, I would feel things but I didn't let them control me. Until you came around. You kinda shook that up for me. I am not saying it is a bad thing either. I just didn't know what it really meant to feel something until I met you. Now I can't stop feeling."

I bring my arm down around her and start rubbing her arm. I can feel her staring at me. I am scared to look at her though, I don't really want to know the expression on her face. I let out a slow breath, "When did you start painting?"

I can feel her smile on my chest, "I have always drawn. Mainly, charcoals growing up. But after I left St. Francis, I was able to get a few scholarships and I went to New York Academy of Art.

"That is where I got my Master in Fine Art degree. I focused on painting though I still did charcoals as well. That was where I met Mark actually. He was at an exhibition with his family when he saw my work."

I smile at her story, I honestly do want to know everything, "So, you knew him for a bit before you were married then?"

She lets out another small laugh, "Yeah. He wanted to get married like a month after we met. I did not. Honestly, I never had any intentions of ever getting married. It just wasn't something I really had a lot of faith in." I hear the pain in her voice, the resistance in her words. What happened to her?

She takes a deep breath and continues, "But he finally wore me down. I knew that marrying him was the smart move. We were best friends, ya know. He was a good man. He was stable and financially secure. He wanted to provide a good life for me. He checked off a lot of the boxes."

I rub her arm again, kissing the top of her head, "But you were never in love with him?"

She tenses up a bit at the question, "I know that makes me a horrible person. But he knew. He knew that I loved him. But he also knew that I was just not the kind of person to fall in love. There is just a lot of history on that topic and it isn't something I like to talk about."

She reaches up and spreads her fingers out on my chest.

I reach down with my other hand and clasp hers, "That is fine baby. You don't have to tell me anything you aren't ready for either. There is absolutely no rush."

She squeezes my hand back and then lifts her chin to look in my eyes, "I never planned to fall in love with you, ya know. When I first heard Ares sing, I was just drawn to the pain in your voice. The torment felt like a piece of home to me. It comforted all the broken parts inside, letting me know it was going to be okay. Then when I met Gideon, it just felt all too real.

"I was physically drawn to you before I even knew who you were. That night at the bar. I was so nervous and just so taken aback by you. You were so confident and bold and sexy. I was instantly entranced."

She smiles at me and her cheeks turn a bit pink, as if she is keeping a secret to herself.

I smile down at her, "What? What are you not telling me?"

She buries her face in my chest, giggling then looks back up at me,

"The day at the gym. After I left. I literally ran to my suite. The door was barely shut and I had a vibrator between my legs. I hadn't had an orgasm in almost a year. I came so fucking fast it was almost laughable."

I belt out a loud laugh and then turn to look at her again,

"After watching you, all hot and sweaty running on that treadmill, singing my songs. I was as hard as steel by the time you rejected me and took off. I jerked off in the shower for a half hour after that."

She smiles at me, "You thought of me the entire time?"

I nod and pull her chin up for a kiss, "The entire time."

She kisses me back and smiles again, "Good."

I laugh into her mouth again, kissing her a bit harder than before. She wraps her arms around me and pulls me in tight. I hold onto her until she pulls back a few moments later, "We should probably get some more sleep. I am pretty tired."

I push some hair behind her ear and nod back at her. She rolls onto her side, facing away from me and I pull her in close to me. I feel her settle in as I run my fingers down her side, onto the curve of her hip then back up again.

She lets out a soft sigh and I lean in and kiss her softly on her neck. I smile as she nudges her ass into me a bit further. I run my hand around and slide it down to her center. She lets out another soft moan as I run my finger across her clit.

She lifts her leg and rests her ankle on my knee, giving me plenty of room to work with. I let my fingers roam lower, collecting some of her wetness then I roll them back up over her clit again.

She moans as her back arches slightly. I pull my hand back then reach down and slowly slide myself inside her.

She lets her leg fall back down as she leans forward just a bit. I slowly thrust in and out of her, reaching around and kneading at her breasts. She starts to push back on me in the same rhythm of my thrusts.

I kiss her neck again as I feel her starting to flutter around my dick. I push myself all the way in then lean into her ear,

"I love you, Lillith Marie Banks."

She pushes herself back into me further and reaches back to grab my ass tightly. She turns her head just enough for me to see her smile,

"I love you, Gideon Jonathan Taylor."

I start thrusting into her faster and harder. She begins to pant and I see her gripping the blanket around her hand so tight that her knuckles are turning white.

I slam into her a few more times as she lets out a deep growl that I have never heard before as I feel her tighten around me. I cling to her tighter as I throw myself into her 3 more times before growling my release right back into her ear.

She smiles as she falls asleep with my dick still inside her.

I wake up around 9 am the next morning. Lily is still curled into my side, purring softly in her sleep. I reach down and tuck a strand of hair behind her ear. It has become my new favorite hobby.

Pushing those long dark strands behind those beautiful little ears so I could see the masterpiece that is her face.

I trace her face from just above her eye down her cheekbone then to her lips. I rub my thumb across her pouty lower lip then lean in and kiss her. I feel her smile into my mouth as she kisses me back.

She pulls back, eyes still closed, "Good Morning."

I grin back at her, "Good Morning."

She stretches her arms high above her head then opens her eyes. I have never seen her eyes right after she wakes up. They are almost as black as mine.

She blinks a couple of times and her pupils instantly shrink leaving behind two storm clouds, flecked with hints of blue and silver. She stretches again, a low groan escaping her throat.

"What time is it?" Her voice is deep and gravely before her morning coffee.

I grin at the sound of it, "Almost 9."

She nods her head then closes her eyes again, "When do you have to leave?"

I run my hand down the side of her face, "What day is it?"

She grins, pulling back and opening her eyes. She raises one eyebrow, "Sunday. Yesterday was your show in Norfolk."

I smile back then let out a sigh, "Our last show is in Savannah. We don't have to be there until Friday."

She smiles then sits up onto her elbow, "What do you mean we?"

I pull her chin to mine, "You are coming with me."

She giggles as she sits up fully, wrapping the sheet around her bare breasts, "Really?"

I nod at her as she smiles back then looks out across the room. "What are we going to do until then?"

She hasn't reached my gaze yet so I reach out and turn her face back to mine, "Spend time together. Get to know each other more. Normal couple stuff."

She smiles at me, "We are a couple?"

I nod my head at her, "Yes Lily. We are a couple. You are my girlfriend. I am your boyfriend. Eventually, we will be engaged. Then we will be married. Afterwards, there will be versions of us running down the halls."

She puts her hands up, "Whoa Whoa Whoa. Let's calm that talk down."

I laugh as I sit up beside her, "You married Mark. Why wouldn't you marry me?"

She laughs nervously, "That, that was different. That was a relationship of mutual respect. This. Between us. This is different."

I lean into her, peppering her neck with kisses, "You would think if this is the real thing you would be all about it."

She swallows hard as she turns and slides out of bed, "I am not saying never. I am just saying baby steps is all."

I watch her walk across the room and grab another summer dress out of the closet then turn to the dresser to grab some undergarments.

She turns back around to me, with an inquisitive look on her face, "I have a question."

I laugh as I swing my legs around my side of the bed and stand up. I watch her eyes roam over my body as I stretch, stopping and staring along the way.

"Excuse me ma'am but my eyes are up here." I point to my face.

She laughs back at me, shaking her head to force her eyes elsewhere, "Sorry, anyways. What is the rest of the band going to do until the next show?"

I shrug my shoulders, "Probably hang out at the hotel. Maybe hit the pool or a few bars. The normal."

She steps into her underwear, then slides her bra on, "What if they came here?"

I freeze and look up at her, "Why?"

She smiles again as she slides the summer dress over her head then straightens it down her body, "Well, I mean if I am going to travel with you guys. I should get to know them, right?"

I nod at her as I slide my jeans on, "Yeah, you should but there is one pretty important piece of information you should know first. And I am not entirely sure how you are going to take it."

She tilts her head at me, looking at me worried, "What?"

I take a deep breath as I walk around to the end of the bed and sit on the edge of it, "Simone is Hera. She is our bassist."

She nods her head then turns her back to me, facing the dresser. I see her shoulders rise and fall as she turns back towards me. She walks up to me and steps in between my legs, wrapping her arms around my neck,

"Did you love her?"

I shake my head,

"No. There were never any feelings involved. On either side. Everything that has ever happened between us was just animal instinct. I have never thought of her that way. She has never thought of me like that either.

"Actually, after everything that happened before, she went with us to your house. She wanted to tell you to your face that there was nothing there and never would be. But you were already gone."

Lily nods and leans down putting her forehead to mine,

"Have you been with her since?"

I pull back looking into her eyes and rubbing a hand across her cheek, "No baby. I haven't been with anyone but you since I met you. I don't want anyone but you."

She smiles back at me then looks past me towards the window, "Okay."

I lean back grabbing her attention, "Okay?"

She nods, "Okay. I mean does it make me uneasy, yes. But if this is going to work, I have to trust you. I trust that you will not hurt me like that again. I trust that you only want me. So....okay."

I smile as I pull her in for a deep kiss. Breathless she pulls back, "This doesn't mean I want to be her bestie. She is not braiding my hair and I am not giving her boy advice."

I bark out a laugh, "I don't think that will be a problem. She is not your typical girl's girl."

Lily nods then pulls back from me,

"Okay, so invite them to stay here this week. They will have privacy. We can all get to know each other. There is plenty of space for you all to rehearse if needed. I think it would be fun. I mean, we have tons of room here. There are 8 fricken bedrooms. Might as well make use of them."

I stand and walk over to her. I place a hand on each cheek and pull her into me, "Thank you."

She smiles as I kiss her forehead then pull back, "For what?"

I look over every inch of her face again, "For accepting this. For letting us fix this. For understanding what is important to me."

Lily wraps her arms around me and puts her face into my chest, "Gideon, you are your music. I would never try to come between that. Your band is your family. That makes them my family now. I want us all to put the past behind us and move forward. This is my olive branch."

I lean down and kiss her hard again. I pull back looking into her eyes, "I will invite them on one condition."

She smiles back at me with a curious look on her face. I grin at her again, "You have to invite Susie too."

Lily lets out a loud cackle, "Why would I need to invite Susie? You have already met her."

I smile back down at her, "Because she is a part of your life. An important part of your life. I need her to know me just as much as I need to know her. I don't want there to be any hang ups between us. Any of us."

She finally pulls away, laughing, "Okay, I will call her. I am going to go fix us some breakfast. Do you drink coffee?"

I smile and nod, "Yes love. I am going to call Matthew and have a chat. I will be down in a minute."

She grins at me again as she turns and leaves the room. I am the luckiest man alive. I can't believe that this is my reality. We have come back from the depths of hell stronger than ever. I smile again as I pull out my phone and hit the button for Matthew.

It rings 3 times before a half asleep asshole answers the phone,

186

"What?"

I laugh as I sit down to slide my socks on, "Good Morning to you too."

I hear him grumble in the background again, "Bruh, it's like 9:30 in the morning."

I look at the clock, smiling again, "Yeah, sorry about that. But I have news."

I hear him shuffling around on his side, more than likely scooting a groupie out of bed, "What's that?"

I slide my shoes on and stand up smiling as I look out the window at the ocean before me, "Lily and I are good. We are together. We are happy. We are gonna make a go of it."

I hear him chuckle, "Thank fuck for that. You are an asshole when you're not getting laid."

I laugh at him again, putting the phone on speaker and throwing it on the bed, "There is more. She has invited the band to come here, to her summer house. There is more than enough room for everyone. She thinks it would be good to get to know everyone since she is going to be around awhile."

I was met with nothing but silence, "Are you there?"

Matthew clears his throat, "Does she know about Simone?"

I pull my shirt down my body and straighten back up, "Yes and she is cool with it. We talked everything out."

Matthew lets out a sigh, "Yeah I mean, it sounds fine to me but I have to clear it with everyone else first. The girls will be upset to not have a pool for a week but they will get past it."

I smile at the phone, looking out over the back porch,

"Not to worry, she has a pool here. Also a private beach on the oceanfront. And I am pretty sure I am looking at a hot tub as well."

I hear Matthew chuckle again, "Are we really sure she is not in the mafia?"

I laugh as I hear behind me, "Why does everyone fucking think I am in the mafia? Other people have money that wasn't obtained by illegal drug trades and arms deals!"

Matthew and I start laughing at the same time, "Hello Lily."

She walks over to me and hands me a cup of coffee, "Hello Apollo."

He groans again, "This is weird. Just call me Matthew when the mask is off."

She smiles as she takes a sip of her coffee. I turn back to the phone, "Just text me if you are coming. You still have the address."

She smiles at the phone as I hang up, "Do you think they are going to come?"

I smile back, "I don't see why not."

Lily takes another sip of her coffee when her phone dings. She pulls it out of her pocket, smiling at the screen. She lets out a chuckle then turns the screen for me to see a message from Susie.

"Are you fucking serious? Yes! Fuck Yes! I will be there in 2 days, max! OMFG! What am I going to wear!?"

I laugh loudly and look up into Lily's eyes. She smiles back at me then puts the phone away and turns to head back downstairs.

We have a light breakfast then just sit at the table, chatting about everything and nothing. We talk about life on the road. We talk about her life, before me, before Mark. She tells me about Susie and high school. I could listen to her tell stories for hours. She gets so animated with her words and arm gestures.

A half hour later I receive the text that they will be making it to the house around 3. Lily becomes instantly excited. She starts running around like crazy and making shopping lists.

She hands me a list of things to get from the store then goes upstairs to make sure that the bedrooms are ready. Make sure there were clean towels and such. She smiles as she buzzes around the house. I never would have imagined seeing her this excited over company. She honestly struck me as more of the loner type, but I am not hating this side of her either.

I volunteer to run to the store and get everything on her lists. It isn't long after that she is pacing the kitchen with a glass of whisky and a whole lot of nervousness raging through her veins.

What the fuck am I thinking? This is going to be insane.

I am about to have the entirety of Carnal Decay in my fucking house. And then Susie will be here in less than 48 hours. This is going to be fucking chaotic. It is crazy enough that Carnal fucking Decay is going to be here, but Susie and Carnal fucking Decay. There is no way this is going to end well.

I have lost my goddamn mind.

Gideon seems calm as can be with his feet kicked up on the coffee table watching me pace the living room. I feel like my heart is going to erupt out of my chest. They are all going to be here at any minute.

Simone is going to be here at any minute.

Insecurities are riddling my brain. No amount of deep breathing or pacing is going to change that. I know this is good. They've accepted my olive branch.

That means maybe they will accept me and Gideon. But I still feel this impending doom just sitting on my shoulders like the devil himself is trying to hold me underwater.

I roll my shoulders back again then take another long drink of whisky. I walk over to the bar, grabbing another bottle of Dalmore and set it on the counter. I grab the open bottle and fill my glass to the rim. I take another long drink when I hear voices from the front porch. I turn and look wide eyed at Gideon, "I'm gonna puke."

He smiles at me, "Babe. Breathe. They are just people."

I nod my head, taking another drink before setting my glass down and smoothing my dress in front of me. I should have changed. I try to breathe like Gideon said but my mind is going to a million different places at once. I feel like the gremlins are back with their pick axes just going to town on me.

I probably look like a fucking nanny or grandmother right now. I try to breathe through my impending doom but I know I have to look half crazy right now. I roll my eyes and put a smile on my face as they all start to walk inside.

I step up beside Gideon, feeling him drape his arm across my shoulders, then smile to everyone, "Hey guys. I am so happy you accepted the invite."

I watch the eyes of all 4 people that walk in as they take in the house around us. They are all wide eyed looking from room to room, even up the stairs. I know they are seeing the antiques, the embellished furniture and art on the walls. I roll my eyes again and sigh as my shoulders drop,

"I swear, I am not in the fucking mafia alright?"

They all let out a laugh at this. Thank god. I smile again, waving them towards the stairs, "Come on, I will show you where the bedrooms are."

They all follow me up the stairs with their bags and some of their instruments. I glance back downstairs and see Gideon moving what looks like a drum set into the dining room.

I point out mine and Gideon's room then show them the others as the hallway wraps around and goes up to the 3rd floor. They all disperse out quickly finding their desired room choices.

Edge, the quietest of them all decides he wants the room with the turret, which was really fucking surprising.

It's the smallest bedroom in the house but he can't quit smiling at it as he walks around then sits his stuff down. It is hilarious. This man literally looks like he walked out of a "guys your mother wouldn't want you to date" catalog and he likes the girliest room in the house. I don't have the heart to tell him that Susie is probably going to kick him out of it tomorrow, since that too is her favorite room to stay in.

I leave them to settle in and I go back downstairs to finish my obnoxiously large glass of whisky. Gideon steps up behind me, rubbing his hands up and down my arms, "You know, you can breathe. No one will fault you for it."

I give him a sarcastic smile and take another swallow of my drink. I am going to have to run 20 fucking miles tomorrow to work all this alcohol off but I don't care. I need something right now to cut the arms off the gremlins.

I hear footsteps coming down the stairs and hand Gideon my glass. I walk around the bar and pull out more glasses, setting them on the counter just in case anyone wants to join me.

I look over to Edge and Simone laughing and talking as they round the corner.

I look her up and down and instantly begin to feel self conscious again. Simone is so fucking pretty.

She has blonde hair and dark eyes. She has an array of tattoos covering the majority of her body. She just looks so young and free. And not like me.

I feel the smile falling from my face again as I wrap my arms around myself. Gideon runs his hand down my arm and I look up, giving him a painted grin.

I take my glass from his hand, "I am going to go upstairs for a minute. You are all welcome to anything. The bar is here, the kitchen is back there. The pool and hot tub are through the double doors over there. Treat it like home."

192

I turn quickly to avoid the look I know Gideon is giving me.

I run up the stairs, passing Matthew in the hallway. He turns like he wants to say something but I run into my room, quickly shutting and locking the door behind me. I finish the last of my whisky and just sit here trying to breathe.

What the fuck am I doing?

I feel like a fucking babysitter crashing a party. I roll my head onto my shoulders, groaning into the empty room. I walk over to the window and look down to see Gideon showing Simone and Mona the pool area.

I let out another sigh and look out over the ocean waves wishing that they would just crash into me and put me out of my fucking misery.

I look back down towards the pool again but they must have all gone back inside. I sigh as I put my back to the wall and slide down it. I hold my head in my hands trying to just get a fucking grip.

He loves me. I love him.

None of this other shit should matter. I pull out my phone and quickly dial Susie's number. Just when I think voicemail is going to pick up I hear an exasperated Susie, "You do realize I am trying to pack and not have a fucking coronary at the same time right?"

I laugh back into the phone. I need her. I need her to tell me I am not doing something stupid, even though I probably am. "I am kinda freaking out."

I hear something glass rattling around on the other end of the phone as I stand to glance back out the window at the ocean, crashing into the land in gentle strokes. Susie lets out a sigh, "Why? All that matters is how you and Gideon feel about each other. If they care about him at all, nothing else will matter."

I nod my head at the glass in front of me, "I know but it's not just that. They are all here now and I have locked myself in my bedroom. Susie, Simone if fucking gorgeous! I have only seen her from behind. I mean I kinda caught a glimpse of her profile that day in the dressing room but being this close to her. I am really fucking intimidated."

I hear Susie moving around still then she lets out a heavy sigh, "Yeah I didn't talk to her but I saw her that day at the brownstone. The day after you left. You are not wrong, she is beautiful but you need to remember. He chose you. He could have had her, he has been with her. But you are the one he wants."

I nod my head into the phone, "I know. It is just really overwhelming to actually be this close to her. I am just trying really hard not to fuck this all up."

I hear a suitcase slam shut, "Here is what you are going to do. You are going to relax. You are going to get comfortable. You are going to let them in, let them get to know the real you. And when I get there, if there is any bad blood at all we will just set them on fire and throw their charred remains into the ocean where they will never be found. Sound good?"

I belt out a laugh, "Yeah, sounds good."

Susie chuckles into the phone again, "Okay, I have to go and try to make it through this day without quitting my job and running straight to your house."

I smile into the phone again, "Susie, you are the fucking boss. Of a non profit. They will survive if you aren't there."

She laughs back at me, then lets out a heavy sigh, "Yeah, I know but I just want everything in order before I leave. I don't want them calling me every 5 minutes with questions. I want to get to know this band. Especially Apollo. Is it in my head or is he really cute? He is, isn't he? None of them said anything to me that day at the brownstone. I don't know who was who!

"I saw the girls standing outside and Apollo and I am assuming Dionysus sat in the living room with me. But who I am assuming is Apollo just looked around nervously and maybe Dionysus stared at me like I was his next meal. It was creepy. Wait, Apollo, my god, does he have an accent like Gideon? I swear to Christ Lily. I will cum on the spot."

I cackle at her again as I turn to look at the bedroom door, "Yeah, he is cute. Yes, he is British. They all are actually. But I think you might be more interested in someone else."

I hear complete silence, "Uh who?"

I smile as I think of the man staying in her favorite bedroom, "Dionysus."

I hear nothing but silence back. For a moment I think the call has dropped, then I hear Susie, "The dude with the scary ass mask? The one that stared at me like he wanted to fucking murder me and not even worry about hiding the body? I don't know about that one. I don't know that he is my type."

I smile back out the window, "Trust me. He is your type. Get your shit taken care of so you can get here. You are leaving out tomorrow morning right?"

Susie lets out another exasperated sigh, "Yup, hopping a flight first thing. I will just take a cab to the house. I am so excited. I love you sweets, I will see you tomorrow!"

I smile back at her as I hear the call disconnect on her end. This is going to be insane. But having Susie here will help keep me in check. She knows how to calm me better than anyone I have ever met. Though Gideon is coming in at a close second.

As I think about Gideon, I am immediately inundated with thoughts of Simone. Then about how much older I am than all of these people. I am going to have to get this age difference shit out of my head if I want this to work. It is just a hard reality to swallow knowing I was going to bars when they were in 7th grade.

I laugh out loud, shaking my head at my insanity. Then I hear something. I turn my head to the side.

Are they jamming?

I walk over to the door and put my ear to it. They are. It sounds like they actually did set up in the dining room. I smile into the door and then my breath stills as I hear Gideon begin to sing.

Every fucking time I hear his voice it feels like the blood stills in my veins. I step over to the closet and pull my dress off, throwing it into the hamper. I look into the back of the closet at the few boxes of old clothes I have brought from the brownstone. I open one of the boxes smiling as I see all my favorites from when I was at NYAA.

I dig through until I find an old David Bowie t-shirt I had turned into a crop top.

I pull it over my head, immediately relaxing in the familiar feel of the cheap cotton polyester blend on my skin. I reach further into the box and pull out some old black cut off shorts. I slide the shorts on then step around to the dresser.

I pull my hair up into a messy bun. Again, I know I don't look 34 but I am. I am going to be 35 soon. That is almost 40. Gideon is fucking 26.

I just stand there looking at myself until I finally decide it is time to stop hiding. I step barefoot back out into the hallway with my empty glass. I make it almost all the way down the stairs when it hits me. Fully hits me.

Gideon is Ares.

Ares is in my house.

Gideon is my boyfriend.

That means Ares is my boyfriend.

This is really happening. I take the last few steps slowly then turn and lean into the doorway. It is weird seeing them all out of character and playing together.

Gideon is at the keyboards so Mona is just sitting on the floor staring at them all as she bobs her head on her shoulders. Edge has even helped Matthew set up his drums.

I know the house is spacious but shit. I turn and walk across the hall into the sitting room and pour me another glass of whisky.

I stand there listening to Gideon sing song after song when something changes within me. I instantly feel the urge to paint. The pull of the canvas is screaming at me.

I smile as I top off my glass then step out the side door into the sunroom. Turning on all the lights, I decide to leave the door open so I can still hear him. Something about hearing him live is just raw and inspiring.

I set up an easel quickly and grab a dozen different paints. Before I even know what I am going to draw, the basis of the painting has already begun to take shape. I have two different brushes sticking out of the bun in my hair and my arms are covered in paint.

The music that pours through the doors is being channeled through my fingers. I take a step back, the painting is starting to tell its story.

It is a cemetery with a woman dressed in 1800s vestments staring at the full moon overhead. There are rows of headstones in front of her and a gothic inspired mausoleum to her right. You can see the pain in her face. You can see the reservation in her stance.

She is in mourning.

Her life has passed her by and now her love is in the ground before her. I frantically paint until I realize the music has stopped. I look down at my watch realizing that I have been in here for hours. I look out the windows behind the painting to see that the sun has already gone down.

I sit the palette down on the table next to me and turn around. Everyone is sitting in the living room staring at me. Silent, not saying a word just watching me paint.

I instantly feel self conscious again. I grab a rag and try wiping the paint off my arms unsuccessfully because it had dried hours before.

I grab my glass and head back into the bar, "Sorry guys. I kinda got lost in that. What does everyone want for supper? I can cook whatever or we can order in or go out. It's whatever everyone is fine with." I am rambling again.

I pick up the bottle of Dalmore, my hands shaking so badly I can barely pour my drink.

Gideon steps up beside me and places his hand on my lower back, calming me. I smile into the glass then look up at him, "I am so sorry. I didn't know I had been in there that long. I was trying to stay out of everyone's way while they rehearsed."

Gideon smiles then leans down and kisses me.

He pulls back still smiling, "You have nothing to apologize for. This is your house. If you want to paint, then paint. I must say though, you were fucking brilliant to watch. Truly."

I smile and nod at him then look around the room. Only Edge is sitting there now but he is still looking directly onto the sun porch.

I follow his gaze and realize that Simone, Mona and Matthew have all gone out there and are staring at my painting. I let out a heavy sigh as I step into the room behind them. I lean into the doorway watching them as they all move around the piece, looking at it from all angles. Simone turns around with tears in her eyes, "Lily. This is fucking beautiful."

I am taken back.

Gideon had said she wasn't a girls' girl but here she is, crying over an oil painting. I give her a soft smile, "Thank you."

Matthew continues moving around the room, looking at the canvas from different perspectives it seems.

Mona turns around, "Why did you paint a cemetery?"

I shrug one shoulder. Staring into the painting behind her, I can't really put into words what had made me do it.

Matthew turns around, "You started this when we were rehearsing Evermore didn't you?"

I smile and nod then take another long drink of whisky. Matthew just stands there shaking his head at me for a moment before turning back to the painting, "Bloody fucking brilliant."

I smile again, "Thank you."

Simone turns back to me then takes a few steps closer to me, "Have you always been an artist?"

I give her a short smile then look back to the painting, "Yeah. For as long as I can remember."

She smiles back at me, "What made you start?"

I shrug again, "I just started. I just grabbed some charcoal one day and just started drawing. I had a pretty sheltered childhood at one point. I didn't really have anyone to confide in so I just drew my feelings"

Mona turns around, "Do you have anything else here?"

I scrunch up my nose, "I have a few sketchbooks upstairs but nothing else really of this size. I am pretty sure they still have some of my work on display at NYAA and on their website too."

Mona smiles back at me, "Badass."

She turns back to the painting and I finish off my glass of whisky. I stand up to go put my glass in the sink when I hear Simone, "Can I see the sketchbooks?"

I look around at all the faces staring back at me.

I nod slightly, trying not to show the fear that is trying to crawl out of my chest, "Yeah. I will go get them." I sit the glass down on the table.

Nervously rubbing my hands together, I make my way up the stairs to a spare room down the hall that basically holds my life in it. Most of the stuff in here I haven't looked at or thought about in years. After I had it all shipped here from the brownstone, I honestly meant to burn it all, throw it away.

I flip the light on and step to the far back corner of the room. I open a few boxes,

"Where the fuck are they? I know I put them in here."

I hear someone clear their throat behind me and I jump, turning around and screaming.

Gideon starts to laugh loudly, "There are 6 people in this house right now and you are still scared?"

I flip him off, laughing, then turn back around to look through the boxes in front of me.

I hear him moving around behind me, "What is all this?"

I frown into the box in front of me, moving it out the way to grab another one,

"This room is me. It is everything I owned when I moved in with Mark. I meant to burn it all to ashes years ago but never did. Not sure why."

I feel Gideon move behind me then his hands are on my sides,

"Why would you burn it all?"

I lean back into him, "There is just a lot about me that you don't know."

He leans into my ear, "It's the mafia isn't it?"

I smack his hands away and reach over to grab another box. I pull the flaps back,

"Yahtzee! Found them."

I pull out the 4 different sketchbooks and turn around.

200

Gideon is standing behind me holding a framed photo of my parents, me and my sister.

The smile immediately leaves my face. My blood runs cold. Everything starts flooding back into me. I can hear Nikki's voice, her laughter. My dad, as he is walking away from me. My mother, standing in the center of our dilapidated kitchen, holding a bloody carving knife in her hand.

He looks at me grinning from ear to ear, then sees my face and he instantly sits the photo down then steps to me, "What's wrong little one?"

I continue to look down at the photo, whispering,

"Where did you find that?"

He looks down at the photo then back at me, "It was in that box over there by the door. Why?"

I look back up at him, shaking my head and putting on a fake smile,

"Nothing. It's nothing. Come on, let's go back downstairs."

I walk past him quickly trying to put as much space as I can between me and my past. I try to shake the memories of Nikki. The memories of that day. I try to focus on what I have now, what I have ahead of me, not what is stuck in the past. I try to feel the warmth from his words asking me what was wrong and his apparent little pet name for me. I continue shaking my head, not sure where my emotions are going to land yet.

Gideon is about two minutes behind me when I get back downstairs. I lay the sketchbooks out on the coffee table then step into the kitchen to grab my phone and order pizzas.

Gideon rounds into the kitchen right as I am hanging up, "Pizza will be here in 30. I got a little of everything, not knowing who liked what."

I sit the phone down, staring at the counter. I can still see my mother's face, the anger in it. The fear, resentment. I close my eyes tight, trying to force some other image into my brain.

Gideon steps up next to me and pulls me in close, "Are you okay?"

I nod into his chest, "Yeah, I am fine. Come on, let's go back to the sitting room with the others."

I can't be alone with him right now.

I refuse to do this in front of everyone.

I will not allow myself to break down right now. No matter how overwhelming the need to cry is. He grips my hand tightly in his and leads me back to the others.

They are all in awe over my charcoals. It makes me feel honored that they are all interested in my work so much. I smile at them as they flip through the pages like kids in a candy store. I turn to Gideon and see he is holding a sketchbook as well.

His eyes are stormy though. He looks at me then turns the sketchbook around showing me a picture I had forced myself to forget about years ago.

It is my sister laying on the kitchen floor. The only color on the page is the pastel red pool surrounding her body. Getting darker the closer it gets to her body. I know my eyes are wide right now. I instantly get flashes of seeing Nikki laying on the floor. The way that rusty crimson seeped out around her body. My mother standing there frantic then just staring at the knife in her hand. I start to hyperventilate. I have to get the fuck out of here. I can't do this.

I should have destroyed that fucking thing years ago.

Fear grips my heart tight like a vise.

I can feel myself start to shake, sweat. I feel the smile fall from my face once again.

This was a horrible idea.

I never should have invited them here.

202

I never should have gone in that room.

I grab my phone tight in my hand, putting on another painted smile, then turn and run out the back door.

16
Ares
All Around Me - Flyleaf

I watch her run from the room like it is on fire.

I turn the sketchbook back around, memorizing every single inch of the drawing. The formica table and chairs, the dingy looking counters, the broken refrigerator door barely holding on.

I instantly recognize the girl in the drawing.

She is the same girl in the photo with Lily upstairs.

I feel Edge step up beside me and look at the photo, "God damn. What in the fuck would have made her draw that?"

I look down at the bottom where she had signed her name. In the corner it says Lillith 1998. The year I was born. She was just a child. I look back over the drawing then turn and hand it to Matthew. He looks down at it with his eyes wide, "Jesus."

I point to the corner where her name is signed, "She did this in 1998. She would have been 8 years old."

Matthews' eyes go wide, "Holy shit man! What in the actual fuck?"

Simone steps over, examining the drawing as well, "Do you think this is something that she saw? I mean she was just a kid, how could she come up with this kind of drawing on her own?"

I look from Simone's face to the back door.

204

"She said she lived in an orphanage growing up. She was never adopted. She also told me that she promised herself when she was just a child that she would never fall in love."

I turn back to Matthew, "I saw a photo of this girl upstairs. I think it might have been her sister."

Matthew shakes his head as Simone looks closer at the drawing, "I can see that. She looks a lot like Lily. You don't...I mean. We don't think she saw her sister die, do we?"

I look to the back door, "I will be back."

I hurry to the door and crack it open, trying not to scare her again. I can hear her on the phone, her breathing is erratic, almost as erratic as her movements,

"Susie, I can't do this. I can't fucking do this. Not again. I can't keep reliving this torture. I can't even fucking breath right now."

She is pacing back and forth by the hot tub, staring out at the ocean. She starts breathing in deeply through her nose, blowing it out slowly from her mouth. She does this 3 times before turning back towards the ocean,

"I know. I know he would understand but I just don't think I can fucking tell him. Fuck, I never even told Mark everything. I never fucking expected us to be this close. I never thought he would see it. I should have burnt the fucking drawing and the picture. Why? Susie, why didn't I just fucking burn them all? Why do I keep leaving myself these little fucking morsels of pain to find later?"

She starts shaking her head,

"No. I know that. It is just all too fucking real."

I see her shoulders fall again,

"Yeah. I know he would still love me."

She leans over the railing,

"I know it wasn't my fault. I just, I never thought I would have to live through telling this fucking horror novel again. I

205

mean I know he would understand. Fuck they all would. I was just a kid. I was just caught off guard. I didn't expect to be thinking about Nikki tonight. It is just a lot."

I sit down quietly in a chair watching her walk back and forth. I know I shouldn't be eavesdropping but I have to make sure she is okay. The panic and fear that had fallen over her face before had literally scared me. I have never seen someone get that spooked that quick.

Lily pauses, looking out over the ocean in front of her, "No. I promise. I am not going to use. I am not even thinking about it. Plus, I wouldn't have the first idea of where to even score around here. I just, I just want to forget. I want it to be someone else's past, not mine."

I hear her tell Susie she loves her then she hangs up the phone. Use? What is she not going to use? What fucking secrets is she hiding from me? Seeing her in this light, I can see all the cracks in the surface. It is like this light is just shining through them showing me all the broken and beaten parts of her. Lily leans forward and holds her head in her hands. I see her shoulders shake. Then she turns around and sees me sitting in front of her.

She doesn't even look surprised.

She looks defeated.

Her face is pulled taut with worry and fear. She looks fucking exhausted. Lily takes a few steps towards me and I open my arms for her. She sits down in my lap then puts her face into my chest.

I rub her back, "You tell me whatever you want to tell me in your own time. This is your story. I will never rush it." I feel her squeeze me back harder.

It isn't a few minutes later and Edge is poking his head out the door,

"Foods here guys."

206

I throw a hand up to let him know we heard him as Lily leans forward then stands up.

She smiles down at me, "Come on. Let's eat."

Lily is silent for most of dinner. She doesn't even eat a full slice of pizza. She just keeps to herself.

She includes herself in the conversation but seems distant for the most of it. I can tell as the time ticks away though, she is starting to settle back into herself.

Still, I can't help but wonder, what is up with that drawing? Was it a memory? Was it just something from her imagination? Or was she holding something in that could be a lot more dangerous?

Mona leans into the table,

"So what now? The night is still young."

Lily looks around the table,

"Honestly, there's not a lot to do here on a Sunday night. Do we want to maybe make some margaritas or something and hit the pool? There is a hot tub too. There isn't a lifeguard so, ocean at your own risk."

Edge leans forward, scrunching up his nose,

"Not sure on the margarita front. Do you have straight tequila?"

Lily smiles as she leans forward,

"Bitch, please."

She stands up and walks to the far side of the bar. She smiles straight at Edge as she pulls up two bottles of Patron and a bottle of Don Julio.

I see the wicked smile falling over Edges' face as she turns behind her and reaches into the refrigerator producing a small bowl of quartered limes.

She grins back at Edge while grabbing a salt shaker,

"Who's up first?"

1 hour and many shots later we are all preparing to get in the pool. I follow Lily up to our room, smiling at her trying not to trip over her own feet as we walk up the stairs. She was finally able to compartmentalize her emotions and there has been no sign of the earlier freak out rearing its ugly head again.

She closes the door behind us, giggling as she turns around,

"Tequila does this every fucking time. I could drink my weight in whisky and nothin. One shot of tequila and I am drunk in a cornfield in the midwest somewhere."

I laugh out loud at the visual,

"Why does that sound like a story you have told before?" She turns back to me grinning and tapping her nose with her pointer finger.

I step up behind her and run my hands along her waist until they meet in front of her shorts. I kiss her neck softly as I unbutton her shorts and slowly bring the zipper down.

She tilts her head up to me, smiling, "Sir. We have guests."

I smile back down at her, "And?"

I slowly slide the jean shorts over her hips until they fall to the ground on their own.

She steps out of them and turns to me,

"And we can't be rude and stay up here fucking while they are all downstairs."

I let out a heavy sigh and pull her in close,

"Why not? They would do it to us. I guarantee that shit."

She laughs as she reaches her arms around me, locking them at the base of my back.

She smiles up at me and I can't help myself. I lean down and kiss her fiercely. I feel her hands flatten out against my back

208

a moment later. I inhale her scent deep into my senses then pick her up by her waist sitting her down on the dresser behind her.

I continue to run my hands all over her body when there is a quick knock at the door,

"We are headed down. See you in a few."

I pull away and lean my forehead into hers,

"Fucking Matthew."

Lily smiles as she looks up into my eyes and pulls her shirt over her head. She ticks her head to the right a bit as she throws the shirt behind me then brings her hands up to her tits.

I inhale sharply, "Tease."

She laughs as she reaches behind her and unclasps her bra, setting her tits free in front of me.

I grin devilishly at her, "Fuck them. They can wait."

I pick her up and turn her around to lean over the dresser. She smiles over her shoulder at me as I forcefully pull her underwear down and spread her legs apart with my foot. I can feel the heat radiating off of her.

20 seconds later, I am slamming into her from behind. She is already gasping and moaning. I reach my hand around the front of her neck, clutching her tightly. She bites her lip as I continue to slam into her. Grabbing a handful of hair, I watch her back arch up.

I can see her face in the reflection of the mirror now,

"Look at me."

Lily opens her eyes, heavily hooded and smiles at me when her eyes meet mine in the mirror. I grit my teeth and start to slam myself into her harder.

Her mouth falls open in a delicious O shape as her eyes roll up in her head. A few moments later her eyes meet mine again in the reflection, with a husky voice she begs,

"Make me cum baby. Please."

I understand the fascination now.

As soon as she breathes out the word please.

As soon as I hear her begging for it, I turn fucking primal on her. I push her down flat with one hand and begin thrusting harder and faster into her than before. I watch the muscles in her back roll along her spine as she takes the beating I am giving to her. Her pearl white skin glowing from the force of it.

It isn't but a few moments later that I feel her clamp down on my dick. I look at her face and she is biting her hand hard so she doesn't scream out for the whole house to hear.

I look down to where we are joined and watch myself destroying her. Her grip on me is so tight that I can't hang on any longer. I feel my balls clench up close to my body and I growl out my own release just a moment later.

We are both completely out of breath.

I continue to slowly slide in and out of her until I feel her release me. I watch her remove her knuckle from her mouth and see that she has bitten right through her own skin.

I smile down at her, at what I have done to her. She looks up in the mirror and smiles back at me before standing up completely, letting me fall from her entrance.

I reach my hands around and grab her tits tight as I pepper her neck with kisses,

"I could fuck you all day and never be completely satisfied. Every single time I am inside you I get taken higher than before." She smiles as she wraps her hands around my own, squeezing her tits harder.

She leans back into me, "We should go downstairs."

I groan into her neck again, "Fine."

She laughs as she pulls away from me then throws me a towel from the hamper to clean up with. Moments later I am watching her put on a string bikini that shows nearly everything.

I step up behind her after changing into my own trunks, "Uh. No."

She smiles into the mirror then turns around to face me, "No What?"

I point a finger at her from her head to her feet, "No."

She smiles back at me and slaps my chest, "Okay. Don't be that guy."

I smile at her and put my mouth to her ear, "Edge and Matthew are going to want to fuck you when they see you like this. Shit, Mona and Simone might want to as well."

She smiles into the mirror, "Then it looks like you might need to step up your game to keep me around. All those offers getting thrown my way might be too much to resist."

I turn her around quickly and slam my lips into hers. I reach down and grab her ass tight as I pull my lips from hers then growl into her lips,

"This is MINE. No one else gets to go anywhere near it. You hear me?"

Her eyes blow wide as she stares into mine. She nods her head slightly. I grip her ass even tighter,

"Say it."

Her voice sounds small,

"It's yours. No one else's. Only you."

I smile as I kiss her roughly again, not even understanding myself where this possession fixation is coming from. I just know that if anyone, and I don't give a fuck who, tries to touch her I will fucking kill them.

I feel her hands come up to my face and I pull back slightly. She looks a bit concerned,

"Gideon. I was joking. I don't want anyone else. I don't care who offers what. I only want you."

I give her a small smile,

"I just wanted to make sure we were on the same page."

She smiles as she grabs my hand and leads me out of the bedroom and down the stairs.

I was right, everyone is staring at her like they want to fuck her. But the best part is that she only has eyes for absolutely no one but me.

She swims in the pool for a bit then as the night starts to stretch on she finds me leaned back in a chair and she sits in my lap. We just enjoy each other's company while watching everyone else get shit faced and splash in the pool.

I am completely fine with this being the new normal.

The next morning we putter around the house. Everyone else sleeps in but Lily and I spend the morning wrapped up in each other. I moved the sketchbooks back into the room with the boxes while she took a shower. I picked up the framed photo of her and who I assume is her family. I was definitely right, the girl in the drawing is definitely the girl in this photo. I glance into the box that I pulled the framed memory from last night but there isn't anything else laying in there besides a few books. I wish she would tell me what is going on. But I won't push. I will let her come to me in her own time. I put the picture back in the box, then close the door as I step out into the hall.

Edge is rounding the stairs, rubbing his eyes and yawning, "Dude. I am never going shot for shot with your woman again. I think I am dying."

I laugh back at him, seeing him drag his feet down the hallway. He is clad in only sweatpants and hair going in every fucking direction. I laugh at him as he heads to the stairs, "My girl knows how to hold her liquor. What can I say?"

Edge rolls his neck across his shoulders, letting the cracks be heard down the hall, "Seriously. Is there coffee, do you know?"

I smile and step up with him, "Follow me."

10 minutes later we are sitting on the back porch. Edge with a large cup of coffee, me with a water bottle. I stare out over the ocean when I hear Edge give a heavy sigh, "This place is fucking beautiful. We don't have anything like this back home. I could honestly live here forever."

I smile back at him while I take a drink of water and watch the waves crash into the shore. There are a few families spread out down the beach but it seems that her little slice of paradise really is a closed beach. All for us.

Hearing the door close behind us I look up over my shoulder and see Lily smiling back. She puts her hands on my shoulders and smiles out over the water, "Susie is going to be here in a few hours."

Edge instantly sits up, somehow completely awake now. My eyes narrow at him, knowing exactly where his mind is at, "Down boy."

Edge flips me off then turns back to Lily, "Susie is coming here? Is she staying or is she just stopping by for a visit?"

I turn my gaze up to Lily, smiling her maniacal grin at Edge. She lets her fingers dance across the muscles in my shoulders, "She is staying for the rest of the week actually. She will probably head home in a few days when we leave for Savannah."

Edge is now smiling from ear to ear. Seemingly completely awake with no sign of a hangover to be found. I fucking knew he would have a thing for her. Lily continues to drum her fingers on my shoulders, "You two might have a little fight on your hands actually." She is still smiling at Edge as his face turns questionable.

He looks to me then back at Lily, "Why?" She runs her hands flat down my chest as she leans over putting her chin on my shoulder before turning slyly back towards Edge, "You'll see. I don't want to ruin the fun of it."

Edge's eyes light up with a scary dose of intrigue mixed with thirst. I smile at him then turn back towards the ocean, "Fucking called it!"

Lily is giggling into my neck as Edge turns to me, "Called what?" I smile back over at him, "That you would have a thing for Susie. I thought it the first fucking moment I met her."

Edge smiles back at us before leaning back in his chair, taking a large drink of coffee. He glances at Lily a few times like he wants to ask something. Or maybe he is just fishing for information.

Lily steps around me and then sits gently down on my lap, wrapping her arms around my neck. She looks at Edge with a devious smile, "She is not seeing anyone ya know. She has a few situationships going on but nothing serious."

Edge smiles and sits up in his seat. He gives me a wink then looks back to Lily, "I can work with that." I let out a loud laugh, this is going to be an interesting 48 hours.

17
Lily
Fuck Me Like You Hate Me - Jutes

Hands down my new favorite comedy is watching Edge freak out over a woman. And not just any woman but Susie. He has been pacing around the living room for the last hour. I am pretty sure at some point he has sat in every single seat in the room, but only for a measly few seconds at a time then he is back up to pacing about the room.

I smile as I lean into Gideon's ear and whisper, "Ten bucks says he clams up when she gets here." Gideon smiles as he watches Edge pace the room, looking out the window then trying to calmly pace back towards the kitchen. "I will take that bet. I have seen this man in action before. He may look like he will hesitate but I promise you, he won't."

I look up into Gideon's face then follow his gaze towards Edge. I smile as I let a plan to win unfold in my brain. I saunter into the living room with a devious smile on my face and turn towards Matthew, "So Matthew I have to ask. Are you seeing anyone?"

I hear Gideon settle into a chair behind me while Edge continues to look out the window to the front yard. Matthew looks up at me, hesitantly, "I have been seeing someone off and on. Nothing serious though. Why?"

I glance quickly towards Edge then back down at Matthew, "My friend Susie. You remember her right? She has the biggest fucking crush on you."

I see Edge stop pacing and go stone still. Matthew glances over at him with a small side smile, catching onto what I am doing, "Really? The redhead right? She is pretty fucking hot. Not gonna lie. And she has a thing for me? That is *interesting*."

The smile he gives me if fucking hilarious. He knows we are just fucking with Edge but apparently Edge is not catching on. He storms across the room and leans down into Matthew's face, "I called fucking dibs dude. Not fucking cool."

Matthew and I both burst out laughing. Gideon steps up behind me and wraps his arms around me, "Why are you starting shit? Edge, she is fucking with you. Both of them."

I shake my head, "Nope, she told me with her own two lips that she and I quote 'thinks Apollo is fucking hot.'"

Edge growls at me then looks back down to Matthew, poking his finger into his chest, "I will fucking end you." Matthew starts laughing even harder at the frazzled Edge.

I look up just in time to see Susie standing in the doorway, confused about the altercation unfolding in front of her. She smiles and looks up towards me, "Did I miss something?"

I see Edge's face turn slowly towards Susie. His expression instantly changes to something darker. I watch him scan her from head to toe, taking in her tight shorts and tank top. She has her hair up in a ponytail showcasing her neck and profile. No makeup on and those neon green eyes ablaze for the world to see.

Gideon leans into my ear, "I understand why she said she thought he was going to murder her. I have never seen that look

216

on his face before." I snicker back at him, watching the moment unfold in front of me.

Edge steps up to her, "Hello. I am Edge. Er, Dionysus. Do you need help with your bags or anything?"

I hear a slight purr come from the back of Susie's throat. Knowing it is because of the accent. Edge seems to notice it too as his eyes narrow a bit to stare at her harder. Susie smiles back at him widely, "No, thank you. I am good." She turns to me with her eyebrows raised, "I am going to go put these in my room."

I laugh and step forward a bit, "Well, you are going to have to pick a different room this time."

Susie scrunches up her eyebrows at me. I can feel Matthew and Gideon staring at me as I smile and look towards Edge, "Edge has claimed your normal room. But the one across the hall from him is open. That is actually the only one put together right now. If you guys don't mind sharing the one bathroom up there."

Edge looks at me wide eyed then back to Susie, "We can switch rooms. I didn't know it was your normal room. I have no problem moving my stuff."

Susie smiles from me to Edge then leans over and puts her hand on his bicep. I see Edge instantly flex his arms like he is trying not to reach out and grab her back. Susie grins wider, noticing his reaction herself, "No, that is fine Edge. You can stay in that room. I will just go across the hall. Thank you for offering though."

Matthew lets out a chuckle as he stands up and turns to face Susie, "Hello again Susie. It is nice to actually get to meet you this time. I am Matthew, or Apollo. But please Jesus god, just call me Matthew here."

Susie lowers her arm from Edge and smiles back at Matthew, fawning over him more than she normally would, "It is

217

SO nice to meet you formally Matthew. I know we all saw each other at the brownstone but I am really glad that I get to really meet everyone. We are gonna have some fun." She bats her eyelashes at him and we all hear a growl come from Edge as he steps around her then heads up the stairs.

Susie looks at me smiling, "This is gonna be fucking fun." She turns her gaze back to Matthew, "Do you mind if I use you as a pawn in my schemes?"

Matthew laughs out loud looking from Gideon then back to Susie, "As long as he doesn't kill me. Let the games begin."

Susie lets out a cackle as I walk over and grab her carry on, "Come on. Let's go get you settled in." Susie laughs louder and picks up her suitcase as I lead the way up the stairs.

We round the top of the stairs and see that Edge's bedroom door is cracked, but there is no noise coming from inside. Susie smiles over her shoulder at me then turns back towards her side of the hall, "So, are we gonna hit the beach today? It is fucking beautiful outside. And I brought my new swimsuit. Maybe see if everyone wants to join?"

I smile back at her, knowing exactly what she is up to. I know her type of bathing suits. There is very little left to the imagination. I glance at Edge's door then turn towards hers, "Yeah, that sounds like a plan. I hope you brought extra sunblock though."

Susie opens the door to her room smiling, "Of course I did. Maybe Matthew will help me put some on." I let out a cackle as I hear a door slightly open behind me. I don't even have to turn around to know that Edge is listening in.

I sit her bag down on the bed. I open the top and then sit down beside it on the end of the bed. Susie doesn't even dare look out the still open door towards the hallway. She smiles as she opens her suitcase and pulls out a bikini. I was right, it is more like two pieces of thread. I smile again as I roll my eyes at her.

Susie has always been the more adventurous of the two of us. She was always the one pushing me on to find a man. Find a hookup. Find anything, anyone. Though she herself has kept herself from a relationship of any kind for years now. I mean I understand why, what she has been through isn't something that you can just easily move on from.

She doesn't even hesitate as she winks at me then pulls the tank top up over her head. She turns so her back is facing the still open door and she slides the top over her head and smiles towards me, "Will you tie me up?"

I let out a sigh and stand up but abruptly come to a halt. Edge walks into the room right up behind Susie. Her breath catches in her throat as he leans into her neck, "I will."

With wide eyes, I look between the two of them before slowly side stepping towards the bedroom door, "I am gonna go. I will let everyone know we are hitting the beach." The last thing I see is the crimson flushing up Susie's back as Edge starts to tie the back of her top.

I take off running down the stairs, giggling. Gideon is coming up the first flight headed to our bedroom as I try to stop from running head first into him. I end up sliding across the floor towards him in a fit of giggles as he laughs and catches me. He smiles down the hall and back towards me, "What in the hell are you doing?"

I grin wildly at him as I yell down the stairs, "Beach in 30 minutes, pass it along!" I grab his hand and drag him into the bedroom behind me and lock the door before turning on him.

He is laughing at me as he sits down on the end of the bed, "Are you okay?"

I laugh wildly at him as I start digging through the drawer for another bathing suit, "You are not going to believe what just happened." I slam the drawer shut and place the bathing suit on top of the dresser.

I turn to him then start walking towards him, my hands splayed out in front of me, "I was up in Susie's room with her. We knew Edge was in his room and could hear us so she says, 'Let's go to the beach. I brought sunscreen. Maybe Matthew will lather me up or some shit'. I hear Edge's door open. She takes her fucking shirt off! Her back was to the bedroom door but still. Then...THEN she slides her bathing suit top over her head and asks if I will tie her up."

I am breathing frantically trying to get it all out as Gideon stares at me wide eyed. I grin back at him, "I stand to help her and EDGE!! FUCKING EDGE walks in and says 'I'll do it'. I just about shit myself. She has fucking met her match with this one. It instantly got fucking awkward in there. I took off. I ran down the stairs barely not killing myself and slid into you. Oh My God."

Gideon is laughing out loud at me, "I knew he was going to like her. I fucking thought it the first time I met her. She rolled her fucking eyes up into her head an groaned because of my accent. They are fucking meant for eachother I swear."

I smile as I step up closer to him, "They are going to destroy each other. In a consensual way of course but still. I swear it felt like I was in the makings of a porn or something. I could not get out of there fast enough."

Gideon's eyes go dark as he steps up to me, wrapping his hand around my neck as I look up into his eyes, "Are you excited from watching them flirt?"

I smile back at him, "Uh no. Nervous yes, excited no."

He takes his hand and slides it down the center of my chest, smiling back at me again, "Do you think they are hotter than us?"

I nervously giggle at him, then look at the door. He puts his finger under my chin, pulling my gaze back to him. I give him a soft smile, "I mean, no. But I can see her being way more adventurous than me. She has always been a bit crazy."

Gideon leans down into my ear, whispering, "You would be crazy for me though wouldn't you? You will try anything, right?"

I pull back, looking into his eyes, "I mean, maybe. Yeah probably."

Gideon smiles back down at me and points to my clothes, "Take it all off. Now."

I look up into his dark eyes with shock, "We are supposed to meet everyone at the beach in like a half hour."

He turns his attention back to me fully, with a stern voice he leans down to be eye to eye with me, "I don't give a fuck if we are meeting them in 60 seconds. Take your fucking clothes off Lily. Don't make me do it myself."

I feel the chills run down my spine at his possessive authoritative rasp. I slowly start to peel my clothes off as he steps over towards the dresser and comes back holding a scarf. I finally step out of my underwear then unhook my bra then I turn to look at him. He licks his lips at me then turns me around to face away from him. I feel his breath on my ear, "Get on the bed, on all fours. Now."

I blink rapidly, he has never been this forceful with me before. I didn't ever think I would be turned on by something like this but I am so fucking wet I can feel myself on my inner thighs. I nod my head and do as I am told. I am completely naked, staring at the comforter in front of me. Gideon steps up behind me and rubs his hand across my ass. I turn to look at him as he slides a scarf over my eyes and ties it tight behind my head.

I am panting. This is new. This is not something I have ever done. With anyone. I hear him moving around the room behind me but I have no idea what he is doing. My hearing seems to be supersonic now that I can't see anything. I hear a drawer opening then closing. I hear movement behind me, then I swear I actually hear his clothes hitting the floor.

I am breathing heavily into the bed when I feel his hand on my ass again. He pulls my hips towards him a bit, lowering my body towards him. I hold my breath when I feel something slick roll across my ass. He must have found my lube in the night stand. He takes his hand and slides it down my fold. I try to look over my shoulder but can't see anything, not even a shadow.

He slowly presses his dick into my ass. I gasp at the shock of the intrusion. He gives me a moment to adjust to him and I lean back into him just a bit. Pulling him in deeper. I hear Gideon moan behind me and I smile beneath the blindfold.

I gasp again as I feel my little friend from the nightstand drawer start to vibrate against my clit. Oh shit. I feel myself tighten against him as he slides the toy across my clit then down to my opening. He puts his other hand on my shoulder as he pulls me back further onto his dick.

"Jesus fuck Gideon." I whisper into the bed. I am not going to last long if he keeps hitting me from both sides. I feel the pressure of the toy vibrating inside of me while he is taking me from the back. I have never felt so full in my life. I can hear myself whining into the bed.

He grunts again behind me, "Do you think they are hotter than us now?" He slams into me with the word now. I cry out into the room at the sensations running through my body.

I turn my head, "Fuck me harder baby. Please." He starts to thrust harder into me as he pushes the toy against my walls, letting me feel the vibrations all the way to my core.

222

I bring my hand up to myself and start rubbing fast circles around my vibrating clit. I scream into the bed as my face lowers to the blankets, "Gideon. I am going to cum. Don't fucking stop baby."

I hear him growl as he slams into me harder and starts sliding the toy in and out of my body at the same time. My walls instantly clench around the toy and his dick. He slams into me hard, "Fuck Lily. Fuck me." I slam myself back down onto him, spearing him deeper into me.

I hear him whimper behind me and I smile at the waves rippling through my body, pulsating around him. He slams into me again, "You're just a little whore for my cock aren't you baby? Tell me. Tell me what you are."

I smile again as I feel my walls clenching tighter, "I am a whore. I am a whore for you baby." It feels natural talking to him like this. I am a whore for him. I would do anything he asked me too, at any time. I feel him slamming into me harder at my admission. I smile over my shoulder again, "Cum in my ass baby. I wanna feel you fill me up. Please."

He screams his release when he hears me begging. I can feel him thicken and release inside of me. I cry out again as he pulls the toy out and presses it hard into my clit. I feel myself starting to tighten down on him harder as another orgasm rips through my body. He stays completely pushed into me to his base as he feels me pulsate around him. He reaches up and pulls my hair hard to make me arch my back more. I scream into the air around me as I feel the waves attacking my body.

Finally he releases his hold on me and removes the toy from my clit. He pumps into me a few more times before he pulls out of me and I crumble onto the bed in front of him. I feel him step up behind me and run a cloth over my ass, cleaning me up before he reaches up and takes the blindfold off.

I smile towards him, still unable to open my eyes. He crawls up on the bed behind me and pulls me close to him. I smile into the room around us, "That was fucking amazing baby." I hear him chuckle then let out heavy breath, "I told you we were fucking hotter than them."

I snicker out a laugh as I nuzzle myself deeper into his arms. I don't give a fuck if they are waiting on us downstairs. They can just fucking wait for all I care. I could honestly lay here for the rest of the day, completely fucking spent but instead I hear someone rapping their knuckles on the bedroom door. "Gideon, get off Lily so we can go down to the beach now please!" Susie laughs loudly as she steps away from the door, then charges down the stairs.

I laugh into the room around us as I feel Gideon's chest rising from laughter as well. I roll onto my stomach, still laughing as Gideon gets up off the bed and puts his hand out to me. Palm up. I smile as I rise as well and put my bathing suit on.

I pull a cover-up on then we head downstairs. Everyone is already down at the beach. I smile as I lay out a towel and sit down on it, watching everyone conversing and having a good time. Gideon sits down behind me and pulls me back into his chest. I smile towards the water as he wraps his arms around me and starts rubbing his hands up and down my arms. He is in the middle of some conversation with Matthew as I just sit back and look at my life developing in front of me.

These people are the closest to me that anyone has ever been, besides Mark. Mark would be happy that I am happy. Truly happy. Susie is shin deep out in the water, smiling back at me waving wide. Gideon is holding me close to him like I am the most precious possession he has ever owned. And he does. He completely owns me and I am fine with that.

I tap Gideon on the arms then sit forward. I smile as I stand up and pull the cover up off then run out into the water with Susie. We laugh and joke and splash each other with water. At one point, I turn and look towards the beach. Matthew and Gideon are still talking but Gideon's eyes and smile do not leave me the entire time. I smile back and blow him a kiss before turning back to Susie.

She leans in, "So, you sounded well taken care of earlier." I laugh out loud at her as I splash her with more water. Edge is standing nearby and starts chuckling. I look at him then back at Susie, "It is 100% both of your faults."

Edge turns towards me with a look of astonishment on his face, "How the fuck is it our fault?"

I place my hands on my hips and direct my glare at him, "If you hadn't walked in offering to tie her up then I wouldn't have barrelled down the stairs like a mad woman, ranting about how shit was getting hot and heavy up there!"

Edge laughs and steps up closer to us, "That doesn't explain how that lead to you getting laid."

I blush and look back at Susie then down at the water, "He had to prove to me that we are hotter than you guys."

Susie barks out a loud laugh and Edge leans forward, "I am sorry but what?"

I smile up into his eyes then look back towards Gideon, "Don't worry. He made his point. We are definitely hotter."

Edge steps up to Susie and puts his hands on her waist and her eyes drop as she stills, not even laughing. He leans his mouth towards her ear as her eyes lock onto mine, "Sounds like shots have been fired, love. We should probably try to catch up soon."

I put my hands up and quickly leave the water running back to Gideon's arms. I hear Matthew talking about someone loving some idea before he goes silent and I lean back down into

225

Gideon. I smile at the complete shock and awe written all over Susie's face as Edge continues to whisper in her ear. Yeah, shots definitely fired.

18
Aphrodite
Leave a Light On - Tom Walker

The next morning, I am sitting out on the back deck watching the small morning waves as they crash into the sand. I can see a few people out with body boards, enjoying the day and the surf already. I smile when I hear the back door open and Susie sits in a chair next to me. We continue to sit in comfortable silence for a few minutes at least. Finally, I can stand the suspense any longer as I turn to her, "So, how are things going with Edge?"

Susie gives me a quick sarcastic side eye then turns back towards the expanse of water before us, "There is nothing going on there. You know this."

I sit up quickly. I look at her with the underlying sadness that only she and I would understand. No one knows her real story but me. No one knows what she struggles with inside every fucking day. I let out a sympathetic breath, "Susie, it has been over 4 years. Are you still not ready to try again?"

I watch her give me a sad smile as she shakes her head no at me. She lets out an exhausted and hesitant sigh then continues to stare over the rim of her mug while she sips her coffee. I continue to give her a sympathetic smile but lean back into my chair as well. Still watching her closely though, just to make sure there are no real cracks in her armor.

As if she can still sense my stare at her, she sits forward quickly, "I want to put myself out there. I want to finally move on from this hell I have been living in but how? How do I do that? No amount of therapy has gotten me any closer. I have smashed every rage room in a 50 mile radius. I have screamed to the depths of hell and cursed the heavens. Nothing seems to work."

I lean forward with her, placing my cup on the floor before moving over in between her knees to look up at her, "I know that you want to move on. You deserve somebody that will treat you the way you deserve to be treated. Fuck when you were with Evan, before he lost his fucking mind, the wettest he ever made you was when you would cry. You deserve some fucking passion in your life Susie. Just tell Edge, everything."

She shakes her head at me firmly, while giving me a small chuckle. I squeeze her knees, forcing her stare back up into my eyes, "I know you are afraid. I know that you think he is going to pity you. But that is not what is going to happen. If he really respects you, he will understand. And if he is really interested, the past won't matter. I have learned that more than anyone.

"Look at me and Gideon. Sure, he still doesn't know everything but he has been so supportive. So loving. I don't want you to miss out on that because you are afraid of the possibility of it going a different way. You are always telling me that I have to try. I have to live my life. Now it's your turn Susanna."

I smile at her as she chuckles at me. I know it is because I am using my "mom" tone but I don't care. She lets out a heavy breath, "Okay. I will talk to him."

Grinning back at her, "Good. Pull him to the side at some point today and just explain your hesitations. I have a good feeling about him, Susie. I really think you two could be amazing."

I smile down at her again as I stand and grab my empty coffee mug. I am still smiling with a hopefulness as I open the back door and step into the kitchen. I move to the sink, sitting my mug down as I look into the sitting room. Edge and Matthew are sitting there. Edge looks lost. Like he doesn't even want to be in this house any longer.

I see Susie out of the corner of my eye. She slowly moves towards the sitting room after sitting her mug down on the island. I look towards the stairs and I see Gideon and Simone standing there glancing towards the couch as well. I watch intently as Susie tries to rally all of her nerves as she steps up to Edge and asks if they can talk.

I watch her shoulders fall when he tells her that he is busy. I see her look all around the room in embarrassment. She turns to me and I can instantly see the pain in her eyes. I feel my own heart break. She finally fucking tried and gets shut down immediately. It is all my fault too. I should have never pushed her that far.

She raises her arms out around her as she shrugs her shoulders, "I tried. This is why I don't bother." She turns and looks back down at Edge, who still isn't meeting her eyes. She turns back to me and I see a tear roll down her cheek. I feel the sadness rolling across my own face as I try to not cry for her. She shakes her head at me, "This was a bad idea. It was too much. I am gonna go. I am, I am just gonna go home. I can't be here anymore."

I watch her turn and round the corner to run up the stairs. I look at Edge, seeing him just as sad as she had been. But he had the chance to bring happiness to both of them. Why didn't he do that? Why wouldn't he just give her a few minutes to try to explain some things? I move to ask him those very questions when he and Matthew stand up then move towards the dining room.

229

10 seconds later I hear the soft strum of the guitar. A moment later I can hear the kick pedal hitting the base drum a few times as well. They are going to rehearse apparently. I let out a heavy sigh, deciding to just finish up the few dishes then go find Susie.

As soon as I grab her empty mug, I hear someone running down the stairs. I sit the mug down and hurry quickly over to the bottom of the stairs where Gideon is standing. A flash of red rounds the corner and then I see Susie right up in Edge's face.

I feel my breath still in my chest when she just starts screaming at him, "Fuck You! Yeah, you heard me right Fuck You! Everyone has issues. Everyone has a past. You won't even give me the decency of taking 5 minutes out of your day to listen to me. So Fuck You!"

I watch her as she swipes the angry tears from her face. I can see her neck is completely crimson at this point. I just want to run up to her and hug her. She glances around quickly then turns back on Edge, "I am sorry that your precious little ego got hurt because I didn't have sex with you. I am sorry that you feel like less of a fucking man because I walked away. But you don't even care to find out why. Why I am hesitant to begin with.

"Which just solidifies to me that this, whatever this is that you have been playing at the last day was just a ploy to get me into bed then move the fuck on. Which is fine if that is what you normally do. But that is not me. I am done with being used and tossed aside. I am done with assholes like you thinking I am nothing more than a fucking cunt to stick your dick in then leave in the fucking gutter. So Fuck You Edge. Do not for ONE second think that I ever want to fucking speak to you again!"

I watch Susie as she turns and stomps away from him. I watch her as she begins to crumble walking up the stairs. I turn my glare back to Edge, "You are a real piece of shit Edge!"

I round the bottom of the stairs and run up after Susie. When I find her she is sitting in the middle of the room on the floor. Her legs are tucked up neatly beneath her, her hands covering her face as she sobs. I watch her shoulders shudder and I run to her. Embracing her close to my body as she whispers, "I want to go home."

I am still holding her close to my chest when I hear someone step up behind us. I turn my eyes, "Get the fuck out Edge."

He glares back down at me as he shakes his head, pointing at Susie, "No. She doesn't get to just scream at me and make me feel like shit then just walk away. That is not fucking fair and you know it." I know he has a point but I am just trying to hold all of her pieces together. I will never forgive myself if I don't help hold her together like she has me.

I pull away as I feel her start to stand. I quickly move up with her, watching her like a hawk the entire time. She glares at Edge, "Fine. Say what you want to say so I can fucking leave."

I can feel Edge staring at me so I turn to meet his eyes, "Can we have a minute please?"

I instantly turn back to Susie. I watch her eyes close as she gives me a short nod, letting me know it is okay. I turn my eyes back to Edge, letting a growl out along with my words, "I will be on the stairs. I swear to god Edge if you hurt her anymore I will fucking end you."

I step outside the door, slowly shutting it behind me. I move to the steps where I sit down quickly, staring at the walls around me. I swear to christ if he makes this worse for her....Gideon might leave me because I will fucking destroy this man. I sit here long enough that my ass goes to sleep before Susie sits down beside me.

I turn to her quickly, "Are you okay?"

231

She smiles as she nods at me, "Yeah. I am okay. We are okay. I just lost my fucking temper. Again. We both know that is my go to emotion. We had a really good talk though. I think we both understand each other a lot more."

I nod my head at her as I reach over and take her hand in mine. She lets a low smile come over her face as she turns to me, "I told him. I told him everything. And he still wants to try to make something work with me."

I feel a wide grin cover my face. I knew he wasn't the asshole he had been playing at. I squeeze her hand tightly as I let out an exhausted sigh, "Thank god. I didn't know how many pieces I was going to have to cut his body into so I could carry his remains out by myself."

Susie laughs as she leans into my shoulder and rests there. We both sit there for a few more minutes before I decide I need to start getting shit ready for us to leave in the morning. Then I have an extremely large dinner to prepare. I move to head down the stairs as Edge walks up behind Susie, smiling down at her. I grin back up at him as I stand then turn to move down the stairs, "You are lucky Edge. You have no idea how close to death you just came." I hear him still chuckling at me as I round the corner at the bottom of the stairs.

I have so much shit to pack. We are leaving tomorrow and I haven't even really begun to start packing anything yet. We have already decided to come back here after the concert in Savannah but I hate leaving the house sitting like it is lived in while no one was here.

I am the type to check every locked door twice and the oven 3 times, just in case. We aren't even leaving until tomorrow and I have already reminded everybody a dozen times about what not to forget.

I am excited for tonight though because I am cooking for everyone. I love cooking. I suck at baking but I fucking love Italian food.

I swear I am not in the mafia.

The real problem though is what to make. I have too many options. I end up deciding on Carbonara and Gnocchi. Cause who can decide on just one?

Mona and I have become kitchen buddies over the last few days. It is nice meeting new people. People that don't judge. That is a new and refreshing experience for me. Even after they all saw the sketchbook, no one judged me, or even asked me about it.

It is taking for fucking ever to make the Gnocchi but I know it is going to be destroyed as soon as it is finished.

"So, where did you learn to cook?"

Mona is sitting on the counter, stuffing bread in her face as I roll out the Gnocchi one by one on the little wooden board in front of me.

I smile and turn to answer when we hear Edge from the sitting room,

"They teach it to all the molls in the underground!"

I laugh out loud and turn around to flip him off,

"Fuck off Edge!"

He laughs to himself and goes back to staring at a sleeping Susie curled up on the couch.

I turn back to Mona,

"I actually learned how to cook when I was in the orphanage. I am not saying I was a handful *but* I got bored easily. They were always finding something for me to do."

Mona nods and smiles back at me,

"How long were you there?"

I give her a quick side eye but know it is just natural curiosity,

233

"I went there when I was 6. I stayed till I was 18 then I moved in with Susie. We got an apartment together in Brooklyn and I lived there all through college. Until I moved in with Mark."

Mona nods her head and smiles at Simone as she hoists herself up on the island, "Need any help Lil?"

I smile but shake my head no.

It is really fucking wild that out of all the people to come up with a nickname for me it is my boyfriends ex hook up.

I am certifiable.

"I don't have that much more left then I will get everything cooking."

Simone smiles back at Mona, "What are we talking about?"

Mona winks at me quickly, "Lily's dead husband."

Simone's jaw drops. I laugh out loud ruining the Gnocchi I am currently trying to roll. Susie strolls around the edge of the island, yawning and stretching her arms out to her sides. She jumps up on the counter, claiming the spot beside Simone, "We are talking about Mark?"

I let out an exasperated laugh, "Mona asked me how long I lived at the orphanage. I told her until I moved in with you then left there to move in with Mark."

Simone laughs as she throws a piece of ripped bread at Mona,

"Bitch."

Mona laughs, throwing it back,

"Whore."

I laugh at them both and go back to preparing dinner.

Simone crosses her legs in front of her,

"What was Mark like?"

Susie lets out a chuckle, "Mark was....Mark. He was really prim and proper. But he was a good man. He treated Lily like a fucking queen. He couldn't stand us when we were together, because we were normally getting up to no good but all in all, he was just a good guy to have on your side."

I stand up, smiling and roll my shoulders, trying to loosen up the taut muscles from being bent over the counter for the last hour,

"She is right. Mark was great. Kinda reserved. He was a corporate lawyer so he was all suits and ties and let's play chess. But most of the time he was just a normal guy."

Mona smiles at me,

"What happened to him? If it's okay that I ask."

Susie's eyes go wide then she looks at me with a questioning gaze, probably wondering how I am going to handle myself talking about it all.

I smile at her then Simone,

"No, it's fine. I don't mind. He got really dizzy one day. We thought maybe it was his blood sugar or something. But then a few hours later he was having trouble remembering things.

"Things he would normally know by heart. Like his birthday, our address, stuff like that. I took him to the ER thinking he was having a stroke or something. That was when they found the tumor."

Mona frowns to Simone, "That is just fucking tragic."

I hear Simone groan her agreement.

I look at Susie who is now stuffing a piece of bread into her mouth as well with her legs criss crossed underneath her. I let out another sigh,

"It was. But they were able to put him on a medication that helped to slow the progression of the spread. A lot of days he was fine. He remembered everything. But as it went on, the medicine could only do so much. And an operation was impossible. We kinda knew long before it happened that it was inevitable."

Simone jumps down off the island and gives me a hug from behind,

"I am so sorry you had to go through that."

I smile over at Mona then Susie,

"Thank you Simone. But I am good. Really. I mean I loved him, he was my best friend but I had a lot of time to mentally prepare myself for it."

I feel Simone pull back, "Please tell me if I am overstepping but Gideon had said something about how you loved Mark but you were never in love. What did that mean?"

Susie starts choking on her bread, eyes wide. She puts a hand up to signal she is fine then grabs a glass of water from the tap and starts to chug it down.

I turn around and look at Simone in shock. Surprised that she has talked to Gideon about something so intimate in my life.

I feel a small chill run down my spine but try to keep myself composed. I had never told Gideon not to say anything so that is on me. I just didn't think he would just throw my business out there like that.

I trip over my own thoughts for a minute,

"I ah. Well, it is complicated. I wanted to be married. I wanted to be secure in my life. That was something I had never really had before. And I knew Mark was a good man, he was a great friend so I just kinda went for it."

I wipe my hands off and turn around to face them all,

"I know it sounds harsh. And selfish even. But he loved me. And I cared for him. I hated to ruin what could be a good thing when who knew what that future held. I could have fallen in love with him. In time. We just never really got to have that time."

Simone nods at me then to Mona,

"No, I get it. It's not selfish at all. At least I don't think it is. It was smart. You had to take care of yourself. And it sounds like the life you had before him made you aware of the possibilities of what life could be like without that security. I don't blame you one damn bit. I would have done the same thing."

Susie smiles at Simone then towards me, "I love this girl. Seriously. LOVE. I have been screaming the same thing to her for forever now."

I stand there completely shell shocked that she is able to read the situation like I always have, like Susie always has. I always apologize profusely anytime the subject is breached.

I blink repeatedly before finally breathing out,

"Thank you. I have literally never had anyone other than Susie tell me that before. I just always assumed I was seen as the asshole."

Simone waves her hand at me, "Bitch no. You are smart. Don't let anyone tell you any different Lil."

I smile back at her as Mona leans forward on the counter a bit, "Soooo that being said. You love Gideon?"

I feel my face turn immediately beet red. If Susie had some popcorn, she would be settling in for the long haul. Her favorite movie is me embarrassed.

I look at Simone and she is smiling with her hands up,

"Don't look at me. We just had some fun a time or two. I never saw him as anything more than a dick."

I laugh out loud at her. She winks at me,

"A good time but nothing more. I swear."

Susie leans forward with her hand raised like she is back in Math class, "I too have seen his dick. I would like to add that it looks rather nice. Pretty cute ass too."

Simone turns wide eyed to Susie, "I am sorry ma'am but what??"

Susie starts chuckling then scoots in closer, checking over her shoulder to make sure the guys are still in the other room, "So the night that they got back together, she thought he was still passed out from their escapades upstairs so she was down here with me on facetime.

"She had her phone propped up in the window over there and was looking at her feet or something. Then in walks Well Hung McGee behind her. Completely fucking naked. Just smiling and waving at me. She lost her shit. I have never seen her so red. It was amazing."

We are all laughing now, me more nervously than everyone else. Gideon would probably lose his shit if he heard us talking about him like this. Or maybe, maybe he would like it.

I look around the room quickly making sure no one can hear us. I decide it is time to get a little more detail from his former fling. See if maybe it is just me or if he is like this with all the ladies. There is nothing wrong with general curiosity right?

"Right? I mean, tell me if this is too much but did he ever just become flat out primal with you? Like full ownership of your pussy?"

Mona slides down off the counter and moves in closer so we were all now in a tight football huddle in the center of my kitchen.

Simone's eyes go wild,
"I am sorry what?"
I laugh again,
"Okay, so I guess that is just with me."

Mona looks between us quickly,

Susie leans in closer, "I need examples. Now."

I smile, lowering my voice a bit so no one in the next room can hear me,

"There are times that he just grabs me. He tells me that I am his. Only his. He makes me repeat him. He just grips my ass or my pussy and growls it out. Then there is the begging. I mean fuck me. Right?"

Simone grabs my shoulders and starts shaking me,

"Did you just fucking say begging?"

I laugh looking around again, still not believing I am having this conversation,

"Yes. He well, he begged me to let him cum. He literally said please baby let me cum. I fucking lost my shit when he said it. His voice was all deep and raspy like when he sings. I felt like my pussy was gonna break his dick off. I locked down so hard on him. I swear I have never cum so hard in my life."

I look between them all, staring them all in the eye one by one,

"He is just a completely different person when that door closes. I never know which Gideon I am going to get. One minute he is slamming me into a wall or slapping my ass hard enough to leave a mark. Then the next he is telling me he can't cum until I do, then just just begs for me to cum.

"Just so he could feel it before he loses his load. I just, I mean obviously I have been with other men before but god damn. I have never been with someone that looks at me like he wants to devour my soul straight through my pussy. It's fucking intense sometimes."

I look over to Mona who is now fanning herself,

"Well fuck. Had I known that I would have tried to swing on that pole before it got locked down. God Damn!"

239

Simone laughs out loud slapping Mona in the arm, "You like girls dumb ass!"

Mona laughs back then winks at Susie, "I will try anything once. Sometimes twice."

I laugh along with Simone and Susie as Mona continues to fan herself with her hand. That is when we hear a voice from the other side of the island, "We having fun ladies?".

We all go stone faced and turn to see Gideon and Edge standing there.

I purse my lips together hard and try not to make eye contact with anyone. Simone is slapping me in the thigh trying not to lose her shit. Susie starts giggling uncontrollably and runs around the island and face plants into the couch. Edge watches her smiling the whole way before turning back around to us. Mona, god love her, steps up to Gideon with a smile on her face,

"I have to go change my panties....Daddy."

She just casually walks away from the conversation as Simone and I burst out laughing. Edge smiled back at us,

"What are you vixens in here going on about?"

I laugh at Simone, "Nothing. Nothing. We are just making dinner."

Gideon looks around us towards the stove,

"Is that Gnocchi? God Damn I love Gnocchi. Please babe you have to let me have first dibs."

Simone and I both collapse into each other laughing so hard that we are unable to breath for a few minutes. His begging has now officially broken us all. Susie is clapping her hands loudly from the couch while cackling. Edge just looks between me and her before walking over the couch and leaning over the back talking to Susie about something. I quickly turn around to finish dinner before Gideon can say anything else.

I do not like the stares I am getting at as we sit here eating dinner. The boys have something up their sleeves. I can tell.

Edge won't stop staring at Susie then Matthew and Gideon are being super nice to me.

I don't trust it.

After we have all destroyed dinner we decide a bonfire on the beach is the best idea. I grab a few bottles of Dalmore and lead everyone down to the burn pit at the bottom of the stairs. Edge gets the fire going as we all set in and get comfortable with our drinks.

Mona moans into her glass,

"I swear on God I have never had whisky this good before. I don't think I can drink Jack ever again."

I smile at her, "Thank you. It's my favorite. I always have stock of it. I obviously can drink it like water."

I smile as I take another drink. Susie is sitting on the ground in front of Edge with his legs on either side of her, just smiling into the crackling fire. Edge leans forward in his seat,

"How much would a bottle of this set me back? I may have to buy some while we are on hiatus."

I smile over at him then back to Gideon sitting behind me,

"I uh. I don't think you want to know. Plus, this particular age isn't something you can find just anywhere. You have to order it."

Edge waives his hand at me,

"Just fucking humor me daddy warbucks. How much?"

Susie lets out a deep laugh, "You all are in for the shit now. You might be asking questions you really don't want answers to."

I take a sip of mine then smile over the brim of my glass,

"Right around $10,000."

241

Gideon leans forward almost throwing me onto the ground in front of him,

"I am fucking sorry but what?"

I smile back at him, "$10,000."

His eyes fan to everyone around the fire then back to me,

"A bottle? We have drank like 5 bottles this week alone!"

I nod back at him,

"Yeah, I know. I have already ordered more. For when we get back."

Matthew leans forward shaking his head at everyone in shock then focuses back on me,

"How in the actual fuck do you have that kind of alcohol budget?"

Susie lets out another deep laugh then turns her glare to me, "They truly have no idea do they?" I shake my head at her while giving her the evil eye.

I look around the people in front of me. They all are wealthy from their music but I know it isn't even close to what I have. I have never brought it up because it doesn't matter to me.

But I trust these people. They have all become my friends over the past week.

I sigh loudly,

"Mark had a sizable life insurance policy. We had a nest egg in savings. And the brownstone sold last week. I am more than taken care of. I can promise you that."

Simone leans forward,

"Damn. I really liked the brownstone."

I smile at her,

"It just wasn't home anymore. I put it on the market right after I left New York."

I feel Gideon lean into my ear,

"Because of me?"

I turn and look at him,

"No babe. Because of me. I needed a change. I would have done it regardless of us."

Mona being Mona and giving zero fucks leans forward in her chair, "Just out of natural curiosity. How much did the brownstone sell for?"

I look out again at the eyes staring back at me. Oh someone is gonna lose their shit, probably Edge. I grin back at the faces before me, "After commission I got a little over 12 for it."

Mona spits her whisky back into her glass and Edge starts laughing like a hyena,

"I am sorry bitch did you just say 12 like 12 million?"

I smiled back again, laughing at Edge as well, "Yeah, just a touch over 12 million."

Matthew is shaking his head at me now, "God Damn Lily. I don't want to know your net worth, do I?"

I laugh out loud at him, "No, probably not."

Susie pulls out her phone and types something in then holds it over her shoulder at Edge. His eyes fly wide as he grabs the phone from her and shows it to Matthew, who in turn chokes on his whisky. Susie winks at me and I know she has just guesstimated my net worth and showed them, but even she doesn't know about everything so it is probably a low ball guess.

Gideon nods his head at me, then kisses me behind my ear. I nuzzle back into him when I hear Edge again,

"So you are like....rich rich then?"

I burst out another laugh.

"Yes, Edge. I guess you could say I am rich rich."

Edge sits back in his chair then holds his now empty glass up to Gideon,

"At least you know she isn't in it for the money, am I right?"

I let out a laugh and look at Mona as she says,

"No, she is in it for that dick."

Gideon's grip tightens around me as I start laughing loudly. Loud enough that I snort, making everyone else laugh even harder at me.

Gideon leans forward and looks at me again,

"Have you girls been talking about my dick?"

I laugh again then take another large drink, trying to hide my face with the glass.

"I mean. Yeah. Why wouldn't we?"

Simone busts out laughing and Edge looks like he wants to become the chair he is seated so far back into it. Susie is grinning to herself and staring across the fire. I look over my shoulder to see Gideon shaking his head but chuckling.

Matthew sits forward in his seat,

"As much as I would love to talk about Gideon's dick all night I have another topic I want to approach."

Susie lets out another chuckle, "Are you sure? It's a pretty nice dick. Just saying."

Gideon sits forward a bit, readjusting me in his lap so he can see me better. He makes a face at Susie as he settles me back into his lap. I shift my eyes between them, oh god.

Plans have changed.

I can't go with them.

My heart immediately deflates. I try to hold back the sadness in my voice,

"Okay? What's up?"

Gideon leans forward, "Matthew and I have been talking. We want to throw something by you."

I look around nervously again. Susie is looking up at Edge but he seems clueless. Simone and Mona seem to have no idea what is coming either. I turn more towards Gideon,

"What's wrong? What has happened?"

244

He squeezes my knee smiling at me, "Nothing like that babe. Nothing is wrong. We just want to ask you if you are down for something."

My eyes blow wide and I look between Gideon and Matthew. Edge busts out laughing as Simone and Mona gasp. Susie is now up on her knees looking between me and Matthew, screaming at the top of her lungs, "Yes! Her answer is yes!!!"

I look back to Gideon and he looks shell shocked as well,

"Not fucking that. We aren't asking your for a fucking threesome right here in front of everyone. Jesus God. You fucking females I swear!"

We all start laughing again. My side fucking burns from laughing so hard tonight.

I finally gain some composure back,

"What is it you are offering then? If threesomes are off the table."

Matthew chuckles, "We will put a pin in the threesome idea."

Gideon quickly replies, "No, we won't."

Matthew huffs then continues,

"We were wondering if you wanted to try something out. At the concert on Friday, would you want to possibly paint? Live. On stage? We were thinking that if you painted and we all signed it maybe it could be like a donateable item or even just something to give to a random fan?"

I sit here completely speechless. Susie is staring at me but shaking her head yes, vigorously.

I can not believe they want me to do something so profound. Also, I am scared shitless because how am I supposed to stand in front of thousands of people and paint?

I take another large drink of my whisky, almost finishing it entirely. I breathe in a deep breath then grab the bottle and drink straight from it.

245

I can feel Gideon's eyes on me.

I can feel his heart beat on my back, going a mile a minute.

I clear my throat and sit down the bottle,

"Well I mean. Maybe yeah. But the thing is oils take forever to dry. I don't think it is something we could just hand out after the show."

Matthew shakes his head, then sits back a bit defeated. I hear a small sigh come from Gideon as well.

They really want to do this. They really believe in my work that much.

I turn to Gideon,

"But charcoals and pastels. I can do that. It won't be as vivid but the statement would remain. Is there anything in particular you would want me to draw?"

Matthew has sat back up and is smiling from ear to ear,

"Whatever you wanted to. Whatever you felt in the moment. I think I can speak for everyone here, the shit you paint when we are rehearsing is fucking brilliant. Could you imagine what kind of hook this could be for us? That we have a fucking picasso on stage with us?"

Matthew has jumped up and starts walking around the fire, with excitement in his eyes.

Simone leans into the conversation,

"We could put her between the piano and drums. Everyone could see her there. We could even have a light just on her at all times. Between songs they could project her work on the main screen while we are resetting."

Edge even seems to be into it, he puts his hands on Susie's shoulders as he leans forward in his seat,

"That would be awesome as shit. I have never heard of anyone blending the two together like that. Live music, live art. This could really work."

246

I shrug my shoulders, watching Susie as she stands up and starts wiping the sand off her butt then she turns and goes upstairs,

"And even if it doesn't I am fine with that. But I think it would be fun to at least try. My only worry is knowing there are thousands of people staring at me while I work. That's a fucking lot of pressure."

Matthew smiles at me wickedly as Gideon wraps his arms around me,

"That is why they won't really be able to see you, Aphrodite."

19
Ares
The Way That You Were - Sleep Token

We get to Savannah early enough for Lily and Simone to go to an art store. Susie wasn't able to come with us so Edge has been pouting for hours now. He keeps his phone close to him though, smiling whenever he gets a text.

I still can't believe that Lily and Simone have become as close as they have. I really thought it was going to take longer for Simone to get through to Lily but it only took a matter of days.

I don't know what has happened for that miraculous moment but I am forever thankful for it.

Edge and I met with the stage crew to let them know what we are going to do, what we need.

They seem a little shocked at first but say they could get with the visual crew and make sure everything is set exactly the way we want.

Mid afternoon I get a message from Lily begging for help carrying everything in.

I laugh as I recruit the guys to help.

Mona has already found her a flavor of the night and has retreated to her room hours before with her tasty treat.

We met the girls in the lobby.

Nothing is heavy, it is just awkward for two people to carry alone. We get everything back upstairs into our hotel room and Lily immediately starts divvying it up between two different wooden boxes for her to have on stage with her.

I smile, laying back on the bed seeing her excitement.

I know she is nervous though.

I can still feel it but I know once she gets into it, once the music starts playing that she will lose herself in her work.

I hear a quick rap on the door and I jump up to answer it. Matthew is standing outside smiling like the devil himself, holding a medium sized black box. I give him a grin then open the door for him to come in.

He clears his throat,

"Aphrodite, you have a delivery."

Lily looks up from her supplies confused,

"What is it? And why did you call me Aphrodite?"

She looks at me, still dazed. I smile at her and nudge my chin towards the box,

"Open it."

She looks us both over carefully before lifting the lid of the box. Her eyes stretch wide, as she looks at the items inside.

There is a long black toga style dress covered in white tulle.

Laid on top of it is a white mask that looks cracked from age and time. There are waves rolling across it to symbolize the beauty in the curves of Aphrodite.

Then in the center of the forehead is a red mural of Aphrodite herself.

I watch her hands shaking as she reaches in to pick it up.

She looks to Matthew, tears streaming down her face,

"This is the most beautiful thing I have ever seen."

Matthew smiles widely back at her then to me.

I nod my head smiling as I take the box from him. He continues to look at her in awe,

"You are going to be great Lily. Trust in that."

She smiles at him as he turns and walks from the room. I shut the door behind him then smile at Lily still rolling the mask around in her hands.

She looks at me in amazement,

"This is really happening isn't it?" I nod as I sit the box down on top of the chair beside her,

"Sure is babe. You are gonna be fucking brilliant I just know it."

She smiles at me again,

"I am nervous as fuck."

I laugh out loud to her,

"As you should be. I am still nervous every single time I take to the stage. But don't worry. There won't be any talking. No introductions. We truly believe the fans will figure out really fucking quickly what is going on."

She nods back at me,

"Yeah, I think so too. This is going to be fucking epic. So I guess I am Aphrodite then?"

I smile back at her as I caress her cheek, "Yes, Aphrodite and Ares were lovers. I didn't know how well you knew your Greek Mythology but I thought the reference was fitting. Matthew actually came up with it first. That is your name in his phone."

Her face is beaming.

I honestly believe if she smiled any wider her cheeks would crack from the pressure. I leave her to finish getting her supplies ready for the next day and order us some dinner from room service.

Two hours later we sit there, fully stuffed and drinking the wine I had delivered with dinner.

She looks over at me and smiles gently,

"My sister died when I was 6. She was 16 at the time. Her name was Nikki. My mother was bi polar and had a manic

250

episode. Honestly, I think she might have been schizophrenic as well but was never diagnosed at the time. As I got older, and learned more on the subjects, a lot of the symptoms stuck out to me."

I stare at her in awe. I have no idea where this is going. I am just grateful she feels she can confide in me. I sit here with bated breath, afraid to even move.

She gives me another half smile,

"Nikki was everything. She was so smart. Fucking beautiful. She made everything fun. I mean we didn't have much but she made every moment exciting. I think she was just trying to keep life light for me because it was really heavy most of the time.

"My mom, well a lot of the time she was okay. There were moments that I can remember when she kinda closed off. She hid herself away from us a lot. Or dad would make her hide away from us. I don't really have a lot of memories of him. I just remember mom not being like the other moms.

"Anyways, my mom had a manic episode and she killed Nikki. She didn't say a word, she just grabbed a knife from the drawer and started stabbing her. I hid under the kitchen table and watched it happen.

"Afterwards, she kept saying that she loved her too much to let her live. I never understood it. I never wanted to understand it. I just wanted to make sure I never loved someone to that point. It scared me. That someone could love someone to the point of killing them. I didn't understand that she was sick. I was just a kid. I just assumed that is what love did. And it scared the hell out of me."

I have sat up in my chair, sitting my glass down. I put my hand on her knee.

She takes another long drink,

251

"Mom was committed. She was deemed insane so she never stood trial. My dad left right after Nikki died and I never heard from him again. Mom is in a state hospital near Boston.

"I haven't seen her since her trial when they decided to have her committed. I have never checked on her either. I didn't speak to anyone for 7 years after the murder. The first person I spoke to was Susie when I met her freshman year at St. Francis'."

I take her glass from her hand and sit it on the table.

I stand and pick her up bridal style and just hold her.

She sighs into my chest,

"I have never talked to anyone about it except Susie. Mark knew my mom had issues but he didn't know what she did. I have always been afraid of telling people for fear of them thinking I would turn out like her. Like it was hereditary or something. I have never had any of the symptoms of either. I have seen many different therapists over the years."

I carry her over to the bed and sit down on the end of it with her still holding closely to me.

I kiss the top of her head as I feel a tear run down my cheek.

It all makes sense now.

Why she fears love so much.

Why she felt so broken that night.

I hate myself for breaking her as deeply as I have. I feel her pull back and I look down into her eyes. She smiles as she turns in my lap so she is straddling me and hugging me.

I nuzzle my face into her neck, "I am so sorry Lily. I had no idea. I would have never guessed that you had been through so much." I hold onto her rocking back and forth.

She leans into my chest, staring towards the window, "I did a lot of shit to try to mask the pain. I stopped talking, I ended up addicted to coke and had to go through rehab. I cut it out of my life completely. I had to. For my own sanity."

252

Her words rip through me like a knife. That is why she got so fucking angry about keeping it from her. I had no idea that having my own issues with it was going to be something that could have taken her away from me entirely. Had I known, I would have just made sure I was clean before we even started anything. I stroke her hair, feeling another tear run down my cheek. My own fucking demons could have killed her.

It seems like hours pass before she pulls back, smiling lightly at me,

"I have given myself to you now. Totally. Scars and all. I want you to know and understand that you are my end. I have ran from this my entire life but I can't run away from you. I love you too much to leave.

"You have a way of taking all the pain inside me and turning it into something that can be healed. I have never really felt that kind of power from someone before. You are my world now, if you are okay with that."

I let out a raspy choked gasp as I push her hair behind her ears on both sides of her head,

"I love you. I love you for your flaws. I love you for grace. I love you for your humility and your fears. I love you because that is what I was born to do. I was born to hold you in my arms until there is no strength left in them. Will you let me do that Lily? Will you just let me hold you and you never leave?"

She smiles back at me as she leans in and gives me a soft kiss,

"Yes. I will."

I wrap my arms tighter around her and pull her closer into me. If I could open up my chest and put her inside, I would.

I can never get her close enough.

I hold her until both our eyes are heavy. I lay back on the bed and we both scoot up and lay there staring at each other until sleep overtakes us both.

I wake up around 2 in the morning and she is gone. I sit up, rubbing my eyes and see her sitting on the other side of the room in the picture window.

I hear her speak into her phone, "Yeah. I know."

She smiles out into the night,

"He is everything Susie. It makes me physically hurt when I think about how much I love him. I can't ever be without him. He has healed me in so many ways I will never be able to repay him. I don't even think he would let me try honestly.

"He just, he sees me. He sees through all the bullshit I put into my everyday exterior. It's like he just looks past it and sees the real me that is hiding behind the curtain."

She nods out the window as she wipes a stray tear off her cheek,

"No I would. I would marry him tomorrow. I would have a million of his babies. I would adopt 700 dogs and start a chinchilla rescue if he wanted. I don't care. I am done hiding and running. I am his, ya know?"

I don't dare breathe or even move.

I don't want her to feel like her conversation has been intruded on but even more I want to hear what she is saying.

She is healing all of my wounds with her words.

It is somehow more meaningful hearing her say them to someone else not knowing I can hear her. It doesn't feel forced.

It is just her, raw and exposed.

I have never known anyone in my life that I have felt was truly dedicated to me. Not Ares, just me. She loves all of me. I never even allowed myself to dream that this would happen.

She smiles into the phone again, "I love you too Susie. I will call you tomorrow and let you know how it goes."

She hangs up her phone and continues to stare out the window.

I hear her sigh deeply,

"How much of that did you hear?"

I smile to myself as I sit up in bed and move to the end of it,

"I don't know what you are talking about."

She smiles again then looks back at me.

I smile back,

"So a chinchilla ranch sounds....gross. I don't want that. Ever."

She laughs out loud as she stands and walks towards me.

I stand meeting her halfway. I turn her so her back is to my front and we move closer to the window, overlooking the city below. I feel her take a deep breath,

"I meant every word."

I spin her to face me and take her cheeks in my hands,

"I know. I love you."

She smiles as I bring my lips down to hers.

She wraps her hands around my neck holding my lips to hers. I grip her hips tight, clinging onto her for dear life. She pulls away from me and slowly pulls her shirt over her head.

I watch her reach down and slide her pants down, never breaking eye contact with me as she steps out of them. I hold her eyes as I remove my shirt as well.

She steps up to me and unbuttons my jeans, sighing as she slides her hands over my hip bones to pull them down. I step out of them then turn to sit down in the window seat.

She leans down, kissing me before settling into my lap. She straddles me, kissing me deeper and harder than ever before.

I wrap my hand up in her hair, flattening the other hand on her back holding her close to me.

She starts to kiss me down my neck then back up to my ear. I hear myself sigh into the room.

I use one arm to lift her up before holding my dick and sliding her down onto me.

She moans as she lays her head back between her shoulders and starts to rock her hips into me. She looks down into my eyes,

"This is the only time I feel complete. Like I have found the final puzzle piece."

I kiss her deeply as I start moving her hips up and down on me. She bites down on the soft spot between my neck and shoulder and I pick her up then carry her to the table. I hold her to me with one hand while clearing everything from the table in a sweeping motion with the other.

I lay her down and bring her knees up over my shoulders as I lean into the table and start to thrust into her harder, deeper. She reaches above her head and grabs the far side of the table as I continue to spear into her.

Her mouth is cracked open as she pants and moans to me. I watch her full tits as they move with the force of my intrusions.

I start to slam into her harder when I hear the table start to creak. I wrap my arms around her back and lift her just in time for the table to break beneath her.

She doesn't even look down as I continue to pummel her. I take two steps and hold her up to the wall with her legs still wrapped around me. I look into her eyes as I wrap my hand around her neck and lift her ass higher with the other.

I can feel her getting close.

She moans a whimper as I feel her nails running down my back hard enough to draw blood.

I slam into her again, "I promise. I will fuck you this hard for the rest of our lives. You will never be left questioning how I feel about you."

She moans louder as I continue to thrust into her in a frenzy. She opens her eyes and looks into mine, "I am yours. Only yours."

I slam into her again forcefully, feeling my release building in the base of my spine.

I kiss her roughly as I continue to pin her to the wall. I pull back and put my forehead to hers when I hear her beg,

"Please Gideon. Please let me cum. Let me cum all over your dick."

I growl loudly and turn her to lay back on the bed. I push her thighs wide enough to stretch the skin. I slam myself into her until I hear her scream and feel her clench onto me.

I open my eyes, staring at her with my mouth open, breathing heavily into her face. She is throwing her head from side to side before her eyes fly wide and she screams my name,

"Gideon! Fuck Gideon!"

I feel her explode around me.

I let out my own scream as I let loose inside of her. I can feel her still riding out the waves of her pleasure as I continue to throw myself into her.

Her entire body is shaking and I feel a literal explosion. I realize what I have just made her body do and I continue to throw everything I have into her.

She has her legs and arms wrapped around me as she whimpers in my ear,

"Fuck baby. Oh my god. Oh fuck me baby. Oh god."

She finally starts to come down and I slow my thrusts.

257

She looks up into my eyes, her own brimmed with tears. I smile down at her and kiss her deeply. She is smiling, eyes still closed when I pull back,

"Jesus Fuck Gideon."

I smile back at her, enjoying this victory more than any other in my entire lifetime.

I slowly pull out of her and lay down beside her. She looks down then turns back to me,

"Housekeeping is getting a very large tip and apology tomorrow."

I laugh out at her and pull her in for another kiss. We scoot to the far side of the bed and hold each other as we fall back asleep.

20
Aphrodite
Read All About It, Pt. III, Emeli Sandé

I wake up with butterflies in my stomach.

I have never been so nervous for something in my life. Gideon is still sleeping beside me as I slide out of bed and walk over to my suitcase.

I change into some work out clothes and smile at him as I grab a notepad and leave him a quick note letting him know where I am going. I grab my room key, phone and air pods then head straight down to the gym.

I grab an open treadmill and put my air pods in.

I settle myself into some Freya Ridings as I steadily raise the speed and incline until I am sprinting uphill.

I run longer than normal. I have to work out some of this nervous energy.

After I have run for more than an hour, I finally start my cool down walk. I grab my water bottle and drink it down eagerly. I step off the machine moving to the wall holding towels, grabbing one and wiping myself down.

I turn to see a man sitting on a lifting bench staring at me and smiling. I give him a quick smile back then toss my dirty towel in the hamper. Not paying any attention I move to go back upstairs.

He waves his hand to me, trying to get my attention and I pull the air pods out of my ears. Smiling,

"Sorry, did you say something? I couldn't hear anything."

He stands up smiling back at me,

"I was asking what your name is. Maybe see if you would like to get some lunch or something?"

I know I am looking at him incredulously. I am not one to get hit on often. Which is fine by me because I am awkward as fuck.

I look over his shoulder, seeing Gideon, Edge and Matthew walking in. I smile at Gideon as he stops and looks us over quickly.

I look back at the man,

"Sorry. I am spoken for."

I move to step around him to go to Gideon when the man smiles again,

"Oh now. That can't be true. I don't see a ring on your finger."

Gideon steps up like he is going to say something but in turn hears me laugh and look at the man,

"Yeah, the only ring we need is the one he slides on his cock for me."

I point to Gideon and Edge busts out laughing. The man looks between me and Gideon quickly as I step around him and lean into Gideon for a kiss.

I see him keep his eyes on the man as he reaches down and grabs my ass while shoving his tongue down my throat. I watch the man walk past us and out the door without another word.

I pull back from Gideon smiling. He has that feral look in his eyes again so I pull him close,

"Yours. Only yours."

He smiles as he smacks my ass and I move to sit across from the boys and watch them work out.

An hour later we were taking a shower, taking out our nerves in a much more serious and pleasurable manner.

I haven't been able to eat all day when Simone sits down beside me looking out the window of the hotel,

"Open."

I look at her smiling as I open my mouth so she cram a chunk of focaccia in my mouth. I chew on it, grateful for a friend.

I lean my head down on her shoulder as she continues to feed herself. I let out a sigh,

"I am going to choke."

She laughs, lifting her shoulder so I will raise up my head. She turns to me, shoving another piece of bread into my mouth,

"No you aren't. You are fucking brilliant and we all know it. Do you know how much nerve it takes to step up on that stage? I nearly shat myself the first time we had a live gig. I held onto Edge until we were on stage then he pushed me away and that was that.

"It has been amazing ever since. You just have to focus on the stage. Don't worry about what is going on beyond it. You have no control over that. Just what is happening on the stage at that moment."

I smile, opening my mouth for more bread. Simone continues to feed me like a baby bird until it is time to start getting ready. I stand in my bra and underwear as I let Simone paint my body an ash grey. Everyone else is painted black.

But me, I am a mixture of light and dark.

Ares' sun in the darkest of nights.

I leave my hair down.

267

I don't straighten it so it has a natural beach wave to it as it sweeps across my lower back. I in turn paint Hera, then we get dressed.

I look myself over in the mirror. Still completely unsure of what the fuck I am doing. I grab my mask and slide it over my face as the guys come in. I let my eyes roll over the shape of the mask, how it sweeps to my jawline, leaving my mouth and lower cheeks exposed.

I flatten my dress down and look in the reflection to see everyone behind me settling their masks as well. I smile into the reflection. We are a family. Granted a fucked up family but a family all the same.

Ares steps up behind me, his cloak chained around his neck. I give him a small smile in the reflection as he whispers,

"You are the most beautiful creature I have ever seen."

I turn around, placing my grey hands on his chest,

"I love you too."

The crew has us all set up on the stage by the time we make it to the venue. We still have a little over an hour before it is lights down.

I carefully step up the stairs taking in the layout of the stage from a whole new type of vantage point.

I move up to the center of the stage then turn around to look out into the empty venue. It will soon be filled with thousands of screaming fans.

I turn around memorizing the layout. I step up to my little section of stage and open up my wooden boxes.

Making sure my canvas is ready. I hear Ares behind me,

"Can we get a light check on Aphrodite?"

I smile at the canvas before slowly turning around into the white light that is now shining from overhead.

262

Ares nods, "Now the screen."

I watch Dionysus and Hestia step up on stage settling into their instruments, making sure they are ready for the night's festivities.

I look at the large screen over the drumset and see my blank canvas there. I let out a slow steady breath. It is real.

This is about to happen. I hope that it turns out as wonderful as we are hoping. I rub my hands together and roll my neck on my shoulders. Ares steps up behind me, I can feel his presence without even turning around.

Then I feel his hands on my waist. I smile into the canvas.

I hear him breath,

"I was thinking. Right before they hit you with the light for the first time I am going to say Aphrodite. That can be their cue but also, I want everyone to know who you are."

I nod and turn around to face him, "I am fine with that. Can it be like 2 songs in? That way the music will have already hit me and I will be lost in the canvas."

He rubs his thumb under my chin, "Of course baby." He reaches down and grabs my hand to lead me back to the green room.

Hestia and Hera have shots waiting for us when we walk in.

Apparently it is a ritual. I smile as I grab my shot of vodka and feel the burn reach my chest. I let out a long sigh and look from mask to mask. It is about to begin.

We step off stage right, hearing the screaming crowd is overwhelming. That was me on the other side of that stage not long ago.

Ares turns around and rubs his thumb over my bottom lip. His smile is the last thing I see before the lights go out.

The crowd is overwhelming from here. I feel Hera's hand wrap in mine as we watch Ares, Apollo, and Dionysus step up on stage.

Hera gives my hand a tight squeeze before her and Hestia follow suit. I shake my hands out quickly then climb the steps myself.

I step over to my spot on stage and make sure all the charcoals and pastels are easily accessible. I hear the beginning chords of Evermore and smile over at Apollo on the drums beside me.

He knew what he was doing starting with this song tonight.

I close my eyes then grab yellow, then orange, then red. I depict a firestorm with asteroids coming for us.

I continue to smear and blend colors together with my fingers bringing them to the perfect shade.

Two songs later, I hear my name leave Ares' mouth.

I feel the light come on above me and the crowd loses their fucking minds. I don't even have it in me to feel nervous.

I am being fueled by them. I don't dare stop.

I continue to blend and smudge and scry. The band comes to their first stage reset and I see my easel projected right above me.

I glance up briefly as I grab my charcoals and start to draw a large church pew. I rub some brown into the black to give it the perfect hue.

5 minutes pass and the next set has already begun.

Ares and Dionysus are behind me moving around the stage.

I take a quick glance over my shoulder seeing Ares grinding into Dionysus from behind.

264

I smile and turn back to my work. The light is on me the entire time. I continue to create my masterpiece. I move into perfecting the features of each member's face.

All of us are sitting on the pew. All except for Ares.

He is leaning over me, in the center of the pew with his arm extended down the center of my torso. Grasping his hand at nothing but air. I sketch his face turned into my neck with my head slightly tilted to the side.

I lean close to the canvas, perfecting each and every person's mask. Hestia, Apollo, Dionysus, then Hera.

I grab the spray bottle I had prepared last minute and take a deep breath. I hear Firestorm start behind me.

Indicating the end of the show.

I raise the spray bottle and lightly spritz the canvas with what looks like blood but is only red paint slightly diluted.

I hear Ares weeping into the microphone behind me.

I had thought of this midway through the show. I think it will be okay. I turn and step down off my pedestal and slowly walk up to Ares.

He is on the ground leaned back onto his ass, chest out to the crowd, head tilted back absolutely weeping into the microphone.

As I hear the last word leave his lips I lean into him, pulling him to me like a lost lover. Kneeling beside him, bringing his head into my chest. The crowd goes fucking ballistic as the lights shut off.

He is sweating and shaking but I feel him grab my hands and squeeze them tightly. He stands up, putting his hand out to me, palm up. I smile as I reach up for his hand as the lights come back on.

The crowd goes carnal again.

They watch me accept his hand and stand before them.

265

As Aphrodite with her Ares.

The rest of the band comes down to us to take their bows, I put my hands into a praying stance and nod my head to the crowd. I turn and walk back to the canvas.

I grab the large black sharpie I have brought. Each member steps up signing their name. Top corner it simply states Aphrodite 2024.

I hand the canvas to Hera then Apollo and Dionysus jump down with the guards. The crowd is losing their fucking minds being this close to the band. Hands are reaching, scratching, clawing for just a touch. I look at Ares as he steps over and kisses me.

In front of everyone.

An entire feral fucking arena of Carnal Decay fans losing their fucking minds. I can hear people screaming,

"Oh My God!"

"What the Fuck!"

"What is Happening!?"

I smile as I sit down on the edge of the stage and put my arms out straight to my sides. Apollo on one side, Dionysus on the other, they lift me off the stage and sit me down on my feet just before the barrier holding the crowd back.

I turn back to the stage as Hera hands me the canvas. I walk down the front of the crowd just waiting for the owner of the canvas to make themselves known to me.

I catch a glimpse of a young girl.

All in black, piercings and tattoos everywhere.

She smiles at me and I instantly know who she was. She is wearing a black and red corset with a tight leather skirt. Her purple hair down around her shoulders.

I seem to float directly to her and her eyes go wide. I smile as I lean into her ear,

"Your taste in clothes was wonderful, love. The cougar hunt was a success."

I stand back up seeing the shock across the young girl's face as she realizes who I actually am. The beaming smile she returns me with is the only gift I will ever need. I lift the canvas over the rail and place it into her hands. The people around us go fucking insane.

I try to keep my smile to myself but it is fucking challenging. I turn and follow Apollo back around to the back of the stage.

I can barely breathe.

He turns to me gripping me in a tight hug and screams in my ear, "Bloody Fucking Brilliant!"

I grin so wide it makes my cheeks hurt.

He grabs me by the hand and we walk to the green room. As soon as the door opens, Ares is on me. He wraps his arms around me and kisses me deeply, harshly.

I pull back slightly seeing Hera beside him. She pushes him out of the way and grips me tightly and hugs me with a fierce intensity,

"You fucking amazing girl!"

I smile over her shoulder at Ares. I am crying but thankfully no one can see it.

Ares moves to his chair and I take my place at his side. Sitting on the arm of the chair as fans start to filter their way in. Not thanking them is the hardest thing for me to do. But there is no talking.

That is the rule when the masks are on and other people are around. Instead of thanking them for their admiration I lift a hand to their cheek and nod ever so slightly.

It seems fitting for Aphrodite.

267

21
Ares
Emergence - Sleep Token

I can not believe this woman. She is bloody magnificent.

She has created this amazing piece of art just by listening to our music. Every single time it is a different piece.

Nothing is ever the same. It is like the images are just channeled into her as she hears the songs begin.

Now she is just sitting on the arm of my chair. Accepting all this attention that I know she hates. She would raise a hand to each person's face as if she is blessing them.

It is beautiful. She truly is a goddess in her own right.

After a few hours, the green room is cleared and we can all breathe freely. We agree to stay in costume until we make it back to the hotel. As we are becoming more popular, it seems the fans are becoming more feral.

At any time, there will be people waiting around corners to get a glimpse at us. I hold Aphrodites' hand as we walk to the SUV.

I hold it as we walk into the hotel as well. I want it very apparent that she belongs to me.

We enter the hotel room and she turns and collapses to the bed on her back. I laugh at her, taking off my cloak and mask, throwing them both in the chair.

She sits up and tilts her head slightly at me.

268

She is beautiful. Her hair, loose and wavy around her body. The mask that hides her identity has seemed to bring her new life.

I watch her as she slides it off then runs a hand through her hair. She turns her back to me and I reach down and unzip the back of her dress. She steps out of it, placing it over my cloak with her mask on top.

I reach up and caress her cheek with my hand, watching the ash grey turn darker with each swipe.

I step closer to her and take her into my arms. I feel her melt into my chest wrapping her arms around my waist.

I kiss the top of her head and pull back slightly to look down upon her,

"Will you go to London with me?"

She blinks rapidly, "Yeah, I can do that."

I smile and give her a kiss. I pull back and she looks at me quizzically, "Why?"

I run my hand down her face again,

"I know about your past. It's time you know about mine."

Lily smiles up into my face and nods her head. We decide to shower then call it an early night.

I wake up before her. She is tangled up in my arms like she has tried to hibernate inside of me in her sleep. I attempt to pull my arm out from under her and she lets out a low moan then rolls onto her back.

I pull the sheet back looking at her naked form. She is still trying to convince me that she is 34 but I just don't see it.

Honestly though, I won't care when she is 64. It is her soul that stole me first. Her body is a signing bonus.

I let my eyes scour her skin. I run a solitary finger from her collarbone over her left breast then down to her abdomen.

269

I look at her face but she is still sleeping.

I let my finger wander further as I lean in and kiss her. I slide that finger inside of her and I feel her lips part underneath mine.

I skate my tongue across her teeth before slithering inside her mouth taking the kiss deeper. Her hips are already starting to move on their own. I open my eyes and look at her as I slide another finger inside.

Her eyes slowly open then close as she reaches a hand up and pulls me on top of her. She spreads her thighs to me as I remove my fingers then replace them with my dick.

She holds me close as I continue to push in and out of her. I put my cheek to hers and wrap my hands around her ass as I continue to make love to her.

This is different. This isn't just sex.

Not just a primal desire to consume her.

I love her. I hear her whisper into my ear, "Gideon."

Her voice is breathy and still gravelly from just waking up. I slowly continue to surrender myself to her.

I pull my face back from hers and just watch her expressions as she lets me own her body. I pull one hand up and start to roll her nipple between my fingers as I begin to speed up my thrusts.

She smiles as she runs her fingernails down my back. I accelerate my pace again and she starts to pant.

I can feel her quivering around me as I slam myself into her. She lets out a meek yelp and then moans again.

I continue to run through her faster and faster when her eyes fly open and her mouth drops.

Her eyes are the color of mine.

Black as night.

I feel her seize me from the inside and she cries out in ecstasy. I lift myself off of her and brace myself on either side.

I begin to fuck her harder as I watch her eyes go to pin pricks. She lets out a scream and her nails are on my back again.

She is grasping for anything to hold onto as she screams her release into the room around us. I follow right behind her panting and grunting into her body.

I lay myself back down on her as she lets her legs go limp and she lazily runs her fingers up and down my back as our breaths start to even out.

I roll off of her and she curls into my side. She reaches her hand up and spreads it open over my heart,

"Good Morning."

I smile at the ceiling,

"Good Morning."

She starts making shapes on my chest with her fingers, "I think I could get used to that type of alarm clock. Or should I call it an alarm cock?"

I belt out a laugh wrapping my arm around her tighter.

"I truly fucking love you."

She lifts her head smiling and sits her chin on my chest. I look down at her, "What?"

She smiles back at me quickly then shakes her head, "Nothing."

I pull her chin back up to my chest, "Tell me."

She smiles and starts drawing shapes on my stomach then looks back into my eyes. She gives me a half grin then rests her hands under her chin, "Do you wanna get married?"

I feel my heart stop in my chest. I sit up a little further, "Excuse me?"

She blinks repeatedly, "Nevermind. It was just an intrusive thought that won. Forget I said anything."

She slides to the end of the bed and runs to the bathroom. Lily just asked me if I wanted to get married.

Lily.

The girl who swore to never fall in love.

The girl so full of fear to give her heart to anyone. I can sit here and know in full honesty that she has never spoken those words to anyone but me before.

I stand up and step around the bed to the bathroom door.

As soon as the door opens, I have her in my arms and lift her around to the vanity. Her eyes are like saucers and I can tell she is trying so damn hard not to cry.

I smile at her, "When? Now? Yesterday? Tomorrow? Please?"

She smiles widely, the tears breaching their dam. She shakes her head, "I don't care when. I don't care where. I just want us to never be apart. I want to be yours forever."

I smile as I lean in and kiss her deeply.

I pull away still shaking my head at her. She tilts her head to the side and gives me a soft side smile. I lift her off the counter then lead her back towards the bed, "Can we do it in London?"

She lets go of my hand halfway and starts to pull clothes out of her suitcase. She smiles up at me nodding, "I am fine with that. I would just have to fly Susie over."

I nod back at her. My heart is going a mile a minute,

"Okay, so we get on the next flight to London. We pick a time far enough out that the entire band and Susie can be there. My mum is going to lose her shit. She is going to love you by the way. I am just...I don't know what to say. I am overloaded at the moment."

She smiles back at me sweetly.

I step up to her and take her hands, "Are you sure? There is no rush. None at all."

Lily looks up to me, squeezing my hands,

"I have spent my life believing I would never allow love into my life. Now that it is here, I want the world to know it. I want the entire universe to know that I picked you. Out of everyone, you are my one. You are my constant."

I lean down and kiss her again before pulling back and finding some clothes to put on. I smile at her, "You find us a flight. I am going to go scream this to the world...aka Matthew."

I hear her continuing to laugh as I run out the room and down the hall. I beat on his door for what feels like eternity.

He finally opens it and I see Simone curled up in his bed.

I smile at them both, "Good you're both here."

I push past him into the room as he walks back to the bed and slides back in next to Simone.

I pace the end of the bed, "I have news."

Simone yawns loudly, "Can't you tell us like after lunch?"

I laugh, turning back to the bed and spreading my hands out in front of me, "We are getting married."

Simone sits upright, wrapping the sheet around her, eyes wide. Matthew starts laughing hysterically.

I roll my eyes at him, "Really?"

He sits up coughing as he reaches over and lights a cigarette, "You finally talked her into it huh?"

I cross my arms over my chest and smile at him, "She asked me."

Simone is now on her knees jumping up and down, "No she fucking didn't! Oh my fucking god!"

I smile at her, "Right?"

Matthew continues to laugh at us as he coughs along with his morning cigarette. I clap my hands together,

"So we are going home. I will send everyone a date when we have figured it out. It won't be far off though so be ready to be in London at any given time."

I point to Simone, "You are expected to wear a dress cupcake so suck it up and be a girl for a day."

Her face instantly falls as I turn and point to Matthew,

"We have to figure out a theme for clothes because you are my best man."

Matthew splays his hand out on his chest and mutters around the cigarette in his mouth, "Oh my god, He chose me!"

I flip him off, "Shut up. So are we all clear with everything?"

Simone, still excited, starts to nod her head when there is a knock at the door.

Matthew sits back up, "What the fuck is going on this morning?"

I laugh as I run over and open the door to see Lily standing there smiling at me with Mona right beside her. Mona runs inside around me and jumps on the bed next to Simone smiling from ear to ear, so she has obviously heard the news.

Lily steps in, noticing Simone in bed with Matthew and smiles, pointing between the two of them, "Nice."

Simone chuckles at her as Mona looks like her head is going to explode. She turns and grabs Simone's hand and squeezes it then looks at Lily and starts nudging her head towards Simone.

I stand back trying to understand the new female code language being introduced.

Lily steps up beside me and smiles, "Simone. Would you be a bridesmaid for me?"

Simone's eyes blow huge again and she jumps off the bed fully naked and runs to Lily wrapping her in a hug.

We all burst out laughing, including Simone who pulls back crying, "Are you sure? I mean really sure? I fucked your man. Are you super super sure?"

274

I close my eyes and sigh heavily as I drop my face to the ground. Lily laughs so loudly again that she snorts,

"Jesus fuck Simone. Yes I am sure. I don't care that you fucked him. I am the only one that gets to ride that fire pole from now on!"

I throw my hands up in the air, "I am right fucking here!"

Matthew has already put out his cigarette because he was laughing so hard he was choking.

Simone squeezes Lily again, "Yes, a thousand times yes!"

Lily smiles back at her and gives her a kiss on her cheek, "Love you bitch."

Simone smiles back, "Love you more Lil."

Mona laughs and hands Simone a robe, "Could ya. Please?"

Simone slides it on, barely tying it together.

I clear my throat,

"So as I was saying. Be ready to be in London on a moment's notice. I don't know where yet but we will figure out all the details soon."

Lily raises her hand up like she is in a classroom, "I have some thoughts."

I wrap my arm over her shoulders and fan my hand out in front of me, "The floor is yours."

Simone throws her hands up,

"WAIT!"

She takes off running around the room until she finds her phone. She quickly punches in a number then hits a facetime call. 15 seconds later we see Edge and Susie staring at the screen, still half asleep.

Lily smiles and waves at Susie getting a cheesy grin in return. I hear Edge let out a yawn, "What is going on? We are trying to sleep over here."

Lily smiles again,

"As I was saying. I have thoughts. I was thinking maybe like an abandoned factory or something outdoors with ruins. I was also thinking at some point wearing the masks and using it promotionally. Every seemed to go fucking crazy about it at the arena. I figured the news has probably already hit the wires about me anyway so why not?"

I squeeze her shoulders,

"You know that if we go that route you have to go full speed with the anonymity right? I mean we have to keep it up in public at least. For the most part."

She smiles back at me, "I am fine with that. If it gets too crazy I will just pretend to be a roadie or something."

Edge sits up closer to the phone, "This is great and all but what the fuck are we talking about?"

I smile down at him, "Lily and I are getting married."

Edge smiles widely, "Nice man. You finally got her to lock it down huh?"

I smile around the room again, "Why is it so hard to believe that she asked me?"

Edge laughs, "Yeah. Okay."

I hear a banshee screaming from the phone and my eyes go wide watching the camera on their side go in 40 different directions as the same. Eventually, I see it come to a stop on Susie's face. She is beaming from ear to ear, and apparently hanging off the side of the bed, "Are you fucking kidding me right now? Lily?? Oh my god! Did you really propose?"

I look back to the phone as Edge looks towards Lily and he sees her nodding. He looks back around the room,

"Well fuck me then."

Susie lets out another banshee scream as Edge sticks his fingers in his ears and makes a face at her like she is a screeching owl. She looks at Lily, "You ARE calling me later and giving me a play by play!"

276

Lily smiles back at her, "Yes mom. I promise."

Susie smiles again, "I love you!!!" She is still screaming when Edge reaches up and hits the end call button.

Matthew leans forward again,

"Serious question now. Does this take the threesome off the table?"

I glare at him as Simone grabs a pillow and slaps him in the face with it. Lily busts out laughing, "Sorry Matthew, I only have eyes for Gideon. Sometimes Mona."

Mona pumps her arm in the air, "Fuck yeah, still in the game!"

We all laugh as I hold her tighter against me.

This is really happening. We all agree to meet in London in a week's time for another run down on the plans and a timeline.

I smile wickedly to myself for the rest of the day until we board a plane for London.

I smile as my mother hugs Lily. I was right. I knew I was right. I knew from the moment I met Lily that my mum would love her. Mum finally lets go of Lily as she leans back into me, I smile at my mum,

"So I know you just met and everything but how would you feel about Lily becoming part of the family?"

My mum's go wide as she grabs Lily again, hugging her tightly and smiling at me over her shoulder.

Mum finally lets her go and holds her cheek,

"I know I just met ya but I think I love ya."

I smile down at Lily as she hugs my mum back. When she pulls away she is crying. She looks at me and waves a hand in her face. I square her up to me,

"Are you okay? What's wrong?"

She lets out a sigh then looks over to my mum then back to me, "I've never had a mom. Not one that I felt actually liked me. I am just kinda overcome right now. I will be okay, just give me a minute."

My mum takes a deep breath and wraps her hand around Lily's, "You have me now, Love. I will be all the mum you need I promise ya."

Lily lets out another strangled laugh as she pulls my mum tighter to her, "Thank you."

I watch my mum smooth Lily's hair down the back of her head and I realize the two most important women in my life are standing here holding each other.

I smile wider.

We stay with mum for a few hours before heading over to my apartment. I had it cleaned while I was gone so at least it doesn't look abandoned when we get there.

I take our luggage to the bedroom and walk back out to see Lily walking around looking at everything.

She smiles as she looks at photos of me growing up. Me and Edge in high school. Matthew, Mona and Simone going through their emo stage. She runs her fingers across the keys of the piano then smiles at me. She looks to the left of the piano and points to a photo,

"Who is that?"

I look around her, noting the photo. I let out a sigh, "That is Emily."

She nods, picking up the picture then looks back to me, "And who is Emily? A sister or something?"

I slide my hands into my pockets, "No, not a sister. I am an only child by the way. No, she is my ex-girlfriend."

Lily's eyes spray wide, "Oh."

She sits the photo back down and steps around me to the couch. She sits down, staring across the room at the picture then quickly looking out the window.

I sit down beside her, "I had that up before I left here months and months ago. I will get rid of it."

She reaches over and grabs my hand, squeezing it, "You don't have to do that. She is part of your past. She was long before me, right?"

I nod at her, "Yeah, she left a few years ago."

She nods at me again and looks distantly out the window. I pull her chin back to me, "What? Say it. Please."

She smiles at me, "It's nothing. I am going to go call Susie. Let her know we made it safely."

I try to say something but she stands and walks quickly from the room. I look over at the photo of Emily. I stand up and grab it, throwing it into the trash can in the kitchen.

I move into the bedroom to start unpacking when I hear Lily in the bathroom. I promised myself I would quit spying on her. I continue to unpack, still tempted to step up to the door but withholding from the temptation just barely.

A few moments later Lily emerges from the bathroom. She gives me a soft smile as she moves to her suitcase and grabs her make up bag and takes it back to the bathroom.

I watch her movements. Her mannerisms.

Something is off. Something is wrong.

She holds back from me the rest of the night.

My own fucking insecurities are going to fuck up my life again. I can just feel it. I want to talk to Gideon about it but I feel like I am this big pile of whining. That eventually he will see me for the messed up piece of crazy that I am and leave.

It is just a little fucking thing too. Nothing huge.

He said Emily had left, not that they had broken up.

So, of course my brain kicks into overdrive and the devil on my shoulder starts whispering,

"*She left him. He didn't want her to leave. He still loves her. You should be worried.*"

I sit around the entire night pouting to myself.

I am sick and tired of these internal struggles. I know he loves me. I know he loves only me. It shouldn't matter who he was with before. But seeing the photo of that beautiful blonde, young woman I instantly feel unworthy.

How can I compete with that? I can't....that's how.

I feel defeated again. For no fucking reason other than my own insecurities having a fucking MMA fight in my head.

I am not trying to keep myself away from him but by the time 9 pm has rolled around I know he thinks something is seriously wrong. I mope around the apartment while he takes a shower. I notice immediately that the photo is gone. I wonder what he has done with it.

Probably put it somewhere private so I don't have to look at his model ex-girlfriend. I sit in a huff at the piano and start touching random keys.

I am instantly engrossed in it. I have never sat at a piano before. I test out random keys to hear what sounds they make then start to think of what they sound like in Evermore or Firestorm.

It isn't 10 minutes later and I look up to see Gideon sitting cross legged on the couch just staring at me. I smile over at him,

"Do you feel better after a shower?"

He nods at me without saying a word. I turn towards him,

"Are you mad at me? Have I done something?" He shakes his head no but tilts his head to the left a bit,

"Why didn't you ever tell me you could play piano?"

I laugh out loud at him then stand and walk to the couch, "Uh, cause I can't."

He turns towards me, "You were just playing. I sat right here and watched you."

I look over at the piano and laugh, "I was just messing around. I have no idea what the keys are or anything."

Gideon stands up and walks to the piano, "Come here, sit with me."

I smile but humor him walking over and sitting beside him on the bench. He turns to me, "Close your eyes."

I laugh at him again, shutting my eyes, "Mhm someone's getting kinky."

I hear him chuckle as he starts to play a few keys, it is from something I have never heard from them before. I smile, "That's nice. I like that."

I feel his hand on my leg, "Open your eyes."

I open them and look at him. He points to the keys,

"Play what you just heard."

I laugh at him again, "I don't know the keys."

He crosses his arms across his chest, "Just humor me. Mess around until you think you have found the right notes then play what I just played."

I smile at him, "Uh, okay."

I put my fingers on the keys and start playing around until I find what sounds right. I listen to the little chorus he has just played in my head then try to play it back as best I can.

To me it sounds like nails on a chalkboard.

Gideon stands up and moves behind me, "Try playing Firestorm."

I look over my shoulder at him, "I have no idea what I am doing though. I don't even know what the little pedal thingies do."

He smiles back down at me and wraps his arms around my neck and points below the piano,

"The one of the right you want to use if you think the note you are playing should sound out longer. The one in the middle, it will keep playing one note but let you play others as well. You won't really use that one as much as the others. The one on the left, it softens the note you are playing. You want to use them like shifting gears in a car. You don't have to use them right now if you aren't comfortable with it though."

I watch his long fingers point to each pedal as he explains what they do. I nod along,

"But if I want to use them, how do I know when to push them down?" He smiles again, pointing,

"So once you are pressing the key you want, press down whichever pedal you want. This will kind of blend them together. Make them not sound choppy."

I nod at him and put my fingers on the keys,

"I will maybe try that later. I am not for sure how good my hand eye coordination actually is."

He laughs at me then stands up, placing his hands on my shoulders. I smile down at the keys then press a few down to make sure they are what I am hearing in my head.

A few moments later I start to play the opening of Firestorm. I am always so emotional when I hear that song though, I tend to listen more to his voice than the music. I play what I can remember then look up over my shoulder at him.

Gideon is standing behind me, shaking his head back and forth. I let out a heavy breath,

"I know. I butchered it. I told you I don't know how to play. I don't even know how to read sheet music. It all looks like Latin to me."

I turn around to face him. He smiles down at me, "You got it nearly fucking perfect."

I shake my head at him, "Don't fucking humor me."

I laugh as I smack his thigh. He leans down into my face bringing my chin around to face him, "I am not fucking lying. You got it almost perfectly. There were maybe 3 notes that were off. You have never played piano before?"

I shake my head back at him, "No. I have never played any kind of musical anything before."

He stands back up to his full height, "Bloody hell."

I glance back at the piano before looking back up at him, "I really didn't butcher it?"

He smiles as he leans down and kisses me, "You really didn't butcher it. It was impressive. Now I have someone other than Mona to play with."

I smile back at him rolling my eyes, "Yeah, I don't know about that."

He laughs back at me as I stand up and head back over to the couch. He sits down at the other end then motions for me to lay into him. I smile as I lay my back onto his torso with his legs on either side of me. I run my hand up and down the outside of his right leg,

"How tall are you?"

I feel his chest rise and fall with laughter, "Fucking tall."

I smile again, "I know you fucking tower over me. But I am short. I think I stopped growing freshman year."

He laughs again, letting that deep timbre float through my ears, "I am like 6'2" 6'3"ish."

I nod as I continue to stroke his leg while looking across the room and out the window. I feel his arm come around my chest holding me,

"What made you ask?"

I smile, "I just wondered how tall of heels I would have to wear to be eye to eye with you. My brain has random useless questions like that rolling around at any given time."

I hear him laugh behind me again, "I would say at the very least it would have to be 6 inch heels."

I laugh back at him, "I would probably break an ankle in anything taller than that."

He softly strokes my arm, "I wouldn't let you fall."

I smile again as my eyes fall around the room. I let out another sigh and he sits up behind him, forcing me to turn towards him, "Will you tell me what is wrong? Something has been off all day. It is starting to worry me."

I let out a small sarcastic chuckle, "My fucking brain. That is what is wrong."

I feel his hand on my cheek and I turn my eyes to him, "What do you mean?"

I exhale roughly again, standing and walking to the window wrapping my arms around myself, "You wouldn't understand."

I feel his shadow fall over me as he steps up beside me, "Try me."

I look at him briefly then back out the window, "It's like my brain is in a battle with itself. I know that none of it makes sense. I know it is just my own insecurities but it is just so fucking heavy. It's like this weight is sitting on my chest not letting me breathe. It's just stupid."

He leans against the wall, facing me, "What are you insecure about?"

I laugh again, "What am I not insecure about?"

He smiles, "I don't see insecurity when I look at you. I see a beautiful woman who struggles with accepting that she is all I want."

I give him another side smile, "I know that I am all you want. You have made that abundantly clear."

I let out another heavy breath and lean against the wall to face him,

"I have spent my entire life listening to this inner drama in my head. Wondering if I am turning into her. Wondering if I should have myself committed or something. Then I figured out, everyone has some type of insecurities, that this is normal for the most part."

I scan my eyes back outside,

"I guess it really is just my own fault. I never let myself get so attached to someone that I was afraid that I would lose them. I was destroyed when Mark died. But even that doesn't compare to the fear that I feel in my chest when I think that you could walk away. You could find someone else, more confident, more secure. Someone that is your own age, that you can relate to more than me. You deserve that kind of love. I just sometimes feel like you are settling."

Gideon strides over to me and takes my face in his hands,

"You are all I need. You are all I will ever need. I don't care about the age shit. I never even think about it. On God, I don't. I have loved you since the first moment I saw you.

"Because of your presence. Because of your expressions. Because of your heart. I love you, Lily. Nothing will ever change that. I am not going anywhere. And if I do, you are coming with me."

I smile at him as I lean into his chest and wrap my arms around him. He kisses me on the top of my head,

"The sooner you get that through that big brain of yours the better off we will be."

I laugh into his chest and pinch his side.

We spend the rest of the night just talking. About anything and everything. But whenever the topic of previous relationships comes up I can feel myself shutting down again. We go to bed silently, but he still holds me as I fall asleep.

The next day we sleep late. Completely content on spending the day in bed just wrapped up in each other. We finally stray away from each other mid afternoon. I make my way to the kitchen and quickly realize there is absolutely nothing in the refrigerator.

I move back to the bedroom and start getting dressed. Gideon leans forward on the bed, "What are you doing?"

I smile back over my shoulder at him, "We are not going to survive on air and scotch. Is there a grocery store around here nearby?"

He scoots off the side of the bed, moving towards the dresser, "Yeah, there is a supermarket nearby. Let me get dressed and we can walk there. It's only a few blocks away."

I nod my head at him as I lace up my sneakers then stand stretching out the jet lag I have been left with. 5 minutes later we are walking hand in hand down the street. This city is

286

fucking glorious. I never get tired of being here. It seems like around every corner is another bit of history just waiting to be remembered.

We stock up on a small amount of groceries then head back home. I make us a small dinner and we sit and eat in silence. I know I am still distant. I can feel his eyes on me throughout the entire meal. I clean up the kitchen after we are done eating then sit on the couch to watch him playing a new song on the piano. His eyes come to meet mine and he stands to move in front of me. He pulls me to my feet and wraps me in a hug.

I lean back, looking into his eyes, "Take me somewhere. Anywhere. Somewhere you love. Somewhere you have history."

He smiles down at me then looks out the window,

"Okay. But it is almost 10 pm. Won't you turn into a pumpkin or something?"

I lean forward and bite his nipple as he yelps and jumps backwards,

"Sweet Jesus woman. At least wait for the bedroom, god damn."

I laugh at him as I walk to the other side of the room and grab some sneakers. He smiles as he walks into the bedroom, coming back out a moment later with a t-shirt on. He grabs his keys and reaches out his hand to me,

"Come on. I know the perfect place."

I smile as I take his hand and follow him out the door.

Twenty minutes later we are in what I can only describe as a midwest pool haul. Every fucking thing in here is wood. There is a bar and a jukebox. To the left is a room with a couple of billiard tables. The bartender smiles at us as we walk in,

"Aye Gideon! I haven't seen you in a while mate. Where have you been hiding?"

I smile up at Gideon as he wraps an arm around me, "I was off in America finding this little minx."

I slap him in the chest then turn back to the bartender, "Ignore him. Hi. I am Lily."

I stick out my hand to him. He looks at it funny then smiles back, "Hiya. I am Robert. What can I get you both to drink?"

He shakes my hand briefly then steps back. I smile at him,

"I would love a whisky. Anything top shelf please."

He nods at me then looks at Gideon. Gideon nods,

"Give me a stout. Don't care what."

Robert nods and turns around to get our drinks. I look around the room. I am definitely the oldest person here. I look back up to Gideon,

"So why here?"

He nods to a booth in the far corner so I turn and look,

"That is where we decided to actually form a band. Like a real band. We had all known each other for ages but in that little booth we decided to forge our own paths."

Then he turns and walks us towards the opening into the other room. He points to a pool table on the other side of the room,

"That is the table we played at to decide what our name would be. We thought that was more fair than flipping a coin."

I laugh at him, "Sounds about right."

He smiles again as he points out the window and across the street to a library,

"That is where I had my first kiss. Her name was Rosemary and we were 12 years old."

I nod my head as I look across the street, "You hung out in libraries when you were 12?"

288

He smiles as he pulls me in close to him, "Truth be told, I was only there because she was there. I had a crush on her for months before that."

I chuckle at him, "So what happened to Rosemary. Why isn't she walking around with the last name Taylor?"

He shakes his head, "Ya know, I really have no idea. I am assuming she went on about her life. I think I was just a summer fling for her or something."

I laugh again, "Yeah cause all pre teens have summer flings."

Robert motions to us that our drinks are ready. We step up to the bar and pay our tab, taking our drinks. Gideon links his hand in mine and we step into the billiard room.

He nods towards a table, "You play?"

I smile at the table then to him, "I have yeah."

He nods his head again, sitting his stout down on a nearby table, "Alright then. Let's do this."

I smile at him, "Okay, but what are we betting?"

He turns back to me, "Betting?"

I smile, "Yeah, I mean you gotta make it worth my while right?"

Gideon racks the balls as I pick out a cue stick that feels right. He smiles, stepping up beside me,

"How about whoever sinks a ball the other person has to answer a question of their choice? Truthfully. Any topic."

I smile at him,

"Okay, just don't come crying to me when I know everything about you and I am still a mystery."

He laughs as he holds his hand out to the table, "Your break then."

I stand up to the end of the table and line the stick up to the cue ball. I let out a soft breath as I hit firmly and send the balls scattering across the table. I turn to Gideon, smiling, "I am solid."

He gives me a chuckle and a nod as he walks to the other side of the table and lines up a shot.

He looks directly at me then sends the cue into a stripe, sinking it directly in a corner pocket.

Well fuck.

I pick up my whisky and take a drink. Sitting the glass back down I wave my hand out in front of me, "Okay, ask away."

Gideon smiles as he stands up, "Who was your first kiss and where?"

I smile as I lean against my stick, "His name was Jarod. I was 14, almost 15. He kissed me behind the bleachers at a dance. My first sophomore dance I might add."

He nods and leans back across the table. He lines up another shot, dropping another stripe in a side pocket. He smiles back up at me as I shoot him a glare, "Are you a fucking hustler or something?"

He laughs as he walks back around to my side of the table and leans his ass against it, "Maybe. Next question. What attracted you to Ares in the very beginning? Before you ever even met me."

I smile at him, turning my head a bit to think about it. I turn back and step closer to him,

"It was something in your voice. I wanted you before I even knew what you looked like. When you sing, I feel this overwhelming sorrow in my soul. And it's weird because it is sorrowful but it makes me feel better. It was like your voice recognized everything broken in me and it was comforting. It made me feel seen, really seen for the first time in my life."

Gideon doesn't smile.

He doesn't have any expression on his face at all. He shakes his head then leans over the table, missing his next shot.

290

I laugh, "Ha! My turn."

I move around my side of the table, sinking a solid into the side pocket. I smile at him as I stand up, "What did you really think of me when we first met at the bar?"

He smiles as he turns around and takes a deep drink of his stout then turns back around to face me,

"Well, when I first met you at the bar I thought you were just this adorable little thing that had no clue how gorgeous she was. I saw you sitting there all alone, smiling at a glass of whisky and it was just amazing to me that you didn't have a flock of men around you."

I smile as I nod to him then begin to walk around the table.

He rounds to the far side of me as I go to line up another shot,

"But that is not what I thought the first time I saw you."

I look up at him from the table.

He is leaning his forearms onto the edge of the table, looking at his hands, "When I saw you at the restaurant. When you turned and your eyes met mine, the world stopped spinning. I know it was only a brief moment but I saw my entire life in your eyes that night. I saw us wrapped up in each other. I saw our children. I saw the life that was waiting for me inside those beautiful storm clouds in your eyes. It was only for a moment but it stunned me. I had to turn away from you so that I didn't chase you out into the street and beg you to come home with me."

I am completely entranced with him. I didn't even realize he remembered seeing me at the restaurant. Of course, I remembered him. I knew it was him as soon as he stepped up to me at the bar later that night. I smile back at him meekly,

"Oh."

He smiles again and points to the table, "Your shot."

I lean into the shot completely missing by a mile. I chuckle at myself, "Fuck. Well now it's your turn."

He smiles as he steps up and sinks another ball. I roll my eyes and take a drink of my whisky. He steps around the table and leans back on it in front of me. He gives me a smile,

"Why did you really get so distant after we got to my flat?"

I feel my heart rate tick up again. I am supposed to be completely truthful. That is the rules. I exhale heavily as I look everywhere but at him, "I am telling you now. It is stupid. I know it is stupid. But it bothered me when I asked about your relationship with Emily."

He smiles at me, "Babe, that was years ago." He is rubbing his hands up and down my arms giving me a knowingly smug grin.

I shake my head, "Yeah, I know it was years ago. It just sent me spiraling the way you said it."

He tilts his head to the side a bit, "How did I say it?"

I look past his shoulder again, "You said she left you. You didn't say you broke up."

He stands up in front of me, looking at me confused, "Isn't that the same thing?"

I shake my head and step around him to the far side of the table, "No. It is definitely not the same thing. Breaking up is a mutual thing. Both parties involved know what is happening and are letting it. When you said she left you, that just told me that she left and you didn't want her too. That you loved her so much you couldn't even agree to a break up."

He nods his head at me, looking down at the table. The cluster of balls left there. He rolls the cue stick around in his hands for a minute,

"Well, the truth is, she did leave me. She wanted something different. I didn't. She meant a lot to me. I did love

292

her. But her leaving didn't destroy me completely. Yes, at first, it was bad. It was really fucking bad. But then I found a sort of peace in it. I had held onto us for so long, even through all the bad that I was unable to see it for what it really was.

"She wasn't meant for me. I found a way to let it all go. I only found this real clarity a few months before I met you actually. That is why her photo was still there. I hadn't even been home yet to get rid of it."

I swallow the lump in my throat the best I can.

Why does it hurt so much to know that he loved someone before me? The man is 26 years old, I shouldn't expect to be the only person he has ever had feelings for. Letting my insecurities get the best of me I meekly ask, "Are you sure she is really in your past?"

He leans over the table at me, smiling,

"If she was in this very room right now I would have no idea because my heart only beats for you. No one else. Ever."

I smile at him again then shyly look down at the table, "Your shot."

Gideon smiles at me as he leans over the table and sinks another ball. All he has left is the 8 ball. I throw my hands up,

"God damn man. You could at least be a gentleman and pretend to let a girl win!"

He laughs at me then steps around next to me. He leans into my ear,

"My last question. How do you want me to fuck you tonight? Do you want me to tie you up and bring you to the brink of ecstasy then tease it away? Do you want me to sink my dick into you so fast and hard that you forget your own name? Or do you want me to let you ride me until you can't feel your legs and you can't imagine coming so hard again ever in your life?"

He pulls back and looks me in my eyes as I catch his glare, panting with need. I blow out a short breath,

"That is a very big decision. I should probably finish my drink before I answer that."

He smiles again as he turns around and sinks the 8 ball into the corner pocket right after he calls it. I put my pool stick up and quickly finished my drink. I smile at him,

"I am gonna go to the little girls room. I will be back in a minute."

He smiles at me and points past the bar in the other room,

"Around the bar, to the left."

I smile back at him, trying to keep my pussy in my pants.

Jesus fucking christ. I round the bar heading to the bathroom and I can still feel his eyes on me. I quickly pee then wash my hands, unable to stop smiling as I look at myself in the mirror. This is my new reality. I couldn't be happier. I wish I would have just talked to him about Emily earlier. I make a vow to myself right here staring into my reflection, that I will not let things simmer inside anymore.

I will approach him. He loves me.

I don't want him to worry. I don't want to give him any reason to think I am just going to walk away from this. I quickly dry my hands then step out of the bathroom.

There is a man walking out of the men's room next door at the same time. I glance up briefly,

"Oh Sorry. Excuse me."

I feel him move up close beside me, "What is your name dah len?" His voice is slurring like he has been here much longer than just for one drink.

I look up at him again then towards the bar, "I am sorry. I don't have time to talk. I have someone waiting for me."

I try to step around him but he blocks my path. I look back into his eyes, "Dude. Seriously. I am spoken for. Get the fuck out of my way."

I try to push him aside but he grabs me by my biceps and spins me around to the wall behind me. I scream, trying to pry his arms off of me, "Let me fucking go you piece of shit!"

He leans in close to me like he is going to try to kiss me. His breath reeking of cheap beer and even cheaper tobacco. I try not to gag,

"Oh come on baby. I can give you something you have never had before."

I continue to struggle when I see a fist come from the left punching the man in the jaw. He falls to his right as I scream again.

I look over to see Gideon standing there with fire in his eyes. His chest is heaving in anger and his neck is maroon like his blood pressure is through the roof.

He reaches down grabbing the man by his shirt collar and punches him again then again. I grab at his arms,

"Gideon Stop! Gideon your gonna fucking kill him STOP!"

It is like he can't even hear me. He pushes me back with one hand against the wall without even taking his eyes off the drunk on the floor. The air flies out of my lungs as I am flung back into the wall again.

He punches him and blood flies out of the man's mouth onto the floor and walls. Gideon kicks the man hard in the stomach and leans down closer to him,

"You put your hands on my wife, you piece of shit. She is fucking mine. You are going to fucking remember this the next time you hear a woman say no you pathetic bitch!"

He kicks him again in the gut. The man is groaning as he tries to crawl away from Gideon. I run in front of him, his eyes wild. I bring his face down to face me, "Gideon, I am here. Baby, I am fine. He didn't hurt me. See? See me? I am okay."

Gideon looks from the man to me then grips my hand tight and starts to pull me through the bar. The cold night air hits me like a slap in the face as I hear the bar door slam shut behind me. Gideon is still dragging me behind him,

"Gideon. Slow down. Please. Babe come on."

It feels like my shoulder is about to get popped out of place. He is yanking that hard on my arm. He rounds a corner into an alley still dragging me behind him. He turns me and slams my back into the wall. I feel the air as it is yanked from my lungs yet again. He is on me within a breath.

His lips slam into mine as he lifts me up by my thighs and pins me to the wall. I feel his tongue as he shoves it into my mouth. He grips my ass tight in one hand and my hair in the other. He is leaning so hard into me that I can feel the gravel of the wall biting into my exposed skin.

I try to push him away but he holds his grip on me. I bite his lip hard and he pulls back, eyes still wild. I try to shove him off me and get my feet back on the ground. He watches me struggle as he pushes me back into the wall again,

"You are fucking mine."

I go still. Afraid to look away. Afraid to breathe.

His eyes are echoing with this sovran phrase over and over.

You are fucking mine.

You are fucking mine.

I place my hand on his cheek, slipping deep into the onyx pools in front of me, not able to see the bottom,

"I am yours, Gideon. I am yours."

He nods his head to me, quickly, fervently then places his forehead on mine. I put my hands on the back of his neck,

"He didn't hurt me, baby. I am okay."

He continues to nod his head as I see the tears fall off his jaw and onto my chest. I can hear his heart beating so loudly it sounds like drums in my ears. Then I hear sirens in the distance,

"Come on. Let's go home. Okay?"

He continues to nod as he lowers me back down to the ground. I wrap his hand in mine as we step back out onto the sidewalk and turn towards home.

23
Ares
Sleeptalk - Dayseeker

I am shaking. I can still taste my own blood in my mouth from where Lily had bit my lip, begging for me to let her go.

I am fucking mortified with myself for my actions. I don't care about what happened to that man but what I did to her. It is unforgivable.

I don't speak the entire walk home. I don't even feel worthy enough of her anymore. How am I any better than the guy I pulled off of her? I lost control. I slammed her into a fucking wall. I'm disgusted with myself.

I didn't even fucking ask her if she was okay. I just saw red. I saw myself losing her and I lost all touch with reality.

She shuts the door quietly behind us as we walk back into the apartment. I slowly walk and sit on the piano bench looking out the window onto the street below.

Lily steps up beside me, standing close. She gently places her hand on my shoulder and I scoff it off. She takes a step back, lowly whispering,

"Okay."

She turns and leaves the room. I hear her crying as she steps away from me. I sit there staring into the night sky.

What the fuck is wrong with me? Why did I do that?

I had just felt at that exact moment that if I didn't kiss her, claim her, that she wasn't real. That she isn't even here.

I have never in my entire life felt like I have been in a dream that turned into a nightmare so quickly. The only thing that could ground me was her.

Her breath.

Her scent.

Her touch.

That didn't give me the fucking right to try to own her very being. I stand up and punch the brick wall in front of me until my knuckles are bleeding.

I hear myself scream at the wall. I feel my skin breaking open as I continue to smash my fist into the wall. It feels like there is something inside of me trying to claw its way out from my very core.

I stand there, breathing heavily, blood dripping on the floor beside me. I turn to see Lily standing in the doorway to the bedroom crying. I look back out the window and sit back on the piano bench, hearing the bedroom door shut again.

I sit there for what feels like hours, just staring out into the night. I hear a quick knock at the door that jars me out of my thoughts.

I turn and look to the bedroom door seeing it still shut. I stand and walk across the room to the front door. I open it to see Matthew and Simone standing there. Simone slides past me,

"Fucking idiot."

She quickly runs to the bedroom slamming the door behind her. I look back at Matthew then take a step back to let him in.

He walks in looking me up and down, noticing my hand. He points to the small island that separates the kitchen from the living room and points,

"Sit down."

I shut the door then turn and take a seat at the island, placing my forearms on the countertop in front of me. Of course she called them. She hates me. She has to hate me. I feel completely fucking empty.

Matthew walks back into the kitchen from the bathroom with a small first aid kit. He cleans my knuckles, putting butterfly bandages on them,

"You probably fucking need stitches."

My eyes never leave the counter in front of me, "No, I don't."

He closes up the last knuckle then throws the first aid kit on the kitchen counter behind him.

"What the fuck were you thinking man? You scared the shit out of her!"

I look towards the door to avoid his glare. He leans onto the island, "You just punched a fucking brick wall until your knuckles busted the fuck open dude. What the hell happened?"

I look back towards him, "Didn't she tell you?"

He nods his head, "She said some dude hit on her at the bar and you lost your shit. You beat the hell out of him then wouldn't speak to her. Then when you got home you beat the fuck out of the wall, screaming like a fucking madman."

I close my eyes, she can't even bring herself to say what I did to her. I have never felt as worthless as I do right now. I place my hands palm down, fingers spread on the counter,

"After I beat the fuck out of that guy, I dragged her out to the fucking alley and pinned her to the wall. I forced myself on her. She had to bite my lip to get me off of her."

Matthew lets out an exhausted and heavy huff, "God dammit Gideon. What were you thinking?"

I look up at him,

"I wasn't. It felt like none of it was real. I saw him pin her to the wall. He had her by both arms and was trying to kiss her. I watched him lower his body to hers and everything turned off. I just went black. Then we were in the alley and I just needed to touch her. I just needed to know she was real. That she wasn't lying dead in the bar. When I finally started to calm down, she was crying and leading me back to the apartment."

Matthew reaches on top of the fridge and pulls down a bottle of scotch. He unscrews the lid, trying to hand me the bottle but I turn back towards the door again.

I hear him take a long drink from it before screwing the lid back on and setting it on the counter. I continue staring at the door,

"She is going to leave me. And I am going to let her." Matthew huffs again as he leans back on the counter, "You don't know that man."

I look at him, defeated, "I want her to leave me."

I see movement out of the corner of my eye. I look towards the bedroom door to see Lily standing there wide eyed.

My heart breaks into a thousand pieces.

She nods her head slowly. An unreadable expression on her face. She reaches into her pocket and takes her phone out slamming it into the hardwood floor in front of her.

We all jump at the force of it hitting the floor and bouncing into the kitchen. She turns back into the bedroom and comes back out with her messenger bag.

She gives Simone a kiss on the cheek then steps up to the trash can. She pulls Aphrodite out of the bag and throws the mask on top of the trash then slams the lid shut.

I feel myself flinch and then a tear slides down my cheek.

She walks past me. I reach out and touch her hand. She stops and turns to me. No tears in her eyes.

I scour her face for some hint of emotion but nothing is there.

"You don't deserve what I have done to you."

My heart feels like it is going to explode. She nods her head,

"You're right. I don't deserve the love and happiness and contentment you have given me. I don't deserve the security. I don't deserve the pure pleasure you have brought into my life. Just go on without me. Go back to being the way that you were. Before you ever made the mistake of meeting me."

She drops her hand from mine and takes another step towards the door. She turns her face over her shoulder, "I love you. Just throw all of my shit away. I don't need it anymore."

Then she is gone.

I pick up the stool I am sitting on, screaming I throw it across the room. I flip the coffee table then fall to my knees around the scattered remains of the broken table.

I can't even see anything in front of me. I am crying so hard. I brace myself on the floor with my fists so I don't fall flat on my face. I shake my head back and forth,

"I had to make her leave. I would have hurt her. I couldn't live with myself. I don't even want to live with myself now."

Simone walks over to Matthew.

"I don't like the way she was talking. Why would she have us throw all her shit away? She told me in the bedroom that she didn't think she deserved the devotion he showed her."

I laugh into the open air in front of me, "Devotion? Fucking devotion? I pinned her to a fucking wall and tried to force myself on her!"

Simone turns to me,

"Because you couldn't imagine the fact that you might have fucking lost her seconds before. Then you refuse to fucking speak to her. You won't even let her touch you then you tried to take down a brick fucking wall with your bare hands.

"Are you really this fucking dense? Are you really this fucking stupid? She thinks you want nothing to do with her because loving her made you that way. That you didn't scare yourself. That she scared you. She was going to leave anyway. Because you made her think that she was destroying you."

I turn and look at Simone as she fumes at me. She starts shaking her head back and forth then turns to Matthew, "She just kept saying it is happening all over again and she couldn't stop crying. What the fuck is happening again?" I stare at her, unable to believe the words she is saying. I look to the door as Simone turns back to me,

"Your a fucking idiot Gideon! I have never in my fucking life seen one person make so many fucking mistakes in a row. Now she is out there, by herself. No way to get ahold of anyone because she destroyed her fucking phone. All she has is the clothes on her back, walking around London of all god damn places in the middle of the night in the rain."

She puts her hands to her forehead, "How are you this fucking stupid? Then you said you wanted her to leave. It just confirmed all of her god damn fears."

She turns back to Matthew as I sit there staring at the floor in confusion. "I am going after her. This dumbass needs to wake the fuck up. Did you hear her? She fucking kissed me before she left!"

She turns from Matthew back to me, "She didn't say goodbye to you. She said goodbye to everything. How can you not see this!?"

My eyes reach Matthews as Simone runs out the front door and down the hallway. I hear her words in my head again,

I don't deserve the love and happiness and contentment you have given me. Just go on without me. Go back to being the way that you were. Before you ever made the mistake of meeting me.

She wouldn't.

She wouldn't. Not over me.

She wouldn't.

I stand and run down the hallway after Simone. I take the steps two at a time then I am running out onto the street. The rain is coming down in sheets now.

I look both ways but don't see Simone or Lily. I turn to my right and run down to the end of the block looking down the street seeing nothing. Matthew runs out the front door, "I will go this way. You keep going that way!"

I nod as I continue to run looking down every street. I have probably made it 10 city blocks when I feel my phone vibrate in my pocket. I pull the phone out seeing it is Simone,

"Where is she? Did you find her?"

I hear her intake of breath, "No. I couldn't find her. She is just gone."

I lean back and scream into the night, "FUCK!"

I inhale deeply, "Keep fucking looking Simone. We have to fucking find her."

She hangs up as I continue to search every corner, every alley. I run through the rain for over an hour. She is gone.

I turn and start to make my way back to the apartment.

If she does what we fear she is going to do. If tomorrow she is no longer breathing the same air as me, laying under the same sky.

How can I live with myself?

Knowing I broke her so deeply. More than her mother. More than her sister. I just don't want to hurt her anymore.

It takes me another hour and half to make it home. I round the corner to the apartment. I glance across the street and see someone sitting on a park bench. I blink heavily through the rain. I can see just a small figure sitting stone still. Then I see her messenger bag draped across her body. I finally realize it is

304

Lily. I run across the street at full speed, not even bothering to check for traffic. I sprint up to her, crouching in front of her.

She won't even look me in the eyes. She continues to stare at the ground at her feet.

"Baby? Lily? Lilith?"

Nothing.

She continues to stare wide eyed at the sidewalk.

I cradle her small body to mine like a baby as I carry her back upstairs. She is freezing and completely drenched. She has been out here for hours, completely fucking alone.

I kick open the apartment door sending it flying into the wall beyond it. Simone jumps off the couch, "Matthew he is here! He has her!"

Matthew comes running out of the bedroom. I run past him into the bedroom and sit her down on the end of the bed. She continues to look past me at the floor. I grab her bag and pull it off her body, tossing it to the side.

"Simone, help me get these wet clothes off of her. Please!"

Simone kneels beside me and pulls Lily's shoes off. I watch her peel her socks off as I pull her jacket down off her shoulders throwing it on the floor as well, "Matthew grab a towel."

He nods in my direction and turns to the bathroom for a towel.

"Baby, I am going to lay you back so I can get these wet jeans off you okay?" She doesn't even blink.

She just continues to stare in front of her.

I lay her back on the bed gently. I struggle to peel the drenched denim from her body. The fabric clings to her skin like a newborn to its mother.

Finally freeing her of the soaked garment, I throw it behind me into the ever enlarging pile of wet clothes collecting into a puddle on the floor.

Matthew rushes back in and tosses me a towel. I pull her back into a sitting position and wrap the towel tightly around her.

"Lily? Can you hear me?"

She doesn't even blink. Her eyes are fully dilated like when she first wakes up. She has no emotions, no expression on her face at all. I look at Simone,

"Check her bag. Make sure there isn't booze or something in there. She must have drank something."

Simone nods and pulls the bag up onto the bed. I continue to dry off Lily's arms and legs with the ends of the towel.

I look at Simone as she pulls a small white baggy out of the satchel. I would recognize those little rocks in powder anywhere.

I pull her into me, cradling her body to me,

"God FUCKING dammit! She is fucking high."

Matthew grabs the baggie from Simone and leaves the room, two seconds later I hear the toilet flush.

Simone runs around the end of the bed to me, "Come on. We have to get her warm."

I nod as I pick her up and Simone pulls the blankets back on the bed. I wrap the blankets tightly around her body. Lily continues to stare at the wall until finally her eyes close hours later.

24
Aphrodite
Pretend My Pain Away - Citizen Soldier

I am done.

I am nothing.

I am ready to go back to the life I was intended to have. With nothing and no one. I crack my eyes open, flinching back at the sunlight coming through the window.

How? How am I still fucking here?

I did three times as much coke last night than I used to do back at St. Francis. I can't even fucking kill myself right.

I blink rapidly, trying to adjust to the light in the room. I see Gideon jump up and run over to me. He must have been sitting on the floor between the windows. I do not want to see him. I can not face the person I have turned him into.

I am disgusted with myself.

I scoot back further into the bed trying to get away from his grasp. He still reaches forward, grabbing me and pulling me to him.

He weeps as he cradles me in his arms,

"I thought you were fucking gone. Lily. I thought you were fucking dead. Then you were just here. And you were drenched. You wouldn't say a fucking word. Then we found the coke. What the fuck were you thinking little one? Why would you do that? I almost lost you."

I have nothing to say to him. I am nothing.

I continue to stare past him out the window.

He pulls back from me after I have not even dared breath. He tries to look in my eyes and I turn my gaze in a different direction.

He lays me back down on the bed as he falls back on his ass on the floor. I roll over to face the other wall and close my eyes again.

I can't do this.

It is too much.

I pull the covers back off me gently. I look at my arms and see handprints. I look at my stomach seeing more fingerprints there too. Black and blue mares my skin but I don't care. I just want to be anywhere but here.

I see my clothes thrown in a corner and my bag half spilled out onto the floor. I close my eyes. I remember everything that happened last night. I couldn't do anything. I couldn't move, I could barely even breathe.

They never even saw me right across the street. They didn't see that guy approach me, they didn't hear me asking him where I could score some blow. I sat there, under the cover of a tree as I snorted half the damn baggie into my system. When I finally moved back to the bench, I put a rock under my tongue. I just let the effects of my actions take over my being.

I let out a small sigh then stand and walk to the dresser. I pull out some leggings and a t-shirt. I sit on the end of the bed and slide some socks on. I walk past the bed to the closet slowly yanking my suitcase out. I sit it on the end of the bed, unzipping it and throwing the top open.

Gideon jumps off the floor moving to me swiftly.

He grabs the top of the suitcase and slams it back shut,

"No. No. We are not going to keep playing this fucking game. This fucking merri go round we think is a relationship. You are not leaving."

I stare past him at the wall.

As soon as he turns away, I throw the lid of the suitcase back open and turn to the dresser to grab my clothes. He picks up the suitcase, throwing it across the room.

I let out another sigh as I sit my clothes down on the bed then walk over and pick the suitcase up.

I try to sit it back on the bed and Gideon pulls it from my hands, flinging it behind him,

"Why are you doing this?"

I turn away from him and grab my overnight bag. I start to clear my perfume and lotions from the top of the dresser.

Gideon steps up to me,

"Will you fucking SAY something!? Why are you fucking doing this?"

I turn and look him dead in the eyes, "Because you want me to leave you."

He takes a step back like he has been shot.

I take advantage of the moment. I step around him and pick the suitcase back up, laying it on the bed. I flip the top open and he spins me to him,

"Why the coke? Were you just trying to get back at me for before? Trying to fucking make me feel what you felt?"

I shake my head no to him. He shakes me, "Fucking talk to me Lily!"

I turn away from him, "I wasn't trying to get back at you."

I reach into the dresser pulling out more clothes. He grabs them from my hands and throws them onto the bed,

"Then what? What the fuck was that about?"

I turn to him, somberly,

"It's the only thing that has ever made the noise stop. It seemed like the easiest way to get it to all just stop. The

309

screaming, her voice. Your voice. I just didn't want to hear it in my head anymore. All I could do was just sit there, just hearing you say over and over that you wanted me to leave you. So I did."

I turn and sit down on the bed. I stare at the dresser in front of me, "I am cursed."

Gideon kneels in front of me, "You are not cursed baby. You're not."

I pull my hands back from his, "Please don't fucking touch me. I ruin everything that I touch."

He rocks towards me onto his knees, "Don't fucking say that. Lily, don't fucking talk like that."

I look into his eyes. He reaches up and puts a strand of hair behind my ear, "Why? Baby why did you do it?"

I blink back the tears,

"Because I love you too much to let myself live."

He wraps me in his arms and just holds me. He is shaking so fucking hard. I just want him to let me go. I want to just disappear. He coughs loudly over my shoulder, choking on his own tears.

I push him slightly to make him pull away from me. I look back down at my clothes thrown on the bed, the half packed overnight bag.

He isn't going to let me just take my stuff and go. He feels guilty for what I did. I turn to him,

"It was my choice, ya know. I didn't do it because I don't love you or because I don't think you love me. I did it because.....because that is the only way you are ever going to be free. You are only still sitting here right now out of pity. Because you couldn't live with yourself if I followed through with it. That is no way to live Gideon. You deserve so much more than I can give you. I have said it from the beginning and I will say it until my dying breath. You deserve so much fucking better than me."

I stand and walk from the bedroom into the living room.

I see the bent metal of the stool he threw against the wall. I see the shattered remains of the coffee table across the floor.

Simone and Matthew are sitting on the couch just staring at me as I walk by. I turn to Simone,

"I am sorry. I didn't think about what any of this would do to you. To either of you. I truly apologize for that. As soon as he lets me leave, I will be gone. None of you will have to ever deal with me again. I promise."

Matthew wraps his arm around Simone pulling her closer. I can hear her whimper out a cry but I just don't have the strength for anything right now. I walk past them to the piano.

I sit down and start to play Firestorm. Out of my periphery, I see Gideon step into the living room. The words just begin to flow out of me,

"We're a disaster waiting to happen,
a bomb set to explode at any moment

Our love is a wildfire, burning out of control
Leaving nothing but ashes in its wake

And when the flames finally die down,
when we're left standing amongst the ruins

Only then do we realize what we've done,
Only then do we feel the weight of our actions

But by then, it's too late isn't it?
The damage has been done, and we can't turn back time

We can only stand here and watch as our love falls apart in front of our very eyes."

I pull my hands off the keys and stare at them. I step over to a weeping Matthew and reach into his coat pocket pulling out his cigarettes.

I take one lighting it quickly then toss him back the lighter. I move back to the piano bench and crack the window open behind it. I turn to the window, bracing my feet on the window sill and stare out across the city before me.

A few minutes later, I hear the front door shut. Then I see Gideon picking up the pieces of the broken table and start putting it into a trash bag.

I continue to smoke my cigarette watching the people below. Gideon sits on the end of the couch closest to me, "We will go get you a new phone today."

I shake my head, "Don't bother. I have no one to talk to anyways."

Gideon lets out a sigh, "I have really lost you haven't I?"

I look at him briefly before flicking the butt of my cigarette out the window. I turn back to the piano and start to play something that is just sitting on my chest.

I can see Gideon sit up, not recognizing the music. I close my eyes as the tears start to fall.

"We painted our worlds in colors so bright,
But time faded the hues, and took away the light.

I reach for your hand in the cold, lonely air,
But find nothing but shadows, where you used to care.

Love that's lost, where did you go?
A broken heart, a shattered dream,
In the silence, your absence screams

The echoes of laughter, they linger in my mind,
But the warmth of your touch, I can no longer find.

I walk this road alone, with tears in my eyes,
Searching for the pieces of a love that died

Love that's lost, why did you have to go?
The heartache echoes, a relentless refrain,
In the empty spaces, I whisper your name."

I pull my hands away from the keys again and slowly close the lid. I turn back around on the bench and look out the window. Gideon comes up beside me and crouches down beside the bench, trying to get down to eye level with me.

I feel his hand on my chin as he turns my face towards him. I let my head turn but keep my eyes closed.

I can't look at him. Everything is gone.

Everything is broken and I don't know how to fix it.

I let out a breath, "I am sorry. What I did. I shouldn't have done it. I just wanted it all to stop. This viscous fucking cycle of hurting. I just wanted it gone. It was selfish and I am sorry."

Gideon strokes my cheek with his hand,

"When I realized what you had done, I felt so much guilt. Anger. Resentment. All at myself. And I deserve it. Every last bit of it. I don't want to lose you Lily. I don't care if that is selfish. I don't fucking care about anything but you. But, please, don't hurt yourself again. Can you promise me that? Please baby?"

I open my eyes, really looking at him for the first time. He is just as broken as me. He has his own scars but they match mine.

I am finally starting to notice all the defects in his facade. All the cracks in his armor. I nod my head to him then turn back to the window. I let out a heavy breath,

"I love you Gideon. I love you so fucking much. But I will only destroy you. I think I have proven that."

Gideon moves in front of me, sitting on the windowsill,

"Baby, we have destroyed each other. We can't keep doing this. We love each other. I made mistakes, you made mistakes. We both have to stop doing that. We have to trust in each other. If you want to leave I will not stop you but please know, I don't want you to go.

"I couldn't see everything from your perspective. I thought you were going to look at me as a villain. I should have just told you what I was fearing. I shouldn't have left it pent up like I did. I love you Lily. I can't live in this world without you."

I nod at him,

"I love you too, Gideon. I love you so fucking much. I just don't want it to make you something you're not. You turned into a different person last night. I thought you hated me for it."

He reaches out and grabs my hands,

"No baby. I don't hate you. I acted that way because of how much I love you. And this isn't justifying it at all. But when I saw what he was doing, my brain went to the worst possible scenario. I thought you were gone. I thought you were taken from me. Then we were in the alley and you were there and I just had to feel you. I had to prove to myself that you were real. I am so fucking sorry."

I reach up and touch his cheek,

"Why didn't you just tell me that?"

314

He looks at me,

"Because I was ashamed of myself. Disgusted with myself. You deserve so much more than that Lily. You deserve the world."

I shake my head,

"No. I don't want all that. I just want you. Only you."

I stand up and move to his lap. I wrap my arms around him and hold him tight as we both weep.

It has been two weeks since our fall. Two weeks since we arose from the ashes, like a phoenix reborn.

I have fallen in love with her a dozen more times since then. Her smile, her soul, her inability to give up on me. On us.

Lily is air. She is my pulse. She is my beautiful little disaster. We don't speak about that night.

What I did. What she did.

We buried it. Where it will remain.

She did agree though to start seeing a therapist. It took me, Susie and Edge to convince her it was for the best but we finally got through to her. She needs to figure it all out inside of her head. To try to sort through her past. To help her have a future. I agreed to go with her. We need to keep each other in check. Make sure those demons really are gone for good.

Susie and Edge showed up the afternoon after it all happened. I have never seen someone so pissed and grateful at the same time. Susie refused to go home. She said she is staying with her family, with her sister. I am amazed by the strength that woman permeates.

I hear the knock at the door, smiling that I know exactly who it is and what time it was. I open the door to see Matthew standing there in black tux, black shirt, satin white cumberbund.

Holding Apollo in his hand. He smiles as he raises it up, "Are you ready to do this?"

I grab Ares off the counter, "You best fucking believe it. Let's go."

I follow him out the door, locking it behind me.

We make our way down to the street and climb into the stretch SUV that is awaiting us. I smile at Simone and Mona.

The last stop is at Edge's house then we will head to the ceremony. Not much longer and it will be official.

We will be married. Finish line met.

I smile as we pull to a stop and Edge jumps in holding Dionysus in his hand. Simone hands us all a shot of vodka,

"Let's do this shit!"

We all take our shot and slide our masks on.

We stop just outside of the abandoned granary that Mona has found. It is fucking perfect. Yeah it doesn't have much of a ceiling left and 45% of the walls are missing but that kinda fits us. We all have crumbling walls and pieces of us missing. But we are still making beautiful things out of what is left.

There are a lot of cameras everywhere but that is what we had agreed too. We made this an open event for the media. With one exception, no video. They can take all the pictures they want but no audio, no recording. We want to be able to say our vows in peace. Without them being leaked onto the web within 2 minutes of saying I do.

We will all be in costume until the very end.

The SUV door opens and Apollo steps out then reaches his hand back in, palm up for Hera to take. After Dionysus slides out, doing the same for Hestia.

I am the last one. I take one last deep breath then slide out into the frenzy of cameras awaiting me.

I don't say a word to anyone. I don't stop and pose for a picture. I stride directly through the black gothic style columns the abandoned building has been decorated with. There is black tulle draped across the open ceiling in long sheets.

The runway has white linen to walk on to get to the preacher standing behind a gothic podium at the back of the building. There is a music-only rendition of Evermore playing in the background.

I take my place at the end of the aisle. Standing perfectly still waiting for my que. This is me becoming Ares a bit more. Forging my path with the woman I love.

The music changes to Firestorm and I know it is beginning. I turn slowly to see Hera in her long black satin gown holding a single white rose being led to the front by Apollo.

A few moments later Hestia is being escorted down by Dionysus in the same long black satin gown as Hera holding a simple white rose.

I smile at my friends as they settle beside me, across from me. I turn back to see Susie, wearing a long red satin dress to match the style of the other girls.

Her face is half covered by a white satin mask. She smiles at me and gives me a thumbs up as she settles into her maid of honor spot in front of the other girls. I glance over my shoulders at the guys and Edge is starry eyed staring at Susie.

I smile at him because I understand exactly how he feels.

The tempo in the music changes, becoming slower. I close my eyes and turn to face the aisle again. I know she is there. I can feel her presence. I hear the intake of breath from everyone watching.

I hear cameras flashing like crazy. I let out the breath I am holding and open my eyes.

Aphrodite is slowly moving towards me in a long off white lace dress. Completely see through to the black negligee underneath.

Her long silky black hair flows down her back. The closer she gets to me I can see that the lace has a pattern to it.

It looks like waves on the ocean. She steps up to me, holding a bouquet of white roses. I quickly realize that we are almost eye level.

I glance down at her 6 inch heels and smile to myself. I look back into her eyes through the mask. I can see her mouth pulled into a smile.

I lift the lace veil off her face and Susie leans forward to smooth it down her hair.

She smiles at Susie, handing her the bouquet from her hands. She turns back to me and takes my hands as the preacher starts the ceremony.

The preacher was hand picked by Lily herself. With some help from Simone. She smiles out into the crowd, "Friends, family, we are gathering here today to bear witness to the love shared between these two amazing individuals. Through hardships and falters, they have held onto each other with a grace and perseverance that should be envied by all of us. I would like to share with you this moment, this one ripple in an ocean that will reach time itself."

The preacher smiles at me then to Aphrodite. She leans forward just a touch, "The bride and groom have decided to say their own vows. Please be respectful of their wishes and turn your phones or recording devices off if they are not already." She continues to smile across the room but pin almost every single person with a stare. I chuckle at her as Aphrodite smiles back at me. She looks to the preacher who gives her a curt nod.

Aphrodite turns her eyes back to mine, "I never intended on finding what we have. I never knew that this type of power even existed. I have spent a lifetime struggling, just trying to make it through the next day with some type of mental clarity that would allow me to continue. The night that I met you changed all of that. When you smiled at me, my walls instantly crashed down.

"When you seeked me out, there was no way that I would have ever been able to find the strength to say no. You have had me, all of me from the moment our eyes met. I promise to spend the rest of my life loving you, being in love with you and showing you the power of that love every second of every day. You are my constant. You are my end. You are my everything."

She continues to smile at me as I feel the tears running down my face. She squeezes my hands and I glance to the preacher then back to Aphrodite, "You have altered me in ways that I don't think even I understand. You have ingrained yourself into my very soul. I cannot imagine a world without you in it. I have wandered this earth, a hollow shell of the person I thought I was becoming. The moment you smiled at me, I was yours. Your essence, your mercy, your forgiveness have all become gifts that I am afraid I will never be able to repay.

"But I will try to, every single day for the rest of my life. You have taken all of my demons, my flaws and polished them. You make me a better person. You are my breath and I intend to be the same for you until the gods call us home. Even then, I will still be by your side."

When it comes time to exchange the rings I turn to Apollo as he hands me the antique style white gold band I had custom made just for her.

I see a tear fall off her jaw when I slide it onto her finger. She turns to Susie then back to me as she slides a black titanium band flecked with gold onto my finger. The preacher then pronounces us as man and wife.

I wrap one arm around her back and dip her deeply. Kissing her with as much passion as our masks will allow.

We stand back up, holding each other tightly as everyone joins us and we pose for a few photos. She takes her bouquet from Susie and holds it high above her head as I take her hand and guide her back down the aisle.

I pass my mother, blowing her a kiss as she cries into her handkerchief. We stop back out front, just holding each other. Staring into each other's faces. We did it. We made it. I can still hear the cameras going crazy behind us so I lean in close to Edge and whisper, "Two days time, party at the hotel. Inner circle only." Edge smiles as he pulls back from me then wraps his arm himself. He smiles loosely at me, "We will be there."

I grin back at them before turning and waving to everyone then move further towards the road. We make it back to the awaiting limo and give one last wave to the crowd before we crawl inside.

Aphrodite turns to me as soon as the door is shut and pulls the mask off my face then slams her lips into mine. I hold the back of her head as she continues to lean deeper into me.

She pulls back breathless a few moments later. I look down at her dress,

"Is that a fucking garter belt?"

She bites her lower lip and nods her head, "Yes."

I let a growl slip out of my mouth as the driver hurls us closer to Claridges, which will be our home for the next 2 weeks.

I slide my mask back on as we pull up and readjust myself so everyone doesn't get a whole different type of show as I step out of the limo.

I hold my hand out to her, palm up and she gently places her hand in mine as we make our way inside. There are more photographers waiting lining the doors.

But fuck if I care. I just want to be inside with her.

She smiles at everyone as we pass by them.

Then as we move to go inside, she hands her bouquet to the doorman and slaps his bicep with a smile. He smiles back and nods his head to her.

As soon as the door shuts to the honeymoon suite, she is in my arms. I take her mask off and throw it across the room, followed quickly by my own.

I grip her face in my hands,

"I haven't seen you in almost 2 days. I was dying."

Lily laughs back into my mouth, "I saw you waiting at the end of the aisle for me and I almost dropped on the spot. You are so fucking handsome. My ovaries almost exploded."

I smile back into her mouth as I kiss her harder. She pushes my jacket over my shoulders and lets it fall to the floor.

I reach back and unclip the cumberbund as she slides the suspenders down my arms and starts to unbutton my shirt.

I pull back looking down at her dress,

"How the fuck do I get this thing off? Did they fucking paint it on you?"

She smiles as she slowly peels it over her shoulders then down her arms and hips until it lands in a puddle at her feet.

Without the lace dress I can see the lingerie set she is wearing is black but I can see straight through it.

I look back up at her, "You wore this for everyone to see?"

She smiles back at me, "I offered myself up, bare for only you Gideon. Only you."

I growl again as I pick her up and spin her closer to the bed. I rip the rest of my shirt open, buttons bouncing off the floor.

She laughs at me as she reaches down and unbuttons my slacks and pushes them off my hips.

I reach up behind her and start to unclasp the back of the corset until it finally opens up to me and I pull it from her. I sit her down on the bed as I unclasp one garter strap clip then move to the other side unclasping it as well, never taking my eyes off of hers.

I reach up and slide the lace underwear down her legs. She reaches down to start to roll down her stockings and I put my hand on hers,

"Leave them."

I smile at her as I unclasp the garter belt itself from her waist. I lean in, kissing her hungrily.

Lily smiles at me as she starts to lean forward and push up from the bed. I turn sitting on the edge of the bed watching her walk before me in nothing but black stockings and 6 inch heels.

Every fantasy I have ever had in my life coming true in that one moment. She steps over to the bar and grabs the bottle of chilled champagne.

She turns back to me as she smiles and pops the cork on the bottle. Slowly, she makes her way back to me, stopping half way as she tips the bottle to her mouth, taking a deep drink.

I watch champagne roll down her chin and onto her chest.

I stand and prowl over to her, finally feeling released from this prison I have been holding myself in for years.

Her eyes meet mine as she pulls the bottle away and I lick the champagne from her chest all the way up her neck and to her chin.

She lets out a deep moan as she tilts her head back and closes her eyes, smiling at the ceiling. I wrap the back of her hair around my hand and pull hard enough that her mouth falls open in front of me.

I kiss her so sharply that it seems to surprise her. I take the bottle of champagne from her and take a big swig of it before I turn the bottle and pour some into her open mouth. She smiles as she turns towards me and kisses me, pushing the champagne from her mouth into mine. I hungrily drink it in. I turn her and start walking her towards the window. I sit the open bottle of champagne on the table as I continue towards the window.

As she stands there in front of me, I move beside her and push the curtains open. She can see the city spread out before her.

I take her right arm, raising it above her head, tightly wrapping the sheer curtain around it. I grab her left arm doing the same then stand behind her.

I press her naked form into the window, arms spread wide and held over her head. I reach my hand down from behind and feel her dripping for me. I lean into her ear,

"You are running down your legs Lilith."

I let my fingers collect her wetness back up her leg as I push her thighs apart and run two fingers down her center.

Lily lets out another breathless moan as I watch her turn her face, pressing the left side into the glass along with her tits. I step up behind her, now that the heels have made her the perfect height and slam myself into her entrance.

Her hands grip the curtains tight as I put one hand on the window to brace myself and wrap the other around her body to clench it around her neck.

Lily is pushing back into me with as much strength as me shoving my cock inside her. I can hear the curtain rod tense with every thrust into her body.

Her eyes still closed she heavily breathes out, "Fuck me Gideon."

I tighten my grip on her throat as I continue to throw myself up into her. I can feel myself hitting the walls inside her as she starts to moan my name louder with every thrust.

I slide my hand down her chest until my fingers are sinking into the heated folds between her legs. I smother my face into her neck as I continue to push further, harder into her.

I kiss her gently on the neck then bite down right above her shoulder.

She screams my name as I feel her start to clamp down on me. The curtains moving with the force of me slamming into her pussy.

I wrap my hands around her hips and pull her ass a bit higher for me. I lean my head back into my shoulders and start grunting louder as I continue to hammer myself into her from behind.

I feel her clamp down on me hard and I lose all sense of space and time. I wrap one hand around her, laying it flat against her pussy and I steady her writhing body with the other and continue to make her scream with my intrusions.

I reach up quickly and unwrap her hands from the curtains and pull her a step back with me still in her.

I bend her forward making her splay her hands out on the glass in front of her. I grip her hips tight as I watch myself fucking destroy her from behind.

She starts moaning again and I know I am going to make her cum again. I slap her ass hard, "Cum all over my cock baby. Fucking do it."

Her head is hanging low between her shoulders as I feel her start to tremble around me again. I smile as I take my thumb and reach up, shoving it into her mouth. I feel her suck on it and roll her tongue around it before I pull it out then slide it into her asshole.

Her back arches again and I feel the flutters inside start to pick up as I fill both of her holes.

I hear her muttering to herself,

"God fucking dammit. Oh my god."

I smile wickedly at the back of her head as I pull my thumb out then wrap her hair around my hand again.

I hear her moan my name as I pull it roughly back towards me, making her arch her back ever lower.

I slam into her again and I feel her clench onto my dick even harder than before.

I lean forward into her, "I am gonna cum baby. Cum on my cock. Do it now."

As if my wish was instantly granted, she screams out my name as I feel her start pulsating in waves down my dick.

I scream her name as I continue to slam into her, releasing everything I have. I continue to pummel her until I feel her waves starting to subside.

I slowly pull out of her and lean down to kiss her ass cheek where my handprint now resides. She stands up, a bit wobbly but smiling and turns to me.

She wraps her arms around my neck and kisses me hard. Harder than she ever has before. I lift her up bridal style carrying her over the bed and lay her out before me.

I lean down over her and slowly slide off each heel then roll each stocking slowly down her legs.

I slide back up the bed parting her thighs and lowering my face to her center. Her eyes come down to meet mine and I smile,

"I am not going to make you stop cumming until you are crying my name."

I lean in and lick her straight up her center, flicking her clit with the tip of my tongue.

She arches her back up on the bed and lays her head back into the pillow. I lean back into her licking, nibbling, sucking her clit into my mouth then biting down gently on it.

Her hands are on the back of my head pushing me further into her. She spreads her legs wider as I continue to claim every sweet inch of her pussy.

She lets out another scream a moment later and starts thrusting her cunt into my face.

I hold her hips down and continue to suck on her clit until I can hear her weeping. I smile as I look up at her.

Her make up completely fucking destroyed and running down her face in streaks from her tears. I kiss the inside of her thigh then climb up her body and kiss her lips.

She wraps her arms around my neck and kisses me back with enough heat to even make the sun want to explode.

I lay down beside her, running my fingers up and down the center of her chest between her breasts.

Her breathing is slowly coming back to normal when she turns to me smiling with her eyes still closed,

"I am a fucking wreck. You just fucking destroyed me."

I let a deep chuckle leave my chest,

"I am just getting started. I thought I would give you a moment to breathe. The next two weeks baby, my dick is never leaving your body."

She smiles again, opening her eyes to me,

"I have never heard better words in my life."

I smile at her as I lean in and kiss her deeply then roll myself back on top of her to claim her again.

The only time we leave the bed in the next 48 hours was to eat, bathe or use the bathroom. We invaded each other for hours on end. Barely sleeping as we explore each other deeper than before.

We finally come up for air long enough to get dressed and meet everyone down at the hotel bar for drinks and to officially celebrate the nuptials with our friends, our family. Lily and I sit at the bar sipping our drinks, smiling at each other. I lean into her shoulder, "Have you talked to Susie since the wedding?"

327

She smiles but shakes her head no, "I have not but I have a feeling she is going to have a lot to say to me tonight. As far as I know, she has been staying with Edge since she got to town."

I let a deep chuckle leave my chest as I sit back up and look towards the door. They aren't here yet but I am sure they will be soon. We may have to find somewhere else to go since this place is a bit too nice for the kind of trouble we usually end up getting into. I take another sip of my drink when I see Lily's eyes light up and look past me. I turn in my seat to see Matthew and Simone walking in.

I smile towards them, "Hey guys. How is it going tonight?" Simone walks up and smacks me in the arm, "Shut up and hug me! I am so fucking happy for you both. Seriously!" I laugh as I hug her back. She then promptly pushes me away and moves to Lily. I hear her whispering in her ear, "I love you so fucking much Lil. I am so happy for you guys."

Lily smiles as she looks at me, "I love you to Simone. I am so grateful that you are one of my best friends. I don't know how I ever survived without you." She closes her eyes tight then smiles wider.

Matthew puts his hand on my shoulder, smiling, "So how does it feel to be married off you old fucker?" I smile laughing back at him.

I glance at Lily then back towards Matthew, "Satisfied. I feel very *very* satisfied." Matthew shakes his head and rolls his shoulders, "Too much info man. Too fucking much." I laugh out loud at him as Lily and Simone finally part.

Lily grabs her glass then turns back to Matthew smiling, "So I guess since I am an old married woman that pin is gonna have to stay in the threesome huh?" I laugh at her then glance back at Matthew.

He smiles devilishly, "That pin can be removed anytime you want to baby." I lean forward and smack him in the chest as

328

he starts laughing. Moments later everyone else starts to filter in. I notice pretty quickly that Edge shows up 5 minutes after Susie. Maybe they aren't together after all.

Susie is smiling from ear to ear, like nothing is wrong at all though so I just let it pass. Edge is standing beside me but I notice his eyes straying to her every few minutes. He seems to be getting more and more annoyed the more she doesn't look back towards him. I stand and nudge him over to the side, "Spill it man."

Edge looks from over my shoulder back up to my face, "What?"

I smile back at him then block his view of Susie, "Fucking spill it man. What is happening?" He rolls his shoulders and downs an entire glass of whisky before slamming the glass down then wiping his mouth with the back of his hand.

He looks back up at me, a hint of something unfamiliar to me in his eyes, "I don't know. I don't know what is wrong. We were doing fine. Great even. Then she just closed off. She decided to get a hotel room and hasn't really spoken to me since. Nothing more than hello or goodbye. I don't know what I fucking did."

I nod my head at him then look over my shoulder at Susie as she stands with her back to us. Like she is purposefully making herself stand like that so the temptation to look at him isn't too great to withstand. I turn back to Edge, "So, you didn't fuck and forget then? You actually think you might want something with her?"

Edges eyes come back to mine then he looks around the bar quickly then back to me, "We haven't fucked."

I take a step back, completely in shock. They were staying together and haven't fucked? How is that even possible? They are the two horniest people I have ever met in my life. It is why I thought they would be perfect together. "Like, nothing. Have you tried? Did she shoot you down?"

He motions to the bartender for another drink then turns back to me, "I mean we have done...stuff. She gave me head, no gag reflex by the way. And I got her off a few times but we never officially fucked. We were just laying in bed a few days ago talking and she just got up then packed her shit and left. She said it just wasn't going to work. She told me she plans to go home after this party sometime. I just don't know what the fuck I did."

I look him over intently, he isn't lying. He has no idea what he has done. I hand him his drink after the bartender sets it down then pick up my own again, "Okay, here is the plan. We are gonna go somewhere else a little less stuffy. I will keep to you so Lily has a chance to figure out what is what. I will try to find out what is up for you. Yeah?"

He nods his head at me then looks around my shoulder again at Susie's back. He lets out a loud sigh, "I don't know what I could have done."

I take another drink, then lean forward, "What were you talking about when she just got up?"

He shrugs his shoulders, "I don't fucking remember."

I roll my eyes at him, that sounds about right. I turn towards Lily and she gives me a confused look so I smile back at her. I turn towards Matthew and wave him over to join us. He walks up and leans against the bar beside me. I turn back to Edge, "Try to remember. You must have said something that rubbed her the wrong way."

He lets out another breath and points his face towards the ceiling. A few moments later he lowers his chin, "We were talking about all the homeless people around London. She made some comment about how she was sad to see a lot of women and kids out there. I told her something like that is just fucking life.

330

Shit happens, or something like that." I let out a heavy breath and look towards Matthew.

He starts laughing. Loudly. To the point that he has to sit his drink down so he doesn't spill it. Edge looks at him like he is insane, "What the fuck are you laughing about man? This isn't really all that fucking funny." I look at Matthew just as confused as Edge, as I watch him try to get some color back to his face that isn't red.

He finally starts to simmer down and puts his hand on Edge's shoulder, "Have you ever asked her what she does for a living?" Edge just shakes his head and looks at me, "No, I don't think so. Have you Gideon?" I shake my head back to him as Matthew starts laughing again.

He turns his head towards the girls, "Lily, hey come here for just a second." I look over my shoulder and smile as Lily walks over and wraps her arm around my waist, smiling at Matthew, "Yeah what's up?"

Matthew chuckles again then looks at Edge, "We are just over here talking. What is it that Susie does for a living again? Simone told me but I forgot."

Lily smiles back at him then looks around at all of us, "She is the president of a non profit back in New York." Matthew nods his head again then grins while looking at Edge, "What kind of non profit?"

Lily looks confused from me then to Edge, "For homeless women and children. To get them off the streets and into some sort of shelter. Why?" Edge's face falls as the color drains from him.

Matthew starts cackling again as he reaches over and pulls Lily into a hug, "I have never loved you more than I do right now." I laugh at his antics and the unfortunate wording of Edge's conversation with Susie.

Lily pulls back from Matthew, looking more confused than before, "Um, yeah. Okay. Love you too. I am walking away now, you guys are weird." She turns and walks back over to the girls. I turn and look pitiful at Edge, "You are so fucked."

His shoulders drop and he lets out a groan, "Fuck me. Okay. I have to figure out a way to fix this." Matthew starts laughing then tapping his watch, "You better move quick she is gonna leave soon."

Edge looks up at Matthew with concern, "What do you mean?" Matthew raises his shoulders, "Pretty sure she told Simone she is leaving first thing in the morning."

Edge stands a bit taller at this. He turns to me and I smile at him, "Go get her. Take her somewhere. Fix your shit." He smiles at me then downs the last of his drink, "I fucking owe you man." I laugh back at him, "I will not forget you just said that."

I laugh with Matthew for a few moments before I see Edge leading Susie out the front door. I see them stop on the sidewalk as he tries to talk to her. She looks in the window and I swear to god it looks like she is going to start crying at any moment. He has his work cut out for him.

Not 5 minutes later we see him walking past the bar towards the elevators. Susie is following behind him slowly. She looks into the bar, looking directly at Lily. I glance down and see Lily smile at Susie as she points towards the elevator. Susie kicks her shoes off, grabbing them in one hand and starts running full speed towards the elevators.

I smile down at Lily before turning back towards the bar, "Well I guess we will see how that goes huh?"

Lily laughs back at me, raising her drink to her mouth, "I still think she will be the one to break him."

I laugh out loud, finishing my drink off, "I will take that bet. He is basically a walking, talking dumbass when it comes to her."

Lily laughs as she turns back towards the girls, "You're not wrong there."

20 minutes later we decide to call it a night. There is just too much going on. Matthew and Simone leave together but Mona hangs back at the bar with her phone in her hand. We slowly make our way to the elevators and wait for the doors to open. When they do we see a pair of green high heels laying in the middle of the space.

Lily laughs out loud, "Let's go find out what room they are in." She reaches down and grabs the heels with one hand while wrapping her other in my hand so we can go to the front desk.

We laugh the entirety of the elevator ride to his floor, which is one floor below ours. We make it to their room and I reach up knocking loudly. We don't hear anything coming from inside. Lily smiles as she leans into the crack of the door, "Open the door assholes, I know you are in there!"

I laugh at her as she leans into the door frame waiting for it to be opened. A few moments later the door opens to Susie standing there in Edge's shirt and obviously nothing else. I let out a soft laugh as Susie thanks Lily for finding her shoes. I am looking over the top of Susie's shoulder as I see Edge approaching the door, butt ass naked.

I glance down at Lily in time to see her eyes fly wide. She immediately turns and looks at me. I start laughing so hard I don't even hear what everyone is saying. Then Edge smiles wide, "I figured it was only fair. Susie has seen you, so now Lily has seen me."

I continue to laugh when Susie says something about some guy named Brian. Lily laughs up into my eyes, "It's about fucking time. I would hug you but Edge still isn't wearing pants so I am not turning around."

333

I laugh down at her then watch as Edge picks Susie up by the waist and the door is being shut quickly. You can hear giggling on the other side of the door. I look down at Lily smiling, "So whose dick is bigger?" She quickly smacks me in the chest then starts stomping towards the elevators.

26
Aphrodite
Hold Me Down - Halsey

Gideon laid so much claim to my body for 14 days straight that I am pretty sure he is going to change his p.o. box to be my pussy.

We were either in bed, or the shower, or the floor. He bent me over the couch. He took me back pressed against the windows. He devoured every inch of my body until I didn't even feel like it was my own any longer. The only time we left the room was to go to the hotel bar one night to meet up with everyone for a few hours. Then we were right back in that suite destroying each other all over again.

I don't know entirely what happened between Susie and Edge but she decided to stick around for a bit longer. Until the tour starts at least. It has been fantastic having her close to me again. She keeps me sane. She keeps me straight.

Two weeks after we return home he begins spending the majority of his days back in the studio. Some days I will go with him, other days I just explore London.

He spent days learning the words to the song I had sung that day in the apartment. Putting his own spin on it.

Making it just as much a part of him as it was me. I play the piano and he would sit beside me and sing his soul out.

As the UK tour starts to get closer I practice my own craft some more. Using different types of canvases. Different types of mediums. I have so many ideas of what to do going forward.

I can't wait to get back on stage. To feel him in his home, welcoming me beside him. I never feel as powerful as I do when he is beside me.

I will sometimes just sit and cry at the unexpected turns my life has taken. It was a fucking painful path, but without that pain, without the destruction we never would have survived the eye of the storm.

Coming out the other side unscathed. Well not completely unscathed. I do still have some demons but I have been making some real progress with my new therapist. I finally found one that fits well with me. It is refreshing to have someone else on my side.

Gideon settles beside me on the couch, "Where is your head right now?"

I laugh as I continue to organize my TBR and motivational pics for the tour, "Somewhere north of my shoulders, I think."

He laughs as he wraps his arm around my shoulder and pulls me in closer, "No I mean, how are you feeling? The tour starts in a few days."

I laugh as I lean into him, "I am stoked honestly. I am excited to get back up there, see what kind of magic these puppies will produce."

I waggle my hands in front of his face. He chuckles at me as he wraps his hand around mine and kisses my knuckles.

He leans over and kisses the top of my head,

"Whatever you create will be marvelous. Also, we need to talk about something. Something kinda big actually."

I lean forward, looking back at him a bit worried and confused. He gives me a quick side grin but didn't seem to want to meet my gaze,

336

"I have something to confess. You are probably going to be pissed. But....my birthday was a few weeks ago and I didn't tell you."

I turn on him and slap him in the arm, "Gideon! Why didn't you tell me?"

He laughs at me as he rubs his arm, "Because you have always made such a big deal over the age thing. I didn't want you to get in your head about it. But I also didn't want someone to say Happy Belated Birthday and then you strangle me, so there. My secret is out."

I shake my head at him, "I would have made cupcakes or something."

He nods his head back at me, "That is another reason I didn't tell you. For fear of you baking."

Again I slap his arm, harder than the first time, "Jackass."

He laughs again as I turn to face him, sitting crisscrossed beside him,

"Well I can't be too mad. My birthday came and went as well and I didn't say anything either."

He turns to me wide eyed, "And you slapped me? That is just rude."

I laugh at him, taking his hand in mine and rolling his wedding band around his finger, one of my new favorite pastimes,

"When was it?"

He smiles as he watches his ring spin on his finger, "August 7th."

I stop twirling the ring and look at him slowly, smiling, "Gideon is a Leo? Interesting. That honestly explains a lot about you. You know Leos are known to be like natural born entertainers. Also they are a fire sign. If that isn't you I don't know what is." I lean forward and give him a soft kiss on the lips.

337

He lays his head on the back of the couch, "When was yours?"

I smile back at him, watching his chest rise and fall, "August 7th."

His eyes crash down on mine, "Shut the fuck up!"

I laugh, "What are the fucking odds? Seriously?"

He laughs out loud again, "That just solidifies it. We were born for each other."

I grin at him as I lean in and kiss him on the neck, "Yes we were."

The first stop on the tour is of course London. Quickly to be followed by Birmingham, Leeds, Manchester, Liverpool, Glasgow, Brighton and Bristol. Susie did end up going back to New York but I have a sneaking suspicion it won't be for too long. She is getting close enough to Edge that she has stopped confiding in me. She only does that when there are certain personal aspects that she wants to just be between her and her man. Edge is fucking miserable with her gone but I see him on his phone all the time now, smiling at the screen. They are going to be fine.

It is going to be a hectic 8 weeks but I am ready for the adventure. Here I am in London. I stand on the stage in full character, rubbing my palms together. Excited for the moment, the energy, the electricity to fill the room.

An hour later, Ares is behind me screaming his lungs out as my fingers smudge and roll over the canvas. They have started the set with a new song, Sunset.

It gives me a whole new thought process to tackle and wrap my soul around. The background is dark blues and purples.

All 5 members of the band are on their knees, their chests facing away as I stand before them, walking towards the rising moon.

I smile as Firestorm finally starts and I throw my charcoals back into the box beside me. I turn towards Ares, kneeling and bringing him to my chest again.

When the lights come up and I am lowered to the crowd. I find a young man, probably no more than 18 years old, just weeping. He is beside himself with emotions, anxiety and is just utterly wailing.

I step up to him and place my hand on his cheek, wiping away the tears. I lean forward and whisper in his ear,

"You are the world. Never believe you are anything less."

I lean back, smiling at him then lifting the canvas over the railing and placing it in his hands. His grin makes my entire month.

Every single show is like that. I will create then cradle my love. I will find someone in the crowd whose soul just draws my attention then I will give them a blessing from Aphrodite.

Some type of encouragement for them to continue living their truths. Everything seems to be falling into place. This is our normal life on tour. I absolutely love it.

Until we hit Glasgow.

Glasgow fucked me up.

I am mid creation, completely wrapped up in myself when I hear the beginnings of my song starting to play on the piano. I turn around and see Hestia at the keys.

I take a step forward as Ares walks out of the shadows and kneels before me. He starts to sing the words, my words and I completely fall into myself. No one told me they were going to perform it. I fall to my knees, completely beside myself.

I feel like a real member of a real family.

I had taught it to him, he had taught it to Hestia.

They play it to show me that I am one of them.

No matter what my brain says, no matter what number follows my name to represent the amount of time I have spent on this earth. I am just reborn into the family I never knew I wanted but somehow always knew I needed.

After the song is over, I am finally able to compose myself. I finish the show's art rendition and continue on like normal.

But the weight of the gift that has been given to me sits on my chest like an anchor. Holding me steady in the massive hurricane that is Carnal Decay.

As the show is ending, I move to each member of the band. Every single one of the members of my new family and hug them tightly. Making sure each and every one of them feel the love I am radiating for them. When I step to Ares, I pull myself so deeply into his chest that I can't even tell whose heart is whose. Hestia gives my drawing away that night because I physically can not be away from him. I have to touch him, to continue to tell myself that this is real.

This is real life.

That night I have my first dream about Nikki. I have not let myself think of her for so long. It isn't that I have forgotten her, I never did. I just can't allow myself to obsess over her death, her life any longer.

She is sitting in the field behind our shitty apartment building. I am running, picking dandelions and chasing butterflies. I turn around and she smiles at me.

Forever 16.

Forever beautiful.

I continue to chase my childhood as one does. She stands and steps over to me pulling me into a hug. She pulls back and looks into my face,

"He is going to find you."

I sit up sweating, shaking almost to the point of not being able to control myself.

Gideon is still sleeping softly beside me. I slide out of the bed and start pacing the room, shaking my hands out. I grab my phone and run to the bathroom.

Noting the time, Susie will definitely still be awake. I dial her number quickly but it goes to voicemail.

I step from the bathroom noticing that Gideon hasn't even moved from his spot. I pull a chair up to the window and sit down, still shaking.

I feel the nerves run through me like a train. I haven't heard her voice in years but I knew instantly that it was her. I could have been in a room full of people and still been able to point her out of the crowd.

I let out a slow steady breath. Trying to bring my pulse down enough to try to decipher what the fuck has just happened.

I remain there staring out the window for the rest of the night. I don't dare go back to sleep.

I am scared to close my eyes at all. My phone rings around 9 am. I look down, quickly answering it then glancing back at Gideon. He is still sleeping soundly.

"Susie?"

I know I am still breathless. I don't know what the fuck is starting this tormented cycle all over again.

"Hey babe. You rang?"

I nod towards the window, "The dreams, they are starting again."

I hear her sigh on the other end of the phone, "Nikki?"

I feel a tear roll down my cheek, "Yeah. Just like before."

Susie lets out another sigh, "Fuck. Okay. What has changed? What do you think is starting this shit again?"

I shake my head, looking back at Gideon briefly before staring back out the window,

"I have no fucking clue. Nothing has changed. Everything is exactly as it was. I haven't been thinking of her or them. I just. We have two more shows on this tour, then we get another few months off before the US tour starts. I can't lose my shit now. There is no time for this right now."

I laugh into the window in front of me. Only because laughing is the only thing that is going to keep me from crying.

I hear Susie chuckle on the other end of the phone,

"Babe. You are just stressed from the tour. Breath. Stay calm. Talk to Gideon. Let him know what is up, what is going on. You will be back home soon and we will have a girls day. Just me and you. We will even go to Boston to see Nikki if you want."

I shake my head at the window again,

"No. If I go to Boston it will be with Gideon first. He should meet her too."

I can hear Susie pacing on the other end of the phone,

"Have you thought anymore about your mom? Maybe it is time. Maybe seeing her will give you the closure you need. Maybe that is what it is going to take to get this shit to finally stop."

I lean my head back in the chair and look to the ceiling. Instead of seeing the smooth ceiling tiles, I see Gideon staring back down at me. I give him a soft smile,

"Susie, I gotta go. But I will think about it. Love you babe."

I can hear her smile in her voice,

"Love you. Hey, things are wrapping up pretty nicely here so I am going to try to surprise Edge at the next show. Don't tell him. Oh and Smack Gideon's ass for me a few times. I will be seeing you soon. I promise. Bye."

342

I smile at the phone as I hang up and look back into the two black pools staring down at me,

"Good Morning."

He smiles as he runs his hand down my chest, between my breasts and stops at my navel, leaning in and kissing my neck, "Good Morning. You were up before your alarm cock this morning."

I lower my head staring back out the window. I smile again as he kisses me again before pulling back and heading into the bathroom.

I continue to just sit there, staring, unable to decide what the fuck to do next. Gideon comes back out of the bathroom and sits in the window sill opposite me, breaking my view of the city.

I smile at him gently. He reaches over, rubbing his hand over my knee,

"How long have you been awake?"

I put my hand on his, "A while."

He squeezes my knee bringing my attention back to him, "What happened?"

I look past him, into the city beyond, "Just a bad dream was all. Couldn't really fall back asleep."

He leans forward, taking both my hands in his, "Do you want to talk about it?"

I shake my head, "Nah. It was really nothing. I will be fine. Just couldn't sleep."

He smiles as he nods at me. He stands walking behind me then kissing me on top of the head before starting to get ready for the day. I continue to stare out the window, not knowing if lying to him is the best for him or for me.

I notice that Lily's sleep is getting progressively worse.

She won't talk to me about it though.

After that first night she mentioned some kind of nightmare, she never said anything else to me about it. I just assumed that she was fine.

But I have been waking up in the early morning hours noticing she isn't in bed with me. I think what is beginning to scare me the most though is that she isn't calling Susie anymore either.

At least when she is calling her, I know she is getting whatever it is out of her system.

But now.

Now it just seems to be dragging her down.

She is a fractured version of herself right now and I have no idea what to do. I don't even know what is wrong, how am I supposed to help fix it.

Every time I approach her with it, she will give me a fake painted smile and say everything is okay.

Everything is definitely not okay.

She has started to start getting dark circles under her eyes and she just looks exhausted all the time. She is losing weight too but I just don't know how to approach it. The tour has at least closed so she has a few months to recover from whatever this was.

I start to wonder if this life isn't really something that is going to work for her.

The touring is too much.

Too much pressure, too much anxiety.

I can't blame her if it is. This is not the life she picked for herself, this is just the one that presented itself to her. Granted she has steam rolled it like a trooper but I can see how it could wear on her after some time.

I can see her sitting on the couch, pretending to read a book but she has been on the page for over 20 minutes now. I have seen her clear a novel in just a few hours.

I make her a cup of tea and sit down at her feet, sitting the cup for her on the new coffee table. She smiles over the book at me as I lift her feet and put them in my lap, slowly massaging each foot. After a few minutes and the page still hasn't turned I reach over and grab the book, sitting it on the table as well. She raises her eyebrow at me,

"Can I help you sir?"

I smile back at her, then look at her legs,

"I am going to talk for a minute and I just want you to listen. I don't want you to get upset. I don't want you to get angry. I just need to say my peace and then you can do what you need to do. Is that okay?"

She sits up a little straighter, instantly looking more worried,

"Of course babe. Please tell me what's wrong."

I turn to her,

"That is the thing. I don't know what is wrong. You have been distant for weeks now. You haven't been sleeping or eating. You haven't even been talking to Susie. I don't know what is wrong and I don't know how I can help you if you don't talk to me.

"I am really, seriously starting to get worried. I feel like you are drifting away from me and I don't know what to do to pull you back to me. What is going on, Lily? What is so scary that you can't even talk to me about it?"

She looks out the window, nodding her head to what I am saying but instantly looks jaded. She is tearing up but her jaw is set to the side like she is trying not to get pissed at me.

I reach out and touch her hand and her eyes meet mine for just a moment before they go back to the window.

I pull my hand back and let out a heavy sigh.

Leaning my head back into the couch, I throw my hands up,

"I don't know what the fuck to do. Have I done something? Why are you angry right now? I don't know what the hell is going on Lily. I am fucking terrified right now."

I see a stray tear run down her cheek as she angrily wipes it away, "I am not angry at you. You haven't done anything. I am angry at myself. For not fucking being a better actress apparently."

I take her hand again, wrapping it in mine, "Lily tell me what is wrong."

She lets out another deep sigh, "I told you that I had been having a nightmare right?"

I nod my head. She looks back towards me,

"When they started happening again, they were the same as before. I used to have this recurring nightmare growing up. It was always just me and Nikki. She was watching me play in a field behind an old apartment we lived in. The apartment.

"At the end of each dream it was always her telling me like, 'why didn't you save me?' 'why did you let her do that?'.

346

Always things like that. But this time. This time they are different."

I rub my hand over hers, "What is different about them baby?"

She turns to me and just starts weeping,

"I am so fucking scared because I don't know what it means. I mean is it just my subconscious or am I turning into mom? Could Nikki be trying to tell me something? I don't know what to do."

I pull her close to my chest and hold her as she sobs,

"What don't you know the meaning of? What is happening in them?"

She lets out another small wailing sound,

"She just, at the end of them, right before I wake up she has been saying different things now. The first time she said 'He is going to find you.' then a few nights later it was 'He knows where you are.' Now it is just getting progressively worse and I just don't even want to sleep. I am scared to death to close my eyes."

I watch her, slump over and defeat,

"How is it getting worse baby? Tell me what she says."

She looks up at me then rolls her eyes while wiping her tears away,

"She says things like 'He is coming for you' and the last one she said 'You have to hide now' I feel like I am losing my fucking mind Gideon. I don't know what to do. I don't know how to fucking fight something that I don't even understand.

"Who the fuck is he? Why is he coming for me? What the fuck is actually happening? Why? Why is my brain fucking doing this too me now? When things are finally starting to go right for me."

I pull her close to me again and rock her back and forth as she continues to sob.

This continues for a half an hour before she finally calms down enough to sit back against me without crying. I move the hair from her forehead,

"Do you want to go see someone?"

She rolls her eyes at me then turns on the couch,

"No. A fucking therapist won't help. I have tried that before. Nothing fucking helps."

I nod at her words, staring at the coffee table,

"What about a psychic? Or even a oneirocritic? I am sure we can find one here. You can fucking find anything in London I swear it."

She turns to me, "What in the actual fuck is an oneirocritic?"

I give her a small smile, "It's someone who interprets dreams, honey. Maybe they can help you figure out where all this is stemming from."

She nods her head and looks at the coffee table. She lets out a heavy sigh, straight from her diaphragm,

"My gut is saying psychic. I don't know why but maybe. Maybe they can see something I am not. I don't know. I don't know what to put my faith in right now. I don't know what to do. This isn't really my thing. This is more Susie's track to take. But her and Edge are finally together again. I don't want to ruin things for her."

She puts her head in her hands, shaking it back and forth. I pull out my phone and find Silene's number, hitting the button and putting the phone to my ear.

Lily turns and looks at me when she realizes I have called someone but I put one finger on her lips to hush her, smiling while I do it.

"Sup Bitch?"

I laugh at Silene, "Hello to you too. Hey, weird question. Who is the psychic you go to? They are local right?"

Silene laughs on the other end, "Yeah, her name is Maura. Why?"

I nod to Lily, giving her a smile, "Can you send me her information?"

Silene chuckles again, "Am I finally making a believer out of you?"

I laugh back at her, "We will see how it goes before I ever admit that. Can you send it to me?"

She cackles out loud again, "Just texted it. Let me know what she says is awaiting you in your future. I say it's my size 7 up your ass but who knows."

I laugh again as I hang up the phone. I pull up the text getting the women's information.

I turn back to Lily again,

"Do you want me to do this? I don't want you to feel like you are being forced into it. If you are not comfortable just say so."

She looks to the ceiling and lets out a heavy breath, "Call her."

I nod as I make the call. I make sure to mention that we were referred by Silene and also that money is no option. The sooner the better. 3 hours later we are walking hand in hand into Maura's studio on the other side of town.

Lily looks uneasy from the jump but luckily Maura is extremely warm and approachable. There are no eccentric decorations, no chicken bones in a pile, nothing that screams run.

349

She has a small studio that seems inviting and just gives you a good feeling when you walk in. I half expected to see a poster of a kitten saying 'Hang in There' on the wall.

Lily seems to relax almost immediately. Maura is probably in her mid to late 40s and for some reason that eases the majority of the tension in Lily's shoulders.

I breath a sigh of relief, the last fucking thing I want is for her to hate the one person that might help her get some kind of comfort.

We sit down at a small table in a windowless room. The lighting is lowered and there is sage burning somewhere because my eyes are on fire.

I keep blinking rapidly, but I don't care.

This isn't about me. Maura has many different services that she offers but she smiles as she explains,

"So, Silene. For one, she is bat shit crazy and I love her for it. Two, she usually takes a whatever you can give me approach, so we combine the services. She gets a small tarot reading, some palmistry glancing, sometimes even an aura reading. We can do whatever you are comfortable with. Is there something specific that you are looking to find out or?"

Lily glances at me quickly then sits her hands on the table gently,

"I have been having some really strange dreams. I had this recurring nightmare as a child and teenager. It went away for the longest time but now it is back with a much more ominous tone to it"

Maura smiles and sips her cup of tea, nodding to Lily,

"Please continue."

Lily gives her another smile then looks to the table, drawing small circles in the wood,

"So my sister died when I was very young and I actually witnessed it. It has haunted me, sleeping or not for a very long

350

time." Lily goes to continue but Maura holds up one hand while setting down her tea cup.

She leans over, her fingers just mere centimeters from Lily's,

"I noticed something right away when you walked in. Your aura, just the atmosphere around you is heavy. Just like there is this dark weight that is just holding you down.

"Now you said that you are having these dreams. But they are much darker now aren't they? They seem to begin the same but you are getting basically not warnings but threats? Did the messages start as just a heeding but now they are more intense, more vocal, more direct?"

I look at Lily but all I see is her eyes wide, mouth parted as she slowly nods her head yes.

I turn back to Maura, in awe myself actually.

Maura nods her head then closes her eyes. She tilts her head to the right just a touch and her face scrunches up like she was confused or frustrated.

Her voice resonates around us,

"There is someone trying to tell you something though. She is younger than you, maybe 16 or 17 years old. She is strong, but somehow weak at the same time. Like her presence is strong but physically she is not. Maybe this is the sister you mentioned that has passed. I am not entirely sure but she is seeing something coming. Someone. She is trying to prepare you I think."

Maura opens her eyes, looking at both of us hopefully,

"Is there someone from your past that may be trying to reach you? Like a relative or something along those lines? I just keep feeling like someone close is looking for you."

I turn to Lily, who is sheet white now, and she shakes her head no,

"No. No one. My only living relatives I haven't had contact with in years, decades even. They would have no way of even knowing who or what I am now."

Maura smiles again as she pulls out a deck of Tarot and sits them in front of her. She does some movements, reshuffling before she turns three cards in front of her, nodding towards them each time,

"So these cards represent your past, then present, then future."

She points to the first card with her pristine fingernail.

The card depicts a woman clutching her knees tightly to her chest. She has pure despair written on her face as she weeps up into the skies.

There are 9 swords all of equal length pointing at her from different angles.

"This is your past. This is the Nine of Swords."

Maura lets out a soft breath,

"This is a difficult card to see. For anyone, regardless of past, present or future. This card shows us that you have endured a moment or time frame of severe emotional distress. Filled with despair, anxiety, depression. This card is troubling because something of that magnitude is hard for anyone to try to get past, regardless of their current emotional and psychological situation."

I squeeze Lily's knee but she doesn't dare look away from the cards while she nods her head.

Maura smiles and looks from my face to Lily's as she points to the next card.

It shows a man and a woman embracing while staring deeply into each other's eyes. The sun is shining brightly between them, beams reflecting off of the couple.

352

"This is your present. This is the Lover's card. I am sure you can probably guess what this symbolizes. A deep connection. A union that is embraced with attraction of course but something more than that. It shows a euphoric encirclement of the divine. It is something that most people beg to witness just once in their lives. Not a lot of people actually attain that level of affinity for another."

She reaches her hand out to Lily's, placing it gently on top, watching a tear roll down her cheek.

She smiles at Lily again, pulling her stare to her,

"Hold onto that at all costs. It is the most precious gift you can ever be given."

Lily nods at her then looks at me with more love than I ever knew one person could possess. If I had not been sitting, I would have fallen to my knees from the power possessed in her eyes at that moment.

Maura lets out another sigh and starts tapping the last card.

This card depicts a woman walking away with two swords drawn behind her back, with five others piercing the ground around her.

She is walking into a blood red moon.

I have no idea what Maura is about to say but I am petrified.

I could feel my blood still in my veins. Maura continues to look at the card as she taps it,

"This is your future. This one worries me the most. The Seven of Swords is well known to stand for deceit or some form of trickery. You are going to be presented with a choice. It is going to be a hard one too. You need to be prepared for what is going to approach you.

"I can't see if it is dangerous or what its true intentions are but I can tell you, I have never seen this card and a person walking away from it unscathed. Whatever you are approached with, it will affect you either way. You are the only person that can determine for yourself if you are being fooled, manipulated."

Lily lets out a smooth breath onto the table as she continues to stare at the Seven of Swords.

She nods her head, "In my dream, she said that someone is looking for me. That I should run from them. I feel like I should listen to her. She, in death or life, would have never wanted any type of harm to come to me. She was my protector."

Her red rimmed eyes turns to me as she tilts her head,

"I think I just need to follow my gut and listen to Nikki."

I nod back to her,

"I will not let anyone hurt you baby. I swear on my life I will not let that happen."

Maura takes Lily's hands in hers,

"You are stronger than you know. You have a power within you that is viscerally entwined with your spirit, your aura. You will get through this. Whatever decision that has to be made I know it will be the right choice. It may not be the easiest choice but the outcome will be the best for you.

"When this moment happens, when it approaches you. You will know it. You will feel it immediately. Listen to your gut. Don't listen to what your head is telling you it thinks you should do. You weigh the options and you go with whatever is safest and healthiest for you. For your life as it is now. Now what it was, not what it will be. Can you do that for me?"

Lily is crying harder than before but nodding her head. This was the best decision we could have made.

Silene is getting her own bottle of Dalmore.

Before we leave, Lily gives Maura not only the longest hug in history but a tip that made her behave like she should not be accepting that obscene amount of money.

Lily smiles at her,

"You are worth every single fucking cent of it. You have calmed me more than anyone has ever been able to before in my life.

"You have given me this bottomless amount of clarity that I didn't even realize I needed. You deserve this for being you. I will not take it back. Do not even try."

Maura hugs her back and we make plans to see her in a month.

The journey back home is a hell of a lot lighter than it had been on the way there.

Lily smiles.

She makes jokes.

She leans into me and just talks to me.

I can see that things are finally processing in her brain the way that they should. It takes every fiber of my being not to show the fear that is setting seed in my stomach.

Who is coming? What does he want?

Will she make the right decision?

Because we don't know what is going to be the right decision until after it is made. We can't see everything. We can just prepare for the moment and hope for the fucking best.

And that is terrifying.

28
Aphrodite
Infinite Baths - Sleep Token

I decide after meeting Maura that she is right. She is also my new best friend, lover, and going to the top of my christmas card list.

I can't be more grateful for Gideon or Simone or Maura.

I just couldn't see the forest for all the trees.

I have never had people, other than Susie and Mark, that actually care about my well being. I just never really saw myself as a loveable person. Too broken, unfixable.

I look to Gideon as we step into the apartment,

"You do know you are the best husband ever. Right?"

He shuts the door and turns to me smiling,

"I am just glad we are able to put a positive spin on this whole situation. I hate seeing you lock yourself up like you did. I feel like you were slipping away and I couldn't stop it. No matter what I did or said."

I step to him, wrapping my arms around his center,

"My biggest fear in life is that I am going to turn into her. My mother. Anytime I feel like I am going down a path that could even come close, I just get scared. Ya know. I don't know how to turn it off. I am sorry that I scared you. That was never my intention."

Gideon pulls me in tighter,

"I know, baby. Just promise me, you will talk to me. Whenever you feel like that dark cloud is sweeping in on you, please just talk to me. I will always listen. I will never leave because of it."

I go up on my tip toes and kiss him, as deeply as a short girl can. I took a step back,

"I am going to take a shower. Then maybe I can fix dinner?"

Gideon nods,

"That sounds good, babe. I have some chords to work on."

I smile as I turn to leave the room, pinching his ass hard, then giggling and running away.

I wake up at 2 a.m. again.

Sweating. Not crying though.

Not shaking. Not terrified.

I run my fingers down Gideon's back and he cracks an eye at me, "Are you okay?"

I smile down at him as he rolls onto his back to face me.

I can hear the dream echoing in my head.

I can see my sister's smile as she gives me another piece of information. I lean down and kiss Gideon.

He seems surprised but wraps an arm around me and pulls me closer. I palm his dick and he let out a groan into my throat.

I smile as I feel him harden, long and hard beneath my hand. I squeeze him again as he reaches down and tries to slip my bottoms off.

I smile, helping him then pulling his own down.

Then I make love to him.

I am slow. I am careful. I am steady and attentive.

Afterwards when he holds me close, I look into his eyes,

357

"Tonight. Nikki told me to stay with you. She said 'Gideon is your guardian now. Stay with him.'"

Gideon pulls back a bit and looks down at me stunned. I feel the tears welling up in my eyes,

"Do you have any idea how amazing it was to hear your name come from her voice? And that she approved."

I smile from ear to ear as he kisses me deeply again. He pulls back again, "I hope I do her proud. I am trying to at least."

I trace my fingers down his face, "You already have, baby."

Almost two full weeks have gone by and I haven't had one nightmare. I forgot what it feels like to sleep through the night completely. It is invigorating to start waking up in the morning and not be totally exhausted.

We only have about a month left before the US tour starts up. Kicking off in none other than Boston. I think that was Nikki's hint for me to come and visit her. Susie said she might be going to go home to New York when the tour starts. But I don't think she is going to be able to handle being away from Edge for very long. She is fighting herself. I get it. I lived it. I have to let her figure it out for herself. I know she is in love with him. Hell she has probably already told him so much. But she has to realize that she is better with him than without. That is when shit will change, for the better.

Gideon has been spending most of his time in the studio, recording the new album. He has asked me to go with him a dozen times but I don't want to hear the new music until they play it live.

Hearing something new from them always makes my soul sing along with them. It is the feeling I get that rolls through my veins like pure ecstasy.

I am happily going about my day, window shopping new art supplies when my phone rings. I instantly realize it is not a number I know. I also realize it is a Boston prefix.

My insides immediately clench up thinking my mother has found me. I send it to voicemail.

I look up and down the street, officially done with shopping for the day. I hear my phone ding letting me know that a message has been left for me.

I make my way back to the apartment and sit on the couch looking out the window when Gideon makes it home. I don't even hear the door.

"Hey babe."

I smile and turn to him. I lazily get up and walk to him then wrap my arms around his waist. I inhale the scent of the sea and smile into his chest.

I feel his arms wrap around me so I look up into his face, "How was work dear?"

He chuckles back at me then throws his keys on the counter behind me. He puts his hands on my cheeks and gives me a heartfelt kiss. I smile into his mouth as he pulls away, "I have wanted to do that for hours."

I grin at him then step over to a stool and sit down while Gideon walks to the refrigerator, grabbing a beer. I lean into my fist as I watch him slowly take a deep drink.

I promised him no more secrets. No more hiding in my own head. He is so going to get annoyed with me but,

A promise is a promise.

"So, something weird happened today."

Gideon brings the beer down, raising one eyebrow at me, "Weird how?"

I stretch my arms out in front of me across the countertop, "I had a call from Boston."

Gideon nods back at me. I lay my face down on the counter facing him, "The only person I know from Boston anymore is my mother."

Gideon sits the beer down on the counter and leans into it, arms straight just staring at the wood, "And what did she have to say?"

I sit up and sigh loudly, "I have no clue. I let it go to voicemail and I haven't listened to it yet."

Gideon walks around the island and wraps me in a hug from behind, resting his chin on top of my head. "Do you want me to listen to it?"

I shake my head and use my hands to spin me around on the stool so I am now facing him, "No. But maybe you could just listen to it with me? Just in case?"

Gideon smiles and I move to the coffee table to grab my phone. I stare at the little image on the screen indicating I have a voicemail waiting. I feel Gideon step up beside me and I lean into his side. I slowly sit down on the couch. I glance over at Gideon as he sits beside me. I look back down at my phone, finally getting enough nerve built up to hit the button.

10 seconds later I hear the beep and the voicemail begins, as the words tumble from my phone I turn and stare at Gideon.

"Lily, Hi this is John. Your dad. I uh, I just found out that your mom has passed away. This is the last contact number the hospital had for you. I uh, I hope that maybe we can meet up sometime. I would really love to see you bug. I know I have a lot to make up for but still. Just give me a call when you can. 8575550990. I hope to hear from you soon."

I stare at Gideon while he stares at my phone. I let out a breath and sit the phone down on the table in front of me like it is a bomb.

Gideon puts his arm around my shoulder,

"Wow. I mean, I am sorry about your mum. But your father sounds like he wants to connect again."

I nod my head, still looking at the phone. I turn my head and look out the window. That is when I see a butterfly land on the windowsill. I stand up and move slowly to watch it flutter then fly away.

I watch it until it blends in with the setting sun. Nikki.

I smile and turn back to Gideon,

"I don't care. I don't care that mom is dead. I don't care if dad wants to get to know me. He left me when I needed him the most. He is the reason I was in the orphanage. I know that most people would think a reunion would be magical but I don't. He is toxic."

Gideon stands smiling at me,

"Fucking good for you. Do you think maybe this is the confrontation that Maura had been talking about?"

I nod my head and glance back out the window.

I smile towards the sun,

"Yeah I think this is what Nikki was warning me about. My gut says not to let him in. So I am not letting him in. He will only try to destroy me again, I just know it."

Gideon steps up to me, "I am so fucking proud of you."

I wrap my arms around him and just hold him. Gideon pulls back from me after a few minutes have passed,

"Can I play you something?"

I look over at the piano then back to him, "I told you I want to be surprised with the new songs."

He nods his head, laughing, "Well there are 12 songs, hearing one isn't going to destroy the mystery."

I smile and sit back down on the couch, fanning my hand towards the piano across the room. Gideon chuckles at me then walks to the piano and sits down. He starts playing a slow ballad, the melody is slow and honestly kinda sexy. His voice starts to carry across the room to my soul and I close my eyes and smile.

"In a world full of shadows, we wandered alone,
Carrying the weight of the dreams that we'd sown.

Through the firestorms and heartaches, we fought through
The night,
But I found you in the darkness, my beacon of light.

We're soaring like butterflies, dancing on air,
Two souls, finally found, a love that we wear.

Through the trials and tears, we rise above,
In a garden of hope, we've blossomed in love.

Every scar tells a story, each battle a page,
Now we're stitching the fabric of love on this stage.

With every whispered promise, hearts open wide,
We'll weather the storms, forever side by side.

And when the skies are heavy, I'll be your reprieve,
Together we'll find strength in this love we conceived.

With you, I've discovered the beauty in pain,
Through the chaos and the calm, it's all in the gain.

So let's dance through the memories, chase dreams that
We trust,
Two wandering souls, now grounded in just us.

In a world where the shadows can never confine,
You're my heart, my forever, my love divine."

Gideon turns to me and sees me utterly wailing.

What a dick!

I laugh at him as I wipe the tears from my face then stand and march over to him and wrap him in my arms. I can feel him smile into my chest. He puts his hands on my waist and I pull back to look down at him,

"That was cruel."

He laughs out loud at me, squeezing my waist with his hands,

"How was that cruel? It is a love song. For you. For us."

I smile at him and shake my head at him before leaning down and kissing him rough and deep. His hands roam around my back, pulling me closer to him. I am cupping his face, kissing him sweetly as he slips his hands under the back of my shirt. I feel him unclasp my bra and I smile into his mouth again.

I open my eyes and pull back to look at his face. This man, this man is my entire world. I trace his cheekbones with my thumbs, looking into those sable eyes where I can see my future, my present, my past. He is my everything.

I kiss him deeper as he stands up and lifts me onto the keys of the piano. My ass makes a horrible noise on the keys as he sits me down but neither of us even seem to notice. I lift my shirt over my head and slide my bra off my arms.

Gideon watches me as I slide off the keys and slowly lower my yoga pants and step out of them. I slide myself back onto the keys of the piano and spread my thighs for him.

His eyes turn dangerous as he pulls his shirt over his head. Then he is on his knees, looking up into my eyes as he spreads me with one hand and lays his tongue flat then licks straight up my center.

I instantly start to convulse. I smile as my eyes close and I wrap my hands around the back of his head. He takes each leg and puts them over his shoulders as he leans back in and starts to devour me.

I feel him slip two fingers into me and then he flicks my clit with his tongue. I look down at him and he is still staring at me. He pulls my clit in between his teeth then he groans.

I feel the goosebumps cover my entire body. I am panting now, but I don't want him to stop.

He continues to pump two fingers into me as I feel myself getting wetter by the second. I look down at him and wrap my hands around his face to pull him up to kiss me.

He slithers up my body then kisses me forcefully. I can taste myself on him and I smile. He quickly removes his pants and boxers then lifts me up by the back of my thighs. I smile as he walks us over to the couch and sits down with me straddling him.

I can feel him hard beneath me as I pull back and look into his eyes again. His eyes scour my face as if he is looking for something he may have lost. He closes his eyes briefly,

"Please, Fuck. Please let me inside Lily. I need you so fucking bad right now."

I smile at his use of the word please then lift up and steady myself to slide back down on his dick. He moans as his hands go flat on my lower back, pulling me closer to him.

I begin to slide up and down on his cock as he starts panting. He opens his eyes at looks at me as I pull back, fire burning in my eyes,

"This is mine. This is my cock. You hear me? No one else, ever. You fucking belong to me. And this pussy, it is yours. Never anyone else's."

364

I am slamming down onto him with every single word. His eyes are hooded as he moans then grips my ass hard. Hard enough to leave marks I am sure. I smile again as I slam down on him again and start to feel my release building at the base of my spine.

Gideon uses my ass to slide me up and down his cock as I lean my head back, smiling at the ceiling. He leans in and takes my nipple in his mouth, circling the peak with his tongue before biting down.

"Fuck Gideon!"

I start slamming into him harder than before. I am panting and my release is about to hit me at any moment. Gideon raises his hips to meet mine,

"Cum on me baby. I wanna feel you break around my dick."

I start screaming his name as I feel myself clamp down on him. The waves of pleasure rolling across my body like I am the beach and he is the ocean. I continue to throw myself into him. I feel his hands grip my ass harder as he screams his release into the room around us,

"Fuck me Lily. God Dammit. Fuck me baby, fuck me!"

I continue riding him as the waves start to dissipate and I can feel myself slowly releasing him. He slams into me again and I feel the pulsating starting back up.

My eyes wide I look at him,

"I am gonna cum again baby. Please don't stop. Please baby."

His eyes go feral as he turns us, laying me down on the couch. He pushes my thighs flat as he starts spearing into me, grunting and moaning. I let out another scream as I feel myself lock down on him again. It feels like he is everywhere all at once. It feels like every prayer I have ever silently whispered is being answered.

He throws himself into me again then goes still as he screams my name. A few moments later, as his second release is still riddling his body he slowly starts to push in and out of me again. I still have my eyes rolled up in my head as he slowly brings me down from my high.

He leans down and kisses me gently. He pulls back just barely,

"Let's have a baby."

I stare up into his face, smiling,

"Are you sure? You don't think it is too soon?"

He kisses me again, holding me close, "It would never be too soon to start our family. I want us to raise little versions of us. I will teach them piano, you can teach them how to draw and paint. I want to give my child a better life than I had. I want to get everything right that my father got so wrong."

I caress his cheek before pulling him into another kiss. This is a huge step but his dream is my dream too. I want to create this with him. I pull my face back and nod my head at him, "Yes. Let's do this. Let's have a baby."

He smiles wider than I have ever seen him smile. He is my life and I am his. We are going to burn this world down around us. Until all that is left standing is us and the family we have created.

A few short weeks later we are in Boston. Susie was going to come with me to the asylum but I wanted it to be Gideon. I want him to meet Nikki. I want to face this part of my life with him. Susie completely understands. She is enjoying spending all of her time with Edge anyways. I am happy to see her happy. I am elated that it is with Edge.

I am still looking out the window as I feel the car coming to a stop. I am nervous as hell. And I don't know why. She isn't

366

here anymore. I am just here to collect her stuff. Probably throw it all in the trash immediately.

Gideon holds my hand tightly as we leave the SUV and stare up at the cold stone building in front of us. This was my mothers home for the last 27 years. It is just hollow and emotionless. Just like her. We slowly make our way towards the large doors then step inside and to an open window.

I smile at the lady behind the partition, "Hello. My name is Lillith Taylor. I am here to collect my mother's personal items. Her name was Miriam Banks." Gideon squeezes my hand tight as the woman flips through some paperwork.

She smiles up at me gently, "She didn't really have a lot. There was a notebook and then I have her death certificate. Give me just a second and I will be back with both of them." I give the woman a slight nod and look up into Gideon's face. I lean into him, feeling his arm wrap around my shoulders. He kisses the top of my head and I smile at the familiarity of it.

The woman steps back up to the window and slides through a notebook and an envelope. I smile at her as I take the items, "Thank you so much." She nods back to me and I turn to head towards the door. I stop at a trash can and hover the notebook over it. My heart is telling me just to drop it in but my gut is telling me there is something for me inside.

I pull the notebook back towards me and smile up at Gideon. He opens the door for me and we head back to the car. We settle inside and I give the driver the address of the cemetery. I want Gideon to meet Nikki. And it has been forever since I have visited her myself. Gideon takes the notebook and envelope, sitting them beside him as he pulls me in close again. I smile at him as I reach down and pick up the envelope. I unfold the paper, reading over all the jargon until I see Cause of Death: Suicide by Affixiation. I sigh heavily as I fold it back up and look up at him, "She hung herself."

367

Gideon pulls me in tight again and holds me there until we make it to the cemetery. I tuck the envelope into the front of the notebook then open the door and slide out of the vehicle.

Gideon smiles down at me, taking my hand as I begin to lead him deeper into the stone labyrinth. I finally come to a stop in front of my sister's final resting place. I lean down and wipe my hand across the front of the stone marker.

I stand back up and look at Gideon, "This is my sister. I know it says her name is Nicole but if you were to ever call her that she would have kicked your ass. Her name was Nikki. She was my best fucking friend and I miss her every single day." Gideon squeezes my hand as I turn back to the stone,

"Nikki, this is Gideon. He is my husband, my best friend and the kindest human you will ever meet in this world. He has saved me from myself more times than I can count. You would have loved him." I smile up at him, "He is also the father of your niece or nephew, not entirely sure which it is yet. I am only a few weeks along."

Gideon's eyes blow wide as he looks from my face to my stomach then back to my eyes. I have never seen him smile as wide as he is right now. He places his hand on my stomach, "Are you fucking for real?"

I laugh back at him, "I found out a few days ago. I have been waiting for the perfect time to tell you."

Gideon smiles even wider somehow before he leans down and takes my face in his hands and kisses me deeply. With every particle of his being. I smile at him as he pulls away.

Out of the corner of my eye I see a man approaching. I recognize him immediately, though he is much older than the last time I saw him. Gideon's eyes recognize the look on my face and he turns his gaze towards the man that is approaching. I grip his hand tight as the man comes to a stop right behind us.

He smiles up at us, his eyes seeming to linger on me, "Hello. Uh, my name is John. I am Nikki's father. Did you know her?"

Gideon's grip on my hand tightens as he instinctively tries to protect me. I place my free hand on his bicep and smile up at him with a wink. I turn back to my father, "She was a really good friend of my sisters. I try to visit her whenever we are in town."

John nods at us then looks around me towards the headstone. I smile at him then start to pull Gideon behind me. I turn back towards him again, "Have a great life." Gideon squeezes my hand as we start to briskly walk away from my past. My father. My sister. My mother.

Our future is what we carve. It is not up to my past or his. It is what we do together, going forward. We are going to be a family. A real family. I smile as I see a butterfly flitter in front of us. I knew Nikki would love him.

A Sneak Peek
Of
The next installment

Fractured Existence

I

Edge
Rain - Sleep Token

From the moment Lily told me that Susie was going to be showing up at the beach house, I felt my stomach muscles harden and my brain turn to mush. That day at the brownstone when we had gone to see Lily, Susie rounded the corner from the living room and I fell instantly. She was perfect.

Red hair, personality just as fiery. These bright green eyes that honestly reminded me of the color of uranium glass under a black light. Her porcelain skin martyred with small freckles covering her cheeks and nose. I still don't know how her slim build can hold such a personality captive.

When she leaned over the railing of the stairway to yell up at Gideon, I could see the muscles flex in her bare legs. The lines in her shoulders were taut like she was trying to hold something back. She shouts, "I was lying then, I'm not now!" then turns back to Matthew and I with a look on her face of pure annoyance mixed with sadness.

She obviously did not like the situation that was going on between Gideon and Lily. I can't say that I blame her, Gideon royally fucked up. But in his defense, he never expected Lily to love him as much as she already did. He would never have hurt her intentionally.

We sat in the living room all just staring at each other while Gideon tore the house apart looking for Lily. But she was already gone. He stepped up behind Susie and asked where Lily had run to but of course Susie couldn't answer that. It wasn't her secret to tell. Gideon wasn't able to see it but I watched a silent tear run down her cheek. She didn't even make eye contact with me but I could feel her pain radiating straight through my bones. She obviously loves Lily. More like a sister than a friend.

And now she is going to be here. At the beach house. With me. As soon as Lily told me, I started to unravel a plan in my head. My initial thought was how much fun this was going to be. Flirting with her, teasing her a bit. See how fiery she can really be. But now that she is going to be here any minute, I can't stop pacing around the room. I have probably looked out the window a dozen times in the last half hour. Basically, I am annoying the hell out of myself.

I hear Lily and Gideon talking about something but I don't really have the time or patience to pay any attention to them. Where the fuck is she? Seriously, it doesn't take that long to get here from the airport. I try to calm my brain down but it is too late for that, I am in full blown hyperfixation mode. I continue to pace as Lily steps up to Matthew asking some other completely mundane question.

I part the curtains again, annoying myself even more with the incessant sidewalk checks when I hear Lily say the name Susie. I immediately turn around and perk to attention. I listen as Lily tells Matthew that Susie has a crush on him. HIM? What the fuck? No. No. No.

Matthew smiles back at Lily, "Really? The redhead right? She is pretty fucking hot. Not gonna lie. And she has a thing for me? That *is* interesting." Before he can even bat an eye, I am lurching around Lily, pointing my finger in his face, "I called fucking dibs dude. Not Fucking Cool."

Matthew grins from ear to ear as he puts his hands up in surrender. He knows I called dibs. I called it the day at the brownstone. He told me then she was fair fucking game. I will fucking end him if he ruins this for me. I turn to Lily as she smiles, "Nope, she told me with her own two lips that she and I quote 'thinks Apollo is fucking hot.'" I turn back to Matthew, letting a deep rasp roll from the back of my throat as I poke him in the chest, "I will fucking end you."

I am glaring down at him as he smiles back at me when I hear the voice that has been echoing in my dreams for months now, "Did I miss something?"

I feel my eyes blow wide as I slowly raise my head to see Susie standing behind the chair Matthew is sitting in. The light is radiating from behind her as she perches there in a light blue ribbed tank top and short little white cut off shorts. Her hair is pulled up into a tight ponytail with her long red curls dancing across her shoulder. Her skin is fucking glowing as she turns those verdant eyes towards me with a slight smile on her face.

I feel my body start to harden from toes to fingertips as I take her in slowly. She is just as stunning as the first day I saw her. I slow my gaze down as I see two pert little nipples saying hello to me through the tank top and I silently thank Lily for having the a/c turned on right now. I feel my pulse quicken as I continue to raise my gaze back up to those emerald eyes. Something about this woman stuns me every single time I see her.

I shake myself out of the brain fog I am currently experiencing and step up towards her, "Hello. I am Edge. Er, Dionysus. Do you need help with your bags or anything?" I sound like a fucking toddler trying to become teacher's pet but I don't care. I would do anything to keep her eyes on me a moment longer. I watch Susie's eyes darken just a bit when I speak to her and I could have sworn I heard a soft moan leave her lips. I can feel a groan growing in my own chest in response.

She smiles widely back at me, "No, thank you. I am good." She gives me a slight side nod of her head and then turns

373

her attention back towards Lily. She gives her a devious grin, "I am going to go put these in my room." She turns to go upstairs when Lily waves at her, pulling her attention back towards the sitting room, "Well, you are going to have to pick a different room this time."

Susie screws up a confused glance towards Lily. I look at her as well, not understanding what she is talking about when I notice that both Gideon and Matthew are smiling cheekily at me. Lily turns towards me, smiling wildly, "Edge has already claimed your normal room. But the one across the hall from him is open. That is actually the only other one put together right now. If you guys don't mind sharing the one bathroom up there."

Of fucking course I would chose the one room that Susie uses every time she visits. I just liked it because it felt like I was in a castle or something. The vibe it gives makes it feel like it is just tucked away from the world. Away from the chaos. I feel my eyes fly wide as I turn back towards Susie, "We can switch rooms. I didn't know that it was your normal room. I have no problem moving my stuff."

I watch as Susie continues to smile at Lily and I could swear I see her wink at her. She slowly turns her gaze towards me then reaches out and places her hand on my arm. I instantly feel chills run up my arm, down my spine and straight to my balls. My breath catches in my chest as she smiles at me, "No, that is fine Edge. You can stay in that room. I will just go across the hall. Thank you for offering though."

I try to calm my nerves as she smiles then slowly removes her hand from my arm. I can still feel the heat from her palm wrapped around my bicep. I can't look away from her. The majestic creature standing in front of me. I don't even notice Matthew is moving until he is standing up next to me, "Hello again Susie. It is nice to actually get to meet you this time. I am

Matthew, or Apollo. But please Jesus god, just call me Matthew here."

I turn my glare from Matthew back towards Susie as she starts fluttering her eyelashes at him. I even see her neck start to turn a soft pink color like she is fawning over him even speaking to her.

She places both hands back on the handle of her suitcase as she gives him a sexy little grin, "It is SO nice to meet you formally Matthew. I know we all saw each other at the brownstone but I am *really* glad that I get to really meet everyone this time. We are definitely gonna have some fun."

I watch her fangirl over him for another moment before I feel the roll of anger coursing through my veins. I glance at Matthew just fast enough to see him wink back at her.

I step around her as I feel a growl try to leave my throat. I have to get the fuck away from everyone right now before I make a right ass out of myself. It doesn't help that I am also rock hard from her touching my arm. I don't even glance back down the stairs as I take them two at a time until I am back on the third floor and walking into my room.

I leave the door cracked just enough to basically torture myself. I know she is going to stay down there talking to her crush for hours and I am going to be sitting here staring at my watch counting the seconds until I hear her enter her room.

I throw myself back across the bed and carefully readjust my extremely uncomfortable hard on. I stare at the ceiling, counting the fucking seconds in my head when I hear Lily and Susie coming up the steps. I smile as I sit back up, looking at my watch, 48 seconds. Suck on that Matthew. I brace my forearms on my knees then lean towards the door just a bit to try to hear them better.

I hear them crest the top of the stairs then that sweet voice rolls down the hall towards me, "So, are we gonna hit the beach today? It is fucking beautiful outside today. And I brought my new swimsuit. Maybe see if everyone wants to join?"

I feel another low moan leave my throat as I imagine her in a bathing suit, standing knee deep in the ocean. The waves licking around her thighs with her hair flowing through the wind around her. I am instantly hard again.

I hear Lily let out a small laugh as they round into Susie's room. I stand up, stealthily moving to lean closer to the cracked door so I can hear them better. Lily's voice carries across the hall to me, "Yeah, that sounds like a plan. I hope you brought extra sunblock though."

I hear the slide of the handle of Susie's suitcase go down then it sounds like she is lifting it to sit it down somewhere. I can hear the humor in her voice, "Of course I did. Maybe Matthew will help me put some on." I reach out and grab the doorframe as the anger travels down my fucking veins again.

He will not be touching her. I will cut his goddamn hands off and he will never be able to play drums or beat off again. I was not joking when I said I would fucking end him.

I hear her unlatch her suitcase and I glance through the open crack of the door to see her pulling out a tiny little white bikini. There is more fabric on a fucking wash clothe than on the totality of this little bikini she is pulling out of the suitcase. She turns away from me and pulls the tank top over her head and tosses it down on the bed.

I see her bare back in front of me. I am left in awe at the inkwork on display before me. It looks like a large light blue ink blot is splashed across her back with a side image of a woman wearing a colorful floral wreath on her head.

She is holding a goblet in her hands. Her long blonde hair wraps around her body to cover her bare skin. Below it in

376

calligraphy it looks like it says the words, "Queen of Cups". My eyes travel back up her body and I can see the side swell of her tit as she reaches for the bikini top then pulls it over her head.

I don't even realize that I have the door entirely open as I just stand here, mesmerized by the woman in front of me. I see her turn her head to the side as she smiles down at Lily sitting on the end of the bed, "Will you tie me up?" I feel my legs moving into the room before Lily even has a chance to notice me.

Out of my periphery, I see Lily stop and her jaw drop. I continue stepping forward until I am leaning into Susie's bare back, whispering in her ear, "I will." Susie goes stock still as I see Lily start to side step out of the room. She mutters something but all I can focus on is Susie. I reach down and grab the two white strings dangling at her sides.

I hold my breath as my fingers skim her bare skin. Then I run my fingertips across her back to tie the two strings into a knot in the middle. Susie slowly turns and looks from my hands up to my face.

I am a good 5 inches taller than her so her gaze has to climb a bit to reach my eyes. I watch her skin flush across her neck and chest. I smile knowing that I am the one having an effect on her. Not fucking Matthew but me.

Susie finally meets my eye and smiles back at me, "Thank you, Edge."

I smile back down at her, "Happy to help. Do you need me to tie anything else up?"

Susie lets a deep chuckle leave her throat as she looks at my lips and smiles, "Not right now. But ask me again in a few hours."

I continue to smile at her as I slowly back out of the bedroom then turn to head back into my room. I turn around to face her as I shut my door and she is smiling right back at me as she slowly shuts her door as well.

I lean my forehead against the door after I have shut it and let out a laugh laced with a heavy sigh. Jesus christ this woman is going to be the death of me. I am going to have a fucking heart attack at the age of 28.

I roll myself around so that my back is now flush up against the door and laugh out into the room before me. I take a few more deep breaths to settle my nerves before I push off the door then find my swim trunks.

I change quickly, making sure I look alright in the mirror before I open the bedroom door then step across the hall. I don't even remember the last time I checked myself in a mirror unless I was about to go on stage.

I smile at Susie's door as I bring my knuckles up and lightly rap on it. Two seconds later it is swinging open and Susie is standing there wearing her scrap of cloth, smiling from ear to ear. I grin back at her, "You ready?" She nods her head as we both turn and start to head down the stairs.

I let her move slowly beside me, happy to make our little alone time last as long as possible. We round the stairs to the second floor and hear someone scream. We both stop and stare at the bedroom door in front of us.

I raise one hand and point at the door as I hear a loud grunt come from behind it. I smile still pointing towards the door, "Well, I guess they are busy then." Susie blurts out a laugh along with me as she sashays her cute little ass over to the door.

She raises her hand to knock again and we both hear Lily scream again. She slowly turns her wide eyes back towards me, letting a devious grin come over her face as we hear Gideon from behind the door, "Fuck Lily. Fuck me."

I smile back at her and take a few steps towards her until I am flush up against her side. I smile as I lean my face into her neck, "Maybe we should just let them finish up before we bother them." I look at her neck before me and I can see a vein pulsing extremely fast.

I pull back and turn my eyes towards hers. She is almost panting, she is breathing so hard. I take a step into her until her back meets the wall behind her. I take my arm and raise it onto the wall beside her head as I lean in close to her again. She doesn't break my stare the entire time.

I raise my left hand and use my fingertips to trail down the side of her face, then her neck before coming to a stop at her collarbone. She lets out a small barely audible moan and I smile while staring at her parted lips.

I grin a bit wider, "Are you enjoying listening to your best friend getting railed behind that door Susie?" Her eyes fly up and meet mine as she grips the sunblock bottle in both hands tightly.

She glances quickly at the door then back at me, "No. That is not it at all." I lean in a bit closer to her so her tits are pushed up against my chest. I hear her breath intake sharply.

I smile back at her as I put my lips to her ear, "Yes, you are. You are getting wet just thinking about someone pinning you to this wall and fucking you senseless. Aren't you?"

I pull my face back from hers to watch the skin down her neck and chest start to turn a crimson red again. She smiles as she steps up into my space, "What if I am? What if I am thinking about someone bending me over that railing behind you and just slamming into me until my knees buckle? Until I can feel them running down my legs. What of it?"

I stare at her dirty little mouth as she whispers her fantasies out to me. It takes all of my fucking strength not to make her wishes come true. I smile back at her, "I am sure Matthew is free. Do you want me to go get him?"

Her eyes narrow at me as she gives me a sly grin, "No, I will let him know for myself *exactly* what I want from him. And I am sure he will be happy to help out."

She steps around me smiling smugly to herself as she raps her knuckles on the door. She turns and stares me right in the eyes, "Gideon! Get off of Lily so we can go down to the beach now please!" I smile at her as she turns and struts her fine ass down the stairs. I roll my neck over my shoulders. Good lord this woman is going to fucking destroy me. I smile after her, hoping that she does.

I follow behind her down the stairs and watch her swing around the furniture then head straight out the back doors. I smile while moving slowly, watching the show. As soon as her feet hit the sand, she is running towards Matthew as he is laying a towel down on the sand while laughing with Simone.

I stand at the top of the stairs as she smiles at me then hands him the bottle of sunscreen then turns her back to him. I smile widely as Mona steps forward and starts to rub down her front while Matthew gets her shoulders and back.

I slowly walk down the steps and casually walk past them, "Better rub that in good Matthew. Don't want our little peach to burn." I continue smiling as I walk straight into the ocean and dive into an oncoming wave. I swim a few strokes then breach the surface, turning around and floating as I watch Susie gingerly walking into the water until it is mid thigh.

I continue to hover in the water as I watch her cup water in her hands and pour it down her body. Thank god I am under water so no one will be able to see the effect she has on me. I start to push myself a bit closer to her until I feel the sand beneath my feet again. I walk towards her but stay far enough back that I am still in the water above my waist.

I continue to tread water as I see Lily barrel into the waves and start splashing Susie like they are in grade school. It is something to see. Lily is always so quiet, so reserved. Like she is afraid of something but she is nervous to admit to anyone what it actually is. Then to go from scared little mouse to this wild woman spraying water at her best friend. I laugh as I watch them play around for a while before Lily turns and catches Gideon's eye then blows him a kiss.

Susie looks at me with a side grin then turns back to Lily, "So, you sounded well taken care of earlier." The little mouse then turns back to Susie and plumes a wave of water at her with her hands. I start chuckling to myself again. These two fight like sisters I swear. Lily then turns her gaze towards me and starts pointing between me and Susie, "It is 100% both of your faults."

I stand up a bit straighter, looking from Susie's laughing face to Lily's accusing glare, "How the fuck is it our fault?"

Lily turns to me and puts her little mousey fists on her little mousey hips, "If you hadn't walked in offering to tie her up then I wouldn't have barrelled down the stairs like a mad woman, ranting about how shit was getting hot and heavy up there!"

I laugh out loud and step up a bit closer to Susie, who is laughing right back at me, "That doesn't explain how that led to you getting laid."

Lily's hands drop back down in the water and she averts her gaze for a minute before blushing and looking up at Susie, "He had to prove to me that we are hotter than you guys."

Susie belts out a laugh loud enough to pull everyone's attention from the beach. Sleeping Simone included. I chuckle and lean in towards Lily while looking across the sand at Gideon, "I am sorry but what?"

Lily looks at me then back over her shoulder at Gideon before smiling, "Don't worry. He made his point. We are definitely hotter."

Susie starts chuckling as I step up to her and place my hands on her hips, pulling her around to face me. I lean in so she can feel the heat of my breath on her neck, "Sounds like shots have been fired, love. We should probably try to catch up soon."

I pull back just in time to see Lily charging back out of the water and towards Gideon. I smile back down into Susie's sparkling eyes, my hands still on her hips. She smiles back and places both of her open palms on my chest. Her eyes meet mine again, "Edge. This is fun and all but I don't know if you can handle all the demons that I carry around with me. There are so many of them, they have their own club."

I lean in closer, pressing her chest into mine, pulling her hips towards my own, "Baby, my demons would bend yours over. And then they would make you fucking beg for more."

www.ingramcontent.com/pod-product-compliance
Lightning Source LLC
Chambersburg PA
CBHW010513100726
47903CB00009B/2721